Louise Fuller was once a tomboy who hated pink and always wanted to be the Prince—not the Princess! Now she enjoys creating heroines who aren't pretty push-overs but strong, believable women. Before writing for Mills & Boon she studied literature and philosophy at university, and then worked as a reporter on her local newspaper. She lives in Tunbridge Wells with her impossibly handsome husband Patrick and their six children.

Lela May Wight grew up with seven brothers and sisters. Yes, it was noisy, and she often found escape in romance books. She still does—but now she gets to write them too! She hopes to offer readers the same escapism when the world is a little too loud. Lela May lives in the UK, with her two sons and her very own hero, who never complains about her book addiction—he buys her more books! Check out what she's up to at lelamaywight.com.

T0337242

WHAT THE BILLIONAIRE WANTS…

LOUISE FULLER

LELA MAY WIGHT

MILLS & BOON

First published in Great Britain 2024
by Mills & Boon, an imprint of HarperCollins*Publishers* Ltd,
1 London Bridge Street, London, SE1 9GF

www.harpercollins.co.uk

HarperCollins*Publishers*, Macken House, 39/40 Mayor Street Upper,
Dublin 1, D01 C9W8, Ireland

What the Billionaire Wants... © 2024 Harlequin Enterprises ULC

Boss's Plus-One Demand © 2024 Louise Fuller

Italian Wife Wanted © 2024 Lela May Wight

ISBN: 978-0-263-32037-4

12/24

This book contains FSC™ certified paper
and other controlled sources to ensure responsible forest management.

For more information visit www.harpercollins.co.uk/green.

Printed and Bound in the UK using 100% Renewable Electricity
at CPI Group (UK) Ltd, Croydon, CR0 4YY

BOSS'S PLUS-ONE DEMAND

LOUISE FULLER

MILLS & BOON

CHAPTER ONE

Harris Carver's private members' club, New York

'IF YOU'D LIKE to follow me, Ms Truitt. Mr Carver is waiting for you in the members' lounge.'

The man in the suit turned and Sydney Truitt followed him. She had no idea where she was. She had been picked up at the airport and then driven by limousine into an underground car park. But this must be some kind of private club, she thought as she followed the man in the suit along the wood-panelled corridor.

He stopped in front of a door, knocked briskly and then opened it and took a step back to allow her to pass. 'Mr Carver will see you now.'

At first she thought the room was empty, but then she saw him.

As Harris Carver rose to his feet and walked towards her, she felt her shoulders tense. Up until now, most of her clients had been smaller businesses, but there weren't many businesses as big as HCI.

'Ms Truitt.' He held out his hand and she shook it. 'Thank you for meeting me here, and for signing the NDA. I know it must all feel a little "cloak and dagger" but, given my position, it's best, I find, to err on the side of caution.'

She smiled politely. 'Of course. And thank you for considering me for the contract, although I'm not actually sure what it is I'm being considered for.' The phone call had been brief and vague enough that she had been slightly afraid that they had called the wrong person.

'It's a short-term contract. Just three days but you will be handsomely rewarded for your time. Take a seat.'

'Could I just ask why you've approached me? It's just there are bigger and better-known people who do what I do—' She could think of at least two firms of white hat hackers here in New York who could carry out a legitimate 'attack' on HCI to find and fix any possible security issues within its network, and yet he had chosen her.

He shrugged. 'I had a shortlist of suitable candidates. Everyone was on a par skill-wise but it was your background that gave you the edge.' He hesitated and then he smiled, a predatory smile that made her whole body grow still and tense. 'You see, I need someone who is not just technically capable but who is, how can I put it?' He paused. 'Ah, yes, ethically flexible. Growing up in your family would suggest you have that quality.'

'My family?' She frowned. This wasn't how these conversations normally went. 'What do you know about my family?'

He held her gaze. 'This contract is sensitive. I needed to know that you would be fit for purpose, so I had my people take a closer look. Don't worry. They're thorough but discreet.' Still holding her gaze, he paused, his face expressionless. 'Unlike your brothers, who seem to have made quite a name for themselves with the local law enforcement in your home town.'

He was right. All three of her brothers had followed the same well-trodden path as their father and uncles. Only, that was the problem. They had the wrong role models and even before they could walk or talk, people had made assumptions about them. But they didn't know them as she did. Just because they had criminal records didn't mean they were bad to the bone, because they weren't. Far from it.

'My brothers are not—' she began, but he held up his hands placatingly.

'I'm not judging, just stating the facts, which are that they have broken the law and are now facing the consequences. I'm sure you must be anxious to help them, but help is so expensive, I find. The good kind anyway. The kind that delivers the required result. Which is why I think you're the perfect fit for this job.' He paused again, his grey gaze sweeping over her assessingly. 'I think you are someone who can help me.'

She swallowed. 'Help you do what?'

'It's a business matter. Tiger McIntyre has stolen something from me. A piece of intellectual property. I want it back. I need it back so that I can prove he did what he will undoubtedly deny doing. Which means I need someone on the inside. Someone who can pose as an employee while she hacks into his server.'

Harris Carver's voice faded and thinned, swallowed up by the heavy, persistent thud of her heartbeat. He wanted her to pose as an employee? Was he out of his mind? Tiger McIntyre had a reputation for being as fearsome and ruthless as his namesake. And as beautiful. Her pulse accelerated. Not that she had met him, but she had seen his picture often enough that she could almost picture his sculpted face and arresting gaze.

'It will mean crossing a line so I understand if that's giving you pause for thought.'

Harris Carver was leaning forward slightly and she blinked, trying to refocus her mind.

'You're a very wealthy, powerful man, Mr Carver, so I wanted to give you the chance to pretend that I misunderstood what you were suggesting. Because it's not just crossing a line, it's illegal.'

He held her gaze for a few uncomfortable seconds and she had to clench her jaw to stop herself from looking away.

'Something which your family knows all about.'

She got to her feet unsteadily. This was not who she was. It was not even who her brothers were, deep down. Only explaining that would mean revealing more than she was willing to do, had ever done, because even just thinking about it still had the power to make her shake inside.

'But I'm not my family so I'm afraid I'm going to have to decline your offer because if I get caught it would ruin my reputation—'

'Then don't get caught.' She felt her muscles tense as Harris Carver typed something onto his phone and then held it out so that she could see the numbers flashing on the screen.

'Just so you know how appreciative I would be.'

Her eyes widened. That was a lot of money.

'Very appreciative,' he said then, and he touched the screen of his phone lightly.

She blinked. Okay, that was a lot of zeroes. It was more money than she had earned in the last year. For a couple of days' work. It would pay for a good lawyer. Actually it would pay for the best lawyer in the country, she thought, her stomach knotting fiercely with relief and hope. It would mean she could keep her brothers from a life behind bars and how could she not want that? They had freed her from a different kind of prison, and yet this was a line she had never crossed or wanted to cross,

She shook her head. 'Even if I didn't get caught, I wouldn't be comfortable with what you're asking me to do.'

'Why?' There was a note in Harris Carver's voice that she couldn't place. 'Tiger McIntyre is no angel. From the outside, he looks like a winner but winning comes at a price. Yes, he's smart and determined, I'll give you that. He works hard but he also breaks the rules. Cuts corners. Crosses those lines that you're being so squeamish about. There is nothing he wouldn't do to get ahead. No one he wouldn't trample over to reach his goal. If you don't believe me, just read the Internet.'

He was telling the truth, she thought slowly, picturing Tiger McIntyre's intense, challenging gaze. McIntyre had a reputation for sidestepping laws and using any number of dubious tactics to get ahead. He took what he wanted and he got away with it because of his looks and his wealth and his power. Unlike her brothers, he never had to suffer the consequences of his actions. But maybe it was time he did.

'You don't need to feel bad about this, Ms Truitt. Believe me, this isn't the first time Tiger McIntyre has taken something of mine. But it will be the last,' Harris Carver said, leaning forward, and such was the venom in his voice that she had to press herself deep into the seat to stop herself from flinching.

Steadying her breathing, she cleared her throat. 'You said this was business, Mr Carver, but it's sounding awfully personal to me.'

There was a short, pulsing silence as he leaned back languidly against the cushions. 'Oh, it's personal, all right. You see, I know McIntyre is a thief, but he's picked the wrong person to steal from this time. So, first I want you to find what he stole, and get it back for me.' The grey eyes had narrowed on her face. 'And then I'm going to ruin him.'

Ten days later, Tiger McIntyre's private jet.

'So what was your gut feeling? Did we get it or not?'

Shifting back in his seat, Tiger McIntyre let the question

from Nathan Park, his head of research and development, hang in the air. He knew the answer, of course. He always knew the answer. It was one of the reasons he had risen so far and so fast, turning his father's failed business into one of the front runners in the race for off-world mining.

It was a growing industry now, the exploration of the moon, but McIntyre was leading the race. Not just leading. Its AI-powered robots were lapping its rivals. Or all but one of them.

He tilted his head to let his gaze drift up past the endless blue of the stratosphere. Sometimes he dreamed about living on the moon. Of course, there would be negatives. But up there he would be able to just stop and pause for a moment, sit back and enjoy the view, because surely the demons that drove him ever onwards would be unable to follow into space.

But until then—

'On balance, yes.' He turned back towards Park, a slight smile pulling at his mouth. 'We have everything they want. Everything they need.'

In truth, there was only one other serious contender for this historic and extremely lucrative contract with the space agency. HCI. No surprise there, he thought, his lip curling. He and Harris Carver had been rivals for more than a decade now and their ongoing duel looked likely to extend into the foreseeable future and off-earth.

But then Harris had all the credentials. The college education, the astronaut father, the intergenerational cosmic bond. Whereas he had nothing.

Now was not the time to let Carver take up any more of his thoughts. In fact, he didn't want to think. Big meetings always made him horny as hell. It was that mix of adrenaline and testosterone. But currently he was in the usual state of being single so sex was out of the question, unless he could face calling one of his exes.

'Excuse me, Mr McIntyre.' It was the steward. 'Just to let you know that we will be landing in roughly twenty minutes so if you could fasten your seat belt.'

He nodded, but instead of buckling up, he reached for his phone and scrolled down the list of numbers. When he was younger, it had been different. Back then he had been happy just to casually hook up with women when he wanted sex.

He let his gaze drift back towards the window. Of course, that was no longer an option. He was too wealthy, too high profile. His security people would have a meltdown. So these days it was simpler to have a long-term but impermanent girlfriend. Although the friend part was a little inaccurate. He didn't do friends, female or male, not since college when he and Harris had fallen out big time and he had realised that trusting anyone, even someone you thought of as a brother, was riskier than firing a rocket into space. Although, truthfully, Harris had come late to that particular party. Watching his father's car crash of a love life over the best part of two decades had made it clear to him that the downside of relationships, particularly the romantic kind, was too high a price to pay.

But he was always upfront about what he wanted, which was exclusivity coupled with an understanding that the relationship was never going to end with an exchange of rings in front of witnesses.

And it worked. Okay, he only really saw them for sex and special events, but as his 'girlfriend' they got an entrée into his world and, besides, he always made his intentions clear from the beginning. It wasn't his fault that they assumed he would change or that it would be different with them.

Sometimes they got clingy, wanting him to meet their

family or to get a place together, and that was a signal to end things. Other times, they would lose patience or their temper and break up with him. Either way, it wasn't a problem.

Usually.

But sometimes the timing was bad. Like now.

His hand tightened around the mobile. This year had been insane, in a good way. The business had doubled its profit in the first quarter and tripled it by the third. He had more than earned a vacation and typically he would head off to Italy, to his private island in the Venetian lagoon, and, in his opinion, September was the best month to visit. Temperatures were still warm but the summer glut of tourists had mostly left and Venice reverted to being the elusive, poetic city he loved.

And then there was the Regata Storica.

The *regata* was the social event of the year in the billionaires' social calendar. Coming hot on the heels of the Monaco Yacht Show, it started with a spectacular pageant on the waters of the famous lagoon and ended with the Colombina masked ball, which was the biggest charitable fundraising event in Europe. Graced by monarchs, heads of state, A-list celebrities and the top one per cent. It would be unthinkable not to attend, particularly as this year he was sponsoring a boat.

But to go alone would be even more unthinkable. For a man like him, a beautiful woman was as essential as an expensive watch or a pair of handmade shoes. It wasn't an ego thing. He didn't want or need anyone's approbation. It was more that perfection was intimidating. It kept people at arm's length and that was how he liked it.

Which left him with a problem.

Alexandra, the latest in his string of ex-girlfriends, was still seething at his decision to unceremoniously end things a few weeks ago. Frankly, though, he couldn't imagine asking her or any of his other exes anyway. Usually, he just asked whoever he was dating at the time, but if he invited them specifically then they would inevitably misread his intentions whatever he said.

What he needed was a woman who would behave like a girlfriend and then just walk away uncomplainingly. In other words, an escort, except he hadn't ever and would never pay a woman to be his date.

Face it, he told himself. *The woman you need doesn't exist and there is no point in hoping you're going to find her.*

She was a creature of fantasy and, unlike his father, he was a man who dealt in facts, not feelings. And as he started to fasten his seat belt, he wondered once again if life might not be simpler on the moon.

Glancing up at the bank of clocks mounted on the wall opposite her desk, Sydney felt her heart accelerate. All of them showed different times. It was seven p.m. in Moscow, midnight in Beijing and five p.m. in London. Here in New York, it was only midday but the fact remained that she was running out of time. This was her last day working for the McIntyre Corporation and if she didn't deliver her end of the bargain to Harris Carver then she wouldn't get paid, and if she didn't get paid...

Her shoulders tensed against the back of her chair.

She could still hear the panic beneath the bravado in her brother Connor's voice when he'd called her from the police station. 'It's bad, Syd. They're saying it could be one to five years for all of us.' He paused, then cleared his throat. 'Including Tate.'

Selling and buying stolen car parts was not the worst crime in the world. But it was not her brothers' first offence. They had been in trouble since the day they could walk, always stupid stuff, avoidable stuff that made their mates laugh.

Until that day when she had called Connor on the phone she had stolen from ex-husband, Noah, and they had driven to Nevada to rescue her and ended up getting arrested for assault. They hadn't hurt Noah. They had wanted to, but, in the end, it was she who had pushed him. She was the one who had punched and kicked him. And in his fury and spite, he had accused them of assaulting him because he knew that would hurt her the most.

And she could have saved them then. She could have gone to the police and told them the truth, but she had been so ashamed of her bruises, so ashamed of her weakness, and her brothers had felt so guilty that they hadn't protected her, that they'd admitted to something that wasn't true. Which meant that thanks to her all three of them had a record for assault.

One to five years in jail. Connor would probably be okay. He was the oldest and knew how to handle himself. Her middle brother, Jimmy, had a smart mouth but he made people laugh so he might get by. But Tate…

Suddenly it was hard to breathe past the lump in her throat. Tate was the youngest of her three brothers. Just ten months older than her. They had been in the same year at school and she knew him inside out. Knew definitively that he wouldn't survive prison. All her brothers were magnets for trouble and not given to deep thinking, but Tate was softer than the others.

He couldn't go to prison. None of them could. And it was her responsibility to make sure they didn't. They had rescued her, saved her, in fact, and she was going to save them. But for that to happen, they needed a lawyer and not just the usual run-of-the-mill sort assigned by the court. She needed someone fierce and smart, which meant expensive. And that wouldn't be the only cost. If they managed by some miracle to avoid prison time, they would all be facing hefty fines.

Which was why she had taken this temping job at McIntyre.

Her gaze dropped to the ID badge hanging around her neck.

For her the hardest part wasn't having to live a lie. She had done that when she was with Noah. Kept the big secret of their marriage. It was just there was so much more riding on this than any other job. This was about more than money or her reputation as a white hat. It was about giving her brothers a second chance.

And you can do this, she told herself again. It was what she did every day for other businesses across the country. Tiptoeing her way around their cyber-security systems, using reverse-engineering malware to break down lines of code so that she could figure out how a virus worked and how to stop it.

Self-taught, she had worked hard to break into the industry and her business, Orb Weaver, was growing fast, and she wanted it to keep growing, which was why she had agreed to meet Carver in the first place.

And now she was working for the two biggest fish in the pond, only neither job was what she had imagined herself doing.

Gazing across the office to Tiger McIntyre's empty office, Sydney shivered. She still wasn't entirely sure that she had made the right choice. But she was here at the McIntyre headquarters off Fifth Avenue legitimately employed as an administrative assistant called Sierra Jones. And once she found the IP and returned to Carver, she would be paid. Far more money than was legitimately due for her services.

But then what she was doing wasn't exactly legitimate.

'You okay, Sierra?'

Her colleague, Abi, was staring at her uncertainly. 'You look like you've seen a ghost.'

She pasted a smile on her face. 'I'm fine. I just remembered I forgot to eat breakfast,' she lied.

Abi rolled her eyes. 'I always forget to eat lunch when *he's* in the building. I just get so nervous I'm going to mess up.'

There was no need to ask who 'he' was. He was the boss. Tiger McIntyre. Christened Tadhg but given his nickname because of his ferocious, single-minded pursuit of success, he was a man who had never encountered failure.

But Carver was right. He wasn't a good person.

She had done her research. If Tiger McIntyre had been Connor or Jimmy or Tate, he would have faced far stricter penalties and public censure for a whole bunch of things he'd done. Like when he'd failed to divulge the purchase of shares in a rival company within the required legal time limits. It seemed trivial until you realised that the delay saved him millions. Or, to put it another way, it cost the stockholders whose shares he'd bought that same amount.

Time and time again, McIntyre had got his way with regulators and officials through bravado and intimidation, often backed by his numerous supporters who made their allegiance known *en masse* via social media.

So how did *he* get away with it? Pursing her lips, Sydney tipped her head back slightly to gaze up at the ceiling so that the huge glass-walled office belonging to the CEO was no longer in eyeshot.

Easy. He was rich and powerful. He had people at his disposal who could spin the story so that all those boring regulators and boards with their incomprehensible titles were not gatekeepers of fair play but fussy, hair-splitting enemies of progress.

And now she was one of the people at his disposal.

Not that she had ever met Tiger McIntyre in person. That was the one positive. He was out of the office breaking rules in Zurich or London or Beijing and wasn't due back until after she left.

'Hi, Sierra.'

She looked up, glad for the distraction. This time it was Hannah. She was holding a tray with a covered plate, a glass and some cutlery wrapped in a napkin.

'You need to take this to him.'

'Him?' Sydney frowned. 'Who?'

'The boss, of course.'

The boss! Her stomach went into freefall. Later she would wonder whether it was stress or stupidity that made her question Hannah because obviously there was only one 'him'. Then again, it was an understandable mistake to make. Surely it was reasonable to expect some fanfare if Tiger McIntyre had arrived in the building?

'Sierra?' Now Hannah was frowning. 'Are you listening? Mr McIntyre is back and he wants you to take him his lunch, so if you wouldn't mind—'

She held out the tray.

Sydney stared at her, her heart rate picking up like one of her brothers' souped-up cars. He must know something. A man as important as he wouldn't ordinarily even notice someone like her. Or was having to lead a double life just making her see threats where there were none? It was hard to say. All she knew for sure was that with every passing hour she was feeling more on edge, like an antelope leaping out of its skin every time it heard a twig snap.

She cleared her throat. 'Why does he want me to take it in?' It was one thing working here, quite another to walk into the lion's den.

'What?' Hannah frowned. 'I don't know. Maybe he can see how busy the rest of us are? Just put it on his desk.' She jerked her head towards the towering drinks fridge. 'And take a bottle of mineral water in too. Still, not sparkling. Get one from the back. He likes it well chilled.'

'Should I say something to him?'

Hannah looked horrified. 'No, absolutely not. Oh, and don't touch anything.'

There was no escape, and during the short walk to Tiger McIntyre's office her panic intensified, not helped by the glimpse she caught of herself in the glass of his door. She looked flustered and nervous.

Not that it mattered. It wasn't as if she were here to seduce McIntyre. Wasn't looking to seduce anyone, period.

Taking a breath, Sydney tapped lightly on the door and pushed it open. At first, she thought the huge office was empty, but then she saw him. He was standing at the window, reading something on his phone, and as she stared at his back, her breath caught in her throat and she felt a ripple of panic and guilt scuttle down her spine in the same way it did whenever she saw the blue and white flashing lights of a police car glide past her family home.

But why should she feel guilty? Okay, legally what she was doing was dubious but in essence she was righting a wrong. For all his fancy tailoring and handmade shoes, this man was a bigger criminal than her brothers. All she was doing was helping to expose that.

Keeping her eyes focused straight ahead, she walked swiftly across the room. She slid the plate onto his desk, and then, holding her breath, she unscrewed the bottle and poured out a glass of water.

'We haven't met, have we?'

It was a simple enough question, but Sydney felt the back of her neck prickle at the sound of the deep, masculine voice, and she turned sharply towards its owner.

For a moment, all she could do was stare. Her heart beat in her throat and her skin seemed suddenly too tight and hot, because Tiger McIntyre was no longer just a photo on her laptop, he was here in the flesh, all six feet three inches of him.

'No, we haven't. I only started two days ago.' She watched mutely as he began to walk towards her.

'What's your name?' he said, pocketing his phone.

'Sierra,' she said quickly. 'Sierra Jones.'

As if to expose the lie, the name, which she had chosen because it shared the first syllable with her own, crackled like popping candy on her tongue and her stomach fluttered as he looked at her closely, narrowed eyes appraising her in a way that made her feel as though he were looking beneath her skin, seeing into her soul.

Under any other circumstances it wouldn't have been a comfortable feeling.

But she barely noticed because she was still reeling from the shock of his beauty. Although it shouldn't have been a shock because she already knew what he looked like. Even before she had done her research, scouring the Internet for stories of his unscrupulous and line-blurring behaviour, his face had been familiar, but she had assumed the pictures she'd seen of him had been edited to flatter or that the camera had caught him on a good day.

But the truth was that none of the images she had seen did him justice. His face was arrestingly, astonishingly beautiful with a clean jawline and high sculpted cheekbones that would grace the pages of any Renaissance artist's sketchbook. And those eyes—

On her laptop, they looked light brown, but in person and up close, they were gold like the sun, only they lacked the sun's warmth. Instead, they were hard and glittering and unreadable.

Her own eyes skated across his face. Everything about him was hard, uncompromising, even his mouth. And yet for some reason there was something undeniably sensual about the shape of his lips, so that even though they were currently set in a line she could imagine them softening to fit against hers. The thought made her heart jerk forward and, to cover her reaction, she held out her hand.

'I'm not permanent. I'm covering for Maddie.'

As his eyes locked on hers, she swore silently. What was she doing? She was supposed to be keeping her head down. Not drawing attention to herself.

'I see,' he said slowly, taking her hand in what must surely be a reflex action, but as his fingers wrapped around hers she felt a sharp shock like electricity and she jerked free of his grip.

'Sorry, it's static,' she said quickly. 'I get it sometimes from the keyboard.'

He stared at her for so long that she thought she had missed his reply, but then he said in that same smooth, deep voice, 'Are you enjoying working here?'

'Yes.' Smiling slightly, she nodded, because it wasn't a total lie. She liked her colleagues and, if things were different, she might have enjoyed being Sierra for real, aside from the heels. Walking in them required the use of muscles she hadn't known she had and it was a miracle she hadn't broken her neck. But like the manicure and the designer handbag, they were part of her Sierra costume. And she would be glad to go back to being herself. Leading a double life was giving her sleepless nights. Frankly, she would be happy when five o'clock came and she would be able to put this chapter of her life behind her and get her life and, more importantly, her brothers' lives back on track.

She owed them that. Owed them her freedom, and a life lived without fear.

She nodded. 'Everyone here has been very kind and helpful.'

Two tiny lines formed a crease in the centre of his forehead and his burnished gaze got more intense. 'You're a long way from home, Ms Jones.'

Her stomach lurched sideways like a boat hit by a rogue wave. 'I'm sorry—' She tried to keep the panic out of her voice but she felt it wash over her anyway.

'California, isn't it?'

How did he know that? She lifted a hand to her suddenly pounding heart, feeling the trap snap shut.

His mouth tugged up minutely at one corner. 'We have a research and development test site up in the hills so I've spent a lot of time there and I recognised your accent. I'm guessing San Francisco.'

As relief flooded her, she managed to make her smile stay in place. 'Los Angeles.'

'Ah, the city of angels,' he said slowly. 'Ever visited New York before?' As she shook her head, his gaze moved past her to his desk and then back to her face. 'May I?'

His grip didn't hurt but when it came to physical contact she liked to be in control. Only she was still dizzy and off balance from this sudden breach of her invisibility, so when he took her elbow and steered her towards the window, she didn't pull away the way she normally did when someone touched her without warning or permission.

She could feel the calluses on his fingers, so that story about him working in the mines was true. For some reason that surprised her. She had thought it was just spin, propaganda designed to reinforce his status as the ordinary working man made good.

'This is the only way to see New York,' he said softly, and then he let go of her arm and she felt suddenly confused and angry because for the first time in years she hadn't minded being touched. On the contrary, she could feel herself leaning into his orbit, and her skin was quivering, itching to feel the warm, firm grip of his fingers again.

And not just on her arm.

Her pulse was a smooth, dizzying drum roll of panic and something else. Something deeper, more dangerous. Something she couldn't name. But it didn't need a name, apparently, to make her breath back up in her throat and her mind go blank as if everything she knew were gone, lost, forgotten, irrelevant. As if this was the moment when her life started. And although she knew that was absurd, she also knew it was true.

'So why did you leave LA? Was it a whim or did you have a particular reason?'

Yes, she thought. His name was Noah and he had almost broken her. He had taken her away from her family and friends. First to a flat and then to a tiny, isolated house far from any neighbours.

Far enough that nobody would hear her screams.

She still had the scars from their time together, although his cruelty had not been restricted to physical violence, so some were not ever visible. The bruises from when she had exhausted his patience and he had twisted her arm until she'd thought it would snap, they had faded. The hair he had pulled out had grown back.

There was one burn mark on her arm that had faded to a dull sheen and, of course, the implant she wore to replace the tooth he had knocked out, but it was the scars beneath the surface that had lingered longest and had left the most damage. That quiet rage that was always with her. Rage and a stifling shame at having been that woman. There was fear too that it could happen again. That she hadn't seen the signs then or had wilfully chosen to ignore them. And not understanding why she had let that happen meant that it could happen again.

Noah and the fear his name provoked was the reason she hadn't dated in five years.

'No, not really,' she lied. 'I just wanted a change of scenery.'

For a moment, his molten eyes rested on her face and she had that same strange feeling that he was seeing inside her head, and she felt a rush of panic. She had never planned on meeting Tiger in person, but now she was in his office, making polite chit-chat with him while lying to his face and stealing from him. It was both surreal and nerve-racking. Every word felt charged, and she was terrified she was going to give herself away.

'Well,' she said stiffly after a taut, electric moment she didn't understand but felt everywhere. 'I should probably be getting back.' But she didn't move, didn't look away from him even though she knew that she should because it was this man, it was him, Tiger McIntyre. He was making her feel this way. Making her drop her guard, making her ache—

'Of course. Don't let me keep you from your work.' He was already turning away. 'Oh, just for the record. My preference is for undressed.'

'Sorry.' She blinked as his gaze arrowed in on her in a way that made her body feel taut and loose at the same time.

'The salad. They've put dressing on it. I prefer it without.'

Her heart had somehow shifted to her throat, and she stared at him, trying to breathe around it. Was this for real? Did he actually care about his salad? Or was he just making conversation to keep her here? She felt another flicker of panic. Focus, she told herself. Focus on why you're here. Who you're doing it for.

'Sorry, I didn't know. Would you like me to get you another one?'

But before he could reply, his phone started to ring and he retrieved it from his pocket and switched from English to what sounded like Japanese. His eyes shuttered and he turned away and, recognising dismissal, she turned and walked swiftly out of his office.

For the rest of the day, she kept one eye on her computer screen and the other on the door to Tiger McIntyre's office. Throughout the afternoon, there was a revolving door of suited executives arriving and leaving his office. Occasionally she would catch a glimpse of the man they had all come to see and she would force her gaze back to her computer.

At some point, Hannah had come over to show her the pictures from her wedding-dress fitting. Staring down at the slideshow of frothy white dresses, Sydney had suddenly felt her skin on her face warm without reason and, glancing up, she had almost bitten the inside of her cheek as her eyes had collided with the shimmering gold gaze of Tiger McIntyre and she had felt that same jolt as before, only this time he hadn't even been touching her.

Not her, Sierra, she'd told herself quickly. As Sydney, she disapproved of Tiger. His behaviour. His abuse of privilege and power. As Sydney, she would never feel that strange, ungovernable pull of yearning or wonder.

After that she had kept her focus steady on her screen.

Not that it had mattered. It appeared that quietly and without her permission something inside her had turned itself towards him.

She was switching between screens now. The first was for the work she was doing as Sierra Jones, but she had a second incognito screen where she was working through the list of images, searching for the digital fingerprint that Harris Carver had sent her of his IP. It had taken her less than five hours to bypass the firewalls, but the fingerprint had offered not one image but nine hundred and fifty-three.

It was fine. She had come up with a workaround that had reduced that number to just under two hundred. So, assuming there was no other glitch, she would be walking out of here at five-thirty p.m. Then all she had to do was hand over the flash drive to Carver. It was a bit old school but it would leave no trail. Or not one that could be traced back to him.

Glancing up, she scanned the desks. The office was surprisingly empty this evening. Yesterday and the day before there had been quite a few people hanging around but tonight it was just her.

And Tiger McIntyre.

Her pulse twitched as she glanced over at his office to where she could just see his outline dark against the fading light. It was as if her eyes were being pulled to him by some magnetic force and, gritting her teeth, she glanced back down at the computer and switched screens again. Please be done, she prayed silently. But there were still ninety images to go.

Why was it taking so long? Her hands were clammy and

her fingers felt fat and clumsy as she picked up her phone and her water bottle and slid them into her bag.

How much time did she have left before she had to be out of the building?

When she glanced up again, her heart stopped beating. Just stopped.

Tiger McIntyre had left his office and was walking towards her and there was something purposeful about him, an intensity of focus that made her pull out the flash drive as a tiny flicker of foreboding snaked down her spine. In one smooth movement, she pocketed it, shut down the screen and got to her feet and, stomach somersaulting, she made her way between the desks to the elevator.

'Come on, come on,' she murmured, her heart a dark thud against her ribs, pressing the button frantically. But it was too late. A shadow blocked the light and she turned to find Tiger McIntyre standing beside her, the dark gold gleam of his gaze rooting her to the spot.

'Sierra, I need you to come with me.' There was a warning edge of steel to the softness in his voice and she couldn't breathe for a moment. 'You and I are going to have a little chat.'

To his left, she could see the exit sign for the staircase and it was almost impossible to stop herself from ducking under his arm and making a bolt for safety.

Not that there was such a thing for her any more, she realised in that moment with a shiver. Once an apex predator caught its prey, the chances of escape were somewhere between remote and zero.

'Is there a problem?' she said, trying not to sound as panicky as she felt.

He didn't reply.

He didn't need to. The hard curve to his mouth and the

two security guards hovering discreetly against the walls did it for him. Instead, he jerked his thumb in the direction of his office. That was the last place on earth she wanted to be but what choice did she have? And after a moment she turned and began to walk back the way she had come, only this time with Tiger following a pace behind, his golden gaze boring into her back, muscular body moving with the smooth, silent, slow-motion grace of his namesake.

CHAPTER TWO

As they reached his office, Tiger sidestepped past her, dragging a chair in his wake and dumping it in front of his desk.

'Sit,' he said coolly, and that coolness surprised him because inside his fury was churning like white-hot magma. It was astonishing to him that this was even happening. His firewalls were the stuff of legend, as complex and intractable to unravel as a Gordian knot, but Sydney had somehow hacked his server. But even more astonishing than that was the fact that she was currently masquerading as an employee.

How had this happened? To him? He was not easily duped, particularly by women, but earlier when she'd come into his office, he'd actually thought that his head of IT had made a mistake. Nobody that young could be so nerveless. In part that was why he'd wanted her to bring him his lunch—so that he could meet her in person before he confronted her. Only then he'd got distracted by that soft mouth of hers and the pale curve of her jaw. The same jaw that was currently tilting up defiantly in his general direction.

'You know, actually, I don't think I will. You see, I don't work for you any more. My contracted hours ended three minutes ago so—'

He watched as she took a step back, but as she turned

towards the exit one of the huge security guards moved in front of the doorway to block her escape.

Tiger held up his hand. 'Thanks, Carlos. I can take it from here. I'll let you know when I need you.'

There was a soft but final-sounding click as Carlos closed the door.

'You're not going anywhere,' he said, letting the warning in his words extend to his glittering gold gaze. 'Like I said, you and I need to have a talk.'

'I don't know what this is about but—' she began, but he cut her off.

'You know exactly what this is about. But I'm happy to spell it out. You hacked my system and you stole from me. So why don't you stop with the whole wide-eyed, first-time-in-New-York act and take a seat? And then I suggest you start talking.'

She sat down with such bad grace that it made him want to frogmarch her down to the police station himself. And yet a part of him was captivated by her and the strange, seductive tension between them and this verbal sparring that felt almost like foreplay.

What the—?

He swore silently, caught off guard by the inappropriateness of that thought and, blanking his mind to the pulse of heat beating a slow drum roll down his linea alba, he leaned back against the desk, stretching his long legs out in front of him.

'You've made a mistake.'

His gaze didn't flicker. 'I don't make mistakes.' He wasn't boasting. He was careful, tediously so, and he was happy to exploit any loophole that served his purpose, but the last time he'd been wrongfully accused of something, he'd ended up getting kicked out of university, so he didn't make mistakes.

The memory of Harris's cold-eyed contempt made him feel suddenly adrift, and, hating it still had the power over him, he focused his frustration on the woman sitting in front of him.

'You, on the other hand, have racked up quite a few in the last few days. Although I prefer to give them their correct title, which is criminal offences. There's gaining unauthorised access to a computer system. Stealing data, presumably with the intention of selling it on to a third party. Industrial espionage. But I'm no lawyer so I'm sure that's just the tip of the iceberg.'

That was better, he thought, feeling a sharp stab of satisfaction as her face stilled. 'What?' His eyes held hers as he deliberately let his mouth pull into a shape that could only be described as mocking.

'Did you think you're the first? 'Fraid not. You're certainly not the best,' he said softly, but with a hint of malice because he wanted to punish her, to wound her pride. Watching her pupils flare, he knew that he'd hit his target.

'It's not quite an everyday occurrence but I get a lot of people trying to mess me over.'

Sydney glared at him. 'If this is how you behave, I can well believe it.'

He stared down at her, his gaze bright and steady, his mouth a contemptuous curl, but he could feel the spark of her defiance igniting a flame he didn't normally feel and shouldn't be feeling because this woman, this red-haired vixen who had done more than any man would dare to do, she should be apologising at least or, better still, be on her knees begging for mercy.

A burst of heat, astonishing in its intensity, surged through his veins as his brain offered up all manner of possible reasons for her to be kneeling in front of him that he didn't want to acknowledge with Sydney here in the room.

'The difference with you is that I don't normally have the pleasure of meeting them face to face.'

She held his gaze. 'For the last time, I don't know what you're talking about. Look, I'm a hard worker but I do have to get up from my computer sometimes, and there're people coming and going all day. Any one of them could have done whatever it is you think I did.'

He heard her breath go shallow as his gaze narrowed on her. 'I don't think you did it, I know you did. I have proof. So do you, actually. It's in your bag.' Now, he held out his hand. 'Give it to me.'

'What? No.' Her fingers tightened around the handle of her bag. Her pulse was beating a wild staccato in her throat and just for a second there she had looked scared, and far too young to be sparring with a man like him.

But she had brought this on herself.

'I'm not going to ask again.'

She gave a small, taut laugh. 'Let me guess. This is where you threaten me. Where you tell me that we can do this the easy way or the hard way.'

His eyes met hers. 'Easy's not on the table. Just hard, and harder.'

'There's nothing in my bag.'

'Then you won't mind me taking a look inside.'

'Not if you don't mind me hurling it at your head first,' she snapped back as if he were the one at fault here, and for a moment he was stunned and furious all over again that she should talk to him that way, and yet for some reason he also wanted to laugh.

He settled for shrugging. 'Not the most sensible of responses unless you're looking to add assault to your list of crimes.'

She drew a breath, and he could see she was trying to maintain her composure. 'I haven't committed any crimes,' she said firmly, her eyes fixed on his as she stalked past him and upended her bag and shook it, scattering the contents across his desk. As she tossed the bag at him, her face gave nothing away but he was looking for a flash drive, not remorse, and, taking his time, he sifted through the detritus on his desk before checking the interior of the bag.

'Happy?' she said as his eyes found hers.

'Not yet. But I will be. Empty your pockets, Sydney,' he ordered, pushing away from the desk, and maybe there was something wrong with him, but he found he very nearly enjoyed the small, sharp intake of breath that followed his instruction.

Sydney's chin jerked up, not only because Tiger had got to his feet but because he had used her real name. She stared back at him, panic lifting her up and throwing her down like a dark rushing tide, pulling her under and sweeping her out into the ocean.

She had thought she'd been careful, ultra careful, but normally she was the one looking for the intruder. Not the intruder herself.

'Not a nice feeling, is it? Having people upend your life?' he said softly, so softly that for a moment her brain actually got confused and thought that he was backing off. But then that mouth of his twisted into a smile that made her understand that she was in trouble. Made her understand on a stomach-churning, visceral level just how ruthless he was.

Sydney held her breath. It didn't really change anything, but part of the reason she'd been just about holding it together was because she could tell herself that this was happening to Sierra. Now it was happening to her. Now it felt real.

All of it.

Blood rushed to her cheeks as she remembered that strange weightless feeling when he took hold of her arm, and that longing to get closer—

'How did you find out my name?' she said hoarsely.

He gestured towards the ID tag. 'I called in a favour. An ex-secret service friend of mine ran a facial recognition check and your driver's licence came up. You're Sydney Truitt. You live in Los Angeles and you're the CEO of Orb Weaver, a cyber-security company. A little detail that, oddly, you chose not to put on your CV.'

'It wasn't relevant,' she said as calmly as she could, fixing her gaze at a point to the left of his shoulder.

He didn't respond for a moment and she tried telling herself that it didn't get to her, but inevitably, as she knew it would, her head turned towards him of its own accord. There was a look of dark impatience on his face.

'If you say so. What is relevant is that, approximately seventeen hours ago, my head of IT picked up some unusual out-of-hours activity on your CPU.'

This was the worst-case scenario. She felt her stomach drop. It was a quiet program but she'd had to keep it running day and night.

'They check, you see, and it was low-level, just working quietly away in the background, but your machine was doing something it shouldn't. I'll let you have a few moments to come up with a reason why that was happening, but in the meantime, you can empty your pockets. Oh, and let me be clear—if you don't, I will ask Carlos to do it for you,' he added.

He would do it as well. This was not a man who made empty threats.

She had been cornered before so many times in the past by a different angry man and back then she'd tried to placate, to distract, tried to make herself small because she had been too scared to stand up to him.

Only for some reason she wasn't afraid of this man. Not physically anyway.

Still, though, she felt goosebumps spread across her skin as his glittering, disdainful gaze narrowed on her face. But she couldn't crack now. If she kept her head there was a chance she could front this out. Her throat tightened. She had to front it out.

Reaching into her pocket, she pulled out the flash drive and put it onto the palm of his hand. For a moment he stared at her assessingly, as if she were an animal in a trap and he were deciding how best to put her out of her misery.

'Is that it?'

She nodded.

He turned it over between his fingers. 'I know what you've taken. My question is what you were planning on doing with it. Because we both know that you weren't doing this for fun.'

Sydney breathed out shakily. For a moment she considered telling Tiger that it wasn't her idea. That she had been hired by Harris Carver to do his dirty work. But, really, what would be the point of giving up his name? Carver would deny all knowledge of their meeting and she had no proof.

Except her word, and right now she was pretty sure that wouldn't count for much.

Now it was her turn to shrug. 'Actually, I was. It's what people like me do,' she lied. 'We like the challenge and it's kind of like a hobby, seeing if we can get into a system. And I can see why that might upset you.'

'Is that an apology? Because you might need to work on it a little.'

'You're just sore because I beat your firewalls.'

He looked at her levelly. 'I'm sore because you lied to me and because you tried to steal from me at the same time as taking a salary from me.'

In the past, with Noah, she was always having to defend herself against untrue accusations and at the time she had often thought it would be fairer if she had done the things he'd claimed. But now she discovered that it wasn't a comfortable feeling being accused of something she *had* done, however justifiably.

She took a step forward, her hands balling by her sides. 'I don't steal.'

'Is something getting lost in translation? Because typically stealing is when you take someone else's property without permission.' The sarcastic note in his voice was like a steel scraping against the flint of her temper and she felt a spark catch fire.

'If you'd let me finish,' she snapped. 'What I was trying to say was that I don't steal from people who don't deserve it.'

'Right, because you're just a gender-flipped modern-day Robin Hood.' He didn't roll his eyes. There was no need. 'You're delusional.'

'And you're a hypocrite.' She was practically shouting now, her voice shaking with an anger that was only partially aimed at Tiger but she let it roll through her. 'You make me sick. You break the rules all the time.'

She felt the fury in her words bang into him and bounce away harmlessly because this man was not some soft-handed, Ivy League trust-fund baby. Tiger McIntyre had worked in the mines before he'd pushed his business into the big time. It was going to take more than a few insults to make him back off. Most likely it would take some very big sticks and stones. Boulders perhaps.

'Rules, not laws. Nothing I do is illegal.'

She shook her head, her fury giving way to panic now, because she was running out of options, out of words. She could feel the trap closing around her.

'Just because you haven't been punished doesn't mean you shouldn't be. But you're rich enough to bully and buy your way out of trouble.'

'You don't know anything about me,' he said softly.

'And you don't know anything about me,' she retorted.

'I know you're a hacker, and that you think that makes you different from other criminals, you know, the ones that rob stores and steal cars.'

'I've never stolen anything. This is the first time I—'

He shook his head. 'Even if that were true, what difference does it make? You're still just a thief.'

Tiger watched her eyebrows lift into cool, delicate arcs.

'Well, at least I don't get my kicks from playing judge, jury and executioner.'

He didn't know what he'd expected when he'd stalked back into his office with Sydney. Tears maybe. Possibly hysterics. The contents of her bag hurled in his face. But not this defiance, this bravado, this cat-and-mouse word-play that was entirely irrelevant and extraneous, and yet for some reason he was enjoying it. Enjoying her and the feeling of having her right where he wanted her.

Not that she would admit to that.

Not yet, anyway.

'You have quite a mouth on you, Ms Truitt,' he said at

last. 'Lots of opinions. Lots of accusations. Just not much in the way of cold, hard facts. But I pay my taxes so I guess I can leave it to the police to find those out.'

Sydney stared at him, her face stilling as if his words had cast a spell over her. If he hadn't been watching her covertly since lunchtime, he might not even have noticed the slight quiver to her body as if she was having to hold herself together not just metaphorically but literally.

He felt something pinch inside him.

He had been telling the truth when he'd said that this wasn't the first time his company had been hacked. For any major business, institution or high-profile celebrity it was a constant threat. Some hackers did it for the rush. Some liked the challenge of defeating a worthy opponent. Others did it for the chaos they caused, or simply the money. All had a willingness to break the law.

But, for all her defiance, this woman didn't strike him as being some kind of disrupter. In truth, she seemed altogether too young to be playing games with people like him. And yet there was a wariness in her eyes that didn't match her age, a tautness to her shoulders as if she were waiting for the sky to fall on her.

Only surely it already had. This was it. The end of the world. Disaster not averted. A real-life elimination event involving her reputation.

It didn't make any sense.

Then again, nothing about this woman or how she made him react made any kind of sense. Why, for example, when he should be focusing on the fact that he had caught her red-handed hacking his system, was he so aware of that curl of dark red hair that had come loose from the riotous mass of dark copper strands twisted into a low ponytail? Why could he not tear his gaze away from where it now lay coiled in a question mark over her right breast?

That he was even thinking about her hair, much less her breast, was just one of many things that had happened today that Tiger McIntyre didn't understand. First there had been the moment earlier when she'd walked, no, sashayed into his office with his lunch. Women walked in and out of his office all day every day and normally he barely registered them, but for some reason Sydney had made him stop reading his emails.

He swore silently. And not just any old email. An email from the United States space administrator no less.

But as he'd looked up and caught sight of her reflection in the glass that hadn't seemed to matter. And he had watched her in silence, waiting for her to acknowledge him, confused at his uncharacteristic behaviour because he never watched or waited for any woman.

And they always acknowledged him first, even the ones who thought they were playing hard to get.

But she hadn't.

Because she was a thief, he told himself irritably. Probably she couldn't meet his eye because she was hacking into his accounts, stealing his IP.

Only that wasn't true. She had met his eye. His chest tightened, remembering the gleam of her irises. Espresso brown. That was the colour of her eyes, and as their gazes had locked, he'd felt his heart accelerate and every single nerve ending start to shiver just as if he'd downed several black coffees in quick succession. It had sideswiped him and he'd been completely shaken by the burst of heat and need that had roared through him, so much so that he had taken her arm as if it were the most normal thing in the world to do.

Shaking his head free of that memory, he took a step towards her. 'What did you think was going to happen? That you'd get a dressing-down and then I'd let you walk out of here? This doesn't go away. This only gets worse.'

She was staring past him into the darkness. 'I didn't get that far.'

That made no sense either. Sydney was clearly smart. Smart enough to create a false employment record and get herself hired by the temp agency. Smart enough to hack past the McIntyre firewalls.

And yet he believed her.

'Maybe you should have done, because you accessed my private server without authorisation. You've stolen intellectual property presumably for profit. You're looking at time in a federal prison.'

'No.' Now her eyes found his. She was shaking her head and her voice sounded thin, as if she was finding it hard to speak, but he told himself that he didn't care, that she deserved to feel like that. 'I can't go to prison. I have commitments, responsibilities—'

'You mean a child?'

It was as if he'd been kicked in the chest by a horse. Which was ridiculous. She was a stranger. He had clapped eyes on her for the first time today. More importantly, she was a liar and a thief, and yet the thought of her having had a baby with some man that wasn't him scraped against something inside him.

'No. That's not what I mean. I have bills to pay.'

He felt a rush of relief, sharp and so incomprehensible that it was swiftly replaced by anger. With her, with himself and, as usual, with his father. Because there was no day when he didn't feel angry with his father.

His teeth were on edge, his body so tense now that he thought it might fly apart. 'You should have thought about that before you took me on.' It was out of his hands. There were laws. She had broken them.

'I could work for you.'

He frowned. Her beautiful dark eyes were narrowed on his face and there was a faint tremor beneath her skin.

'You? Work for me.' He repeated the words as if he couldn't believe that he'd heard them correctly, although he knew that his hearing was perfect. 'You think I'd trust *you* to work for me? After this?' He laughed then, showing his teeth, although it was a laugh without a hint of mirth. 'I don't do second chances, Ms Truitt. You cross me once, we're done.'

'I got past your firewall,' she said after a hard pause, and there was a flush to her cheeks. 'That shouldn't have happened. I can make sure it doesn't happen again.'

'An argument which might have more power if you hadn't been caught.' Why was he even having this conversation? He should just let the police deal with her, and, in the meantime, Carlos could babysit her.

And yet, he couldn't quite bring himself to do that, and he didn't understand why. He just knew that at some point in their conversation he had drifted closer to her. Too close. Close enough that he could touch her if he wanted to. Which, in spite of what she had done, he did.

His eyes rested on her flushed face, then dropped to the curve of her mouth.

Such a thing had never happened before and knowing that this woman was the reason, that she was causing this uncharacteristic reaction, made him feel more tense than he'd ever felt. He wasn't that man; had never wanted to be the kind of man who let his need for a woman dictate his behaviour.

His jaw tightened. Unsurprisingly, given that ever since he was four years old he'd watched his father make a total fool of himself with women, watched him confuse lust with love. Gerry McIntyre could casually mention a woman's name over breakfast one day and the next he would have proposed to her.

It was a pattern that had repeated itself over twenty years and cost his father a fortune. By the time Tiger took over following his father's premature death at fifty-nine, the medium-sized mining business Gerry had inherited from his father had been whittled away, hollowed out to fund his multiple divorces. All that had remained was the name, a whole heap of debt and a bunch of unpaid, understandably unhappy employees. Oh, and some very rich former wives.

Not substitute mothers, none even attempting to be. He had been nothing to them. Just a rival pull on his father's time. Not that his father had needed much pulling. Whenever he'd fallen in love, Gerry had been like a blinkered horse galloping for the finishing line.

Tiger had so longed for his father's attention. And there had been times when Gerry would remember he had a son, like when he'd wanted to watch the game. Mostly, though, Tiger had been easily forgotten, a lonely little boy who'd had to be self-reliant to survive. Who'd grown up to become a solitary, elusive man.

Because he wasn't like his father. He had no intention of marrying one woman, let alone six. As for letting Sydney Truitt near his business, forget it. He'd seen his father lose too much from trusting the wrong people. He preferred to put his faith in the evidence to hand and, on that basis, Sydney was not someone he could trust.

His gaze moved to where she stood a few feet away. Anyone else in her position would be pleading by now, or need restraining by the security guards, but there was a stillness to her as she waited for his next move and he found himself admiring her composure.

What the—?

Clearly, he needed a break more urgently than he'd thought if he was starting to admire someone he'd just caught stealing from him. He was obviously suffering from nervous exhaustion. Only, from somewhere at the margins of his mind, an idea was taking shape. Briefly, he tested it for weakness.

But it was sound. Pragmatic. A near-perfect solution to a problem that he had shelved on the flight back to New York.

It was also completely insane, he told himself.

Or was it? In business, if you had your rival over a metaphorical barrel, you took what you wanted, what you needed, and right now he needed a no-strings partner. But just because Sydney would be given access to his private life, it didn't mean that it was personal. This was a transaction like any other.

'You react well to pressure,' he said after a moment.

She stared at him, those brown eyes confused, but curious. Because his non sequitur had piqued her interest. And that in turn had piqued his. Curiosity, the desire to know more and so be more, that he understood. More than understood, he thought, remembering the first time his father had taken him to the copper mine in Colorado. It had propelled him forward, given him wings.

The need to have control over what was his. To not have to sit by, powerless to intervene as it slipped through his fingers, that was the engine that drove him onwards, but his curiosity was the fuel.

'Yes.' As she nodded, the slight movement of her head made another curl slip free of its moorings and watching its progress made him feel light-headed.

'It's part of the job. If you get emotional then you lose focus.'

True, he thought, dragging his eyes away from the distracting curl back to her face. Only that didn't help because now the part of his brain that should be cool and clinical was distracted by the freckles on her face.

She had beautiful skin, smooth and pale aside from a faint flush of pink along her cheekbones, so a perfect canvas for that mesmerising sprinkling of sun kisses. A beat of heat danced along his limbs. Was that all there were or were there others elsewhere?

'That's good to know,' he said, shutting the door on that thought. 'You see, while we've been talking, I've realised I have got a use for you after all. A short-term contract.'

He watched as her shoulders dropped fractionally. 'You won't regret it. I can start tomorrow.' She hesitated. 'But I'll need some kind of security clearance to get into the building. My pass expired today.'

He let her wait, as she had made him wait earlier in the day, liking how it made the colour in her cheeks spread like spilt wine.

Finally, he shook his head. 'You won't need a pass. I don't want you anywhere near my office. But you will need a passport.'

Her forehead creased. 'Where do you want me to go?'

My bed, he thought, his body suddenly hot and tight.

Without the pants, but she could keep that blouse on. His gaze dropped to her spiked heels. And those shoes. It was a cliché, but clichés became clichés because they spoke to something true.

But not enough to act on. Coming to his senses, he met her gaze. 'Venice,' he said slowly. 'That's where I want you to go. Where you need to be.'

'You have an office in Venice?'

'No, I don't. And I don't need your hacking skills. I have

a big event coming up. In Venice. I need a date, a girlfriend of sorts. Just for a week.'

She was looking at him as if he had lost his mind, and to be fair a part of him was thinking exactly the same.

'Is this your idea of a joke?' Her eyes clashed with his, the pupils wide with shock and outrage. 'Because it's not funny.'

'It's not a joke. It's a proposition. A chance for you to avoid a prison term. I'm sure you're familiar with the concept. You see it a lot in the movies. Bunch of no-good criminals are offered freedom and a pardon if they take on a dangerous mission. I believe it's called the "boxed crook" trope.'

She let out a small, brittle laugh. 'And there I was thinking you were just being a typical male sleazebag taking advantage of a situation to get his leg over.'

The mouth on her! Tiger stared down at Sydney, feeling his hackles rise. 'For the record, I don't take advantage of women, Ms Truitt. And in any case, you don't need to worry. I'm very choosy about who I get my leg over.'

'Then I suggest you "choose" some other woman,' she said, and there was an edge to her voice that made him think his words had hit their target. 'There must be one in New York who would enjoy your company.'

'Many,' he said coolly. 'But I can't think of another woman who shares your unique skill set. You see, I need someone who understands that our "relationship" is just for show. Someone who can play a part under pressure. Persuade people that she's something she's not. Lie to their faces.' His eyes locked with hers. 'Someone willing and available to bend to my will.'

Her pupils flared. 'Then you definitely need to choose another woman because I'm neither of those things.'

Watching her face, Tiger wondered what it was exactly

about this woman that drew him to her so intensely. It was maddening to feel this way, but to not understand why.

Most likely it was just this whole set-up, he reassured himself. He was intrigued, or maybe that wasn't the right way to describe how he was feeling but he couldn't think of a better one.

'You misunderstand me, Sydney.' He saw her hands ball into fists as he used her name. 'When I said willing and available, I meant within the context of the alternative being jail time.'

CHAPTER THREE

PUT LIKE THAT, she had no choice, Sydney thought, panic scrabbling in her throat. But, of course, she'd never had one because the choice was between two equally unpalatable options. The classic rock or hard place. Deep blue sea and the devil.

Remembering Noah's twisted face as he'd reeled off her faults in that cold, hissing voice, she shivered. In some ways, too many ways right now, Tiger had more power over her than Noah had ever had. And yet, although he was making her feel nervous and tenser than she'd ever felt, that wasn't the same thing as being scared.

The worst part was that she had chosen Noah. There had been no threat hanging over her. At eighteen she had found his authority and rigour thrillingly exotic. He had been so unlike her family, so articulate and emphatic, and she had been hooked.

Had put herself on the hook, she thought, throat tightening at her naivety. *No*, not naivety. To be naive was to be credulous and clueless about how the world worked. But she was a Truitt, she knew how it worked and, more importantly, how often it failed to work. She had been stupid and smug, believing herself to be different, better than everyone around her. And she had been better academically. She'd worked hard and she'd liked school. There had been rules to follow, and she'd found it relaxing to know what she had to do and where she had to be at what time.

Because home had been far from relaxing. It had been chaotic and overwhelming, and she'd always been on edge, always worrying about what was going to happen next. Noah had seen that, and exploited it, flattering her and isolating her and telling her 'hard truths'; telling her she deserved better.

Now she could see that his 'honesty' and principles were a mask for his cruel, controlling nature, but back then she had wanted to believe him so badly that she had ignored all those red flags in his behaviour until it was too late and she was living in his world—if it could be described as living.

But that was then. Now she understood that to be that certain, that uncompromising, had a dark side. A dangerous side that was best avoided.

Her gaze shifted an inch to where Tiger stood watching her, the potency in his gaze undeniable. Unavoidable.

Because she couldn't avoid this man unless she let him call the police, and faced the consequences. And she couldn't do that. She couldn't fight for her brothers' freedom from behind bars.

Then again, how could she pretend to be his girlfriend?

Her arm twitched, the point of contact where his fingers had pressed against her skin tingling as if he were touching her now. If she agreed to that, then he would have to touch her, kiss her even. And she knew how he would kiss, could see his hand in her hair the better to hold her as he pressed his mouth against hers.

She took an unsteady step backwards, shivers running over her skin, her head spinning with shock and an intense, alien longing for something she didn't recognise or know how to process.

'What about your security team?' She waved her hand in the direction of Carlos. 'And your head of IT? They think I'm public enemy number one. Isn't it going to look a little bit weird if we suddenly start "dating"?'

He shrugged. 'We use white hats all the time to challenge the integrity of the security system. Obviously, it has to look real or nobody takes it seriously. If I tell them this was one of those occasions, then that's what it is. The only opinion that matters on that subject, on any subject in this building, is mine. And it's not just an opinion.' He lifted his chin and there was a dark gleam in his eyes that made her breath catch. 'It's more of a directive.'

His voice was quiet. Matter-of-fact because he wasn't bragging or bigging himself up. He didn't need to. The truth of his words was stamped into every curve and line of his gorgeous face.

Her pulse was racing. Tiger might be the most dangerous man she had ever met and yet she wasn't scared of him in the physical sense. Her fear was that he would somehow sense the heat she could feel blooming inside her.

'Even if that's true I don't see how it's going to work,' she said firmly, because she had to try, had to make him see that she would be better employed as a cyber-security asset. 'This isn't Halloween. I won't just be putting on some costume for a couple hours. You're asking me to convince people that I'm someone I'm not and I'm not an actress.'

He stared down at her, his golden gaze steady and unblinking. 'Are you saying that Abi and Hannah are in on this? That they know you've been hacking my system?'

'No, of course not.'

'Are you sure?' he persisted. 'Perhaps I should have someone bring them in and I can see what they have to say.'

She glowered at him. 'You know they haven't got a clue about any of this.'

Which, of course, meant that she had proved his point for him, she thought furiously, a fraction of a second later. The dark gleam in his eyes told her that he had been waiting for her to reach that conclusion.

Squaring her shoulders, Sydney lifted her chin. 'You're missing the point,' she said, not bothering to hide her anger and frustration. 'I wasn't acting because I *was* an assistant to Katherine.'

'True, but you were also hacking my business for personal gain.' He shook his head. 'Time's up, Ms Truitt. Make your choice.'

'It's not a choice. It's blackmail.'

His mouth twisted into a smile that made her heart thud heavily in her chest. 'No, this is retribution.'

She hated him then. Hated how he was making it seem as though he were being so reasonable when the reality was that he was bending her to his will.

'And just so we're clear, I will take silence as a refusal,' he added softly.

'This isn't legal.'

'But hacking is?' he said coolly. 'My lawyers can find a workaround. All you need to do is sign whatever I send you.' His eyes held hers as he tapped his expensive watch. 'Last chance. Yes, or no?'

'Yes,' she said through gritted teeth and the look of satisfaction on his face made her want to scream and throw things at his head.

'Good.' He sounded calm, relaxed even, as if the outcome of their conversation had never been in any doubt.

'We leave tomorrow. I've had my lawyers draw up an NDA and you'll need to sign that before you leave the building. You can wait out there. Then I'll get a car to take you home and see you to your door. Wouldn't want anything happening to you on your way home. I mean, there are so many unscrupulous people around these days,' he added, pulling his phone from his pocket.

Was that it? Sydney stared at him in confusion and a mounting anger as he began scrolling down the screen.

'You can go,' he said softly without looking at her. 'Unless you want to type out a couple of emails for old times' sake.'

She felt her cheeks grow hot. 'You know, I'm starting to think that maybe prison wouldn't be such a bad option.'

He straightened then, and held out his phone. 'Shall I make the call or would you rather do the honours?' he said in that dark way of his that made her pulse dance along her limbs. 'I guess not,' he added as she shook her head. 'In which case I think we're done here.'

There was a beat of silence.

'Not quite' she said stiffly. Ignoring the hint of shame that flared inside her, she drew a deep breath, because it had to be done. 'We haven't discussed my fee.'

Now his gaze rose to meet hers. 'Your fee?' he repeated, his mouth curving downwards in a way that thudded through her in time to her heartbeat.

The flash drive was in Tiger's possession so Harris Carver wouldn't be paying her now. Not that she was about to share that piece of information with the man in front of her. Finding out that she had a buyer and that it was Carver would be an unnecessary distraction at this point in the negotiations. What mattered was getting hold of some money, and fast. So, she was just going to have to brazen it out. There was no way around it.

'I need money,' she said flatly.

He didn't like that. Didn't like a woman asking to be paid to be his 'girlfriend'. But then it must be a first, she thought, trying to ignore the burn of his gaze. A man as beautiful and wealthy as Tiger McIntyre would have women queuing up to be invited, however briefly, into his bed.

'Tough.' His eyes were dark and dangerous then. 'Your fee is your freedom, Ms Truitt.'

Which was true but didn't make her feel any better. For a moment she contemplated appealing to his soft side and telling him the truth about her brothers. But admitting that her family were petty criminals was hardly going to help her case. And besides, Tiger was not some housecat. He didn't have a soft side.

Suddenly and fiercely, she wanted this over. Wanted to get out of this vast air-conditioned office that somehow felt small and crowded and hot because of him.

She shook her head, because she had to try. 'Right now, my freedom isn't enough.' Which hadn't always been true, she thought, with a jolt. Trapped in the house down that dirt track, miles on foot from the nearest road, body stiff from tiptoeing on eggshells, she had dreamed of freedom as a woman in a desert dreamed of finding water.

Her whole body tensed as he pushed off from the desk and took a step towards her. 'You're in no position to negotiate or make demands, Sydney, and I would advise you against thinking that is ever going to change, because it won't,' he said, and there was a husky softness to his voice that made her shiver. 'But it will vex me, which for obvious reasons I would also advise against.' His gaze narrowed on hers in a way that made her breath go shallow. 'Put simply, if you want to stay out of jail, you need to keep me sweet.'

Her lip curled. 'I thought you were on the record for not taking advantage of women,' she said tightly.

He frowned. 'I don't take advantage of women.'

Her eyes narrowed but the stupid thing was she believed him.

Yes, he was taking advantage of the situation but there was a pragmatism to his thought process that she understood. He needed a partner, a woman on his arm who could be relied upon to smile and gaze up at him adoringly and then walk away afterwards without a murmur of complaint and in a weird but logical way she fitted that remit.

Even more weirdly she had often thought how useful it would be to have a man like that to hand.

Since Noah, she had been single and celibate. She'd tried various dating apps but she was always on edge, constantly looking for the signs that she had missed with him because she couldn't trust them, or herself. Couldn't let them get close or allow things to get too deep. But there were times when it would be helpful or even just more fun to have a partner of sorts. Someone she could meet for breakfast or to take to weddings or even the occasional party. Someone who was calm and kind and intelligent, who would dance with her and laugh with her without expecting more. Someone who wouldn't try to curtail and control her when she wanted to move on.

Because she had to keep moving. Keeping one step ahead was the only way to stay safe, and it had worked just fine until today.

Feeling Tiger's gaze, she lifted her chin. 'Am I not a woman?' she said crisply.

She instantly wished she hadn't said anything because his eyes locked with hers, then moved over her face. Slowly. Then dropped again to the tiny pulse beating at the base of her throat roaming downwards over her quivering body, not missing a detail.

The atmosphere in the office was suddenly so taut that it felt as if it would shatter at any moment.

'Yes, you are,' he said slowly, and she felt her body shiver to attention, breasts suddenly and inexplicably heavy, a bud of heat pulsing between her legs.

Behind him the walls of his office seemed to be losing shape and that thing, that twitching, staticky golden thread between them that she had been pretending not to feel since walking into his office for the first time this morning, snapped taut.

Her heart was running free like a herd of wild horses.

'If there's nothing else,' she said after a moment, shifting her weight from one foot to the other like a boxer squaring up to her opponent, because that was what he was. She was clear about that. 'I'll just get my things.'

She half expected him to move but he didn't and, trying her hardest to ignore him, she reached past him for her bag, only, because she was intent on not touching him, her balance was off centre and she teetered sideways.

His hand snaked out so quickly she didn't see it move, just felt it as he caught her, her breath snatching in her throat as his arm curled around her waist, pulling her upright with such force that she found herself pinned against his warm, unyielding body.

For a moment, she couldn't process the feeling of him, the heat, the hardness. It was too much.

Except it wasn't.

Her fingers curled into his shirt. She wanted more. More heat. More hardness. More of him—

And that was a shock because she didn't like people touching her, didn't like to be touched.

Until now.

'Sydney.' The hoarseness of his voice as he said her name

arrowed through her, kicking up sparks inside her so that she felt singed, and the heat of his hand was telling her things about herself she had never known, making her want things—

Her legs were softening, she was melting inside and she reached out to steady herself.

'Ouch!'

She winced. Her elbow had connected with something and a crash resounded through the cavernous office, yanking her out of her trance-like state.

What the—?

'Is everything okay in there, Mr McIntyre?' The man's voice sounded distant, as if she were dreaming it. But this wasn't a dream, she was here in Tiger's office, his chest pressing into hers, the hard shape of his thigh pushing between hers.

Only how could that be?

Tiger was her enemy, but searching inside herself she could feel nothing like loathing or disgust. Instead, her body felt taut and achy and unfulfilled because his hard, muscular chest was still temptingly within touching distance and as he moved her fingers tightened in his shirt of their own accord.

She could feel his gaze pinning her to the floor. She glanced down and saw the lamp from his desk rolling in slow, lopsided circles on the polished concrete floor. Beside it her bag lay on its side, the contents fanned out around it.

'Mr McIntyre?' The man's voice was taut and urgent now.

'Everything's fine, Carlos.' Tiger released his grip and she clutched dizzily at the desk for support. Her whole body felt hollowed out with a hunger she had never felt for any man and she could only watch dazedly as he picked up the lamp and put it back next to the pile of folders.

'I just knocked something off the desk. It's all good. In fact, Ms Truitt is just leaving, aren't you? So you can walk her to the elevator.'

Out of the corner of her eye she saw the shadowy outline of Carlos move away from the door and then her body tensed as Tiger turned towards her, because his pupils had swallowed up his irises so that his eyes were no longer gold, but black.

'Are you okay?' He stared down at her, his expression hard, glittering and unreadable, and she nodded.

She couldn't have answered Tiger's question aloud. Her breath was gone. Her voice too. Her heart was pounding sluggishly as if she'd been drugged or hypnotised and all her blood seemed to have rushed to her cheeks and her face felt as if it were burning and yet she wanted to lean into him again and the whole thing was so confusing that she couldn't look at him any more and, ducking down, she began to pick up her things.

'Need a hand?'

'No, I don't,' she said quickly, but Tiger was already crouching beside her. His nearness made her skin feel unfamiliar, hot and tender and tingling.

'Don't,' she snapped, snatching a packet of tissues from his hand. Her voice sounded high and thin and she understood that it was revealing too much. But she couldn't do anything to change it without drawing attention to that fact and she had already given away more of herself than was sensible to this man.

There was a long silence as he stared at her for what felt like an eternity and then he spun round and walked around his desk.

'I'm sure you can find your way out. Don't forget to sign the NDA. I'll see you tomorrow morning. Make sure you're ready. If you keep me waiting, it won't be my security team knocking on your door. It'll be the NYPD.'

His eyes roamed down over her body in a way that made her feel unsteady. Unclothed.

'Dress is smart-casual but nothing flouncy or garish. Keep it subtle. Oh, and, Sydney…' He paused as she turned to face him, and now his gaze was as hot and bright and destructive as a solar flare. 'A word of warning. Any little voices in the back of your head suggesting you do a disappearing act— you would be wise to ignore them. Otherwise, you'll find out exactly what happens when you pull a tiger by the tail.'

He hadn't given her a time, she realised as she let herself into the apartment, no doubt on purpose to punish her for asking for money.

But she had no choice. She needed money and Harris Carver owed her nothing because she hadn't delivered. Her spine stiffened as she remembered their brief conversation. She hadn't told him that she'd been caught red-handed, just that she couldn't hack the McIntyre server. 'Thank you for letting me know,' he'd said and then he'd hung up.

And now she was back to square one. Worse than square one, because she had no money coming in. But at least she wasn't sitting in a police station, which was good, and in a week this would all be over, and really how bad could it be? It was just a different version of what she'd already done, only, instead of posing as an admin assistant, she would be posing as his girlfriend. So put like that, it was just more role-playing, only with a few added complications.

Her heartbeat jerked in her throat. That was one way of describing Tiger.

She felt suddenly exhausted, as if she had just finished a triathlon. As she sat down on the sofa, her phone pinged and, gazing down at the screen, she felt her breath catch in her throat. It was the NDA. She scrolled down to the bottom because otherwise it wouldn't let her sign, but she didn't bother reading it. What was the point? She was hardly going to negotiate her terms. Clicking on the screen, she signed in the box and pressed Send.

There. It was done. She wasn't going to have to face the police.

And yet she couldn't properly enjoy the feeling because now it was real. Undeniable. Unavoidable.

Her back prickled against the sofa cushions. Back in his office, it had all felt so surreal, so *unreal*. The whole time she was there she had just kept thinking, This can't be happening to me. And as she'd walked back into the apartment it had felt even more like a dream. Or a nightmare.

She glanced down at the screen, her pulse twitching.

But it was time to wake up and smell the coffee. By signing that NDA she was bound to Tiger.

Bound.

Remembering Tiger's warning about pulling a disappearing act, she got abruptly to her feet and began pacing round the apartment. Round and round as she had once paced the home that became a cage.

Could she run?

No point, she thought, a shiver running down her spine. Nobody could run for ever. Which meant she would have to find a place to hide. Only hiding was worse than running.

Her body stiffened as she remembered what it had felt like waiting to be found. Eyes closed. Braced. Breathing between clenched teeth. Waiting for the sound of his voice, his footsteps. Praying for it in the end because the silence was the most terrible thing of all.

Somewhere nearby a dog barked and her legs slowed then stopped.

No, she wasn't going to run or hide. And she didn't need to. Okay, it hadn't exactly gone according to plan, but everything was under control.

Under control? Heat rose up over her chest to scald her face as she remembered how her skin had seemed to dissolve and fuse with his in those few febrile seconds when his arm had slid around her waist and her body had pressed against his.

There had been no control, no will. She had been a creature of basic and compulsive need, impervious to the danger and absurdity of her actions.

Stalking into the kitchen area, she yanked open the refrigerator door, snatched a can of soda and pressed it against her cleavage. The last thing she had been in that moment was in control. Then again, in some ways it was good that it had happened. Now she knew what he felt like up close and if that was as bad as it got...

Only that was the problem. It hadn't been bad. On the contrary, it had been the most singularly erotic experience of her life.

Maybe, possibly, probably at some point during this sham relationship they would have to get that close again. Maybe they would even have to kiss but it would be brief, performative, but not in any way passionate. It certainly wouldn't involve tongues or open mouths because couples didn't kiss like that in public except in the movies.

And she had no intention of ever being that near to Tiger McIntyre in private again.

Staring at his laptop, Tiger frowned. That was the third time he had read that page of the document on screen and he still couldn't remember a word of it. It made no sense. He was interested in the research, respected the academics who had authored the report, but for some reason it was hard to stay focused. His mind kept drifting off.

He slammed the screen shut and shoved the laptop across the desk so hard that it collided with the lamp and he had to grab at it to stop it falling onto the floor for the second time that day.

His body tensed as a memory of the first time reared up inside his head, hazy at the edges but clear and sharp at the centre so that he could see Sydney Truitt's wide brown eyes and trembling mouth just as if she were standing there in front of him.

Although if that were the case, neither of them would be standing.

He swore under his breath. What the hell was she doing back in his head? Although it wasn't really a case of her coming back because she had never left.

His phone pinged and, glancing down at it, he felt his shoulders stiffen as he stared down at her signature. So that was that. It was official. The game was afoot.

Except it hadn't felt like a game when her body had been pressed against his. Remembering the quivering arc of her body and the way her hand had clung to him, he felt his pulse accelerate. He couldn't think of many games that involved a loss of will and purpose but, in that moment, he had forgotten why she was there and why he was there.

And it had shaken him deep down. Not just the shock of it happening, but that he hadn't wanted to let go of her.

Of course, it was understandable, he reassured himself. He had reacted without thinking and the anger and frustration and intimacy in his office had created some kind of chain reaction that had blown away his logic and willpower. But he was back in charge now and when he held her in his arms the next time, it would be on his terms, not hers.

He pictured Sydney's face, that slight uptilt to her chin, a subtle but deliberate challenge to his authority.

In fact, this whole arrangement was going to be on his terms, as Sydney Truitt would soon find out.

CHAPTER FOUR

THAT THOUGHT WAS still front and centre in his head the following morning when he strode down the aisle of his private jet and he felt a ripple of satisfaction as he saw Sydney. She was sitting in one of the cream leather seats, that gorgeous dark red hair pulled up into one of those half-up, half-down hairstyles with a darker red ribbon, her face determinedly turned towards the window.

But she knew he was there. He could tell by the slight stiffening of her shoulders.

No doubt she was annoyed with him because he had deliberately kept her waiting for just under an hour, only rolling out of bed when Stefan, the driver he'd sent to collect Sydney, had called to let him know they had arrived at the airfield.

'Sorry, darling. I completely forgot the time,' he lied.

Now she looked up at him, slowly, reluctantly, like a prisoner of war greeting her captor, and he felt a sting of wounded pride because, yes, the alternative was being arrested but, still, he was Tiger McIntyre. Most women fell over their high heels to catch his eye but this one looked at him as if he were something that had crawled out from under a rock.

He dropped down into the seat beside her, enjoying the glint in her narrowed eyes as she moved her legs away in one seamless motion. It was a challenge he couldn't resist and he caught her hand and lifted it to his mouth, feeling immense satisfaction as he felt her surprise and then anger. Payback, he thought, for the day before. For the night he'd spent tossing restlessly in his bed thanks to the memory of her soft curves and small, stunned face intruding on his sleep.

It was a new experience for him, this incessant pulse of hunger, and one that wasn't restricted to his dreams, he realised as she angled her body away from his and his eyes followed the movement hungrily. He gritted his teeth. He had no idea why she affected him so. She was a thief and a liar and had yet to show any remorse. By rights he should despise her, and yet he couldn't remember feeling so out of control with a woman.

It was one of the reasons he'd kept her waiting. To prove that he was the one in charge of both the situation and himself. Unlike his father, he was not going to be buffeted about by his fascination for some random woman.

'I'll make it up to you,' he murmured.

'No need,' she said, smiling stiffly. 'I was perfectly happy sitting here on my own.'

'That's what I love about you. Any other woman would be bitching about having to wait but you turn it into a positive,' he said softly.

'Excuse me, Mr McIntyre, Ms Truitt.' It was Carole, one of the stewards. 'If you could put your seat belts on?'

'Of course.' Letting go of Sydney's hand, he watched her buckle up, liking how the movement made her red hair shimmer beneath the overhead lights.

His pulse gave a jerk as the jet began to rumble down the runway. This was it. He could still stop this. And he should stop it. Sydney Truitt was bad news and trouble all tied up with a bow, metaphorically and literally.

Of their own accord, his eyes flicked to the bow on the

back of her head, because all he wanted to do was tug that ribbon loose. Maybe then she would try to kiss him again as she had yesterday, he thought, watching her pale fingers tighten around the armrest as the plane lifted away from the ground.

And just like that, it was too late to do anything.

Twenty minutes later they were at cruising altitude and it was clear that any assumption that this arrangement would be happening on his terms was looking a tad premature.

Yes, Sydney smiled warmly at the stewards and answered their questions in that husky, precise way of hers that he seemed to find so fascinating, but the moment they were unobserved, she would retreat back into silence and present that profile of hers to him like a queen on a coin instead of the thief and the liar that she was.

'Are you hungry?' He didn't wait for her answer, just inclined his head slightly towards the hovering air steward. 'Good morning, Adam. I'd like three eggs, sunny side up, four rashers of bacon and an espresso to follow, and Ms Truitt will have the same. Aside from the coffee,' he added. 'She prefers an americano.'

Sydney's head jerked up and he thought she was going to say she wasn't hungry or that she didn't eat bacon or eggs, but instead she stared at him, two small lines furrowing her smooth forehead. 'How do you know how I drink my coffee?'

He shrugged. 'Intuition.'

That was a lie.

After she'd delivered his lunch and they'd had that strangely charged encounter, he had found his gaze drawn to her again and again throughout the afternoon. At one point he had wandered casually over to stand by the glass so that he could watch her return from the coffee run, her face scrunched with concentration as she made her way across the office. Even at that distance he could tell the contents of the cups from their height and colour and she had distributed the tall, skinny lattes in their cream beakers to her colleagues but kept the shorter black beaker containing an americano for herself.

'Intuition?' She stared at him suspiciously, not sure whether to believe him or not.

But why did it matter if she did or didn't? He'd never cared before what other people thought about him. With a father like his he'd had to force himself not to care, which was not easy when Gerry McIntyre was the punchline of so many jokes.

Tiger felt his jaw tighten. But he'd had the last laugh.

Taking on the name callers, calling out each and every person who thought he was as weak and dupable as his father and making it painfully and unquestionably clear to them that was not the case.

He had never looked back. But then there was no reason to do so. Everything behind him was lost or wrecked. His mother had died before he could remember her, then his grandmother had followed less than a year later. Now his father was dead too and his childhood home was a derelict shell.

All that remained was the business, and that would have gone too if he hadn't single-handedly turned it around. It hadn't been easy. On the contrary, he had earned his stripes. It was during that period of his life that he had cemented both his nickname and his reputation for ruthlessness, despatching his rivals with a speed and savagery that had left him prowling the corporate jungle almost alone so that now he was free to make the rules, not just bend them to his will.

And as the apex predator he had got used to a lot of scraping and sycophancy.

That had changed yesterday when he had generously offered this tightly wound woman sitting beside him the opportunity to be his 'girlfriend' for a week and instead of biting off his hand she had more or less told him to shove his offer where the sun didn't shine.

Such a thing had never happened before. Only, instead of hurling her to the wolves, he had doubled down, astonished and intrigued by her defiance and by the pale curve of her jaw as she'd lifted her chin to meet his gaze, because, truly, it was so alien for anyone to talk to him in that way. Which was no doubt the reason she had this effect on him.

Gauzy rays of early morning sunlight were slanting through the window onto Sydney's face and, taking that as permission to follow, he let his gaze move over her features.

She was undeniably beautiful with that red hair, dark like damp fox fur, curling over her collarbone and that matching flush of colour on those cut-glass cheekbones. The soft pink bow of her mouth was nothing short of perfection.

But instead of yesterday's office armour she was wearing black gingham capri pants, a white blouse flecked with tiny yellow flowers and low-heeled taupe-coloured sandals. His gaze steadied on her toenails, which were painted a soft, pale pink. Smart-casual, he'd said, and she was definitely erring towards the more casual end of smart-casual, but she was all the more luminous and fascinating for that.

'Have you been to Italy before?' he asked.

She shook her head.

'But you have been on a plane?' he persisted, suddenly remembering how she had clutched the armrest during take-off.

'Yes, of course. But I've never been to Europe.' She gave

him a light gleam of a smile that knocked him sideways until he realised that she was smiling at Carole, who had arrived to tell them that their food was ready.

As he sat down at the table, his pulse skipped a beat as he realised that it was the first time he had eaten breakfast with a woman on his own since his grandmother died.

Like everything he did, that was a conscious decision.

He knew most people would think that dining together was the most intimate of meals and it was in the sense that fine food, low lighting and alcohol could and often did lead to sex.

But for him, sex was an end in itself. It might happen more than once. It usually did, he conceded. And then afterwards, he got up, ostensibly to shower because showering gave him a reason to get out of bed, then got dressed and left because staying over could suggest, not unreasonably, a desire to take things to the next level and he had never wanted to do that. Never wanted there to be any confusion about the kind of relationship he was offering, which was mutually satisfying but always impermanent. Sharing breakfast with a woman would simply be a humbling reminder of the mistake he'd made, the risk he'd taken. So, breakfast *à deux* was never an option.

His eyes moved to the woman beside him. But of course, Sydney was different. He *had* to eat with her so it didn't count. And anyway, it wasn't real. This was role-play with the added benefit that he was not just starring in but directing the production. This was nothing like one of his father's affairs, because there was absolutely no risk whatsoever that he would end up marrying her.

'You must have been to Vegas.' Every second person at the test plant in California seemed to have visited Sin City, either for stag or hen dos or as a consolation prize after a messy divorce.

'Vegas?' Something flickered across her face, an expression he couldn't quite place. She cleared her throat. 'Yes, I went there once.'

She glanced past his shoulder almost as if she was bored by the conversation, which was another new sensation for him. Or at least one that he couldn't remember happening since first grade.

Sydney felt everything inside her tip and roll sideways as if she were a capsizing boat. A shiver ran over her skin.

She had been to Las Vegas once, but she never allowed herself to think about it. Not because what happened in Vegas, stayed in Vegas. But because who would want to remember the place where they made the biggest mistake of their life?

It was hard to remember it now. So much time had passed. Mostly, though, it hurt to remember the girl she'd been back then. Younger, yes, but also full of hope for a future that would be different from the kind of life all other Truitts in living memory had led. She would have a husband with a steady job. A partner with principles and a clarity of purpose.

Her fingers pressed against the smooth, pale, puckered skin on her arm. Unfortunately, his purpose had not been to cherish and honour her but to 'correct' her deficiencies. It had taken a month after their wedding before he'd had his first meltdown and thrown his plate across the kitchen because she'd put condiments on the table.

She felt Tiger's steady gaze on her face and realised that she had no idea how much time had passed since she had spoken or even if he had replied.

Fortunately, Carole returned at that moment to serve their food and she was able to legitimately turn away from him.

The rest of the flight passed surprisingly quickly. She had been slightly concerned that Tiger would want to keep on sharpening his claws on her, but, perhaps because he had eaten, he merely made a profuse and completely insincere apology and then opened his laptop and worked for the rest of the flight.

He worked hard. Harris Carver was right about that. Although that didn't absolve him of all his rule-breaking and entitlement.

Still, it was a relief not to be the focus of that dark gold gaze that saw things she needed to keep hidden. Instead, she watched a film, read some of her book and wondered after roughly every third page how his 'real' girlfriends put up with being treated in such a cavalier fashion.

Money probably. But then she was only doing this because she needed something from him too. So how was she different from them?

Nibbling her thumbnail, she listed off all the ways she could think of. Firstly, there was no actual relationship. No trust. No history. No hopes. They didn't even like each other and obviously there was no intimacy.

Her pulse stalled, her memory rewinding like a car spinning on black ice to that moment in his office when she'd almost kissed him.

She hadn't forgotten it. She had tried to, of course, but it seemed to have burned itself into her brain. Thankfully, it was probably a common enough occurrence for Tiger to have dismissed it from his mind but, glancing up, she felt a different shiver scamper through her body. Instead of looking at the laptop screen, he was staring at her in that intent way of his, his pupils flickering. Was he remembering it too?

It didn't matter one way or the other, she told herself firmly.

She couldn't change the past. She knew that better than anyone. But you could choose how to live your life, make decisions about which risks were worth taking and which would be avoided, and kissing Tiger fell unequivocally in the second category.

An hour later, the jet landed with barely a shudder on the runway at the private airfield on the Italian mainland.

There was a car waiting for them on the runway and she knew there was a bridge across the lagoon so she had assumed that they would drive into the city but, after twenty minutes, the driver turned off the main road and she saw the shimmer of water.

'What's happening?'

Tiger glanced over at her. 'We're swapping onto a boat.'

As explanations went it was minimal but there was no time to question him further. The car had already come to a stop, and now the driver was opening the door. It was a short walk to a covered jetty and then Tiger was helping her into a glossy, wooden speedboat.

He sat down beside her, letting his leg graze against hers in a way that was without doubt deliberate, but she was tired now. It had been a long day and the air was cool and his thigh was warm so she could reasonably allow herself to stay where she was. Leaning back against the plush leather upholstery, she watched eagerly for her first glimpse of Venice.

All she knew about the city was from the movies and it felt odd seeing a place so familiar for the first time rising out of the water. But even at night and at a distance it was mesmerisingly beautiful.

'Come si sente suo cugino, Angelo? Ben preparato, spero?'

She blinked as Tiger leaned forward and began speaking

fast, fluent Italian to the driver. He caught sight of her expression, and his mouth curved up at one corner.

'His cousin is taking part in the *gondolino* race this year. I was just asking him if he was feeling ready.'

Tiger talking to the driver of the boat in Italian was distracting enough but when that was combined with the way his hair was being blown in the wind and the glint in his eyes, it was a moment before she realised that the city was fading into the distance.

Her heart thudded against her ribs. 'What's happening? Is there a problem?'

Dropping back down onto the seat beside her, he shook his head. 'No problem.'

'But surely the hotel is that way.'

'What hotel?'

She blinked. 'The hotel we're staying at.'

'We're not staying in a hotel. I don't like the crowds and, besides, I have a villa here.' His mouth did that curving thing again and she felt it thump through her in time to her heart as he corrected himself. 'Not here in the city. It's on one of the other islands in the lagoon.'

Sydney stared at him, her head spinning. She had assumed, wrongly it turned out, that they would be staying in a hotel surrounded by staff and other guests. But that wasn't the case because he had a villa.

Of course he did.

And there was not much point in worrying about it now, she thought as the speedboat accelerated. Finally, the driver shouted something over his shoulder and the boat slowed to a crawl. Her heart gave a thump as Tiger turned towards her and said softly, 'Just remember, you're my girlfriend and you're madly in love with me.'

There was no right response to that statement, or none

that she could think of, but she didn't need to, because they were pulling up alongside a wooden jetty that lit up as they got closer. A young man wearing smart shorts and a black polo shirt stepped forward to pick up their cases.

'*Bentornato, Signor McIntyre, e benvenuti, Signorina Truitt.* I hope you had a pleasant journey.'

Tiger took her hand again to help her off the boat and this time he didn't let go, but she was expecting that. It was incredibly quiet after the thump of the boat, but it was quieter even than that. Almost as if this were a desert island, not a playground for wealthy tourists.

They were walking so swiftly that she had only the briefest glimpse of the villa—large, three storeys, with lots of arched windows—and then they were inside and a middle-aged woman with sleek dark hair stepped forward to greet them.

'This is Silvana. She doesn't speak much English. Most of the staff don't. It means I have to practise my Italian.'

'What about the other tourists? Are they just Italian?'

'There are no other tourists. This is my island.'

Of course it was.

He was walking as he talked and she let him lead her upstairs. 'You can have the guided tour tomorrow, but this is our room,' he added, so casually that it took a moment for the implication of his words to hit home.

And then everything lurched inside her.

Sydney's eyes narrowed and Tiger felt the air sharpen between them.

'Our room?' She frowned.

'Yes, darling. Our room,' he repeated. Yet another thing he had never had to do before. He sensed rather than saw Silvana turn. Moments later he heard the door click shut.

'What the hell do you think you're playing at?' Sydney snapped, her soft mouth curving into a snarl that revealed small white even teeth. She tugged her hand free, her body rigid with fury and outrage.

'I could ask you the same thing,' he said mildly, and with what was an admirable amount of restraint given that they were alone and he knew exactly what it felt like to feel her body against his.

'Meaning?' Her hands curled into fists by her sides.

'You're supposed to be my girlfriend, remember?'

'Only in public.' She waved her hand wildly to encompass all four corners of the room. 'We're not in public here.'

'You and I have a deal,' he said, adopting a soothing tone that was designed to do the opposite of soothe. Because, frankly, why was he having to explain himself? Again? 'I gave you a choice and the choice you made was obviously going to include us sharing a room. Surely you understood that?'

Her hands clenched and unclenched by her sides.

'Why obviously? We've only just started seeing one another. Maybe I have strict parents so I've insisted on separate rooms?'

Separate rooms? For a moment he was stunned by her suggestion. It had literally never happened before, and in this instance, it couldn't.

The reason she was here, the *only* reason in fact, was so that he would have a partner. Having a beautiful woman on his arm was part of his brand. Like the watch he wore and the handmade suits and even his nickname. It was his armour. All of it was designed to intimidate, to discourage people from getting too close, because everyone had their own agenda, particularly women.

He switched his gaze to Sydney's face. 'And what exactly do you imagine everyone is going to think about that?'

'Exactly what you tell them to think, I expect,' she said, and he felt the huskiness in her voice pulse in all the wrong places. 'After all, the only opinion that matters on that subject, on any subject, is yours. And it's not just an opinion, is it, Mr McIntyre?' She lifted his chin. 'It's more of a directive.'

He laughed then. Partly to cover up his astonishment at being bested by her because, damn, she was smart, and she was right too, even though it pained him to admit it. And partly, and this was even more astonishing, because he was enjoying himself.

In the space of forty-eight hours she had ignored and interrupted him, defied and challenged him and now she was making him laugh.

He couldn't remember the last time a woman had done that.

Not because he didn't find things amusing. Despite what most people thought, he had a sense of humour, but laughing meant you were relaxed, and being relaxed would require him on some level to let down his guard and he had never done that with any woman because there was a risk that he might turn into his father if he did so.

But Sydney was different. This 'relationship' was different. He didn't have to worry about things getting out of hand or being misinterpreted. They had a deal, and so he could relax.

Which must be why this felt more real than any of the so-called relationships he'd had in the past.

And maybe him laughing like that caught her off guard or perhaps it was just the sudden break in the tension between them, but her mouth was pulling at the corner and he was suddenly desperate to see the smile that was trying to break free.

'That's how it works,' he agreed, and he had that same sudden intense need to touch her just as he'd had back in his office. He reached out to touch her face—

Her eyes snapped wide open, and she took an unsteady step back, and for a moment she just stared at him in the taut silence that filled the room.

'Unless,' she said at last, her voice a light taunt, 'you were simply bragging. Or projecting. Is that why you suggested this charade? Because you're not the man you pretend to be?'

He wasn't enjoying himself now. Her words had hit home.

Which was ironic, as he hadn't had a home since he was four years old when his grandmother had died and he'd moved back to live with his father. From then he had felt like a guest, and often not a welcome one. His heart thumped against his ribs. But Gerry had been oblivious because Gerry had recently fallen in love again. So Tiger had decided that he wanted no part of love. That love was blind, and it was dangerous.

But now this woman, this thief, this imposter, had got past his carefully constructed walls. And he had let her, invited her in no less. He felt a rush of fury with himself, but mostly with Sydney for turning him into a stranger. For making him feel like the kind of stupid, susceptible man he'd sworn never to become.

'You're getting confused, *Sierra*,' he said coolly. 'You see, I'm perfectly clear about who I am. But maybe I didn't make it clear enough to you, so let me rectify that right now.'

Reaching into his trouser pocket, he pulled out the flash drive and held it up between his fingers.

'I am the man standing between you and a long prison sentence. So if I say jump, you jump. Real high. And you keep on jumping until I say stop.'

Silence.

'Do you like threatening people?' she said finally.

No, he thought, his chest pinching as he stared down at her. She looked as though she was bracing herself just as she had in his office and he didn't like how that made him feel. Didn't like that he was making her feel that way.

It didn't help that those clothes made her look younger than she had yesterday. He might even have said vulnerable, if her chin hadn't tilted up pugnaciously.

It was enough to make him come to his senses.

'Do you like stealing?' he countered, severe suddenly, although he was far more distracted by the flags of colour on her cheeks than was sensible.

Another silence.

Damn it. He glanced round the bedroom, his spine taut with frustration. This was not what he had imagined. Then again, he hadn't actually given much thought to how it would work in reality, just signed off on the concept.

'I'm not sure what you were expecting to happen.'

'Don't do that.' Her voice was hoarse when she answered and her eyes shimmered with a heat that he wanted to immerse himself in. 'Don't try to make me out to be the problem here. This was your idea. You're not going to make me responsible for your lack of forward planning.'

He stared at her, his teeth on edge. It wasn't lack of forward planning that had brought them to this moment, but arrogance and past experience. To put it another way, he couldn't remember the last time a woman had not wanted to share his bed because there had never been one.

'Look, the bed is big enough that we don't have to interact.'

His body tensed painfully as his brain began to offer up a slideshow of several possible permutations of what interacting with Sydney might look like.

'It's not just the size of the bed. It's the fact that you'll be in it. There isn't going to be an "interaction" of that sort between us.' Wide brown eyes accompanied that dismissive statement, but the sudden splashes of high colour on her cheeks told a different story and he remembered that shimmering, explosive moment they'd shared in his office back in New York.

She was stubborn, almost as stubborn as he was. She was also out of her depth and she didn't have his stamina for fighting her corner. More importantly, he could see her pulse hammering against the pale skin on her throat and that glitter in her eyes.

'Nothing is going to happen. Unless you want it to,' he added, because he could still remember her soft, stunned gaze and the way her fingers had splayed against his arm. And he was also arrogant enough to assume that she would be no different from any other women in his life.

Her pupils flared. 'Then I hope you enjoy waiting because I will never want you.'

Wrong, he thought, and he wanted to prove that, to yank her against him and finish what had started in his office. Instead, he took a step closer, close enough that he could see her pulse fluttering down her throat.

'And I hope you enjoy sleeping on the right side of the bed, but if you don't, then I'm afraid you'll have to choose between the floor, the couch or the bathtub because while you're here with me, this is your bedroom, and this subject is now closed.'

She stared up at him in silence, and he felt a tick of irritation.

'Right, I suggest we go and get something to eat.' What now? He broke off, frowning as she shook her head.

'I don't want anything to eat. I'm tired. I want to go to sleep.'

'You can't go to sleep,' he said impatiently. 'It's only four p.m. in New York. Plus, you've missed a meal.'

'I don't care.' There was strain in her voice now but with that same storm in her eyes as before. 'I want to go to sleep.'

'Fine. Have it your way. Just don't blame me when you wake up and can't get back to sleep, because that's what will happen. And when it does, I suggest you think long and hard about how you're going to make this arrangement between us work. Unless, of course, you'd prefer to take your chances with the police, which, frankly, I wouldn't recommend, but given you seem determined to do the opposite of whatever I suggest, knock yourself out.'

Sydney held her breath as Tiger spun round and stalked past her, and the walls shuddered as he slammed the door behind him, and then it was over. He was gone.

She was alone.

She was shaking inside. Not from fear any more, although it was not fear of him but of the idea of sharing a bed with a stranger. Now, though, she felt frustrated. He was impossible. Unreasonable. Thoughtless. And she was stupid for thinking this could ever work.

And for not thinking about the possible sleeping arrangements for their week together. How had she not thought about that?

Mainly because back in New York, and even on the way over to the island, she had been trying so hard to believe that none of this was happening that she hadn't allowed herself to think that far. Her eyes fixed on the bed. Because if she'd thought about 'this' she would never have been able to do what was needed.

As she stared at the bed, her mouth felt suddenly dry. It was a very big bed but the idea of sharing it with Tiger made her heart thud painfully hard inside her chest. What did he wear in bed? And what if they moved while they were sleeping and ended up touching?

That moment in his office reared up inside her, shimmering bright and tactile, and she was flushed with the heat of it, skin tingling, breasts aching and heavy. No, she thought, her pulse scrambling for a footing. That wasn't real. Whatever she had felt then was just a combination of gravity and panic and proximity.

Wasn't it?

And then, quite suddenly, she felt tired, the have-to-sit-down-before-I-fall-down kind of tired that made thinking impossible. She needed to sleep, and now, and, walking over to the bed, she pulled back the cover and climbed in, her eyes closing like shutters as her brain powered down to silence.

Tiger had been right, Sydney thought four hours later as she woke in the darkness and stared blearily at the time on her phone screen. It was three a.m.

Three a.m. here but nine p.m. in New York, which was no doubt why she had never felt more wide awake. Or hungrier.

Except that wasn't true. There had been frequent days with Noah when food had been a privilege, not a right.

But Noah wasn't here. Nor was Tiger. She had known that maybe even before her eyes had snapped open. Which must mean he had decided to sleep in another room. She felt what must be relief only it felt oddly almost like disappointment. Or hunger, she told herself firmly as her stomach rumbled loudly. She reached over to switch on the bedside lamp and she sat up, blinking into the light.

Why was she so hungry? They had eaten lunch and had cakes and coffee in the afternoon, but not enough, apparently.

Maybe a glass of water might help. Her throat tightened because she didn't want to do that. Having a glass of water would mean accepting that food was not an option. It would mean that Noah was still inside her head, controlling her, crushing her, and that wasn't an option either.

She wasn't some cowed prisoner; she was Tiger McIntyre's girlfriend. Or at least that was what everyone believed.

Heart pounding, she threw back the covers and realised she was still fully clothed. Her bags had been unpacked and the contents neatly placed in the walk-in wardrobe. Ignoring the beautiful shirts hanging from the rail, she found the T-shirt she wore to sleep in, stripped, then pulled it over her head.

Back in the bedroom, she picked up the luxurious, quilted bathrobe that was artistically draped over a beautiful linen-covered armchair. It felt glorious, she thought as she wrapped the belt tightly around her waist, soft and thick but light, like being enveloped in a cloud.

The next step was to go downstairs and, not giving herself time to think, she stalked across the room and opened the door. There was nobody there. Obviously, because it was three o'clock in the morning, but there were table lamps lit and she made her way downstairs.

Having not had the 'tour', she had no idea where the kitchen was, but it was the first room she found, which seemed like a good sign. There was no sign of a fridge, but then a house this big would surely have a larder.

It did.

Sydney stared around the regimented rows of condiments and snacks and jars of pasta and flour and grains. Her stomach rumbled appreciatively. It was an Aladdin's cave of food, teeming with every possible ingredient and treat.

And there was a cavernous fridge. Tentatively, she pulled on the handle. Oh, goodness, it had a door within a door so that you could see inside without opening it. She licked her lips as her eyes snagged on a plate of salad with tomatoes and bread and olives.

This would be perfect, she thought, opening the second door to retrieve the dish, then shutting the fridge doors and turning—

She gasped and almost dropped the plate.

Tiger was standing there, laptop in hand, his body blocking the doorway to the larder. 'You know, this is becoming a habit with you. First you try to steal my IP, now you're taking my panzanella.'

CHAPTER FIVE

SYDNEY BLINKED.

Her heart was beating so loudly she was surprised that Tiger couldn't hear it. If only she had stayed upstairs. It was the latest in an ongoing, ever-growing list of regrets she had about the last few days. But there was nothing she could do about that now.

She cleared her throat. 'Is that what this is called?'

Tiger nodded, and then he walked towards her and every single cell in her body exploded with panic, except it wasn't panic. She knew panic all too well, and this was more complicated.

And contradictory.

'It's a Tuscan bread salad. I have my chef make it every time I visit.'

'Here, you have it.' She held it out towards him, and then wished she hadn't as the movement made the robe part around her throat and she felt the flick of his gaze lick her skin like a flame.

'Or,' he said after several beats of silence, 'we could share it.'

They ate in the kitchen. Tiger didn't bother to decant the salad onto a second plate so it was a case of sharing.

'My bad—' Her pulse twitched as his fork collided with hers as they both tried to spear the same piece of tomato at the same time.

'You have it,' she said quickly, fingers tightening around the handle of the fork. She couldn't remember the last time she had shared a plate of food with anyone and it felt oddly intimate. Too intimate. It was the kind of thing a new couple might do on their first date, order a dessert and then smugly ask the waiter for two spoons.

But she and Tiger were not a couple and, even though superficially this had all the component parts of one, this definitely wasn't a date. More it was a ceasefire.

'You're the guest,' he countered.

Her eyes flicked to his face. 'I thought I was a pain.'

In the low lighting of the kitchen, his hair and eyes were dark, only his skin looked golden. 'Oh, you're that too.'

She had been here before with a different man who had made it his mission to point out her flaws. But this didn't feel like that at all. Absurdly it felt as if his words were meant as a compliment.

'I mean, it's kind of what you do, isn't it? Being two things at once.'

That wasn't a compliment but his voice lacked the sting it would have if he were digging at her and the slight up-tilt to his mouth made her want to lean closer and trace the curve of his lips—

Shying away from the ridiculousness of that thought, she let her gaze drop to the plate, staring down admiringly at the olive-oil-strewn chunks of bread and glossy tomatoes, as if that, not him and his all too fascinating face, was the most important thing in the room just then.

'But I was being a bit of a pain too,' he said softly.

Glancing up, she found him watching her in that incisive way of his.

'A bit?' She raised an eyebrow.

Tiger leaned back in his seat, his strong fingers stroking

the rim of his water glass, and she suddenly wished that it were New York time here so that Silvana or some other member of staff would be bringing them food just as they had on the plane, and there would be something to distract her from this intense and intensely beautiful man sitting opposite her.

'Okay, I was a pain earlier. I hadn't thought through some of the hands-on practicalities of our arrangement.'

Hands-on. Remembering the seeking press of his fingers as he had pulled her against him, she felt her face get warm.

'I didn't think about it either,' she said quickly.

He tilted his chin back. 'True, but as you so rightly said, this was my idea.'

It was more of an acknowledgement than an apology but that in itself felt seismic. During her brief, exhausting and terrifying marriage, she had always been wrong and it had taken years to shift that thinking.

'And I should have realised that you might not be comfortable sharing a bed.' She must have tensed because she felt his eyes flick to her face.

'So, I was thinking maybe you might be happier in another room.'

Now her eyes flicked to his. She hadn't expected that and something of her surprise must have shown on her face because he frowned. 'I know I haven't offered you much in the way of evidence but I'm not a monster, Sydney.'

'I don't think you're a monster,' she said quietly. 'And I get why it makes sense for us to sleep in the same room.'

His eyes were steady and precise on her face. 'I can take the sofa.'

'Or you could share the bed.' Her voice sounded different, and now his gaze enveloped her, holding her captive with hypnotic intensity.

'Like you said, it's big enough.'

'It is.' His voice was different now too. 'But only if you're okay with that.'

She nodded. 'I am.' She was. And she knew that shouldn't make sense, and yet it did. Because of him.

Maybe he hadn't formally apologised but Tiger had admitted to going too far; what was more, he was trying to make amends for how he'd acted.

Only this wasn't just about him, it was about her too. About how, even though she was divorced, she hadn't put her relationship with Noah behind her. For so long now, she had been too scared to let anyone get close but, probably because none of this was real, she felt safe enough with Tiger to do so. Not just physically, but emotionally.

After all, she was playing a role. Her actual feelings weren't involved.

And a part of her did miss being intimate, being held, being close to someone, which was completely understandable. Although it was surprising that it should be Tiger who had made her finally admit that to herself. To cover her confusion she said quickly, 'But thank you for giving me the choice.'

'So, you believe me now?' He was watching her with a narrow sort of gaze as if he cared about her answer. 'That I'm not a monster?'

'You're not a monster. I mean, you like getting your own way.'

'You sound like my housekeeper.'

That smile.

She felt her stomach lurch, only this time it had nothing to do with hunger and her heart thudded hard as heat surged through her. A dizzying, dangerous heat that she felt everywhere, almost as if those callused hands were touching her, caressing her—

'What do you mean?' She didn't really care. It was just something to say to clear her head but as his eyes met hers, she was suddenly curious.

A knot formed lower down in her belly as he shifted back in his seat and the crooked smile curving his mouth deepened a fraction at the corners. 'When I came downstairs, she guessed we'd had a row about where you were sleeping. I think it's fair to say that she was surprised, but also pleased. She thinks I have things too easy. With women. She thinks it's bad for me.' His smile twisted. 'She doesn't say so to my face, but she has a way of conveying her opinion with an eyebrow or the slightest of shrugs.'

'And do you? Have things too easy? With women?' she blurted out before her brain could apply the brakes.

Her whole body tensed, the reaction both a learned response and a survival instinct hardwired in her DNA to the sudden tautness in the air that followed her question.

Tiger shifted in his seat.

'I like women. And they like me,' he said, putting down his fork. 'Or they think they do until they realise that I'm not in it for the long haul.'

'And that's a problem, is it? The long haul?'

He nodded. 'I think relationships are best kept simple.'

She agreed. Simple was good but safe was better. Not that she was interested in relationships. For any relationship to work there had to be trust and outside her family she didn't trust anyone. And yet she was having this surprisingly frank conversation with Tiger.

'By simple, I'm guessing you mean that you just want sex?'

He laughed. 'That's maybe putting it a little too simply. But yes, I suppose in an ideal world, I think it would be easier for most people if they accepted that sex was all they wanted a lot of the time. Only humans seem determined to make things more complicated, so we have marriage and romance and love.'

Been there, done that, she thought bleakly, and once was enough. And for her it had not been complicated at all.

Marriage was a cage; romance was a hoax. As for love?

Love was the most dangerous of them all. So much more dangerous than you were told. It was a promise that got broken every single day.

'I'm not interested in any of that.' He pushed the empty plate away from him as if to underscore that sentiment.

'I'm not interested in any of that either.' She hesitated for a moment then, putting her fork down, she said quietly, 'What does interest you, then?'

Her heart slowed to a crawl as silence stretched between them.

'Work. Building my business. And the moon. Ever since I was a kid, I wanted to go there—' He glanced past her to the dark square of sky outside. 'It always felt like it was watching me, seeing me.'

It seemed like an odd thing to say. She couldn't imagine a situation where Tiger wasn't seen.

'I suppose it would be quiet.'

He nodded and there was another long, shifting silence and then abruptly he leaned forward, his eyes suddenly very golden. 'So, was it the truth?'

She stared at him, confused, not just by his question, which made no sense at all, but by the way he was looking at her so closely as if she was a puzzle he was trying to figure out. 'Was what the truth?'

'What you said about your family being strict. Are they?'

No, she thought. Her childhood home had not quite been lawless, but there had been very few rules. And she had hated it, because every morning when she'd woken, anything could have happened. Maybe that was why she was so good at hacking. She accepted the impossible, the random, the topsy-turvy and she had learned to let it flow round her while she restored order.

But she could imagine how that would sound to Tiger, how he would react. She had heard it so many times already, some version of the 'apple doesn't fall far from the tree'. She didn't need to hear him say it too.

'They're not strict,' she said slowly. 'But they have lines they won't cross.'

Her family might turn a blind eye to selling car parts that might be stolen. But they weren't violent or controlling or abusive. For example, they wouldn't bang someone's face against a steering wheel because they had missed a spot of dirt on the windscreen.

The memory had crept in uninvited, but she couldn't look away. One tiny little tooth, white like a pearl, and blood, red, slick, gleaming in the Nevada sunlight. So much blood.

She shoved the memory back forcefully into the margins because obviously she wasn't going to tell Tiger any of that.

Or could she?

The question shocked her almost out of her skin. She was definitely suffering jet lag, she told herself, if she thought that was an option. It was the only possible explanation for why she was considering something that made absolutely no sense whatsoever.

She had never told anyone about Noah, not even the police.

And she especially couldn't tell Tiger. He wasn't her confidant.

He wasn't even her friend.

He was the man who had offered her a way out of the fire

into the frying pan. And he would walk her straight back into the fire without a qualm because nobody got as rich as Croesus by being soft and *simpatico*. It didn't matter that he had sat and shared a salad with her or that she had momentarily imagined feeling safe with him.

If she told him about Noah, then he would ask questions and any answers she gave would raise more questions. Only how could she answer those questions? To do so would mean revealing more than she was willing to share and she didn't want to think about the person she had been back then. Didn't want to show weakness when it felt as though they had reached some kind of equality.

'What about your family? Are they strict?'

For a fraction of a second, she thought he wasn't going to reply but then he did another of those infinitesimal shrugs.

'I have no family.'

He glanced at the expensive watch on his wrist. 'You should probably be able to sleep now.'

It was a dismissal, just as if they were back in the office. Except she was wearing a bathrobe.

'Is there a dishwasher?' She stood up, reaching for the plate—

'You don't need to.'

He moved at the same time, his chair scraping against the floor as he got to his feet, his hand covering hers.

Move, she told herself. But she couldn't. It was as if the touch of his hand had stopped time. Stopped everything. There was nothing but the silence and the darkness and the heat of his skin and his nearness as the air grew thicker.

For a second they both stared at each other. Every single nerve ending in her body was flickering like a malfunctioning circuit board.

Only she didn't feel broken.

She felt whole and right and sure, and she stepped forward and clasped his head between her hands and fitted her mouth against his.

And everything just stopped.

She felt a jolt of shock as if she hadn't decided to kiss him. But then in a way she hadn't. It had been more of an imperative, a challenge to be met, a need to be satisfied. Curiosity and desire in their most primitive and basic form.

She couldn't remember any kiss feeling like this. It was a wildfire tearing through the darkened outback, torching everything in its path. A wall of flame that altered everything it touched. It was possessive and intoxicating. Devastating and reckless and so necessary.

And that was shocking in a different way. That she should want his mouth on hers. That there was no terror pulling her under at his closeness.

For the first time in six years, she wanted this, wanted him.

He was pulling her towards him now, his hand fumbling clumsily at her waist, anchoring her body against his so that she could feel the hard press of his chest and thighs.

The lights beneath the kitchen units spun and blurred behind them, bright and fast like a carousel, but the real world, the world of lawyers and contracts and threats and failure, was so far away.

There was only him.

Tiger.

Here. With his free hand sliding upwards through her hair in one smooth motion, fingers warm and strong, his mouth rough and tender. He parted her lips and deepened the kiss and the fierceness of him took her breath away and she heard herself moan. Then he was lifting her against him and her few remaining thoughts grew gauzy, weight-less, unimportant.

Somewhere in the house a clock chimed loudly and she jerked backwards and her heart, which had stopped beating when he had touched her, started up again at twice the pace.

'If you've changed your mind about where you want me to sleep—' He sounded as shell-shocked as she felt. Nervous almost, although she must be imagining that.

She cleared her throat. 'I haven't,' she said quickly.

'Okay, then.' He was back in control. 'Like you said, the bed is big enough.' He glanced at his watch. 'Why don't you go on up? You don't need to wait for me,' he added. 'I have some work to finish up.'

His dark gold gaze held her captive momentarily and then he turned to pick up the plate and she didn't quite run but she moved swiftly through the silent house and back into the bedroom. Undoing the robe, she let it drop to the floor and climbed into bed, her body shimmering and strange to her, and she stayed that way when he slid in beside her as the light began to creep beneath the shutters.

'Dovrei preparare una caffettiera fresca, Signor McIntyre? Questo è freddo.'

Glancing up at his housekeeper, Tiger shook his head. 'No, *grazie*, Silvana.'

Normally he could drink any amount of coffee without any noticeable side effects at all, but today he had barely drunk more than a quarter of the French press that Silvana had brought to the table and he was already suffering from a sensory overload.

Or maybe the cause of his twitching pulse and headache was not the contents of the coffee press but the contents of the yellow shirtdress sitting opposite him in the soft Venetian sunlight.

He had woken early, but when he'd rolled over, the bed had been empty and the sheet smoothed flat as if she had never been there. As if he had dreamt her.

But she wasn't a figment of his imagination, any more than that kiss.

Yet here she was sitting opposite him, calmly sipping her coffee as if nothing had happened in the kitchen. And he didn't know whether to be relieved or angry. When he'd strolled onto the terrace, he hadn't expected her to smile but her mouth had curved up at the corners because Silvana was there too, he'd realised a moment later. But then she'd tilted her head up so that he'd caught a glimpse of the smooth arc of her throat and he'd leaned in and brushed his lips against hers.

She had stiffened fractionally and then her lips had parted and he'd had to fight against every urge to deepen the kiss because this arrangement was on his terms and that meant being able to pull back.

'*Buongiorno,*' he'd said softly, lifting his mouth and pulling out a chair in one smooth moment as Silvana had returned with a bowl of freshly baked *cornettos*. Sydney had selected an almond-flavoured one and as he watched her pull it apart, he wondered why the process of sharing breakfast with her today seemed so much less of a big deal than it had done on the plane.

No doubt it was because they had already eaten off the same plate last night or the early hours of this morning, depending on which time zone you applied. Although, right now, nothing seemed to matter as much as getting her to keep looking up at him like that so that he could see the pale underside of her neck.

He leaned forward casually. 'Did you sleep well?'

She nodded. '*Ho dormito come un ghiro.* Like a dormouse?'

He raised an eyebrow. It was an Italian phrase, but Sydney didn't speak Italian. 'Where did you pick that up?'

'I did some miming to Silvana.' She pressed the palms of her hands together and rested her head on them. 'She told me what to say in Italian and then I checked on my phone to make sure I hadn't got the wrong end of the stick.'

'Or mistaken fireflies for lanterns. *Prendere lucciole per lanterne.* It's the closest to getting the wrong end of the stick in Italian.'

He leaned a little closer, drawn to the flicker of curiosity in her brown eyes because, other than himself, he couldn't think of a single person he knew who would be interested in learning idiomatic Italian for a week-long trip.

'So, you like languages? I thought hackers were all maths nerds.'

Her eyes narrowed. 'Do I look like a nerd to you?'

No, he thought. She didn't. In that dress, with that hair and those toenails, she looked as if she were about to sashay down the Rio Terà de le Carampane to meet some girlfriends for lunch at Terrazza Cattana.

She shrugged. 'Coding is like a language. Equations are just sentences with numbers. At school I never really understood that. I thought words weren't my thing. Reading, writing was always such a struggle, so my teachers told me to focus on maths.' She glanced away as if she was remembering a classroom somewhere and he found himself trying to picture her as a child. Skinny, he thought. Plaits and maybe a brace, he thought, remembering the way she had covered her mouth sometimes.

'What changed?'

Her shoulders stiffened. It was the smallest of movements, so subtle that another man might not have noticed it. But thanks to his father, he was an expert at reading people and there was something about that infinitesimal shift that made his chest tighten.

'I realised that letting other people set your boundaries was the easy option. Pushing back feels harder at the time. And it feels like an unnecessary risk to take, because you might fail.' There was an odd undertone to her voice that pulled at something inside him. She was choosing her words with care, he realised, not just because she wanted to be clear about what she was trying to say. She was also trying to conceal some things too.

'But if you don't push back, you stop being you. And then every day a little piece of you will disappear until finally there's nothing left.'

Sydney felt her stomach tighten. Tiger was lounging back in his chair, his face bathed in sunlight, one arm resting lightly along the back of the chair beside him, his long legs stretching out casually beneath the table. He was wearing a pale blue, short-sleeved linen shirt and loose cream-coloured trousers and he looked every inch the relaxing business mogul on vacation.

Except his eyes. Which were staring at her intently.

'That's quite a theory,' he said at last.

She forced herself to shrug but inside her head was spinning. It was true, she did feel that way, but she had never articulated it out loud because it wasn't just reading and writing she found hard. Speaking her mind, making herself heard, was also a problem. It was another reason why she liked working with computers. Coding didn't require actual speech.

But there was something about this man that made her eloquent.

No, not this man, she corrected herself quickly. It was the situation. Being here, in Italy, on this island. It felt as though she were outside space and time, outside herself.

'In my job, there's a lot of sitting around waiting for things to reveal themselves so I get a lot of time to think.'

Or she could just say the first, stupid thing that came into her head.

Her words reverberated loudly around the terrace and her jaw clenched tight as Tiger's eyes flicked to her face.

'Am I to assume by job you mean the part in the day when you hack my server in order to steal my IP? Rather than what I was paying you to do?' Tiger said softly. He hadn't moved a muscle but the air around them seemed to shudder a little and she swore silently because they had come full circle. The guarded rapprochement of moments earlier had evaporated and Tiger was once again the man who had stared down at her in his office with such contempt.

'I was just trying to—' she began, but he cut her off.

'No matter. You're here to do a different job now and time is moving on.' His gaze sharpened. 'I'll give you a quick tour of the house and then we need to go over a few things, get our stories straight.'

The villa was beautiful and she would have liked to stop and admire the gilt and the marble and the tapestries and the glittering chandeliers, but the tour was brief and perfunctory, with Tiger opening doors and listing off rooms at breakneck speed so that she had little more than a blurred impression of pink and dark red and burnished gold.

Finally, they made their way upstairs and he ticked off the various bedrooms and bathrooms until they reached their bedroom, where the housekeeper stood waiting by the door.

'Ah, Silvana, *è tutto pronto*?'

The housekeeper nodded. *'Quasi.'*

'Bene.' He turned back to Sydney, gesturing through the door. 'Shall we?'

She stepped into the bedroom and stopped. There was a rail in the middle of the room and hanging from the rail were clothes. Not her clothes, but fluid, figure-hugging couture that came without price tags because only people who didn't care about money would buy them.

'What are these?' She turned towards Tiger, who frowned, unsurprisingly, because it was obvious what they were.

'They're for you to wear this week. It's not just the regatta and the ball, there are other events and you need to look the part. You're welcome,' he added, his mouth twisting, clearly underwhelmed by what he perceived as a lack of gratitude on her part.

'What's wrong with my clothes?' she said, pushing back against the memories of Noah throwing her favourite jeans in the trash. As on everything else, her ex-husband had had opinions on what she should wear. And now Tiger seemed to think he could have an opinion too. Only it was more than that. Ever since she'd talked about her job at breakfast, his mood had shifted. But why was he so angry about something he already knew? It made no sense, only that was the worst kind of anger to manage.

'I knew I was going to have to borrow something for the ball, because I don't have a ball gown, but—'

'Are you being serious?' he said after a moment, his tone cool and sardonic. 'What you're wearing is fine for here, but you need something more high-end.' He flicked the sleeve of a beautiful dark green dress.

'You said smart-casual.'

His golden gaze seemed to tear into her. 'I meant for the

flight. Obviously, I'm not expecting you to wear your own clothes when we're in public.'

Sydney stared at the contents of the rail, a small shiver winding through her body. 'Why "obviously"? My backstory is that I'm someone you met through work. We're not pretending that I come from money.'

'Because that's how this works.' He was impatient now. 'Because I'm not just a guest, I'm a sponsor of the race and the ball and you're going to attend those events as *my* girlfriend, which means you have to wear the kind of clothes that a girlfriend of mine would wear. Most women would be happy, grateful, excited.'

Trying to stay calm and centred, Sydney let her gaze move over the shimmering silks and gauzy wisps of chiffon. 'But I wouldn't wear anything like this. It's not who I am.'

'You are who I say you are.'

His voice was harsh but it was the shrug accompanying that blunt statement that made the floor ripple beneath her feet as if it were made of quicksand, because that tiny, careless shift of his shoulders was more than just proof that he was unmoved by, and impervious to, her point of view, her wishes, her feelings.

It was a sharp, stomach-churning reminder of how quickly her world had shifted and shrunk six years ago.

'Think of it like Halloween. Only there's an upside. You don't have to return the costume.' Now he picked up the green dress and let it dangle mid-air from the hanger like something broken. 'You can keep it. Keep all of them.' He gestured to the rail. 'And as they're "not who you are", you can sell them. Because they're worth a lot of money and we both know that's what matters to you, isn't it, Sydney?'

In the past she would have kept quiet, tried to defuse the situation, but Tiger had reduced her life, her ambition, her essence, into one cutting rhetorical question. Because as she already knew it was only his opinion that mattered.

'Says the billionaire who stays up until three a.m. working.'

A muscle pulsed in his jaw and he looked as if he might move closer. 'This is going to come as a shock to you, Sydney, but some people actually work hard for a living.'

'I work hard.'

His face was like stone. 'In this instance, working two jobs is not some sign of your diligence. Quite the opposite, in fact. Your position at McIntyre was about deceit and ultimately theft, and all theft is about entitlement and greed.'

'I'm not entitled or greedy.'

'Then why were you stealing from me?'

'I told you I needed—I *need* the money. Or are you deluded enough to think I want to be here with you, that I would for one moment consider pretending to be your girlfriend if you weren't continually threatening to hand me over to the police?'

His eyes were burning a hole in her retinas. He didn't like that, but she didn't care.

'Do you think I want you here?' he said coldly. 'You're just the lesser of two evils.'

That hurt more than it should have done but that wasn't why she flinched. It was the fury in his voice.

'But,' he continued in that same cold voice, 'if this is all such a trial to you, Sydney, then why don't I put you out of your misery and call the police?'

'Because I can't help my brothers if I'm stuck in prison.'

There was a moment of stillness and she knew from the way Tiger was looking at her that her face had gone pale, but she was already spinning on her heel, moving, legs reacting before her brain even knew what she was doing—

She heard Tiger swear, sensed him moving, his hand reaching for her.

'*Scusi, signorina.*'

Silvana had returned with a trolley laden with boxes and she caught a glimpse of the housekeeper's startled face and then she sidestepped past her and did what she should have done all those years ago when Noah had first made it clear that her feelings didn't matter. That she only mattered in relation to him, and then only if she put his needs above her own.

Never again.

Never.

Again.

Her strides lengthened and as she pushed open a door into the sunshine, she started to run, feet pounding against warm stone, then grass, stumbling, then running, once, then twice. She had no idea where she was going. All she could think about was getting as far away from that scene in the bedroom as possible. She had shown too much emotion, given too much away. Given him more than she had wanted to.

Too late, she realised she should have gone to the jetty, but instead she had reached a beach.

She slowed, slightly out of breath, her heart shuddering against her ribs, her gaze moving past the dancing white-tipped waves to the pale, shimmering city hovering like a mirage beyond it.

Venice.

It was too far away to make out anything specific but even at a distance she felt its calming effect and, a moment later, she reached down and unbuckled her sandals. Pressing her feet into the sand, she felt a wave of homesickness, and guilt. Because she had let them down. Her brothers had needed her and she had failed them.

What had she done?

Tiger was no pussycat, but he wasn't violent. Except his anger, that blind fury she'd heard in his voice and seen on his face, it had panicked her in a way she couldn't control.

It was still rippling through her now, making her want to cry, because it was all such a mess. Being here with him was so far from the worst place she had ever been. But she had been there before and back then she hadn't acted, hadn't defended herself and everything had got so hard, so fast. She hadn't wanted to make the same mistake again.

So she had made a different one.

And there was no point in trying to take it back.

'I don't do second chances, Ms Truitt. You cross me once, we're done.'

Tiger's voice seemed to echo down the beach and, needing to get away from the consequences of her actions, she started to walk beside the tiny, tumbling waves.

Her feet slowed. Set back slightly from the shoreline was a small stone building. It looked too small to be a home, and anyway who would be living there?

Sliding her feet back into her sandals, she walked towards it cautiously, but as she got closer it was obvious it was empty. Abandoned? Tiger had kicked the owners off when he bought the island?

And then as she turned her head a fraction, she saw him. Her stomach plummeted and she lifted a hand to cover her pounding heart.

He was standing there, watching her, his dark head tilted to one side as if he wasn't entirely sure what he was doing there.

He still wasn't sure why he had gone after Sydney, just that watching her leave had pulled at something inside him. Without any kind of conscious decision, he had made his way through the villa and onto the terrace, his gaze fixed on the comet's tail of Sydney's hair.

'It used to be a fisherman's cottage. If that's what you were wondering. It was empty when I came here.'

It was actually one of the main reasons why he had bought this particular island. It was a reminder of how fragile the things you took for granted could be. For years people had pushed their boats away from this shoreline to cast their nets. They had made their homes here, earned a livelihood and then just like that it was gone.

And Venice itself was one of the most perilously situated cities in the world. Anything could be lost and you had to remember that and do anything and everything to stop that from happening.

Sydney was staring at him as if he were a particularly dangerous animal that had escaped from some local zoo and he couldn't really blame her. Even as he had been talking to her, he'd known that he didn't like how he was acting but he'd still been riled by that comment she'd made at breakfast. Casually mentioning how she derailed businesses as if it were nothing. As if she hadn't been planning to do that to him. It was a blunt reminder of who she was, only, with the imprint of that kiss still front and centre in his brain, he had let himself forget.

And then he had expected her to be excited and grateful when he'd shown her the clothes, but she had acted as if it were a bad thing. What woman didn't like new clothes?

Glancing up, he found Sydney watching him, her face pale and still, her hands clenching at her sides.

'Don't let me keep you.' Emotions he couldn't name moved swiftly across her face and he felt a flicker of irritation that he couldn't read them and that she could keep herself out of reach, defying him, even now.

'You know this would be a lot easier if you stopped turning everything into a fight.'

'There is no "this" any more,' she said, lifting her chin in that maddening way of hers.

'Because I bought you some clothes?'

She didn't answer, but she didn't need to. He knew that the clothes were not important. As for the money?

Her hair had come loose and the breeze lifted it away from her small, stiff face, and he held back. Not to savour the moment but because he knew it would hurt her. He knew because he'd heard the hurt in her voice when she had talked about her family.

'Why didn't you tell me?' he said quietly.

'Tell you what?' Her voice was fierce, hostile.

'About your brothers?'

Her skin looked like paper. 'Because people like you think you're different from people like them. Because you don't want to hear that you're the same.'

His heart twisted, which was strange because that particular organ usually functioned solely as a life force but she was so defiant, standing there with her brown eyes.

'What if I did?'

Her hands were like tight balls now and for a moment he thought she wouldn't answer, but then she took a step closer, her eyes narrowing on his face.

'They run a chop shop. They buy and sell stolen parts.' Her voice was fierce, combative, as if defying him to show his disgust, but it only seemed to root him deeper to the spot. 'They do other stuff. Stupid, small-town, small-time stuff with their idiot friends. And now they've been arrested and with their record they're going to go to prison.'

He opened his mouth to speak but she cut across him, fiercer still, 'Let me guess what you're thinking now. The apple doesn't fall far from the tree. Only it's not a tree, is it? The Truitts have a whole orchard. Misdemeanours. Warnings. Arrests. We're all the same. Rotten to the core.'

'You don't know what I'm thinking. We're talking about your brothers and you. And given how much you loathe being here with me, I'm guessing you must love them very much.'

Her eyes were storm dark but there was a tremble to her mouth that made his chest pinch because she was trying to hide her feelings and failing. Only he wasn't sure if it was the trying or failing that felt like a blow.

'I know how it looks but they're not bad people. They just make bad decisions. I don't expect you to understand,' she said after a moment, as if she needed to manage her voice.

But he did understand. Tiger felt his chest tighten. He understood only too well.

She hesitated. 'I didn't mean what I said earlier about being your girlfriend. I mean, obviously I didn't want to do it but you're not who I thought you were.'

Ditto, he thought as she met his gaze.

'Are you going to the police?'

He shook his head. 'But we have to find a way to make this work. We might not be friends but we can't be strangers.'

'I know.' She nodded. 'I could take another look at the clothes.'

'And you could wear some of your own clothes if that would make you feel more comfortable. Or I could get the stylist to select some other options, and you could choose something more "you".'

It was easy to offer that, and he wondered why it had seemed such a point of contention back at the villa. But then that was before he knew the truth. That she wasn't just the grabby little thief he'd assumed her to be. She had a motive, so, yes, she had still tried to steal from him, but at least he understood why. It wasn't greed that had motivated her but love, and loyalty. She had put everything she had on one desperate spin of the roulette wheel. Her job. Her professional reputation. Her freedom. Gazing down into her face, he felt a stab of something like envy. Who would do that for him? Who would sacrifice anything to save him?

He pushed the thought away. This wasn't about him. It was about Sydney, and that look on her face when she'd turned and seen him on the beach. She'd looked like he used to feel. Lost, alone, angry and scared, but trying not to show it and he'd hated it.

'Your brothers, do they have a lawyer?'

'Yes.' She nodded. 'But they need a better one. I did go to the bank, but I'd already taken out a loan to set up the business. And my parents don't have that kind of money. That's why I was trying to hack your system.'

'Then maybe now is a good time to rethink our arrangement, tweak it a little.'

She stared at him warily.

'Look, if you're still willing to help me, then maybe I can help you. I know plenty of good lawyers. I can make some calls, that way your brothers will get proper legal representation.'

Her eyes widened. 'Why would you do that?'

He held her gaze. 'Because you highlighted the vulnerabilities in my system when you hacked it. So, in a way, you did me a favour. Plus, it would be awkward if something came out about your family while we're together, so if I can stop that from happening… I mean, what's the point of being rich if you can't bully and buy your way out of trouble?'

He watched her cheeks flush as she recognised her words.

'That would be such a relief,' she said after a second or

two, as if she'd needed a moment to pull herself together, and it wasn't that he was surprised, because he knew her better now, but hearing the tremble in her voice felt like a blow.

'Why did they leave?'

He frowned, then realised she was looking at the stone hut.

'The fishermen? I think it was around the time Venice grew. Other islands were just geographically closer to the city. Times change.'

'It's strange to think that people lived and worked here and then they just disappeared.'

'They didn't take everything. There's some graffiti on the wall.'

Her face shifted then, mouth curving into a smile of such sweetness that he felt momentarily light-headed. 'Here, let me show you.'

He held out his hand and, after a second, she took it and he led her into the hut. Maybe it was because the shutters were closed or perhaps it was the shafts of light slicing through the cool air, but he felt as if he were in a dream.

'Look here.'

Crouching down, she gently touched the writing on the stone. 'What does it say?'

'My Latin is pretty basic but I think it's something about a woman he likes. Wants,' he corrected himself. 'He wants her.'

There was a beat of silence and then she took a step forward into the wavering light and the flush on her cheeks was the realest thing he had ever seen.

CHAPTER SIX

SYDNEY COULD FEEL his heart pounding beneath his ribs.

Tiger hadn't moved but the tiny hut seemed smaller, she seemed closer. But maybe that was because every single one of her senses was homed in on him so that she could practically feel the pulse that was beating haphazardly in his throat. Could see the flecks of both green and amber in the gold of his irises and the unchecked desire. The same desire she knew was mirrored in her eyes.

For a moment, they just stared at one another and then she leaned in or maybe he did, afterwards she couldn't remember, perhaps because it didn't matter. Because they both wanted the same thing.

His mouth on hers. Her lips on his. Soft. Unimaginable. Irresistible.

Miraculous. Because for so long, she had felt neutered, fearful of intimacy and touch, and it felt like a miracle to want sex, to want a man.

No, not a man. This man. She wanted Tiger. And he wanted her.

A shiver of anticipation rippled across her skin as he reached behind her neck and loosened the band, tugging it free so that her hair tumbled down her back.

He slid a hand up to cup her cheek, his touch rough and tender, and she took a shallow breath like a gasp and he pulled back a fraction, but then she pulled him close and he was fitting his mouth to hers, opening her and answering the hunger spilling from her lips.

She had never been kissed like this.

Pleasure was fluttering in her stomach and her lips parted, and she breathed him in, then licked inside his mouth, tasting him on her tongue, her hands tugging at his waistband, fumbling clumsily for the button, then the zip. Yes, she thought, as she freed him.

Her head was spinning. He felt amazing. Hard and hot. She could feel the pulse of his blood beating against her fingers.

'Sydney.' He breathed her name against her mouth and the ache in his voice sent something through her, something she had never felt before, something fast and primitive, and she couldn't swallow the whimper rising in her throat.

Jerking his mouth away from hers, he lifted her up onto the window ledge, then dropped to his knees, pushing up the skirt of her dress.

Her heart pounded against her ribcage as he slid her panties down over her legs, then brushed his lips against the triangle of flame-coloured curls. It was like a match meeting kindling. She felt a flare of heat and need and possibility and she moaned then and her hands splayed against his shoulders, pressing down, holding him steady as he flattened his tongue against the pulse beating between her thighs. She rocked against him, moving her hips back and forth.

Heat was swelling inside her; a feverish, dizzying heat that was changing her, transforming her like alchemy from flesh and bone into something eager and liquid. Her fingers bit into his arm and she was pulling him to his feet.

'Inside me,' she said hoarsely. 'I want you inside me.'

'Are you—?'

'Yes.' She cut him off, her pupils flaring, and he grunted as her fingers curled around him and he slid a hand under her bottom to raise her slightly, using his thumb to part her thighs and then he pushed upwards, entering her smoothly, filling her with heat.

Through the doorway outside, just a few feet away, Tiger could hear the soft rush of the waves as they tumbled onto the beach. The sand, the sea, the breeze...all were there waiting for him.

And it wasn't too late. He could stop this now. He knew that. He had never wanted any woman so much that he couldn't stop and pull back. He had the willpower and the strength of mind to resist.

But he didn't want to resist Sydney.

A groan of pleasure climbed up his throat and out of his mouth and he pressed his knuckles into the rough stone edging the window, leaning into the slight pain, needing it to offset the flickering heat that was rolling through him in waves and stop himself from ending things too fast.

Because even though he badly wanted to let go, he wanted to savour this more.

But then she moaned again, arching against him, her hands seeking his face, panting as she pressed a desperate kiss to his mouth.

He couldn't fight both of them and, clasping her hip, he began to move, thrusting rhythmically, using his free hand to protect her head as she reared up against him, her muscles tightening around him, spasming again and again, her breath hot and scratchy as she cried out. No longer conscious of the act itself, he clamped her against his shuddering body, surging inside her with molten force to claim her as his own.

He let his head fall forward, breathing raggedly. His skin

felt as if it were on fire and he leaned into the damp curve of her throat, his heart raging.

For a few fragmented seconds, neither of them moved, they just clung to one another like survivors of a storm. Then he felt Sydney's hands slide shakily over his torso, almost as if she was checking that he was real and that what had just happened was not some fever dream. And he understood that because he couldn't quite believe that it had happened either.

Finally, he pulled back and out, steadying her as he did so, although he felt less than steady himself.

'I'm fine.'

Her voice momentarily caught him off balance. He had forgotten that they were thinking, speaking creatures, that he was, in fact, a CEO in charge of a global business. Right now, he didn't feel in charge of anything and, glancing down at Sydney, he felt an unfamiliar mix of relief and responsibility as he saw that she looked as shell-shocked as he felt.

Although in some ways, was it that surprising that it had happened?

They had been dancing round that kiss in the kitchen like jittery teenagers. Which was not the image he had of himself ordinarily. There was something about this woman that made him feel younger and less complicated than he had in a long time.

'Excuse me.' She reached past him to pick up her panties, which had somehow ended up on the floor. Now that she was standing up, he could see the stone windowsill and it looked uncomfortably hard and their coupling had all been so frantic, so urgent.

'You're bleeding.'

He frowned. 'What?'

'Your hand.' The softness in her eyes made the dust spirals quiver in the air and he felt suddenly and intensely vulnerable.

'It's nothing.' His voice was harsh, too harsh in that tiny room, but it was an instinctive reaction to feeling anything. Feelings, caring, bonding on anything but a purely physical basis were dangerous. He shrugged. 'I just—'

Just what? His pulse jerked as he remembered the moment when he'd had to push his knuckles into the wall to stop himself from climaxing too soon.

'I caught it on the wall. It's just a scrape. What about you? Are you okay? I didn't hurt you, did I?'

Shaking her head, she smoothed down the skirt of her dress and it was far too easy for him to imagine those slim fingers smoothing other things. As she straightened up, her eyes found his. 'That probably shouldn't have happened.'

'It's a little late to worry about that,' he said softly.

Which was true.

But he didn't have any regrets. That simmering tension between them had been chafing at him and clouding things for sure. No wonder they'd had that stupid bust-up about what she should wear. Now they had got it out of their systems, everything would go more smoothly.

As if their thoughts were running on parallel lines, she said stiffly, 'I don't regret it, but it shouldn't happen again. It was just one of those things.'

He nodded. 'I agree.'

At this point in his life, one-night stands or their daytime equivalent were a little too rogue. He might not be as instantly recognisable as a movie star or pop singer, but having a name like Tiger meant people were more likely to put a value to his face and that made for complications that he didn't need in his life. And this was no different.

Okay, it was different in some ways, he conceded, remembering that hunger that was so unlike any that he'd felt before. It had consumed him and his orgasm was more than just release or relief or ecstasy. It was all those things but it was also a kind of oblivion, and an acknowledgement, a feeling that he was being seen and known completely.

He felt a muscle in his jaw knot. Which was nonsense, of course. Nobody got to know him, he made sure of that.

But this whole arrangement with Sydney was hardly a normal set-up. It was unsurprising, therefore, that he was struggling to make sense of it or that his mind was coming up with left-field explanations.

But really, was it that complicated?

With hindsight, being cooped up with Sydney was obviously going to trip some switches because it was several weeks since he had broken up with Alexandra and sex was a primal need. And while he might have a near mythical status in the business world, he was still just a man.

But this hook-up had scratched the itch, which meant that now he could concentrate on the week ahead. And afterwards, when she had served her purpose, he would despatch her back to New York on the first flight out of Venice.

Because this didn't change anything, he told himself, feeling calmer than he had for days. It had simply tidied up a few loose ends.

Walking into the bedroom, Sydney shut the door and leaned back against the cool wood, letting it chill her overheated skin.

The beautiful dresses were still hanging from the rail. The window was still slightly open just as she had left it. The curtains were still fluttering in the light, warm sea breeze coming from the lagoon.

Everything looked exactly as it had when she'd stormed out of the room just over an hour ago. Only how could that be?

It should look different. Changed. There should be some external evidence to reflect the transformation inside her because that was what it was. A transformation.

She scowled, suddenly furious. No, it was just sex, she told herself, pushing away from the door and walking across the room to the rail of clothes. Only describing what she and Tiger had just done in the fisherman's hut as just sex was like calling the Sistine Chapel *just* a ceiling.

There had been a moment when she had looked up from that graffiti to find him watching her and she had known that it was a choice. She could choose to walk away if she wanted to.

But everything she'd wanted had been in that room.

And he had wanted her, she thought, her hand closing around the rail. Not to own her or stifle her or simply to prove that he could. He had wanted to kiss and touch and caress and lick—

She felt her thighs clench.

Gazing down at his dark head, she'd felt like a goddess.

But her thoughts had been more prosaic. So that was what the fuss was all about. Because it felt momentous. Miraculous and, oh, so good that she had almost forgotten to breathe.

She still wasn't quite clear on how it had happened. It wasn't as if she'd woken up this morning and thought today would be a good day to have sex.

And she had done more than have sex. She had orgasmed. For the first time in her life.

She had faked it every single time with Noah. He was five years older than her and, coupled with his certainty about everything, that had been thrilling enough for her to ignore the way sex had been mostly uncomfortable and unsatisfactory. For her anyway. Which he had made clear was her fault, not his.

She knew what passion was now, and pleasure. What was less clear was why her body had chosen to discover both those things with Tiger McIntyre.

It wasn't that unclear, she thought, her pulse twitching as she pictured Tiger's astonishing face. He was beautiful, undeniably so with those flawless contoured features and those mesmerising gold eyes. Plus, he clearly knew what he was doing when it came sex. Only it was more than just technical expertise—he had wanted to please her.

And before that, he had wanted to make sure she was okay.

She felt her body tense at the memory of when she'd realised he had come after her. With Noah, running, hiding from him, had always been a last resort. Mostly she'd just wanted it over with, but also it would increase his rage tenfold.

'Don't make me have to look for you—' he would threaten down the phone on his way home. And sometimes she hadn't. But other times she hadn't been able to stop herself.

A shiver ran over her skin.

Her body had taken charge just as it had in the bedroom with Tiger. Because she'd thought she had gone too far, pushed him too far, and he had been angry, and exasperated, but he'd been controlling his anger. It hadn't been controlling him.

Instead of raging he had asked questions and listened to her answers. They'd had a conversation, and that in a way felt as climatic as her very first orgasm.

She trailed her fingers over the smooth silk, remembering the smoothness of his skin. It was a lot to take in, but not as much as she had revealed. Was it too much? It was certainly more than she had ever shared or wanted to share before. Even just the thought of doing so had made her feel naked, flayed by the curiosity and judgement in people's eyes, but Tiger hadn't judged.

There had been an intensity to his focus, as if he couldn't look away, as if he'd liked what he'd seen and she had liked the way he'd looked at her. Of course, back in the States it would be different. In the real world, she wasn't ready to let someone get close, but this wasn't real, and maybe that was why she had felt safe enough to open herself to Tiger physically and emotionally.

Gazing up at the pale sun that was sliding smoothly up through the cloudless blue sky, Tiger checked the timer on his watch. Two minutes left.

Easy, he thought, accelerating across the grass to the beach and the shimmering sea.

He had slept badly then woken early and decided to run around the island. Because why not? The sun was shining. There was a soft, warm breeze. It was going to be a beautiful day, which was good news because today was the day of the Regata Storica.

It was also, give or take, eighteen hours since he had been inside Sydney's body.

He swore as he lost his footing and stumbled forward onto the sand. Because it wasn't the first time he had lost his footing over the last eighteen hours, metaphorically speaking at least. And the reason for his clumsiness was no doubt still sleeping. In his bed.

Gritting his teeth, he glanced at his watch. That stumble had cost him thirty seconds. Which meant that now he could add time to the list of things that Sydney Truitt had stolen or tried to steal from him.

Walking back to the villa with her yesterday morning, he had confidently assumed that things would go back to normal. Normal being a state where he had already moved on. Variety was good, and control. Relationships, for want of a better word, only happened on his terms, so when Sydney had said that they shouldn't have sex again, he had been completely on board with that.

Or so he'd thought.

Everything had been fine at first. Over lunch, he'd felt calm, relaxed even, but then his body had still been suffused with post-coital endorphins. Then afterwards, Sydney had disappeared upstairs to try on some of the clothes and he had taken some calls from work, but he had found it difficult to concentrate because he could see Sydney from the window of his office. She'd been sitting by the pool, and most women, particularly a woman he'd just had sex with, would be not just wearing a bikini but languidly smoothing sun lotion on herself. He'd seen it all so many times. And the more they tried to tempt him, the less interested he got.

Because he wasn't Gerald McIntyre.

Not even close.

Only Sydney hadn't been rubbing sun cream onto her skin. Nor had she been wearing a bikini. She had been not quite fully dressed, but not far off it, and yet he hadn't been able to look away. He kept remembering the parts of her body he had so briefly glimpsed when they had reached for one another in the half-light of the fisherman's hut.

The curve of her shoulder. That doe-soft skin of her inner thighs. The pale swell of her breast.

But that was it. That was all he was going to get. A glimpse, because Sydney was not looking for anything to happen again.

Was that why she had got under his skin and into his

dreams? That was certainly a first for him, this feeling of wanting more. He had never wanted to be the kind of man who could be controlled by his desires, because that would take him dangerously close to becoming like his father.

But despite this arrangement supposedly being on his terms, Sydney seemed to be full of ways to make him question who he was and what he wanted.

The trouble was he knew what he wanted.

He felt his legs slow beneath him.

It was strange to admit it, given that he'd had any number of sexual partners since he'd lost his virginity in high school, but he had forgotten how pleasurable sex could be. For as long as he could remember, sex had been about satisfying a physical need.

And yet here he was, up at dawn after a night spent feverishly stripping Sydney in his dreams, his body hard and aching and jangling with a need that he couldn't still or stifle, and it felt very personal.

But that would change today, he realised with a rush of relief. The regatta was always rammed. They would be surrounded by people and after the regatta there was lunch and then cocktails and dinner so, basically, the opposite of personal.

Looking down at his watch, he stopped and reset the timer. If he ran fast enough, he would still have time to lap the island and shower before they had to leave. It would be cutting it fine but that was what he did, who he was. He didn't just meet, he welcomed a challenge, and, starting the timer again, he began to run.

Shifting back against the leather upholstery, Tiger gazed at the brilliant, saturated blue water as Angelo guided the speedboat across the waves. The lagoon had its own unique character. It was part of the Adriatic and yet it was separated from the vast expanse of sea, protected by seawalls and the prayers of the population. To him, it felt like an oasis, and Sydney clearly thought so too.

He let his gaze drift over to where she was looking across the water, transfixed almost.

'Are you okay? I can get Angelo to slow down.'

She turned, her forehead creasing above her nose. 'Why would he do that?'

'I thought you might be feeling sick. You didn't eat much at breakfast.'

Her eyes found his, startled, the soft brown irises huge in the sunlight. 'No, I'm fine. I was—' She gave him a small, stiff smile. 'I *am* a bit nervous, but I don't feel sick.'

'Don't be nervous. You've got this.' His eyes moved over her face then dropped to her short-sleeved silk shirt in wide horizontal stripes of sky blue and white and the pleated blue skirt she was wearing. She had put her hair up in some kind of soft, muddled updo and the whole effect was very pretty, very sexy.

'So stop worrying and enjoy the view.'

He watched her head turn. Her lips parted.

'Welcome to Venice,' he said softly.

Her smile snagged at his senses. 'I couldn't really see it properly when we arrived because it was dark.' In the sunlight, she looked excited, her nerves forgotten. 'It doesn't look real. It looks like a mirage.'

'I know what you mean. But we're still some way out. Up close, it will all feel a lot more real.'

Tiger was right, Sydney thought as they made their way through the palazzo to the balcony where they would be watching the races. There were a lot of people. More people than she had ever seen in one place and the noise and the energy felt in-your-face real.

As they walked towards the sponsors' balcony, Tiger was welcomed like a returning monarch, fresh from a victorious battle, although, so far, he hadn't introduced her to anyone. Not that it mattered. He was the one they wanted to get close to, and it seemed as if everybody wanted to greet him and, although she had been telling the truth when she said that she didn't feel sick, she felt dazed by this sudden reminder that he was a big deal. The main event.

He looked the part, all golden eyes and tanned skin and yet another suit that fitted every curve and angle of his body. She wasn't the only one to notice either. Women watched him like hawks. Except that made him sound as though he were a rabbit or a mouse, and he was neither. He was a tiger.

'Tiger, how are you? I thought I heard screaming.' A dark-haired man wearing an artfully crumpled linen suit grabbed Tiger by the arm and pumped his hand enthusiastically. 'I heard you were a sponsor this year. Thought I might see you here for the film festival. Lot of beautiful women—'

He glanced at Sydney as if seeing her for the first time, his eyes narrowing appreciatively. 'But I see you're already covered in that department. Scotty Aldridge, and you are?'

'Heading out to watch the races. Gotta watch my team,' Tiger said smoothly, cupping Sydney's elbow in his hand and sidestepping her past Scotty Aldridge as he leaned forward.

'Is there a problem?'

Tiger frowned. 'What do you mean?'

'You haven't introduced me to anyone. I might as well not be here.' It shouldn't matter. This wasn't real. He wasn't her 'boyfriend', but he had been off with her.

She glanced down at her blouse and skirt. 'Is it what I'm wearing? Do you not like it?'

'I do. I did. I should have said something before. I wanted to,' he said. 'You look beautiful. Too beautiful to be pawed by some man old enough to be your father.'

She bit her lip. 'My grandfather, actually. My dad got my mum pregnant when they were fifteen. It was a shotgun wedding. No, really, her brothers turned up with actual shotguns.'

'Is that a family tradition? I mean, should I be expecting your brothers to roll up at some point?'

'That would be unlikely.' She gave him a small lopsided smile. 'As I haven't told them about us. I haven't told anyone about us.'

He raised an eyebrow. 'And there you were accusing me of being ashamed of being seen with you.'

'I didn't accuse you of that,' she protested as he took her hand and pulled her closer.

'You were thinking it,' he said softly. 'How could I be ashamed? You look beautiful. You are beautiful.' His eyes were dark and steady on her face, and it would be easy to believe him, and for a moment she did. But, of course, he was just saying the kind of things a man would say to his girlfriend.

'You don't believe me?'

'I feel like an imposter. But I suppose you think that's some kind of hubris.'

'What I think is that you're talking nonsense. Every single person in this room is playing a part. Everyone has a hidden agenda. So just because you and I have one, doesn't mean you don't belong. And you are beautiful, Sydney.'

His words made her feel light-headed. Noah had made her feel so ugly and worthless. He had made her believe that she was the problem. That everyone saw what he saw, and that it wasn't good enough. And she knew that wasn't true but hearing Tiger say it out loud made her feel as if she were filling with light that was brighter and warmer than the sun.

'I wanted to tell you before but Silvana and the maids were there and I thought it would look as if I was doing it for their benefit. But I thought it, I still do. You believe me, don't you?'

And the crazy thing was, she did. Because Tiger didn't need to say it. They'd already had sex. Nor did he need to keep her sweet, because theirs was a finite, transactional arrangement. But most important of all, she could see the admiration in his gaze, feel it as it touched her skin, hot and bright like the lick of a flame.

Impulsively she leaned forward and kissed him. For a second, she felt his body tense with surprise and then he was kissing her back, and the heat and the noise from the regatta felt like a separate place.

Her lips parted and she felt his tongue, and she made a soft noise against his mouth as his hand moved to the nape of her neck, and she felt his thumb, sure and firm, holding her steady, which was lucky because her legs were all out of steadiness.

'Get a room, McIntyre,' someone shouted and she pulled back, her breath jerking in her throat, her hands tight in his shirt.

Tiger's eyes held and for a moment he just stared at her, breathing unsteadily, as if he was as thrown by the taste of her as she was by him.

'We should go and watch the race,' he said finally.

'Yes, we should.'

The balcony was heaving with people but the crowds parted like the waves for Tiger and he guided her to the far left corner.

'You'll get the best view here.'

'Can you see? It's your boat.'

'I can see everything I want to,' he said softly, moving behind her, his hand resting on her waist.

She barely noticed how many boats there were or who won. She was only aware of the places where Tiger's body grazed hers. Her waist. Her hip. Her throat when he leaned in to kiss her neck and she leaned back into him, her breath catching as he held her close.

'This is our race,' he said finally as another cluster of boats waited for the starter's gun to fire. 'Can you tell which one is our crew?'

That was easy. Even among the bright colours, the orange and black of *The McIntyre* stood out. There was a band and the crowd roared as the crews began rowing smoothly through the rippling blue water.

Behind her, Tiger was still, but she could feel his tension beneath her own quivering excitement.

'They won. You won.' She turned towards him as the balcony erupted into cheers, her chest tight and swollen with pride and happiness and then Tiger was kissing her fiercely.

'You won,' she said again as he broke the kiss and pulled her against his chest.

He was pleased but he shook his head. 'They won. I paid.'

They watched the last race and then everyone started to drift downstairs.

'What happens now?' she whispered.

'Drinks, canapés, a lot of pointless conversation.'

'Scusi.' A beautiful dark-haired woman glanced up from her phone, smiling approvingly, her cat's eyes flaring at the corner as she caught sight of Tiger. 'No, darling. Let's go to Corbucci's. I heard Harris Carver was there and I want to see if he's as delectable in person as everyone claims.'

Sydney felt her face freeze.

Harris Carver.

He was here.

She felt sick. Looked sick too, she realised a moment later as she looked up and found Tiger staring at her steadily.

'You know Harris Carver.' His eyes were narrowing, and she could sense him moving pieces of a puzzle around, turning them, rearranging them.

'Signor McIntyre, would you like to join the winning teams for a photo?'

It was one of the event organisers, beaming.

'I would.' Tiger cut him off smoothly. 'But unfortunately something has come up. Another time maybe.'

His arm tightened around her waist and he began to frog-march her through the crowd.

'We don't have to leave.'

He jerked her round to face him. 'Oh, but we do. You see, I saw your face back there. You know Harris Carver, and right now all that matters to me is finding out how.'

CHAPTER SEVEN

THE JOURNEY BACK to the island seemed to take no time at all.

As Angelo slowed alongside the jetty, Tiger was already out of the speedboat, pulling her up alongside him and guiding her back towards the villa.

Silvana was waiting for them in the entrance hall but as she stepped forward to greet them she caught sight of her boss's face and changed her mind.

'In here.' Tiger threw open the door to his office and Sydney followed him in, her breath catching in her throat as he stalked past her and turned to face her.

Today in the sunshine with the cheers of the spectators echoing around them as the McIntyre *gondolino* had crossed the finishing line first, she had forgotten this was how it had started. Gazing up into his golden eyes, she'd been lulled into a false sense of security, but Tiger and Harris Carver moved in the same circles and now it felt inevitable that his name should have come up.

'Sit. Talk. Now,' he ordered, folding his arms in front of his body and lifting his chin in that commanding, autocratic way of his. He was practically vibrating with a mix of fury and disbelief so in that sense it was more or less a replay of what had happened in the New York office, except she could see the sea here through the windows and there were no burly security guards hovering at the margins of her vision.

She sat down, her heart thumping jerkily.

This wasn't like before when they had argued about the clothes. Then, his anger had been hot and blurred at the edges with exasperation, and her survival instincts had kicked in and overridden everything so that even though she wasn't physically scared of Tiger, she'd had to run.

But she didn't want to run now.

What she wanted was for things to go back to how they had been at the regatta when he had stood slightly behind her to watch the race, his hands resting on her hips, anchoring her to him, his stubble grazing her skin as he'd leaned in to kiss her softly at the base of her neck.

She stared at him, dry-mouthed, trying to calm her beating heart. He didn't look as if he wanted to kiss her now.

He looked distant. Hostile. And when he spoke, his voice scraped over her like sandpaper. 'Do you think that silence is going to save you? That if you stall for long enough, I'll give up? I won't, I promise you. So why don't you stop wasting my time and tell me how you know Harris Carver?'

'I only met him once.'

'When?' He bit the question off and spat it at her.

'About ten days before I came to work for you.' She swallowed, her brief, unsettling rendezvous with Harris Carver flashing across her mind, so real and vivid that for an instant she could smell the leather of the club armchair and feel its smooth warmth against her back.

'What happened in between?'

'With him? Nothing. I just told you. I only met him once.'

'You've told me a lot of things, Sydney. Most of them are either untrue or a partial truth so I'm sure you'll understand my reluctance to take you at your word.'

His voice was taut and strained. 'Why didn't you tell me all this back in New York? Or out on the beach? I thought we had some kind of understanding, but you were lying to me and you'd still be lying to me now if somebody hadn't mentioned Carver's name. I mean, when were you going to tell me?'

She swallowed.

'I met him once,' she repeated. 'There was no reason to meet him again. But I needed the time in between to create my identity and references.'

'Sounds like you know what you're doing.' Her throat tightened as Tiger's eyes jerked to hers. 'So, the cyber-security company of yours is a front. This is what you do. You tout your hacking services to billionaires. Steal on demand.' His eyes narrowed, and the air in the room snapped tight. 'Does he know about this? About you being here with me?'

'No.' She shook her head. 'He doesn't. I haven't told anyone. And I don't steal on demand. I've never—'

'Stolen anything,' he finished her sentence and the sneer in his voice made something curl up inside her. 'I remember. Back in New York when I confronted you, you said, "This is the first time I've done anything like this," and I didn't believe you. But then I found out about your brothers and I thought you might be telling the truth. But you were lying then and you're lying now, aren't you?'

No, and yes. No, she had never hacked anyone and stolen their IP, but yes, she had done something even more reckless and dangerous. She had taken her ex-husband's phone.

So tell him. Tell him what you stole.

But she couldn't, because that would mean telling him why she had stolen the phone. Which would mean telling him about Noah and opening up a can of worms, opening herself up so that he would see the ugliness of the scars that hadn't faded, laying bare her stupidity and weakness.

And she didn't know why but the idea of him seeing that,

knowing that about her, felt like the very worst thing she could imagine right now.

'It's not what you're thinking,' she said quietly.

'The trouble is,' he said after a moment that seemed to last a lifetime, 'everything I know about you tells me that it is exactly what I'm thinking.'

Her hands clenched. 'He approached me. Harris Carver. His people got in touch with me. It was all very hush-hush. I had to sign an NDA and they picked me and took me to some private members' club.'

He frowned. 'You mean the Millenium?'

'I don't know. We went in via some underground car park. I didn't see anybody except a man in a suit who showed us where to go.'

Tiger reached back and switched on the light on his desk and she had a sudden sharp memory of a different lamp on a different desk and a moment in time that had snapped through her like a lightning strike and left her singed and shaking inside.

'I didn't know what he wanted me to do when I agreed to meet him. I thought he was going to offer me a job. A job at HCI.'

'You wanted to work for him?' His eyes blazed, and if theirs had been a different kind of relationship she might have thought there was a jealousy to his temper.

'Not him. His business. I needed money and HCI is an S&P 500 company.'

'Right, and he's so squeaky clean, isn't he? Harris Carver: all-round good guy.'

She thought back to that nerve-racking meeting and Carver's steady grey gaze. 'No, I didn't think he was a good guy. I felt like I was swimming in a tank with a shark the whole time I was there.'

'But he made you an offer you couldn't refuse.'

'I did refuse it. I told him that I wasn't comfortable doing what he wanted. But it was a lot of money for three days' work.'

'Work?' His mouth twisted into a shape that made it hard to breathe. 'For the last time, what you did wasn't work. It was theft. Here.'

She blinked. Tiger was holding out the flash drive he had taken from her. 'But I'm guessing my word counts for nothing alongside Saint Carver's, so why don't you take a look? See for yourself.'

His anger was different this time. It felt older, and bitter, as if it had been left to fester. As if he, not Carver, had been wronged.

He pushed away from the desk and walked towards the window and after a moment she got up and sat down in front of his laptop and pushed in the flash drive.

Somebody, possibly Tiger's head of IT, had finished running the program she had set up and she clicked through the images on the screen. They were all of some kind of drill bit. More importantly, there was a tiger's head stamped across each image: the tiger's head trademark of the McIntyre Corporation.

Her head was spinning. She sucked in a breath. 'This is your property?'

'Correct.' Tiger nodded.

'So you didn't steal this from HCI.' Which meant that things were back to front. Black was white. Day was night and she wasn't some caped crusader righting wrongs, but simply the thief Tiger had accused her of being.

And all because she had taken Harris Carver's words at face value.

Obviously, she had heard of Tiger, but, up until that meeting with Carver, everything she'd known about him had been based on the third-hand gossip and hearsay and rumours that swirled around the Internet.

But Harris moved in the same circles and he had confirmed what she'd already believed to be true. That Tiger McIntyre was just another fat cat, or, in his case, a lean, muscular big cat who played the system and thought the rules applied to everyone else. So, stealing back something that belonged to someone else had felt more like meting out natural justice than theft.

And then there was the money.

With hot, slippery panic swelling inside her every time she thought about her brothers, she had been eager to find a benefactor. And Harris Carver had known that. That was why he had shown her the amount he was prepared to pay her, because he'd known that seeing it made it real, made it feel as if it were already hers, and then it was that much harder to say no.

It was basic psychology. Fish and bait. Donkey and carrot. *Basic.*

But effective.

And the depressing truth was that it was most effective on the people like her who were desperate to ignore the fact that the wriggling worm was on a hook on the end of a line attached to a rod held by a fisherman.

'Doesn't feel good, does it? Being deceived? Played?' Tiger's gaze felt like an insistent, living thing tearing and mauling her and for the first time she wondered if she had completely misunderstood what had happened when she'd sat down in that quiet, wood-panelled room.

'Because that's what happened. Carver saw that you were someone who could be turned and so he lied to you and used you.'

His words echoed around the room, stark and undeniable,

and she shivered inside because Noah had seen something in her too. A weakness, a vulnerability, a need to be something more than the rest of her family and he had exploited it, flattering her, offering a future away from petty crime and financial insecurity, then isolating her and slowly taking her off the bone.

And she had always thought that a part of why her ex-husband had targeted her was her youth and her hunger to be something more than just another Truitt clogging up the courts.

But she wasn't eighteen any more. She was nearly twenty-five. She owned her own, admittedly small business, but it was still hers. And a year of marriage to Noah had taught her enough about the dark side of life to immunise her against lowering her guard. Curled up on the back seat of Connor's pick-up, she had made a promise to build her barricades high.

Only then Harris Carver had come along with his money and his offer of a way out just as Noah had, and she hadn't questioned his opinions or his motivations. At least not enough to stop herself from making a bad situation worse.

'He did use me,' she said slowly.

She could see that now, and yet she could still see Carver's face, see that shadow of something that was darker, deeper, weightier than professional rivalry. It hadn't been important then. What had she cared about the cause of their conflict? Now, though, it seemed to matter a lot.

'But I don't think he lied to me. In fact, I know he didn't. He believed what he was saying.'

Tiger's face stiffened. 'Because he's the hero of this story, right?' he said, and the harshness in his voice made her chest tighten. 'Let me guess, you started believing him right after he told you how much he was going to pay you.'

'No,' she protested. 'That's not true.' Except in a way it

was, she thought, replaying the timeline of that conversation with Carver. And Tiger, of course, correctly interpreted that realisation on her face.

'It's amazing how convincing money can be,' he said, and the steel beneath the softness in his voice was so ferocious that it sharpened something inside her.

'It wasn't just about the money. I thought I was righting a wrong.'

Two weeks ago, she had been so sure of Carver's story but now those certainties were collapsing. And yet there was still something nagging at her.

'That was what he said to me,' she said after a moment. 'That he wanted me to take something back from you.'

'And now you know he was lying.'

She did. But somewhere inside her head she could hear that note in Carver's voice when he'd told her that Tiger was no angel.

'About the IP, yes, but then he said that it wasn't the first time you'd stolen from him. Only that was after I'd already agreed to work for him. He didn't need to give me another reason, so why did he?'

'I don't know. More importantly, I don't care.'

Except he did, she realised. She could see it in the sudden stiffening of his shoulders, and she remembered the comment that woman had made after the race, the one that had started off this whole inquisition.

'Carver said it was personal between you two.'

Tiger straightened. 'But this, you and I, we aren't,' he said coolly. 'We might have held hands and kissed and looked into each other's eyes all afternoon but that was a performance. You are not my girlfriend. You're the hired help. And your services are no longer required.'

She stared at him in disbelief, fighting for control. 'You're sacking me? No, that isn't going to happen. You don't get to drag me halfway round the world just to dump me over some detail—'

'Detail.' His features contorted. 'This is not a detail. And we are done here.'

He stalked past her, and she watched him go, her body rooted to the floor with frustration and disbelief, her brain somehow still conscious of the lethal, masculine grace with which he moved despite his anger.

And he was angry.

His anger felt defensive, almost as if he needed to keep her at arm's length.

She knew that feeling, that need to have high walls around her. Make that high walls and a moat. It was how she had lived her life for five years. Until Tiger had gone to look for her the other day. Not to have the last word. Or to punish her. Or make her 'see sense', and if that didn't work, then make her see stars. He had wanted to make sure she was okay.

Didn't he deserve the same level of care?

She didn't have to stay with him, just check that he was all right.

The house was quiet, just as it had been that first night when she'd crept downstairs in the darkness to find something to eat, but Tiger wasn't in the kitchen. Nor was he in the living room or in his bedroom or any of the other rooms. Which meant he must be outside, somewhere on the island.

Through the window, the sun was slowly sinking towards the horizon. It would be dark soon and she wasn't a big fan of the dark. But for some reason she wasn't frightened here on the island. She felt oddly safe.

The air was still warm but it would be cool soon and she ducked back into the villa and grabbed a throw from the sofas. Outside, she slipped off her espadrilles. There was no sign of him on the terrace or in the tented gazebo at the edge of the lawn.

Could he have left the island? She made her way down to where the speedboat was moored, and that was when she saw him, standing at the end of the jetty, his elbows resting on the balustrade, his head bowed over the water. He had rolled up his sleeves and lost the loafers and he looked like a model doing a photoshoot for some upmarket clothing brand or watch.

'Why are you still here? Didn't you get the message?'

She froze. Even though she was barefooted, he had heard her, but he spoke without looking up at her, which made it easier to keep walking towards him.

'That you fired me? Yeah, I got that. But I just wanted to make sure you were okay.'

He looked over then. 'You don't need to pretend any more, Sydney, and I think we both know that you don't give a damn whether I'm okay.'

'I never had to pretend in private.'

'I'm fine. Go back inside, it'll be cold soon.'

'I know. That's why I brought you this.' She held out the throw, which he ignored, and, after a moment, she draped it over the balustrade, then rested her hands against the smooth rail.

A muscle pulsed in his jaw and there was that note of impatience in his voice. 'I told you to go inside.'

'I will if you will.'

It was the first thing that came into her head. Her brothers always used to say it to one another when they were younger and they were daring each other to do something stupid or dangerous or both. Her throat tightened as Tiger looked over at her, his golden eyes dark and narrow, and she wondered which category this fell into.

'What are you? A child? Go back to the villa.'

'What are you? My dad?'

There wasn't a flicker of reaction on his flawless face or even in those dark gold eyes, but she felt the air snap tight. 'Clearly not. If I were, you wouldn't be earning a living committing cyber crimes or spending your evenings sipping whisky with random men who pay you to commit those crimes.'

'Crime,' she said quietly.

His eyes locked onto hers. 'I'm not sure that makes an awful lot of difference in law.'

'I think it does. It's my first offence and there were extenuating circumstances.'

'I don't think greed qualifies.'

She changed tack. 'What about coercion? Blackmail? What does the law think about that?'

'Whatever I tell it to think.' He was staring at her, a flare of incredulity lighting up his eyes. 'Are you seriously threatening me?'

'Yes. No.' She fought to keep her voice steady. 'I don't know, Tiger. I've never done this before. I don't even know what this is.'

'This is you throwing away your life for a man who doesn't even value your sacrifice.'

'I didn't do it for him. I did it for my brothers.'

There was a long silence. Tiger stared past her, his chest lifting and rising infinitesimally.

'Sometimes you can't save people. Sometimes they don't want to be saved. Or maybe you don't have what it takes to save them. Sometimes all you can do is protect yourself.'

Yes, she thought, remembering the moment when she had called Connor. It was as if Tiger knew. She was suddenly shaking inside and there was a tense silence broken only by the water lapping gently against the jetty.

But she didn't notice the silence or the water. She was too transfixed by his taut silhouette because Tiger wasn't talking about her and her brothers. He was talking about himself, and that jolted her, only it was so snarled up with the tumult of emotions swirling inside her that it took a moment for her to reply.

'Sometimes you can't even do that.'

Tiger breathed out unsteadily, Sydney's words drowning out the world so that the breeze coming off the water grew still and the jetty and the speedboat and the balustrade seemed to lose shape and fade into the darkening light. Only the woman standing beside him stayed vivid and as sharply drawn as a pen-and-ink sketch on vellum.

'Sometimes.' Make that never, he thought, remembering his father's last, bedridden days, and he felt that same helplessness and sense of waste and loss, and anger. Always anger.

'They can be hard to bear, those times.'

A ripple of water lifted the jetty and he felt it judder through his bones as he shrugged. 'It doesn't matter.' He wouldn't allow it to matter.

He felt her move closer and he wanted to touch her then, wanted to touch her so much, to pull her close and not feel alone. Only that was the reason he couldn't, shouldn't.

To need Sydney like that, not for sex but because she was the only person who could soothe the ache in his chest, would be a sign of weakness and for so long now he had resisted emotional entanglement.

But Sydney had followed, and he was no longer alone. And he found that he didn't want her to go, not when her brown eyes were steadying him as she waited for him to speak, and he was more than tempted, he was struggling to hold back.

That she was here, and that she cared about him enough to put her own feelings aside, stunned him, and swept away the anger that he could now acknowledge was disproportionate and misplaced. She had scraped against a poorly healed wound, but it was Harris who had caused that wound. And it was partly that he had never called him to account that rankled, but also it had stung, finding out that Sydney had this connection with the man who had cast his friendship aside, and over a woman.

More than stung, it had hurt a lot. On more levels than he cared to acknowledge.

And in that moment, he hated that he'd revealed that hurt to Sydney.

But what was worse than all of that put together was knowing that he was no better than Harris. They had both spotted a vulnerability in Sydney and exploited it, and knowing that made him want to smash things.

'It does matter. You matter,' she said in that quiet, husky way of hers and everything tilted sideways as if the jetty were moving beneath them, but he knew that it was him. He was unmoored.

'It doesn't change anything though, does it?' he said, almost angrily because, more than anything, he wanted to believe what she was saying. Wanted it more than anything he had ever wanted, only that would mean straying from the path he'd chosen and following in his father's footsteps.

'If you mean the past, then no, you can't change that. But you can change how you feel about the past.'

'I doubt that.'

'Why?' Her beautiful brown eyes were narrow and dark on his face. 'Because that might mean you were wrong?'

'No, because every time I think about my father, I want to punch things.' He hadn't been going to say that, but the words came out in a rush as if they had been sitting there, just waiting to be spoken.

She blinked, and he felt her body tense beside him. 'Did he hurt you?'

'Hurt me? You mean hit me? No.' He shook his head, appalled. And yet, the answer to her question was yes, he realised, or how else could he explain that dark ache inside his chest that he had carried for so long?

'There are other ways to be hurt by someone.'

'I don't think he knew he was hurting me. Not in the beginning anyway. After my mother died, he was adrift. He couldn't be on his own, and every single time he was so sure that he was in love, so sure they were in love with him, even when it was completely obvious that it wouldn't last.'

'How many times were there?'

'Six. But I only really had to deal with the first four. I went to college just before he married number five.'

'Didn't any of them last?'

'I think the longest was probably four years. She was number three. A couple of them lasted around six months. There was one who lasted three weeks. You would have thought he'd learn from his mistakes but he never did. He'd meet them and he'd be so sure they were the one and the next thing they'd be married and then they would divorce him and he'd be on to the next one.'

'But he loved them?'

'He thought he did. But it always fell apart so easily. And each divorce left him a little poorer but not a little wiser.' His mouth twisted. 'In the end it was just a mess. He had to sell our home and downsize and he did that again and again until there was nothing left. It was the same with the business, although I managed to hold onto one mine and the name.'

'And where did you fit in?'

'I didn't.' It was the first time he'd ever admitted that to anyone. 'None of my stepmothers really wanted me around.

And my father was either distracted or desolate. It wasn't all bad. I mean, I had a roof over my head and there was food on the table and he was smart and funny, and I loved him. I loved who he used to be.'

Gazing down at Sydney, he remembered that ache in her voice when she'd asked him what he wouldn't do to save someone he cared about. The answer was simple. If it meant saving his father from his worst impulses, he would have sold his soul.

'That must have been hard.'

It had been such a long time since anyone had been there for him. Obviously he could draw on the expertise of his staff if he needed financial or legal advice, but he had never been able to let people get close to him.

He'd seen the consequences too many times with his father and then the one time he'd thought he had found someone he could trust, it had blown up in his face.

'School was tough. It was a small town. You know what they're like. Everybody knows everyone else's business. My dad was a great go-to for gossip. What is it they say? No fool like an old fool? And I was the old fool's son.

'I got a lot of grief from the other kids, and I was on a pretty short fuse so I was a bit of a loner. And then I got a place at MIT, and nobody knew who I was or who my dad was and what he'd done. I guess I relaxed a bit. That's when I met Harris.'

'You were at university together?'

'He was in the same halls as me and we just clicked. We had the same interests, same determination, same focus. We were really competitive, but in a good way. We drove each other on. I don't have siblings, but he felt like a brother to me.'

Sydney felt her stomach twist. There was a tension to Tiger's spine that looked painful.

'What happened?'

'He had a lot of girlfriends, we both did. Nothing serious or exclusive. He dated some of my exes and I hooked up with some of his. You know how it is?'

No, she thought. Her sex life had been nothing like Tiger's casual 'friends with benefits' approach to relationships. It had been tense and confusing and limited to one man's view of what it should be.

'But it wasn't like that with Franny. I knew she was different. That they were seeing each other. Anyway, my dad was ill a lot that year and I had to go home because his last wife had left him and he was on his own, and when I got back, she was in my bed.'

Sydney felt a stab of jealousy that was as sharp as it was irrational.

'My roommate had let her in. Apparently, she and Harris had fallen out and she wanted to talk to me about him. I tried but I wasn't, I'm *not*, good at talking about relationships. Anyway, she was tired and I had classes so I told her she could stay and get her head straight. She came to the door to see me off, and she must have taken one of my T-shirts to sleep in. Long story short, Harris saw us.'

'Didn't you tell him what happened?'

A muscle tightened in his jaw. 'He didn't give me a chance. He followed me downstairs and punched me in the face and I lost my temper because it hurt and so I hit him back.'

He pressed the heel of his hand against his forehead. 'Someone called Security and we both got hauled up in front of the dean and Harris said I started it.'

Sydney could hear the pain in his voice. 'Why did he do that?'

'I suppose he thought I'd slept with his girlfriend. The stupid thing is, if we'd both taken a step back things might have been different, but he was angry and I was too angry to back down.' He tipped back his head. 'I didn't know how to back down, so I said a few stupid things and then a couple more just to make sure I messed things up real good and got myself kicked out.'

'What happened to Carver?'

'Nothing. He finished his degree. I didn't see him again for years. Didn't think I ever would but suddenly he was in New York and now our paths cross all the time. Not literally, just we run in the same circles, bid for the same contracts.'

'He needs someone to put him right.'

Glancing down at her clenched fists, he almost smiled.

'Yeah, but not you. I can deal with him.' He unpeeled her fingers and slotted his hand into hers. She felt his gaze on her face. 'I'm the bad guy here, remember? Bullying and buying my way out of trouble.'

She blinked. He was smiling now, that absurd, astonishing smile that made something tug loose inside. 'I might have jumped to some wrong conclusions.'

'I think we're both guilty of that.' He fell silent. 'I miss my father,' he said after a moment. 'Weirdly, I miss Harris too. We were on the same page. I trusted him. But then it was like I was disposable.' There was an ache to this voice then, and she knew why he had reacted in that moment. That punch was the culmination of abandonment, grief for everything he'd lost, all mixed up with the defiance of that small boy who'd had to take on all comers.

But it wasn't vicious or punitive. Tiger could be ruthless and determined but, even in the beginning, he had shown restraint.

'After that, I kind of shut down. I decided it was easier to "walk by my wild lone".' Catching sight of her face, he smiled stiffly. 'It's a quote from this book my grandmother used to read to me. It's about why cats don't trust dogs and why they keep their distance from humans. I guess I sympathise.'

'You didn't deserve any of what happened to you,' she said slowly. 'You didn't do anything wrong. You were a child and your dad thought that meant your feelings were less important than his. But you also said he was adrift. Maybe love always seemed like a risk worth taking. Maybe he saw marriage as an anchor, for you as well as him.'

'Maybe,' he said slowly. 'I think he wanted that; he just went about it all wrong. He kind of said that before he died but I wasn't ready to listen.'

'But you were there for him when he needed you.'

She squeezed his hand, and after a moment he pulled her closer, close enough that their foreheads were touching.

'You know there's not many businesses that could handle this kind of specialist equipment. HCI and McIntyre basically slug it out over the big contracts. That's why we often end up going down the same path, so when I thought about who might be a buyer, I did think of Harris, but I thought you'd have to approach him. I didn't think he was the person who'd set it in motion. Only then I saw your face change when you heard his name at the regatta.'

His mouth twisted. 'I overreacted. I know I did. It was just a shock finding out that you were working with him but I shouldn't have said what I did or fired you and I'm sorry.'

An apology. She stared up at him, mute and undone.

She shook her head, her eyes finding his. 'For him, not with him. He said he needed somebody "ethically flexible". A see-no-evil. Someone who would look the other way for the right price, and he knew all about my brothers, so I guess he thought I'd take the bait.' Her mouth trembled. 'And I did.'

'Because you love your family. That's a good thing, Sydney.'

'But I did a bad thing, and I'm sorry, and I know that doesn't change anything.'

'No, it doesn't.' He reached up and touched her cheek. 'But someone very smart and kind told me once that you can change how you think about the past.'

Their eyes locked and she held her breath, certain he would kiss her but instead he frowned.

'You're shivering.' Reaching past her, he grabbed the throw and wrapped it around her shoulders. 'Come on, you need to get inside.'

Neither of them felt the need to speak on the walk back to the villa but as they walked into the bedroom, he stopped in front of her, his golden eyes fixing on her, so intent and direct that she hurt inside. 'What I said earlier about you being the hired help, I didn't mean it. Well, maybe I did in the moment, but that's not how I see you, and I don't want you to go.'

'I don't want to go either. Staying is the only way I'm going to get my brothers a good lawyer.' But that wasn't the only reason she didn't want to leave. She knew that. He did too. But she couldn't admit to it, because it was just too terrifying. Tiger clearly felt the same way, as he pretended to be taking it seriously, pulling out his phone.

'I can sort that out for you now.'

She shook her head. 'No, I know you're good for it.'

His gold eyes moved over her the way his hands had the other day in the half-light of the fisherman's hut. 'Oh, I am, am I? So if it's not my legal connections, what's making you stay?'

The air around them seemed to tremble. 'This,' she said softly. And she leaned forward and kissed him.

CHAPTER EIGHT

IT WASN'T A KISS, just a brush of her lips against his, but as she pulled away, Sydney could feel her body shaking inside.

'Do you—?' he began. 'Is this what you—?'

'Yes,' she said hoarsely.

If Tiger was fazed by the force of her words he gave no sign, he just closed the door and turned and reached for her in one movement, his mouth seeking hers, and she felt the heat radiating from him, and the hunger. The same hunger that was humming in her veins.

Only Tiger could quiet that chaos.

His hands were moving lightly over her body, caressing, pressing, stroking, his touch making her head spin, making her limbs tense with anticipation.

'Tell me what you want,' he whispered against her mouth. 'Tell me what you like.'

This, she thought, her heart pounding. She liked this. She liked the warmth of his breath and the way his thumbs were drawing circles on her belly. She liked him. Everything about him. But she didn't know what she wanted except that she wanted to see him unravel in the same way she had unravelled by the beach. And she wanted to take her time.

She pushed back from him, swaying a little, dazed by that knowledge, by the certainty of her desire. 'I want it to be slow.'

The shutters weren't closed, and in the moonlight spilling

through the window his golden eyes were molten heat. She saw him swallow, felt her belly clench, tightening hard with need as a muscle pulled at his jaw. And then his mouth was on hers and he kissed her as she had kissed him, softly, his lips barely grazing hers and then he pulled back to nip at her lower lip, taking his time, deepening the kiss a little more each time.

They kissed like that for some time. Just kissing, his hands flush against her hips, not moving, just steadying her and she felt her pulse slow, desire rippling through her in slow, curling waves.

She leaned into him and he lifted his hands so that she could take a step closer, close enough that she could feel the press of his erection against her stomach, hard where she was soft and yielding, and the feel of him made her shudder all the way through.

Yes.

His desire was the biggest turn-on and she arched her back, her hips meeting his, and, breaking the kiss, she tipped back her head, exposing her throat to his hot, teasing mouth.

A shivery pleasure danced across her skin and her hands moved to his chest as she moaned softly. He had a great body. Hard, muscular chest. Broad shoulders. And a stomach that made her fingers pluck his shirt from his waistband.

'Let me help,' he murmured and then he laughed softly as she began tugging at his buttons. 'I thought you wanted to go slow.'

'I want to see you,' she said hoarsely.

His narrowed gaze was trained on her face. 'Then undress me.' His words sent shivers of need chasing across her skin.

Her pulse twitched, and she pulled his shirt down from his shoulders, then unbuttoned his trousers and hooked her fingers into the waistband and tugged them down his thighs, taking his underwear with them.

Oh, my—

He was naked now. And aroused. Very aroused.

Her skin was shivering as if she were cold, but flushed with the heat of her desire.

'My turn,' he said softly, and she tensed, her body hot and damp, and aching as he undid the buttons of her blouse and opened it to his gaze. Her lips parted as he slid his hand over the hot, bare skin of her stomach, and then tugged the blouse down over her shoulders.

Now he turned his attention to her skirt, deftly unfastening it.

She felt the air snap to attention as her skirt fluttered to the floor around her bare feet. She was naked now aside from her bra and panties and she felt his gaze like a caress, a whisper of heat and intent that made everything melt inside.

This was how she had wanted sex to be. Slow and seductive and thrillingly sensual.

He made her want so much. She could imagine his hands on her stomach and on her breasts and between her thighs.

There was a dark flush to his cheekbones and as she met his gaze, her belly tightened, then tightened again as he leaned in and fitted his mouth to hers, one hand cupping her cheek, his thumb brushing the skin there, his tongue, teasing her, stirring her senses. Making a kiss into something more than a kiss. Making it into a promise, a contract without words, that he was going to unravel her.

Heat flared inside her and she tried to deepen the kiss but he pulled back, tipped back her head to stare into her eyes.

'You're so beautiful,' he murmured, and, reaching up, he touched her mouth gently and she tensed for a different reason. But then he moved his thumb away and brushed his lips against hers, calming her.

'You're exquisite.' His hand slid down over her collarbone

to cup her breast and her nipples tightened as he caressed first one then the other, lightly, before reaching round to expertly undo her bra. No one had ever touched her like this. No one had ever made her feel so hungry and uninhibited, so confident of her power to arouse, to take, to pleasure.

She sucked in a breath as he pushed her panties down over her thighs and stepped back, and she had to stop herself from crying out as the seconds ticked by and his gaze grew harder and hotter. And then he touched her lightly between the thighs and she moaned softly, her body instantly hot and tight and aching and damp for him.

Her hands fluttered down his torso to find his hands and then she lifted them up to cup her breasts. He sucked in a breath and now he lifted his mouth from her throat and she saw that he was fighting for control.

Yes, she thought.

She pushed him backwards, and he let her, bracing himself with his elbows as she dropped onto her knees. Her head was spinning. She had never wanted to do this with Noah. But the desire to taste Tiger, to give him pleasure in the same way that he had given her pleasure, was irresistible and, dipping her head, she flicked her tongue over the blunted tip, her hand wrapping around the length of him, and she took him in her mouth.

His hips jerked and he groaned, her clumsiness and lack of expertise no obstacle to his pleasure. Quite the contrary, she thought, his lack of control evident from the uncoordinated twitches of his body.

'Sydney.' He breathed out her name, his hand moving through her hair to still her, and she eased back and he pulled her onto the bed. Leaning back against the pillow, he put his hands on her hips and lifted her onto his lap and slid into her smoothly.

She moaned softly and he leaned forward, his mouth closing over her nipple, and she arched against him, shuddering, her hands gripping the muscles of his arm.

He pulled back then, his golden gaze dark and narrowed. 'Let me watch you,' he whispered and the hoarseness in his voice kicked up sparks inside her and she rolled her hips against his.

His face was taut with concentration, the muscles in his chest and arms bunching as his dark gold gaze held her and he began to rock his hips, one hand fitting into the indent at the base of her back, the other stroking her clitoris with his thumb.

She pressed against him, panting, chasing the flickering heat that was just out of reach and then he thrust upwards, driving into her and now she was trying to grip him, to hold him, to hold back but she couldn't.

Her body tensed, muscles tightening and tightening and tightening, in wave after wave, and he pulled her closer, burying his face against her throat as his body spasmed to a juddering climax.

A washed-out primrose light was seeping through the open shutters when Sydney blinked her eyes open. For a moment, she didn't recognise the room, then she felt the warmth of Tiger's body beside her and she remembered.

She remembered all of it.

Could see his body, so big and hard, moving inside her with shattering slowness. See herself, back arched like a bow, a creature of need and impulse, hardly human and yet all woman. The kind of woman she had always wanted to be. Powerful. Certain. Uninhibited and unafraid to be vulnerable.

It was different from the first time. Then their need for one another had been driven by frustration and a need to purge the jangling, seductive thing that had swirled around them.

Last night, this morning, was about desire and pleasure. Taking it and giving it. Because now she knew what desire looked like, what it felt like and tasted like. And she had wanted to feast on him, to lick every inch of his skin, to give him pleasure in the same way that he had pleasured her.

Now, though, it was time to leave. To give him space. And one less reason to regret what had happened?

Her limbs stiffened, her body protesting silently because she didn't want to leave the gravitational pull of his heat and his strength, and his gentleness. Remembering how lightly he had used his strength, she pressed her thighs together around the softness there and for a moment she let the feeling of being close to someone and not having to wonder if the hand clasping her waist would be tightening painfully around her wrist at any moment wash over her. She could enjoy the dizzying, unthinkable freedom of being in this space, with this man.

It was an astonishing sensation. But then it had been an astonishing, transformative night.

Tiger was a generous, intuitive, expert lover and being with him was revelatory. But it was more than knowing where and how to touch. Whatever was happening, however lost he was in his own ecstasy, she had sensed that a part of him was always tuned into her heartbeat and her breath almost as if they were joined by a thread.

Last night was about more than sex. They had fought and then they had talked. Tiger had talked about his father and his disastrous failed friendship with Harris Carver and she could see why he lived as he did, never letting anyone get close, choosing instead to walk by his 'wild lone'.

The people he had trusted had hurt him, betrayed his

trust, made him feel vulnerable and powerless. No wonder he had decided that he wanted out. It was easier that way. And by easier he meant safer.

Suddenly it was hard to swallow past the lump in her throat. It was such a small ask. To feel safe. To be safe. Even for someone as rich and successful as Tiger, a life without safety meant a life not fully lived. A part of you was always curtailed by fear. Fear of failure. Fear of being hurt.

She hated that he had been hurt, was still hurting, and suddenly it was impossible not to reach out and touch his beautiful, sculpted face.

It seemed incredible to her now that back in New York she would have done anything to get out of being here with him. But it was going to end, and sooner rather than later. Much better to face that now while he slept. To draw a line now, rather than have it drawn for her as had happened so many times in the past. But also, because she was starting to care about him, and maybe she couldn't stop how she was feeling, but she didn't need to let it go any further.

Because last night had also been about reclaiming her power: the power to arouse; the power to act on her desire... and the power to leave.

Sliding out of Tiger's arms, Sydney shifted to the edge of the bed, moving carefully so that her progress wouldn't displace the mattress and disturb the sleeping man.

Get dressed, she told herself.

But that was harder to do than it sounded because her clothes were scattered haphazardly across the carpet like some confessional art installation.

'What are you doing?'

She froze.

Tiger was sitting up in bed, looking at her with sleepy eyes. Her gaze moved automatically to his gym-hard abs and then she remembered that she was naked. Which maybe explained why his eyes were looking a lot less sleepy.

'I thought you might want some space.'

'Don't you want to stay?'

She hesitated. He had told her the truth last night. But she was not brave like him, so this was as much of her truth as she was ever going to share. 'Yes, but I didn't know whether you would want that. I thought you might be regretting—'

'I'm not.' He shifted forward, his forehead creasing. 'Are you?'

His face didn't alter, but after last night she knew what it would have cost him to ask that, to admit a need of any kind, even just physical.

She shook her head. 'Not at all.'

The air in the room shifted, softening as if an unseen tension had lifted. 'So will you stay?'

He was watching her, waiting, she realised, for her to reply, to make her choice.

Her choice. The words fizzed on her tongue like sherbet. He was letting her choose, but he was also letting her know that he had no regrets. That he had wanted her and still wanted her, and knowing that made it easy for her to make her choice. To do what she wanted. To stay with him.

She nodded slowly and he moved then, kneeling up and holding out his hand.

'Come back to bed,' he said hoarsely. The sheet had fallen away from his body and, as if they were being pulled by some force of science or maybe nature, her eyes dropped to the erection standing starkly proud from his mouth-watering body. She felt her abdomen tense and an answering liquid heat between her thighs. He wanted her, and she wanted him. Why make it any more complicated than that?

Taking his hand, she let him pull her back to bed.

* * *

They spent most of the rest of the day in bed. Which was wonderful on so many levels, not least because it stopped Sydney panicking about the ball. The regatta had been fine, but it was more a 'day out' kind of atmosphere. There had been just so many people and so much noise that she had felt, not invisible, but lost in the crowd.

But the ball would be different. Instead of mingling with a drink in hand and smiling, there was a formal dinner, which meant having to make conversation. And then there was the dress. How was she supposed to carry off a ball gown?

'What are you worrying about?'

She jolted back to Tiger, nestling closer to his warm, solid body just for a moment before she answered. Just because she could. And because he was so gorgeous, and for the moment, anyway, he was hers.

'I was thinking about the ball, and the dinner.' Now she tilted her head back, met his eyes, felt another jolt at the curiosity there because he was listening to what she was saying. 'I've never been to anything like this. I mean, it's in a palace, for goodness' sake, and it's hosted by somebody called the Duke of Bergamo and Brandolini.'

Even just saying that out loud made her feel slightly sick.

Her breath caught as he pulled her towards him so that her breasts and stomach pressed against the honed muscles of his chest and abdomen.

'A ball is just a party. A palace is just a big house. And all those dukes and duchesses are just people like you and me.'

She rolled her eyes. 'But I'm not like you. You're like them. You own an island. And a private jet.'

'So, take them away. See what's left. That's when you realise that deep down people are all the same. Just think of it as a tailgate party with masks and champagne. And I'll be there with you the whole time, so you don't need to be nervous.'

As he slid his hand along her cheek and smiled at her, she leant into it, groaning. 'You make it sound so easy.' She sounded casual enough, but her heart thudded inside her chest. With each passing minute, she found herself wanting him more. And she knew it was dangerous to think like that. To think that this was about anything more than sex. But that was hard to remember when he smiled like that.

Tiger waited for Sydney to join him downstairs, his fingers clamped around a slim, rectangular leather box.

His reaction to stress had always been to come out fighting, and his almost omnipresent state of anger with his father, and with the women who became his stepmothers, had left no room for nerves.

Until now.

He glanced up to the top of the staircase, and then swore softly as he realised what he'd done because he must have already looked up in anticipation of seeing Sydney there at least thirty times. And he didn't know why it mattered so much that she saw him looking up at her. He just knew that was what he wanted to do, and that waiting for her was making his stomach churn as if he were some gangly schoolboy on his first prom date.

Except he had been to plenty of proms and the girls had always been eager and ready. Was that why he was feeling so on edge? Because, inevitably, Sydney was making him wait and waiting was such an unfamiliar experience for him.

Maybe. But mostly he was nervous on her account.

He put the box down.

He had been telling her the truth when he said that the ball was just a party, but he knew that it would be intimidating and he wanted to give her this night. Wanted it to feel like a dream and for her to enjoy it and for her to shine, to recognise her own value.

His spine stiffened as he searched inside himself for the anger that had been a part of him for so long, but it was gone. Okay, he was angry with Harris for what he'd done. Mostly for what he'd done to Sydney, exploiting her like that. But it was a different kind of rage. It was clean, righteous, and, this was the biggest change, it was impermanent. Always before, his anger had been limitless and he'd never understood why. His whole life there had been no one to ask. His father, his stepmothers, his teachers, everyone had just seen the consequences, not the cause.

Only Sydney had bothered to ask. She had sat and listened and now he could see that his anger was just a form of weaponised fear. Fear of repeating his father's mistakes, of being used then abandoned. Of being part of someone's life and yet ultimately alone.

He didn't feel alone now. Or angry.

Here with Sydney, he felt relaxed, comfortable in his skin. Extremely comfortable in her skin too. Happy, basically—

His arms prickled and he saw something at the periphery of his vision and he turned, tilting his head back, and all the thoughts slid sideways, colliding with one another inside his head.

Sydney hadn't shown him which dress she was going to wear, but given her nerves he'd assumed it would be something subtle.

She had gone bold. His eyes skimmed the rippling burnt-orange silk. No, it was more than bold. It was fearless, she was as fearless as a goddess, and just as beautiful.

'Don't talk to me,' she said, gripping the banister as she

picked her way down the staircase. 'I have to concentrate otherwise I'm going to trip.'

As she reached the bottom of the stairs, he held out his hand, and she snatched it.

Their eyes met and, tilting her chin up, she smiled, and he smiled too because she knew she looked good and he liked that. But his opinion mattered to her. And he liked that too. He liked that a lot.

'You look good,' she said then.

And he was still so stunned that he just said, 'Thank you.'

Her face scrunched a little. 'I'm the one that should be thanking you.'

'For what?'

'For getting someone in to do my make-up and hair.' He glanced up to where her glorious red hair was coiled into some bouffant updo. 'And for this.' She smoothed a hand over the shimmering skirt. 'I've never worn anything so beautiful.'

His gaze moved over her face. He hadn't even noticed the make-up, but now, glancing down at her glossy lips, he wanted badly to kiss her.

'You look stunning.' His fingers tightened. 'I wanted to say that before… I was going to but…anyway, you look incredible, honestly, you look—'

'Oh, sei bellissima, Signora—'

It was Silvana, her hands fluttering to her cheeks, and he felt a rush of relief that she had arrived to stop him stammering like a schoolboy. And he hadn't felt this out of control since he was a kid. Had never wanted to feel out of control. That was why he lived as he did. Never committing, never allowing himself to care. Only he did care about Sydney. And that should be scaring him.

Then again, what was there to worry about? In a couple of

days, they would go their separate ways, and his life would be back on track.

He cleared his throat. 'We should go.'

Sydney turned from where she was still being admired by Silvana and the maids.

'But first I have something for you for tonight.' He picked up the rectangular box he'd been clutching earlier. 'I didn't know what you were wearing so I went for diamonds because they go with everything.'

Her eyes were wide and stunned.

'Oh, Tiger, it's beautiful, thank you.'

'Here, let me put it on you.'

She turned and he picked up the necklace and looped it around her throat, fastening it at the nape.

It looked exquisite. The facets caught the shimmering fabric so that it looked as though there were flames flickering at the centre. The same flame he could see in her eyes and an answering heat flared inside him. Heat and hunger.

'Are you ready?'

The ball was the reason she was here. The reason he was here, but now he wished that he could just stay here with Sydney and talk and make love—

'Let's go,' he said lightly.

Tiger had wanted the evening to feel like a dream for Sydney. He hadn't expected it to feel like a dream for him too. Despite the glamour, he usually found these events boring and formulaic, but tonight, from the moment they had slipped on their masks and stepped off the *gondolino* and walked into the palazzo's glittering entrance hall, everything had felt as if it were in soft focus and weightless.

Only Sydney's hand in his felt real, and it seemed the most natural thing in the world to be with her. They sat opposite one another at the dinner, which meant he couldn't touch her, but he could watch her, and so while the spoilt heiresses on either side of him droned on, he watched Sydney. Watched and marvelled, because she was holding her own. More than that, she was shining.

After dinner, he got to hold her as they danced and every time her dress brushed against him, he would think about her body and how, even though she was turning heads in that dress, she looked better without clothes, and then he would try not to think about her naked because it made him want to stroke the soft skin of her thighs or trace his hand over the curve of her hip.

'Shall we go back?' he said, leaning in to graze his mouth against her throat.

Her eyes were bright and steady. 'Yes.'

As they walked off the dance floor, someone called his name, and he felt a hand on his shoulder and everything slammed into focus.

'McIntyre! I thought it was you.' Harry Atherton was grinning at him, swaying slightly, his eyes screwing up against the lights, his wife Juno clutching his arm. 'These bloody masks, honestly, if there's one thing I'd outlaw it would be masked balls.' He straightened slightly, his gaze sliding over Sydney. 'I'm sorry, we haven't been introduced.'

She smiled. 'Sydney.'

'Harry—it's a pleasure to meet you, Sydney. So, what are you two lovebirds up to now?'

Tiger felt Sydney glance up at him. 'I think we're going back to the villa.'

'Seriously, mate?' Harry frowned. 'We were all going to play some games upstairs. Come on, it will be fun.'

He tightened his hand into a fist. Maybe it was being recognised by Harry, but he felt suddenly disorientated and for a moment he was torn, but then again—

'Yeah, why not?'

'You know what we should do?' Juno shouted over the music. 'We should play hide and seek. Harry, you count and the rest of us will hide. Come on, Sydney.'

Juno dragged Sydney away and he stared after her, something jamming inside him as Harry started to count. It was just a game, and she was one of the few people on earth who had defied him, but that look on her face had been panic, fear almost.

He was moving before his brain caught up with his legs. Pushing past the other guests and up the stairs. Where was she?

'Hey, McIntyre, you're supposed to be hiding.'

He turned, eyes narrowing, and Harry stumbled back, holding his hands up. There was no reason to feel this panic, Tiger told himself, taking another flight of stairs, three steps at a time. But he couldn't seem to stop it. Yanking open a door, he stepped into the room.

It was small and unfurnished and empty, and he was about to leave when he heard it. The sound of someone breathing, small, panicky breaths almost as if they were injured. And then he saw her. She was pressed against the wall, her eyes closed, body shaking, one hand in front of her face as if she was trying to hide something.

'Sydney,' he said softly. 'Did someone hurt you?'

She was shaking her head, trying not to cry, he could see that now and it tore at him. He touched her wrist gently, wanting to comfort her, and her arm twitched and her eyes snapped open and then he saw her fear, and everything inside him turned to stone.

'It's okay. It's okay. I've got you,' he murmured, scooping her up into his arms. 'Just hold onto me. I'm going to take you home.'

CHAPTER NINE

LATER TIGER WOULD wonder how they got back to the island. He had a vague memory of walking downstairs, of shouldering his way through the crowds of partygoers, but beyond that nothing. Except Sydney's hand curled around his neck, limply, like a rescued animal.

He had felt a new kind of anger then. Not hot, but cold, cold enough to shatter everything it touched because he wanted to raze cities, wipe out populations, smash a world that could hurt a beautiful young woman and still keep spinning in space.

Remembering that blind flinch, he felt a dark heaviness spill through his chest. The pain he had felt as a child was nothing to this.

But his pain could wait. His anger too.

He slipped off his mask, then hers. 'Do you want me to get Silvana?' he said gently as Sydney sat down on the bed, staring past his shoulder, her freckles standing out against the paleness of her face.

She shook her head. 'I'm fine.'

Except she wasn't. Even if he hadn't heard the hollowness in her voice, he knew she wasn't fine. She looked exhausted and frozen to the bones, and she probably was in that dress. Getting up, he closed the shutters and then the curtains and then he crouched beside her. 'I think you should get into bed. I can help you undress or I can leave?'

She didn't answer, which he assumed meant that she

wanted him to leave and he was about to stand up when her hand caught his. 'I don't want you to go.'

Her shoulder blades looked small and sharp like the wings of a moth as she leaned forward so that he could unbutton the back of her dress. He helped her into the T-shirt he assumed she wore in bed when she slept alone and then he undid her hair. And all the time he was helping her, he talked to her about nothing because he wanted to make it feel normal. Wanted to make her feel safe.

As she slid under the covers, he tucked her in. But she was still shivering.

'Let me get you something warm to drink.'

'Could you just stay for a bit?'

He nodded. 'I can stay. I can stay right here.' He stretched out beside her, still fully clothed, his head on the pillow beside her. 'Just close your eyes and try to get some rest. I'm not going anywhere.'

Her chest lifted and fell and then quite suddenly her eyes closed and she was asleep. He had planned on staying awake like some guard dog, but he must have fallen asleep too because he woke with a jolt and thought it was morning. But then he realised the lights were all still on and that Sydney's eyes were open, her face expressionless and watchful.

'Did I wake you?'

Shaking her head, she inched up against the pillows. 'I think I woke you.'

Her fingers were pleating the sheet and his heart felt as if it were going to slam through his ribs, but he had to ask. 'Did something happen there? Did someone hurt you?'

'No. No one did anything. It was my fault. I thought it would be okay. It's been so long, but—'

There was a silence and he could see her trying to marshal her thoughts and he wanted to pull her closer and hold her, but then he remembered how she had felt so limp and diminished when he'd carried her to the boat, and he knew that doing that would be for his benefit, not necessarily hers.

'You don't need to talk about it now. You don't need to talk about it ever.'

'I want to... It's been such a long time... I didn't think it would feel the same, because it was just a bit of fun. The hide and seek, I mean—'

'But it wasn't fun for you?' He knew it hadn't been, but he was terrified that she would shut down again if he pushed her.

She was shaking her head, shaking everywhere. 'I used to hide from him when he was really angry. Which was stupid, because I knew it would make him angrier, make him hurt me more.'

A wave of rage streaked through him like lightning. There was an excruciating pain in his chest, as if someone were snapping his ribs apart.

He looked at her still, tense body. Last night, she had helped him face the shame he had felt all his life. She had made him see his father in a different way and it had loosened the knotted ball of fear and distrust and anger so that it was easier to breathe. And all she had done was let him speak.

'Who hurt you, Sydney?' he said gently.

Her hands stilled against the sheet and for a moment she didn't respond. It looked as if she weren't breathing even, and he knew that she was reluctant to go back there. 'His name is Noah,' she said at last. 'Noah Barker and he was my husband.'

Husband. Tiger stared at her, his heart beating slow and hard in his chest, the air tilting around him. Sydney had been married? 'But not any more?'

The air in the room seemed to ripple as she shook her head. 'I left him five years ago, and then I divorced him.'

He could see then what he hadn't wanted to see in New

York. What he hadn't been able to see because of his anger and confusion. Her defiance was an armour. That need to push back was self-defence learned the hard way.

'How long were you with him?'

'Just over a year. I should have left him after the first time. The first time he hit me. But he was so upset and he said it wouldn't happen again, that he would never let it happen again, and I believed him. Or maybe I wanted to believe him. I wanted what I thought he was offering.'

Tiger stared at her, light-headed with shock, his stomach lurching, the world exploding around him. He could hardly hold onto the thread of his thoughts.

'And he was my first. My only, until you.'

Her voice was scratchy and she seemed young then. He had a sudden, bruisingly clear memory of the two of them out in the hut by the beach. He remembered her hands pulling clumsily at his zip. He had put it down to the urgency of their hunger, but it had been her first time in five years.

'We were in this tiny flat and he thought we needed space, so we moved out to this house way out in the desert, and it was okay for a bit. And then it happened again and it kept happening. Only we were miles from anywhere and he had taken my phone and my credit card.'

She rubbed her forehead with her fingers as if it was hurting. 'I know what you're thinking. You think that I'm making excuses. That I should have left, that if I really wanted to, I would have left.'

Actually, he was thinking of all the ways he could ruin Noah Barker's life. Slowly, painfully.

He shook his head. 'Leaving is a process, not a single act. I sat next to the head of a women's refuge charity at some dinner. She told me it takes an average of seven attempts before a woman can leave.'

'It took me three.' She took a deep, shaky breath. 'The first time he dragged me back into the house by my hair. The second time I tried to take the car and he smashed my face into the steering wheel and knocked out a tooth. This one is an implant. The real one is in the desert somewhere.' Her voice trailed off and she pressed her fingers against her mouth as if she was remembering the pulpy feeling and the taste of blood.

'It kept bleeding so long Noah got worried and he took me to hospital. There was this nurse and she took me off on my own and she asked me if my husband had hurt me. I should have said yes, but I was so muddled and scared. After that I stopped running. I used to hide but that was worse. He used to get so angry.'

She made a small, tense gesture with her hand.

'Did your family know?'

He felt sick. The idea of hurting a woman was appalling but letting her be hurt was just as bad.

Her eyes skated away to the door. 'I didn't want them to know. I know it sounds crazy, but I was ashamed. I felt so stupid, and I thought it was my fault, that I was doing something to make him that way. That I deserved it.'

'Why would you ever think that?'

'Because for so long I hated being a Truitt. I love my family, but they don't make it easy. They're lazy and messy and they do dumb things.'

She sucked in a sharp breath. 'When I was growing up, we never had any money and they were always in and out of trouble, and I wanted to be different. I thought I was different, better than them, and I thought Noah was better because he dressed well and he had an expensive car, and an actual job, a good job. But he was a monster and it was my dumb, lazy brothers who rescued me.'

Her cheeks were shining with tears and Tiger reached into his pocket and handed her a handkerchief.

'The last time he hit me, he was so out of control. I remembered that nurse at the hospital and I stole his phone and I called Connor. I was so scared Noah would find out. He was always checking his phone and in the end I panicked and I dropped it into the oil tank.'

He hesitated a moment then put a hand on top of hers. 'And your brothers got there before he found out?'

Scrunching the handkerchief into a ball, she nodded.

'When Connor saw me, he wanted to kill Noah. They all did, but I wouldn't let them do anything, only then when I went to get my things Noah told me that I was a nothing. He spat in my face.'

Her face was wet again but there was a flicker of light in her eyes, a clear, unfaltering fire that he recognised.

'I punched him and I kept punching and Connor had to pull me off.'

He wanted to laugh, because of course Sydney had punched him, but instead he pulled her against him, kissing her face. 'Good for you,' he murmured, burying his face in her hair.

She looked up at him, smiling weakly.

'I didn't really hurt him but out of spite he must have called the police at some point and told them my brothers had assaulted him. They didn't tell me at first and then when I found out, they wouldn't let me go and tell them what really happened because they knew I didn't want anyone to know about Noah, and they didn't want me to get into trouble.'

'That's why you agreed to work for Harris,' he said slowly.

Her mouth was trembling, her hands too. 'I let them lie for me.'

Leaning back, he took hold of her wrists.

'Look at me, Sydney,' he said gently, but firmly. 'I don't know your brothers but I'm guessing they wanted to do that for you. And, yes, as a consequence they now have a criminal record for assault. But you didn't make them run a chop shop, did you? That's on them. And I won't let them go to prison. Whatever they need, I will make it happen, okay? You don't have to deal with this on your own any more, because you're not on your own. I'm here.' He softened his grip. 'Have you talked to anyone else about your marriage, like friends or counsellors?'

She hesitated, then shook her head.

'I went to a couple of DV support groups, but I didn't speak. I thought speaking about it would make it all come back and I just wanted to forget about it. You're the first, the only person I've told.'

Knowing that she had chosen him as her confidant made everything inside him spin like a pinwheel. 'If you need someone more qualified—'

'I don't think I do, but thank you. It's taken a long time but I can see now that Noah was the problem.' She swallowed. 'I think he knew his own limitations, and because of that he was angry at the world, and he took that anger out on me.'

'He did. He was a bully and a coward.' His gaze held hers, steady and direct. 'But just so we're clear, you did not deserve what he did to you. And you are not a nothing. You are brave and beautiful and loyal, and I am in awe of you.' He traced a line along the curve of her cheek. 'And, as you know, my opinion is the only opinion that counts.'

He pulled her back into his arms and held her tightly, and she tilted her face up to his and kissed him softly on the mouth. Then she pulled back and looked into his eyes and she kissed him again, this time with heat and longing.

'We don't have to.'

'I want to,' she said, finding his mouth again and pressing her lips to his. 'I want you.'

He rolled sideways, taking her with him so that she was on top.

'And I'm yours.'

Sydney stared down into Tiger's beautiful face, the air leaving her body. He meant here, now, in bed. And that was enough, she told herself. He was enough. In some ways, he was too much. Like his nickname, he changed the world as he moved through it.

Look what he had done for her.

Noah had broken her and she had put herself back together but nothing fitted, everything jarred and, because it hurt, she was reminded of the ugliness and the pain and fear. And it wasn't that she wanted to pretend that her marriage hadn't happened, but she couldn't move on.

But who couldn't face their fears with a tiger by their side? Thanks to him she felt whole and strongest along her fault lines. Whole and strong and freer than she'd ever felt before. It was as if she were filled with a golden light.

Her gaze moved shakily to his face, her pulse pounding in her head because it was him. Tiger. He had pushed back the shadows inside her, his strength and certainty, so different from the kind she had known before, pouring into her, hot and pure and clean like sunlight.

She felt dizzy. Her heart felt soft and vulnerable, no longer just an organ beating blood around her body but a rose, petals bursting apart, because that was what love felt like. And she had fallen in love with Tiger.

But how? When? The answer to all those questions was the same. Who cared? She was in love.

'Why are you smiling?'

She jolted back to him, glancing down at his gorgeous, golden face, feeling the press of his gorgeous, golden body, so gorgeous and male it made everything inside her feel sweet and honeyed.

Because I love you.

The words were there ready and waiting to spill from her lips, but how could she say them out loud?

They had known each other for such a short time that it could be counted in days. And he wasn't looking for love or even commitment.

'Because I'm happy.'

Small muscles creased around the corners of his eyes and he touched her face then, lightly, and, caught in his glittering gaze, she felt suddenly almost desperate to feel his mouth on hers, and his hands, and the hard length of him clenched between her legs.

Reaching down, she pulled her T-shirt up and over her head, feeling him still beneath her, and beneath the stillness a pulsing, predatory hunger that matched the hunger that was beating through her like a gong.

'I'm happy too now,' he said softly, and she laughed when she saw him smile, and she thought that if she could have one wish it would be that this moment would last for ever. Then he was reaching for her, stroking the swell of her breasts, and she was no longer capable of thinking.

They woke late again and took a long, warm shower together and then wandered downstairs. Smiling at two of the maids as they made their way out to the terrace, Sydney wondered if anyone could see the difference in her. It felt as if it should be visible because it felt like fireworks exploding beneath her skin. This was love, the thrilling, miraculous, absurd, mysterious, dreamlike, beautiful kind that was only supposed to happen in fairy tales.

And now that she knew what love really was, she knew that what she had felt for Noah was a pale, bloodless imitation of love, a delusion, a cruel trick. When she was eighteen, he'd seemed to represent all that glimmered only for the gilt to flake off and reveal dull lead beneath.

But Tiger, he was a ride on a roller coaster, all dips and tumbling turns and soaring upwards into a never-ending blue. He was also a safe haven, a lagoon in a stormy sea, and when his strong hands touched her skin, she could feel her scars healing. And his hands were touching her constantly. Even while they ate lunch out on the terrace, he kept reaching out to touch her almost as if she were necessary to him, like oxygen or daylight.

His phone buzzed and, pulling it from his pocket, he frowned.

'What is it?'

'It's the office. I'm sorry, but I'm going to have to deal with these emails.' He pressed her hand to his mouth and kissed it and she felt an intense, almost unbearable tug of hunger ripple through her body as she imagined leading him back upstairs to bed.

'Unfortunately, the business doesn't stop when I do.' He kissed her on the mouth then, and she tried not to read too much into his words. Tried to ignore the way it made her feel when he said things like that.

She'd thought he would disappear into his office, but he had lolled beside her on a lounger with his laptop and the fact that he had chosen to stay by her side simply added to the soft-focus happiness that seemed to burst from her skin every time they touched.

'I've been thinking about tomorrow,' he said slowly, sliding the laptop under the lounger.

The happiness oozed out of her. Tomorrow was always going to be her last day. On the flight over she had actually written those exact words in her diary and put a smiley face beside them. But now *my last day* sounded like an epitaph and she didn't feel like smiling any more.

'What are you thinking?' She lifted her hand to shield her eyes from the sun, but also to make it harder for him to see what she was thinking. His gaze seemed even more intense and golden than usual today.

'I've been planning a little surprise for Harris, retribution, you might say, for his meddling in our lives. But he will come out fighting, so I'd rather you weren't in New York when it goes live.'

'That's fine. I was going to go back to Los Angeles anyway.' Her throat tightened, but there was no reason to stay in New York. Or not one she could share with Tiger.

'You don't have to feel responsible for me.'

Her chest felt oddly tight. Or full, maybe that was a better description. But then she was breathing so much more easily today, maybe it was just all that extra oxygen.

'But I am,' he said slowly. 'So just stay in LA. Keep your head down. Maybe move back home for a while.'

'I can handle myself.'

'I know.' His eyes moved over her face. 'So how would you like to spend our last day?'

Sunlight was skimming across his face so that it was hard to see his eyes but all too easy to imagine him stretched out above her.

'So what would you like to do? I want you to choose. We can do anything you want, go anywhere…just tell me what you like.'

'I know you've probably done it a hundred times already, but I'd really like to see Venice,' she said after a moment. 'Properly, I mean. You know, do the touristy things? Only, would that be too boring for you?'

Tiger stared down into her face.

Boredom was the secret curse of the super-rich. To a normal person a palace or a private jet was something you dreamed about. But to the top one per cent, they were assets, the adult equivalent of trading cards that you played with at school. With nothing out of reach, it was perilously easy to get bored.

But he couldn't imagine anything getting boring with Sydney.

It wasn't just the sex either. Right from the start, she had challenged him, challenged his status, and she was curious, which he loved. She wanted to learn, to explore, to lift up stones and see what was underneath. Character traits that made her such a good hacker. Such a good person.

'I can't think of anything I'd like to do better. Except go to the moon, but maybe we can do that next,' he said softly, and he felt his heart beat out a complicated rhythm as she smiled.

Making Sydney smile, making her happy, was not a burden but a pleasure, he thought as they made their way to St Mark's Square the following morning.

The hand that wasn't holding hers tightened into a fist. He couldn't understand how anyone could have hurt her, and with such systematic brutality. He hated to think of her alone and scared and trapped. Her ex deserved to be hung, drawn and quartered. And Sydney?

She deserved so much better. She deserved to be safe and happy, and more, so much more, and he couldn't give her everything she deserved but he could give her this.

He could give her Venice.

He gazed up at the Basilica with its great arches and Romanesque carvings and the four horses that presided over the whole piazza.

When he'd first made enough money to be able to leave the States and travel comfortably, he'd had a tick list of places to visit. All the usual suspects... London, Paris, Rome. But it was Venice that had fascinated him. There was a stubbornness to the city he liked, and an ingenuity that clicked with something in his brain. Then of course there was the architecture and the art and the food.

Since then, he had visited Venice as a 'tourist' on countless occasions, mostly on his own with a ball cap pulled down low over his face, his security detail discreetly matching his stride.

Visiting with Sydney was a whole lot more fun.

The landmarks felt less like scenes from postcards or backdrops to a thousand bloggers' selfies and she was wide-eyed with excitement, wanting to know everything. He had bought her a guidebook and he let her tell him the facts. The names of the buildings. The year they were built, and why. But then he told her the stories behind them.

'Casanova once escaped a tryst with the French ambassador and a couple of nuns by climbing across those rooftops,' he said, as they squinted up into the sunlight to admire the Doge's palace.

'And that house there,' he said, pointing to a long, low building on the Grand Canal. 'That's the Palazzo Venier dei Leoni. It was Peggy Guggenheim's home. She collected thousands of works of art during her time here, and thousands of lovers.'

Venice was not just a city, he thought as they sipped mimosas in Harry's Bar. It was a world of water, dappled and delicate, of reflections in tarnished mirrors, and each time he visited, he discovered something new. And Sydney was the same. With each corner they turned, he saw another, different side to her, each one more fascinating than the last.

And for once, he didn't try to navigate the confusion of side streets and sudden unexpected piazzas, because today the city itself seemed to be leading him somewhere.

They ate lunch in a *trattoria*. *Vongole* and red wine, watching the *vaporetti* glide past. And then, because he knew she wanted to, he suggested a ride in a *gondola*.

'Really?' She rolled her eyes. 'It's not too much of a cliché for you?'

He shrugged. 'I can't remember the last time I did this, so it feels new to me.'

No, that was her. He watched Sydney's face light up as he helped her into the *gondola*. She made everything feel new and fresh and possible.

'Do you really want to go to the moon?' she asked him suddenly.

'Ever since I was a kid.'

'So the world isn't enough? You have to conquer space.'

Here, now with Sydney, it felt peerless but—

'Not conquer it. I supposed I just wanted to be someplace far away where I wouldn't have to deal with my dad's messes.'

She squeezed his hand.

'What do you think?' he asked as they glided down the Grand Canal, past the floating palaces with their filigreed, shuttered fronts.

'I think it's the loveliest place I've ever been.' Her expression was so open and sweet it hurt to look at her. 'Maybe it's the water but there's something about the light here, it feels magical. I can't tell what's real and what isn't. I love it.'

'They say that other cities have admirers,' he said softly, responding to the happiness in her voice. 'But Venice has lovers.'

Their eyes locked. Lovers. The word hovered in the air between them and his blood began pounding fiercely through his body.

Was that what they were? Yes, but only in the physical sense, he told himself, because it was obvious that they were no longer just having sex. They were more than bodies fusing in mutual need. What they felt in each other's arms was more than pleasure. More complicated, but also less. There was understanding there and acceptance. Sydney had helped him face up to the pain of his past and address his anger with his father, and, frankly, that astonished him. She astonished him more and more with every passing hour, and he cared about her.

But love—

Not being angry didn't mean he was ready or capable of loving anyone. His childhood had left scars, and they would always be there and no matter how he and Sydney fitted together in bed and out of it. That wouldn't change.

He didn't want to admit that to himself, but Sydney needed, deserved, more than he could give. She deserved to be loved.

And he had a business to run and scores to settle. That was what mattered, that and not letting a week of intimacy and possibilities make him risk turning into his father.

She was staring at him, her hair loose around her face, brown eyes wide. She looked like a Titian and he had to kiss her then. Leaning forward, he pulled her closer and fitted his lips against hers gratefully, letting himself vanish in the kiss.

As they broke apart, he couldn't look away from the softness in her eyes.

'Shall we go back?' she said quietly.

* * *

Back at the island, they spent the rest of the day in bed, exploring, teasing, seducing one another. Finally, they lay, muscles relaxed, bodies warm and damp, their limbs intertwined, at ease with each other in a way that seemed both natural and miraculous. And yet something was different. He seemed distracted, as if his mind was split. Her heart squeezed a little. Could he be thinking what she was?

'Tiger.'

'Sydney.' His eyes gazed down on her, pupils darkening.

'Actually, hold that thought.' She leaned forward and kissed him on the mouth. 'I have to go to the bathroom.'

In the bathroom, she turned on the taps, scooping up the lukewarm water, to splash her face. Straightening, she stared at her reflection. Her heart was pounding. She hadn't needed the bathroom, but she'd had to leave. She needed some distance because it was getting harder and harder not to tell him that she loved him.

She wanted to, and she would, but she couldn't just hijack him with her feelings. He had been hurt, and just because she was ready didn't mean he would be. And that was fine. This was all still so new for her and she wanted to hold the feeling close and private. This feeling of love, of loving with knowledge and understanding, of loving a man who was worthy of her love, it made her feel strong and as if she were a bird soaring high and free.

For now, though, kissing him was easier.

'What was it you wanted to say?' he said, pulling her against him. She wriggled round so that her head was resting on his shoulder.

'I just wanted to thank you for taking me to Venice. It was the most perfect day.'

His eyes stilled on her face as if seeing her for the first

time. 'It was. And thank you for being there for me this week. And I haven't forgotten about your brothers. I'll get in touch with my legal people on the flight home.'

Flight home.

She'd always known that they would be flying home this evening but hearing him say the words out loud was like having a bucket of cold water tipped over her head.

'So we're leaving this evening,' she said slowly.

He didn't speak or nod but he was already starting to sit up, shifting his weight. Retreating, she thought, her throat tightening.

'I have a meeting tomorrow with the lead on the space agency project. To talk numbers.'

He was standing now, and had already pulled on his trousers. 'And maybe finalise my piggybacking on one of the exploratory missions.'

'So you really are going to go to the moon? That's amazing. I'm so pleased for you.' Her smile was instant and genuine. His face softened a fraction and he pulled her closer, his hand curving around her waist.

'Hopefully, yes.'

He let go of her then without even kissing her and she stared at him in confusion.

'Don't look so worried. You kept your side of the deal and I'm going to keep mine. I'll make sure your brothers get the best legal counsel.'

The deal. She stared at him, trying to breathe past the frozen lump in her chest. He must be trying to reassure her because there was more to this week than the deal they'd made in New York.

'I just thought—'

'Thought what?' he said impatiently. 'Look, Sydney, I

know things have got a little blurred between us but this was only ever a temporary arrangement. '

Her heart stumbled. He was looking at her in the same way as he had a moment earlier and she felt a chill scamper down her spine because she wasn't the stranger here. He was. There was a tension in him now, and a distance.

She cleared her throat. 'Maybe I could come with you,' she said lightly. 'You know, watch your back. Support you.'

He ran his hand through his hair. 'Where is this coming from, Sydney? I don't need supporting. What I need is for you to stick to the terms of our arrangement.'

Glancing down, she realised she was naked and she reached for her robe. As she slipped it on, something flickered in his eyes, desire, and something else she couldn't name.

'I don't care about the terms of our arrangement. I care about you. And I thought you cared about me. You said you did.'

Tiger was staring at her, his eyes not that clear, light gold any more, but opaque, guarded.

'I did say that, and I meant it. In the context of you being here. With me. Now.'

The room seemed to sway a little. Here. Now. The terms of the deal had been clear from the start. Nothing had changed, and everything had. She watched him shrug on his jacket to complete his transformation back into the billionaire tycoon she had met in New York.

He glanced over at her, his forehead creasing. 'I can make sure you're taken care of. I can make things happen for you. Good things. You have excellent skills so maybe so if you still want that job at McIntyre—'

'You're offering me a job?' She felt dazed, drunk almost. 'I don't want to work for you, Tiger.'

'That's fine. If you'd prefer to work for another company, I can make a few calls, put in a good word for you.'

She was shaking her head. Her whole body was shaking. 'I don't want to work for you and I don't want you to put in a good word for me. I love you.'

She had said it before but not understood what it meant. Now she did, and she felt it spinning inside her like sugar turning to candyfloss. 'I love you,' she said again. Because he was worth the risk. They were worth the risk.

But Tiger was staring at her as if she had said a different kind of four-letter word. A shadow slid across the curve of his cheekbone. 'I'm sorry, Sydney. I think you are an incredible woman—'

'Don't do this, don't pretend—'

'But this is pretend,' he said flatly. 'It's only ever been a pretence, a performance.'

'I don't believe you.' Her chest felt tight, and heavy. 'I know you. I know this is real.' It was difficult to breathe, to speak, but she had to try. 'You're not your father, Tiger.'

'Maybe not, but I can't be what you need, what you deserve.' His eyes were dull like beaten metal. 'I'll call my lawyers *en route*.'

'No, I'll find another way.'

His gold eyes were darker than a solar eclipse. 'Do me a favour. Maybe stay here until the stuff with Harris blows over.'

He stared at her for a moment and then he turned and walked swiftly through the door. Outside, she could hear the waves splashing against the shore. The world was still shifting, moving, breathing. But as she slid to the floor, hugging her knees to her chest, she knew she would never be a part of it again.

CHAPTER TEN

SYDNEY HADN'T STAYED on the island.

Tiger shifted back in his chair and stared across his office, remembering that first time he'd seen her out of the corner of his eye, all light curves and red hair.

Because that was the problem: there was too much to forget and so much he wanted to remember.

About an hour after take-off, he'd swallowed his pride and made a call to Silvana. Even though he'd still been piqued by her outburst as he was leaving. It was the first, the only time, he could remember his housekeeper losing her temper with him, and in English.

'Why are you leaving?'

'Because I have a business to run,' he'd countered.

Silvana had folded her arms across her body and stared at him. 'And what about Ms Truitt?'

He'd frowned. 'What about her?'

Her eyes had narrowed. 'Why is she not with you?'

'She's not with me. She never was. This was only ever a short-term thing.'

Silvana had snorted. 'Short term? I saw how you looked at her when she came downstairs before the ball. That is not how a man looks at a woman who is short term to him.'

He had been rooted to the spot. With fury and fear. Because he could still remember how he had felt. *Felt.* So many feelings roaring through him, and he hadn't recognised half of them, and hadn't known what to do with any of them. Or what it meant that he felt them for Sydney.

'I know you are scared of loving.' Silvana's face had softened. 'And it is scary because loving hurts but losing her will hurt worse. So don't leave her here. Stay or take her with you. That is what you want. She wants it too.'

'I can't do that.'

'Then you are a fool.'

No fool like an old fool. It was what people said about his father. That Silvana could say it to him made him see red, and he had stormed off without another word.

On the phone, he had made up some nonsense about papers on his desk. But really it had been an excuse to check that Sydney was okay.

His hands had tightened against the armrests.

'Lei non è qui, Signor McIntyre,' Silvana had said tersely. *'Se n'è andata circa due ore fa.'*

In other words, Sydney had left right after him.

Pushing away from the chair, he strode over to the windows, his pulse beating out of time. He had tried to call her, but her number was out of service and her website just offered a message of apology. In other words, she had gone dark.

He felt a flicker of frustration, and beneath that a nagging anxiety that Sydney was out there in the world without him. Not that he was worried about Harris. When the story finally went live, he would be too busy salvaging his reputation to go after Sydney.

But he couldn't stop thinking about how he'd ended things. Or the look on her face. He had told himself countless times that it had to be that way. That she knew what she was signing up to. All the things he'd told himself in the past, and it had never been a problem before.

Only it was now. For some reason he couldn't explain, he couldn't unhear her telling him she loved him. Couldn't unsee the moment when he'd told her it was a pretence. The look on her face as she'd looked up at him had sliced him open.

Because he cared about Sydney. How could he not after everything she had told him? But this feeling he had, this tightness in his chest that made it hard to catch his breath, and the waking in the night and the inability to focus on anything, it was probably just a virus, something he'd picked up crossing six time zones.

He gazed out across New York, a memory stirring inside him like a flickering flame: of him taking Sydney's arm and leading her to the window to show her the view. It cost a lot of money to own that view. As he looked at it now, it held no value.

Nothing seemed to have any value any more, not even the contract that would take his empire into space.

Because Sydney wasn't here with him.

He let his head fall against the glass, trying to cool his feverish brain, but it wasn't a fever making him feel like this. It wasn't down to something he'd picked up. It was something he'd lost. No, pushed away.

His eyes were burning. The irony was that he had spent his whole life not wanting to be like his father. Not wanting to be tricked by 'love' because he had seen only the falseness of love and how it diminished everything it touched.

But Sydney did love him. He knew that because he knew her. He had fought with her and comforted her and held her while they made love and she had held and comforted him. They had talked and listened and laughed and she had cried.

She loved him. It wasn't a pretence.

And that was why he couldn't be with her. Because he loved her too. He pressed his hands against the glass, framing that truth, accepting it, acknowledging it. Letting it push back all the layers of fear and the assumptions he'd made and clung to for so many years.

He had loved her from that very first day in his office. He just hadn't seen it because he hadn't known what it was. Not even at the masked ball when he had been so hopelessly in love with her that his housekeeper and the maids had known. Give a man a mask, and he will tell the truth. He had told the truth that night, but had been too blinded by fear of falling into the same bad pattern of behaviour as his father.

He saw it now. He felt it now, inside him, burning bright and pure like a votive flame.

Only he was so untested in love, so unpractised, and he wanted the best for her. Wanted to protect her. That was why he'd wanted her to stay on the island. That was what he'd told himself. Maybe, though, keeping her on the island was more about prolonging the fantasy, because the reality of love still scared him. Silvana knew that, Sydney too. But it had taken losing her for him to see it, and his housekeeper was right, losing her hurt more. And it was a self-inflicted pain. By attempting to avoid the pain of love, he had pushed Sydney away and hurt himself. Hurt her too, just as his father had hurt him. Because it was people who hurt each other and sometimes they used love as an excuse.

And he needed to tell her that he'd been wrong, and stupid. A fool, in fact.

Breathing out unsteadily, he lifted his head.

Was it too late?

No, it couldn't be, was the only answer to that question that he could contemplate. But if he was going to be the man Sydney needed by her side, then, for the first time in his life, he was going to have to take a leaf out of his father's book and take a risk on love.

* * *

'It should only take a couple of hours but if you need us, all you have to do is call.'

'Why would I need you?'

Glancing up from the magazine she had been pretending to read, Sydney frowned at her brother. She had been helping out at the auto repair shop for the last few days, partly to have something to take her mind off Tiger and partly because she wanted the judge to know that this was a genuine family business.

'It's lunchtime. Nobody has come in at lunchtime for the last three days.'

Connor reached past her to grab the keys to the pick-up. 'Yeah, but if they did and you didn't know something, you can call us is what I'm saying.'

Her middle brother, Jimmy, nodded. 'We're only talking to her. It's not like we're in court.'

'She's your lawyer. You need to pay attention to what she's saying. Don't take any calls. In fact, switch off your phones.' She put down the magazine, frowning. 'Maybe I should come too.'

This was the penultimate meeting with the lawyer before they went to the courthouse on Tuesday. Kim Shaw had been a good pick. She was smart, no-nonsense but she had also agreed to being paid in instalments. Which was surprising but also a great relief. Sydney hadn't asked Tiger to make good on his promise. She had thought about it. Not seeing him in person—just thinking about that had made her want to curl into a ball and howl. But she had considered calling him—and almost immediately decided against it.

What they'd shared might never have been real to Tiger, but she had loved him, utterly and unconditionally and, despite how it had ended, she didn't regret it. But asking him to get a lawyer for her brothers would take that love and turn it into something ugly and transactional.

'It's fine. We're just signing some paperwork. We're seeing her again on Monday to go through everything.' Her youngest brother, Tate, leaned in and kissed her on the cheek. 'Besides, we need you here otherwise we'll have to shut up shop.'

'Don't forget to switch off your phones,' she called after them. 'And stop looking so shifty.' They were looking shifty, she thought as she watched them leave, her heart thudding against her ribs. But she loved them all the same, and it looked as if they were going to avoid jail time, so having her heart broken by a beautiful stranger had been worth it.

Except Tiger wasn't a stranger to her. Leaving Italy, she had felt bereft, as if she had left her shadow behind.

The journey back to the States was a blur, but somehow she had got to Los Angeles and gone like a homing pigeon to her parents' house.

This was the second time she had moved back home after her life had imploded. The difference was that then the hurt had had relief in it. Now, though, she felt alone and desperately, desperately sad.

She missed Tiger. All the time that she was awake, she missed him constantly and so intensely that sometimes she would have to press her hand against her chest to push back against the ache there. And at night, she dreamed about him. Hot, frantic dreams where he felt so real that she would wake with a start, expecting to hear his voice, talking to her in that same soft, soothing way that he had after the ball. His arms holding her tightly, his heart beating through her and steadying her.

But it was just her, alone, in the bed she had slept in as

a child. And it was there in that bed, alone in the darkness, that she allowed herself to cry.

She hadn't told her family anything of what had happened with Tiger. She just didn't have the words. How could she describe that astonishing, life-changing *coup de foudre* of meeting a man like him and of finding herself in his golden gaze?

How could she describe the intensity of their dizzying chemistry? Or the rightness of his body against hers? It would sound ridiculous when in fact it was miraculous, transformative, a benediction, an awakening.

Thinking about him hurt so much. Loving him was like having a splinter of ice in her heart. But then she should have known. Tiger's heart was off-limits. Hopefully, one day, someone would find the key to set him free and let him love as she knew he could and should love. With fire and fervour.

As for her, she had to rebuild her life. Try to live an hour, then a day, then a week and so on.

And she would do it.

Right now, she had shut down Orb Weaver, but it was only temporary. She needed to focus on keeping her brothers out of prison. And as soon as she knew they were safe and free, she was going to go travelling to Europe. To London and Paris and Copenhagen and Barcelona, and then maybe she could think about going back to Italy.

After that? Who knew? Maybe run the business out of some London town house? Or perhaps she would just come back to LA. Right now, she was taking one day at a time.

Speaking of which, she needed to change the battery in the clock. The time had been stuck at half past ten for about three years now.

But where did Connor keep the batteries? She found them in the end, and she took the clock down off the wall and began pushing them into the slot. No, that was wrong. She had put the positives and the negatives back to front.

The door buzzer made her jump, but she didn't look up. At this time of day, it was probably just the guy from office supplies. She was trying to make the auto repair shop look more professional and less like a hang-out for wannabe gangsters.

'Be right with you.'

'In your own time.'

That voice. The air around her froze. Her whole body stilled, even her heart stopped beating. For days now, it had been as if she were wearing an old-fashioned diver's suit, the kind with the fishbowl helmet, and she'd had to focus hard to work out what the people on the other side of the glass were saying. But his voice had cut through the glass instantly.

She felt a jolt against her ribs as her heart started again and the roar of her own blood spun her round to face him.

No name needed, because '*him*' could mean only one man.

Tiger was standing in the doorway, his fingers loose around the handle. And the world snapped into focus, so real and sharp it hurt, his beauty blinding her like a searchlight. She stared at him in shock, stunned, devastated.

She must be imagining him. Except she wasn't.

'We're closed.'

He shut the door, and flipped the sign. 'Yes, you are.'

Still arrogant, she thought, arrogant and wanting to run things his way.

For an endless, shuddering moment, nothing happened and then he walked slowly towards her with that beautiful feline grace as if he owned this shabby little shop. As if he owned the whole world. But he didn't own her.

She slammed her way round the desk. 'You need to leave.'

'We need to talk.'

'No, we don't,' she snapped, trying to manage the vaulting somersaults her heart was performing beneath her ribs at the same time as stifling the shoot of hope she could feel trying to push its way to the surface. Because seeing him was already too much for her to handle.

'Your phone number doesn't work. Your website is inactive. And you closed your bank account.' His voice was quiet but she could hear his anger and frustration.

'I already know all of that.' Her voice cracked and she stared at him, shaking, not with fear, but with need and longing, and love. But Tiger didn't love her.

Tilting her chin, she forced herself to look into his eyes. 'So, if that's all you came to tell me, I think we're done here.' She didn't want to believe it, but now that she had said it out loud, she meant it.

'Why did you do that? I was going to help you. You need the money.'

She folded her arms in front of her aching chest. 'Not your money. And what I do with my bank account is none of your business.'

Tiger felt his heartbeat accelerate.

Walking into the auto repair shop and seeing Sydney there, whole, not weeping or bleeding or crushed, he had felt a bone-deep relief and such an immensity of love that he could hardly speak. Because he knew what love was now. He knew because it no longer felt like a risk but an adventure, a poem and a blessing all rolled into one.

But it was as if she were still behind the glass counter. There was a barrier between them, thin but unwavering, which was good. He wanted her to be safe and careful. But also bad, because he wanted to take her in his arms more than he had wanted anything, even the moon.

Only he needed to find the right words.

'It is my business. You are my business.' Which were the wrong words, he realised, cursing silently, panic swelling in his throat as he watched her stiffen. He tried again. 'What I'm trying to say is that you're my world.'

'And you're heading to the moon, so you'll be orbiting me at a distance, which suits me fine.'

'Not without you. If I go, you go.'

'You can't do this, Tiger. You can't just turn up and say things like that. I was getting better. So say whatever it is you came here to say, and then go.'

His heart felt as if it were tearing in two. All his life he had seen love as a weakness but now that it filled him from head to toe, it felt like a superpower. Only one that he hadn't learned how to use properly.

Please let me find the words, he prayed.

'It's very simple really. I love you and I need you. And I don't know how to live my life without you. Without you, nothing matters. Nothing makes sense.'

'You're the one not making sense. You told me you didn't love me. You chose the moon, remember?'

'I don't care about the moon. I care about you. And I love you. I love you like I never thought it would be possible to love anyone. And I know you probably won't believe me, but I think I loved you right from when you walked into my office and gave me the cold shoulder. I just didn't know what I was feeling. But I was lucky. I had a couple of people on hand to help me and I took their advice.'

Her eyes, her beautiful brown eyes, were wide and stunned. 'Your lawyers told you to come and find me?'

He shook his head, then he took a step forward. Just a small one, not big enough to scare her.

'When I was leaving the island, Silvana gave me a ticking-off. Made me see that I was sabotaging the only future that's ever made sense to me. The only future I want, and need.'

She held his gaze. 'What did she say?'

He laughed. 'She told me a few home truths.' Another step forward. 'Basically, that I was a fool.'

'You're not a fool.'

His eyes on hers were bright with tears, and as he shook his head, she took a step this time. 'I walked away. I let you slip through my fingers.' He hesitated, then reached out and touched her cheek gently, his heart contracting with relief, and a hope that hurt, when she didn't pull away. 'That would make me a fool in anyone's book.'

'Never to me.' She let herself lean close because he was so familiar, so beautiful and she couldn't not. 'You said a couple of people. Who was the second?'

'My father.' His mouth twisted. 'I remembered you saying that he thought it was worth risking everything for love. And I realised that I was risking everything that mattered to me because I was *scared of* loving you, of losing you. And then I lost you anyway.'

'You haven't lost me.'

Tears filled her eyes as he made a hard, scratchy noise as if his throat were too tight. 'I know that I have no right to ask for a second chance but, back in Italy, you said you loved me and I was hoping you might still feel that way.'

'You know I do,' she said softly, and he pulled her against him now, grateful that he had been given this second chance.

'And I love you. You believe me, don't you?'

Sydney looked up at him, seeing a man with a beautiful face and a loving heart. Strong still, but with the hard edges rubbed off. He had shone a light into her darkness and she loved him utterly, and unconditionally. 'I know you're good for it.'

He laughed again, and they moved closer, then apart, then closer again, like waves tumbling onto the shoreline, amazed by each other, stunned by the miracle of it.

'When did you get here?'

'Yesterday. I've been going out of my mind waiting. But I knew you'd need persuading, so I had to wait until you were on your own.'

'But how did you know I was going to be on my own?' She frowned, remembering Connor's shifty expression. In fact, they had all looked shifty. 'Did my brothers know you were coming here? They did, didn't they? I knew they were being weird.'

'Not weird. Worried. They care about you. A lot.' Remembering the triple-tractor-beam intensity of their gaze, he smiled at her. 'They needed persuading too, believe me. I think one of them mentioned a shotgun and a shovel at one point. But I explained why I needed to talk to you, and I asked for their help.'

'I can't believe you talked to my brothers.'

'Of course, I did.'

'Why of course?'

He shrugged. 'If we're going to be related, I need to get to know them, don't you think?'

Related?

She stared at him mutely. Her head was spinning. She felt as though she were floating. 'I don't understand. What do you mean by "related"?' Her voice trailed off and she covered her mouth with her hand. Tiger was kneeling down on the dusty floor, holding out a diamond ring.

'Marry me, Sydney,' he said softly.

Her legs folded beneath her and she slid down beside him. 'You can't do this. We can't do this,' she said hoarsely.

'Is that a yes?' he managed.

'Of course it's a yes.' Her hands tightened on his arms and for a moment he couldn't breathe past her words. 'But you're here and I don't want to lose you again.'

'You can't lose me. When I got on that plane to fly back to New York, I was fighting you, fighting myself, fighting Silvana because everything I thought was true and necessary for me was slipping away or disintegrating and that scared me because there was nothing left to hold onto. But then I realised that the only thing I wanted to hold was you.'

'But we've only known each other for a few days.'

'Ten.' He smiled at her, and just like that she was lost or maybe found. 'But who's counting?'

'Everyone will. They'll say we don't know each other. They'll say that we need more time.'

'We do know each other, and we're going to have for ever.' He pulled her close, his heart beating like a drum, pressing her close to him, breathing in her scent and her strength.

'And as you already know, although it seems I might have to remind you again, the only opinion that matters on that subject is mine. And it's not just an opinion.' He lifted his chin and there was a dark gleam in his eyes that made her breath catch. 'It's more of a directive.'

'Is that right?'

'It is,' he said softly, and, dipping his head, he found her mouth with his and set about proving that to her.

* * * * *

ITALIAN WIFE WANTED

LELA MAY WIGHT

MILLS & BOON

Emma and Dante's love story
is dedicated to *all* the Birmingham princesses.

The Brummy princess in the high-rise tower with
her black curly hair, the princess in the first-floor
maisonette or the second floor with no hair at all,
the princess in the house with too-thin walls…

One day, your prince will come.

CHAPTER ONE

THE CAR MOVED smoothly down the road. A road that wouldn't dare to have any imperfections. No potholes. No uneven surfaces to jar the elite residents it welcomed home.

And Emma Cappetta was coming home.

She was one of the elite in her chauffeur-driven car. In her designer black skirt suit and red-soled heels with metal tips that clattered on hard floors and sank deeply into newly turned soil.

The car stopped, and Emma stepped out into the night.

Her feet ached, her body hurt and her heart was wounded.

She paused at the bottom of the white stone steps. Her hand resting on the black metal handrail, she stared at the black door and gold knocker, at the entrance to the five-storey Edwardian building she'd called home for almost a year.

She'd only been away for fourteen days, enough to pack up her mother's life and prepare for today, her mother's funeral.

But oh, how easily she'd slipped back into her old life in Birmingham, how easily it had welcomed her back, how comfortable she'd felt in the childhood home she'd shared with her mum. The photos of them on the walls. The warmth. The smell. She'd slept so soundly in her old bed with the neighbour's conversation drifting clearly through the thin walls.

The estate, the crumbling roads, the potholes, the chatter of children out too late playing in the community playground…it had embraced her as if she'd never left.

Two weeks. That's all it had taken. Two weeks to unmask the lie of the life she'd been living for almost a year. She didn't belong here in London, in this beautiful house.

This wasn't…*home.*

The door opened and she moved through it, her throat tightening as she did.

She took the first step, and another, until she stood face-to-face with the dipped head of the butler.

'Mrs Cappetta,' he acknowledged. 'Would you like some tea to be arranged for you in the sitting room?'

Emma smiled, but it was barely a twitch. 'No, thank you, James.' She moved past him, her heels clicking on the marble-floored reception area.

'Is there anything else I can get for you?'

Dante?

Her nose pinched.

She still wanted him.

And that want was like a constant hunger in her stomach. Inside her. Even now, when the veil had lifted from her eyes and she knew the undeniable truth: that she meant nothing to her husband.

She was a fool.

Today had been her mother's funeral, and he hadn't come. Hadn't called. Hadn't sent a card.

The one time she'd *really* needed him, he'd hadn't been there.

Just like your dad.

Emma's heart clenched.

What had she expected? Her husband was only ever there for the thrill. For the sex. For her body. Never for anything…*real*.

'No, I don't need anything,' she told James, because she had no physical needs. What she had needed was her husband's support. His presence. His compassion.

And it wasn't just that he hadn't been there; it was the very fact she needed him at all. That realisation was un-ravelling everything she'd ever believed about herself, about their relationship. And about this life she'd been living with Dante.

Her heart ached acutely behind her breastbone.

'If there's nothing else, Mrs Cappetta…'

'Thank you.'

James nodded and left her alone.

Alone as she'd been all day.

Just today?

The voice in her head mocked her. Because it was true. It had taken the death of her mother, her funeral, for her to understand.

But now she did understand.

The weight on her shoulders doubled, anchoring her to the spot.

Her eyes moved, taking in the plush silk rugs, the hand-carved and intricate side tables with professional lighting installed to highlight the priceless art hanging in just the right spot to awe and please.

It was a museum of priceless artefacts collected and

displayed in a house that showed no signs—no evidence—of the people it housed.

No evidence of *them*.

It was further proof she didn't belong here.

The inner-city girl who had grown up surrounded by discoloured high-rises had no business here in Mayfair.

She had no right—no claim—to any of it.

The tendons contracted in her throat.

She hadn't realised it before, hadn't seen it, but she was in too deep.

Had she already fallen victim in the same way her mother had? Fallen in—

No. This wasn't love.

Love didn't exist. It was an illusion. And her mother had been punished for her folly. She'd been left brokenhearted time and time again. It's what had killed her, led to a heart attack at forty-three.

Emma straightened her spine.

The lie of love had killed her mother.

And it would kill her too if she allowed these feelings to take hold of her.

Emma slipped off her shoes where she stood and made her way to the spiral staircase. Two at a time, she climbed them.

She entered her bedroom. *Their* bedroom.

At the sight of the perfectly made bed, heat engulfed her. She couldn't help thinking of the nights, the mornings or the afternoons she'd spent in it. In his arms.

Sex wasn't the problem. It never had been. In fact, it's what had started it all.

Emma couldn't let herself think of that now.

She moved to the desk positioned by the balcony doors to the view of the secret garden below.

There were only three secret gardens in London. Emma and Dante had visited all of them before they settled on this one. On this view from their bedroom. On this house.

He'd never promised her a home. He'd promised her a year. One year to allow the chemistry that raged between them to burn itself out.

And she hadn't been able to say no.

She'd agreed to the terms of this marriage because she'd wanted what her mother had never had. *Security.* Financially and emotionally.

When had it changed? she wondered. When had she started to want…*more*? More of Dante's time? His friendship? Companionship? Support?

Because she wanted all those things, didn't she? Had needed them today and felt their absence when he hadn't been at her side.

She couldn't really be mad; she hadn't directly asked him to be there. But she'd told him the day and the time of the funeral service.

Emma wanted to wail as the truth assaulted her.

When had she got in so deep that his absence hurt?

She twisted the gold band on her finger.

It meant nothing. It was nothing more than a certificate of purchase. A twelve-month rental plan that she'd willingly agreed to.

And she hated it. Hated herself for how attached she'd become to a man.

For nearly twelve months, she'd waited for him, been ready for him. For him to visit her bed. A bed they shared when he returned from his endless business trips abroad that he'd never taken her, his wife, on. And those trips had got longer. And longer.

Marriage was the lie she'd always believed it was, wasn't it?

Her relationship with Dante was no different from the relationship her parents shared. A relationship where her mother was always waiting for her father to come back to her.

Emma believed she'd created something different. That she'd been in control in a way her mother never had been.

She sighed. *Heavily.*

She was still lying to herself, wasn't she?

It wasn't the marriage that was the lie. The marriage was everything Dante had promised it would be.

She'd changed. She wanted more. More than she knew Dante could ever give. And knowing that would kill her.

Emma padded back across the room and threw open her walk-in wardrobe. So many clothes. So many gifts he'd given her. So many *things.*

And he could keep them all.

These things meant nothing, not to her, not to him.

Even she was a possession he kept shiny and clean, in preparation for the time he'd take her out of her box and display her for his pleasure.

She was only an extension of his collection.

She wasn't part of the elite. This wasn't her home, and what she'd agreed to wasn't a marriage.

Not the marriage *she* needed anyway.

Not anymore.

She opened the drawers and withdrew every velvet box and bag, lined them up on the bed in an array of colours and sizes. Over two dozen gifts he'd presented her with every time he returned to her, right before he'd seduced her. Bedded her. And then left. Over and over again.

She gazed at her left hand, at her engagement ring, the blue stone in its centre. Her birthstone. Then her gaze moved to the plain gold band. Her wedding ring.

They meant nothing. More meaningless gifts.

But the urge was to keep them. To leave them there, to remind herself what happened when you let yourself *feel*.

No.

She slipped the rings off and placed them in the middle of the pile of gifts.

Would he even recognise the symbolic importance of her rings there with all the other jewels?

She pulled out a single piece of paper and an envelope from her side drawer.

What to write?

She was angry at him, but at herself most of all. Angry for wanting things she'd decided long ago that she couldn't have if she was to keep her heart safe.

How did she explain this wasn't about love, that it wasn't him that had broken his promise? It was *her*.

She picked up the fancy ink pen and wrote three words he'd understand. Three words that would have given him the permission to end their marriage.

She collected her rings, and dropped them inside the envelope, with her note, and sealed it.

She placed it on her pillow.

When he returned, *this* would be the first place he'd come. To find her willing and waiting. As she always had been.

Except this time she wouldn't be here.

Emma turned and made her way out of the room and down the stairs. She slipped her heels back on, walked to the front door and opened it. She stepped outside and gripped the handle to the door. She held on tight, looking back at the lie of the life she thought she could have had.

'Goodbye,' she said to the house, to the *things* and to him.

Emma pulled the door closed and let go of the handle. She let go of all the lies she'd told herself for the last year, and readied herself to face the bold truth of what came next.

Divorce.

Two days later...

Dante Cappetta signed his name with elegant flicks.

It was a simple document. It outlined as much as the first contract he'd presented to her. The only difference was the time they'd remain married.

Dante stared at the empty signature box. He didn't imagine it would be empty for long. Soon, so very soon, his wife would sign her name without hesitation and bind herself to him for an additional three years of marital bliss.

Four weeks remained on their original marriage contract, but there was no need to wait until then to present her with a new agreement.

He was...*satisfied*. And he wanted her to have this gift. An early present for being...*perfect*.

He closed the contract.

But he felt it. An easiness. Something close, he supposed, to contentedness, because the urge was not for *more* as it always was with the Cappetta men to climb higher peaks, or to parachute over more perilous terrains.

The urge was simply to keep things with Emma the same. To keep her.

He settled into the leather recliner and watched the lights twinkle over the dark city of London.

The Cappetta Travel Empire had its fingers in every pie: airlines, boats, hotels. They had headquarters in every important travel capital, with offices everywhere else they were required, but never had one city taken precedence over another.

Dante simply went where he was most in demand, and before Emma, women chased *him*. Followed him to any God-given destination, and did all they could to attract his attention.

He'd eventually made a game of which socialite it would be *this* week. Sometimes they'd tried to seduce him in duos.

But never had he travelled for a woman. Never had he returned to any specific destination because his skin ached to feel a woman's touch. Never had he tried to beat the sun to make sure he was in a woman's bed before she woke to wake her with *his* kiss.

But he did these things for her.

For his wife.

Their marriage was a contract; it was not about love or friendship. It was a way of controlling the fire that raged between them. A way for him to have the one woman who consumed him, again and again, whenever he wanted.

He had thought one year would be enough. Enough to satisfy the hunger.

In the past, Dante had played by the rules his father

had written. That playbook had suited him just fine. Until Emma… So many rules didn't apply to her because she was different from any other woman he'd ever taken to bed.

And that's why he was proposing they extend their contract by an additional three. Because the heat between them was too hot to ignore. But most of all, because Emma understood the rules of their marriage and she played by them so beautifully. They wanted the same things.

The plane landed without ceremony.

Dante collected the contract, slipped it inside his briefcase and closed the golden clasps.

He descended the stairs and got into the waiting car.

Ten minutes and he'd be back at the house they shared.

He wasn't so naive. This obsession with her, his little crush, would end. *Eventually*. Then and only then would he end it.

But not yet.

Three more years should suffice. He was sure. And then he and she would part ways amicably.

He hadn't spoken to Emma for two weeks. But his people had informed him his wife had returned safely to their Mayfair residence two days ago.

Funerals, they were horrid things. When his father died, Dante had jumped out of a plane rather than attend. And what would have been the point anyway? Burying an empty casket seemed pointless. When people went missing at sea, there were no bodies.

Besides, funerals were for the living to mourn and weep, and to claim closure. None of which Dante required. He'd never loved his father. Never had a relationship with him that required closure. The only thing his father had left him was his playbook, the only inheritance Dante had ever required.

And Dante knew by heart the script his father had written: *never give away your power. Always be in control. Let no one get too close. Never let them leave first. Never give them the opportunity to hurt you.*

The only woman who had ever done that was his mother.

Technically, she'd left them both. Her husband and her son. But it mattered little. He'd couldn't remember her. He certainly didn't need her.

But Emma wasn't like him. And she had done all the dutiful things she thought a daughter should do for her mother's funeral. She had wanted closure. She hadn't felt the need to run from her past by whatever means necessary.

It was why he had never taken her with him when he was away on business. His work took him deep into dangerous territory, exploring unmapped lands and canyons. Emma didn't want to explore the unknown. She liked the status quo. *Normality.* And that's what he gave her.

That's why they worked so well.

He lived his life, and she lived hers, and then they both came back to each other. No mind games.

If she had a need, he met it. As he had for the entirety of their marriage—as he would continue to do until their marriage ended.

Their arrangement suited them both. And she was content. He knew, because why wouldn't she be happy? His billions give her access to everything she could ever want, including him.

The car travelled through London's sleeping streets until it reached the house he and Emma shared. Swiftly, he made his way inside, depositing his briefcase at the foot of the staircase.

Anticipation shot through him.

For twenty-one days he hadn't touched his wife, hadn't felt the warmth of her skin.

He'd flown through the night to reach her before the sun rose. Before the staff woke. Before *she* woke.

He eyed the curling stairs, with intricate carved patterns adorning the white banister. He knew which step creaked and which whined, which could alert her to his presence. They were the final part of his journey back to her.

His body pulsed.

The slow ascent was agonising. But finding his wife soft and pliant would be worth it.

Bed soft, he liked to call it, when the body was torn between waking and dreams. Everything, every muscle, oversensitised. And she'd come awake, alive with him beside her. Touching her.

He toed off his shoes, shrugged off his suit jacket and let it fall to the floor. He removed his tie. Attacked the buttons of his crisp, white shirt with silent precision, letting it float the way of his suit jacket.

The thrill remained the same as ever. The excitement of making love to her ever present.

It moved inside him now, as strong as the night they'd met.

Need.

He unbuckled his belt and guided his trousers and boxers down his firm thighs.

Oh, God, he was hard. *So hard.*

Naked now, he ascended the stairs with stealthy speed.

Adrenaline pumped through him. He almost growled at the ferocity of the anticipation of surprising her with his unexpected homecoming. But he remained silent.

He wanted to wake her with a kiss. A kiss she'd reciprocate with a speed that always floored him. Excited him beyond measure. Her effortless enthusiasm. Her absolute adoration of him.

Slowly, oh, so slowly, he opened the bedroom door.

Darkness.

He moved towards the bed on silent feet. He couldn't see a thing, but he knew this bedroom. This bed. His wife. Waiting for him. Curled into herself. Her blond hair would be strewn across the pillow, waiting for his fingers to grip it. He would draw her mouth to his.

He slipped between the sheets, reached for her. 'Emma?' he said, calling to her in the darkness. And he could taste it. The longing in every syllable of her name. The yearning to be in her arms and accept her welcome.

Her side of the bed was…*cold.*

It was a large bed. He moved closer. Stretched out his arms, his long legs, his feet—searching for her. The warmth of her tiny toes to stroke against his. Her soft body to pull into his.

Something on the bed—on her side—clattered to the floor.

He slammed on the lights.

Jewellery boxes. A dozen had toppled onto the floor. He picked up the only black velvet bag to remain on the bed, opened it and withdrew a necklace from within. It dangled between his fingers. A white gold chain tipped with the clearest diamond…

Where was she? It was barely four in the morning.

He dropped the necklace and bag onto the bed.

He pulled back the sheets and stepped out of the bed. His toes sunk into the carpet with every footfall as he opened her walk-in wardrobe. Nothing was out of place. Had she laid out all her jewellery to decide what to wear and forgotten to put them away? Had she gone out last night and had yet to return?

He frowned. Irritation crawled over his skin. Where would she have gone? With whom?

He didn't keep tabs on his wife, and he didn't give her a timetable of his whereabouts either. He didn't tell her if *this* work trip was any more dangerous than the last. His clients' needs differed.

He froze.

A white paper edge stuck up at a sharp triangular angle between the headboard and the pillow.

He freed it.

It was an envelope with his name on it.

Dante tore it open.

The contents fell onto the bed.

Her engagement ring.

Her wedding ring.

He stared at them.

She'd taken them off.

She'd never taken off her rings before. Not even in the shower. Neither had he. Not since she'd slipped it onto his finger in the courthouse.

And yet, here they were.

Her rings.

He turned the envelope upside down and shook it. A little rectangular slip of paper slipped free.

Her elegant handwriting swirled before his eyes: "I want out."

His body tightened with a pulse of emotion he didn't recognise. *Didn't like.*

But he felt stripped down. Exposed beyond his nakedness.

She'd left him?

No, she wouldn't leave him. Didn't have any reason to leave—

Realisation dawned.

He'd made a mistake. Miscalculated. By letting his wife know how much he wanted her, he'd given her everything she needed to play him like a fiddle.

She's never played games before.

No, she hadn't. But that didn't mean she wasn't playing games now. So, what did she want? More money? A larger settlement if she remained married to him?

His temples throbbed. It made no sense. It was completely out of character. And yet, she was gone. But that was what women did, wasn't it? They left when it suited them.

Dante picked up the simple gold band and slipped it onto his little finger. And there it sat beside his own.

He let out a deep, calming breath.

Emma would come back.

And when she did, he'd close the door in her face.

CHAPTER TWO

Three months later...

DANTE LOOKED DOWN at the rings on his fingers. He'd kept hers on, not for sentimental reasons, but as a reminder of how close he'd come to losing control. Letting his hunger for his wife become an obsession.

Determination straightened his spine.

He was indifferent to her now. But it was maddening how much of an effect her departure had had. How much he had allowed her to influence his life to begin with.

For three months, he hadn't accepted any jobs that would take him away from English waters. He hadn't been back to London either, but he'd remained close. Japan wasn't happy. Some of their most exclusive clients were demanding they have access to his personal expertise, wouldn't take no for an answer. People came to him, to his company, to provide them with the type of experiences they couldn't get anywhere else.

The Cappetta Travel Empire was built on his father's thrill-seeking adventures. His father had revolutionised a small airline company into a recognisable brand. And Dante had inherited it all.

Being stuck on British soil was unwelcome. But he

couldn't leave, especially not now as he recalled the doctor's words over the phone.

Mr Cappetta, your wife has fallen. Bumped her head. She's confused. She doesn't remember a lot of things.

His mother had claimed she'd fallen too. That was how she'd found out she was pregnant. *A lie.* She'd known all along, but the lie allowed her to manipulate his father. Manipulate his desire for an heir, an heir he wanted little to do with raising but wanted nonetheless. And his mother had got what she wanted too: the means to live her life as she pleased, with the money she got in exchange for her son.

Emma couldn't barter his flesh and blood. Dante had made sure there would never be children in his future.

You never thought you'd have a wife either.

After tonight, he wouldn't.

But the depth of Emma's deception was unexpected. And he hated he hadn't seen it coming. Over the last three months, he'd talked himself in circles. Doubt had riddled him.

She'd left everything behind, including a small fortune in jewels. On the surface, it looked as though she no longer wanted her things. No longer wanted...*him.*

But he understood the truth.

His wife wanted something, because there was no fathomable reason for her to leave, unless this was a play for power. *For more.*

And it was. He was sure of that.

Anyone's palms could be greased with the right lubrication.

'Sir,' the driver said. 'We're here.'

So they were. The drab inner-city hospital in Birmingham was so far away from the life he'd gifted to her. And the knowledge that she'd chosen to come back here speared him in the gut.

Emma's accent was rich. There had been no doubt of her origin when they'd met. But this city was nothing like the capital they'd lived in together. It was closer. The atmosphere was too intimate. The people were too much. Their melodic and soft accents somehow penetrated deeper.

Just like her? Is that why you haven't filed for divorce?

No, that was because Emma had plunged a knife into his solar plexus, and he knew the only way to drive out the blade was to see her again. To confirm that his sweet little wife was just like his mother, who had traded her unborn child for a fat cheque and a private island. Seeing Emma would confirm that she had been manipulating him all along.

He stepped out of the car, and night lights burned in a shimmering rainbow all around him. He looked over the nondescript concrete building with red letters lit up by a white background.

Accident and Emergency.

He moved towards it.

The electronic door slid open.

He eyed the A&E department. Stale and metallic, the air reeked. And it was...*cloying*. The reality of it. Humans littered the chairs and the floors. Zombified, they stared at a string of red letters floating across a screen, announcing an estimated wait time of six hours.

This would not have been the venue he would have expected for an attempt to woo him.

He felt a sense of powerlessness here. Hopelessness. That whatever happened in these walls was out of his control.

Did Emma understand that? Was that why she'd chosen this scenario? To toy with him? To make him feel powerless?

The two double doors to Dante's left opened, and two paramedics exited.

He moved through them, confident he'd find Emma somewhere in this rabbit warren.

The doctor who'd called had said an ambulance had brought Emma in and she was now waiting for the doctor to examine her, but A&E was busy. As her next of kin, he needed to arrive promptly as she was showing signs of distress. *Confusion.* She needed support.

He was sure the doctor's words had been calculated to trigger certain emotions in him. And delivered by a professional, they were all the more believable. Made it easier to alarm him, imagine how vulnerable she was. *Alone.*

He wasn't alarmed, but here he was.

The doors closed behind him.

Drawn curtains equalled full beds, didn't they? He'd never been in a hospital like this, but Dante understood. He'd read the papers. It was easy to see why Emma's doctor had been so easily persuaded to take part in her little ruse.

What if she isn't lying? She's never lied to you before. Never gone to these kinds of lengths to get your attention.

She *had* to be lying. He couldn't allow for any other scenario. He would call her out on her lies, she would sign the divorce papers and they'd be done once and for all.

His ears pricked as the low hum of conversations behind each makeshift cubicle peaked.

He moved. *Listening.*

'Thank you, Doctor.'

His neck snapped to the left as a white, cheap curtain was dragged back on a metal rail. A harried man with a tight smile nodded and withdrew from the cubicle.

And there she was.

Her blond fringe had grown and fell over her eyebrows. Thick silky strands framed her face, teasing at her high cheekbones before falling in a wave over her shoulders.

Oh, how he'd liked to play with her hair. Wrap it around his fist and draw her into his chest as her back pressed into him.

No, he wouldn't go there. He would not indulge in what had always been between them.

He focused himself and let his gaze travel down. Her legs lay flat on top of sterile white starched sheets as she sat up against an almost nonexistent pillow. A white blouse covered her pert breasts and a black pencil skirt hugged her hips and thighs.

The same little outfit she'd worn the night they'd met.

As he brought his gaze back up her body to her face, their gazes caught.

Wide, bright blue eyes met his. And he noted the widening of her pupils.

'Doctor,' she acknowledged.

Was this her attempt at strengthening the ruse?

Slowly, he pulled the curtain back into place. 'No,' he said, dismissing the idea of playing *that* game. 'I'm no doctor.'

'Then who are you?' Her pink lips parted, and his

mouth slickened. Unbidden. 'A nurse?' she pressed. 'A porter?'

'You really don't know who I am, Emma?' he asked, and ignored the pressure building in his sternum. He knew she was faking, and yet... The conviction in her voice was impressive.

'Should I?' She shrugged. 'The doctor said lots of things were going to happen. Someone would be with me shortly to take me to a ward. And then something about a psychiatrist and an MRI. Or some abbreviation of letters. But honestly, I feel fine.'

He moved closer and stood at the end of the bed. 'Of course you do.'

'I do,' she confirmed. 'I've already wasted so many resources. I don't need to be in this bed taking it from someone who needs it.'

'You don't need it, Emma?' he asked, moving around the bed in purposeful strides. 'The bed? You don't require *my* assistance?' he baited. *Watched*. But she didn't flinch. Not a flicker of anything.

'I'm clumsy,' she said. 'It's untreatable, I'm afraid.'

'If you are untreatable,' he said, catching the lie as it was spoken, 'why come to a hospital for treatment?'

'The paramedic insisted.'

'Or *you* insisted?' he countered.

'*He* said he was following protocol.'

'And as the protocol would bring you here,' he said, watching her reaction, waiting for the penny to drop that he understood what she was doing, 'you thought you'd use it to your advantage?'

'My advantage?' she laughed. 'No one wants to be in a hospital on purpose.'

'Not even if it would bring me to you?' he asked.

'What kind of question is that?' she asked. 'I don't know who you are.'

'I don't want to play games, Emma.'

'*Games?*' she repeated.

'Yes. And this is not one you will win.'

'Everyone likes to win, don't they?'

'Some more than most,' he agreed. 'Some stack the deck in their favour. Hide an ace up their sleeve. They underestimate their opponent, and ultimately lose.'

'What are you talking about?' She blew out an exasperated breath and swept the hair out of her face.

He felt the pressure build in his chest until he was vibrating with it. Something feral. *Primal.*

She blinked up at him. 'Did you just growl at me?'

He moved closer to her, raised his fingers to her forehead.

'May I?'

'What are you doing?'

He stalled. 'I need to see.'

Eyes wide, she asked, 'See what?'

His fingers, feather-light, lifted her fringe.

'Emmy...' he exhaled and dropped his hands to his side.

'*Emmy?*' Her fringe fell, once again hiding the long graze on her left cheek and the ugly bruise on her forehead. 'Why would you call me that?'

'You *are* hurt.'

'I'm in a hospital—of course I am,' she snipped. 'But I'll heal. In time. Without medical intervention.'

'You said you fell?' He had to discern the lies from the truth.

'Yes. *I fell.* How many times do I need to repeat myself?'

'This will be the last time,' he promised. 'Tell me. What happened?' he asked, because he wanted to hear it. The detail. The rehearsed script written just for him.

Because there it was again, the doubt that coursed through his veins in sluggish waves.

Yes, she was hurt, he conceded. But she was using it to get to him, taking advantage of the situation she had found herself in, he rationalised to soothe himself. But it did not soothe him. He was conflicted. And that was surely the point, exactly her intention: to confuse him enough that she could influence the outcome of their reunion.

'I've already explained what happened to the triage nurse, the doctor, the registrar…' She scowled. 'I suppose one more time can't hurt,' she said, and raised her knees.

His eyes followed the movement. And this time he really looked at the state his wife was in. Her tights were ripped, split like ladders on her knees. The rungs spread wider as her legs rose to her chest. And there was blood.

His heart thumped harder in his chest. He'd never seen her injured. Not even as much as a paper cut. And yet her knees were scraped raw. Her face… Her head…

'*I* was carrying too much.' She looked at the phone in her hand. 'I went to try and check the time on this.' She threw it on the bed. 'I lost my footing and went down with potatoes.'

'You went down *like* a sack of potatoes,' he corrected.

'No.' She shook her head. '*With* them. The taxi driver

wouldn't help me carry the shopping up the stairs. I didn't want to leave the bags for an opportunist thief. I'm on the second floor of a maisonette so it takes time to get up the stairs. And now that's a week's worth of shopping ruined.' She grimaced. 'Such a waste. And it's horrible waking up to an empty fridge, which I shall be now.' She picked up the phone from her side and held it out to him. 'In fact, maybe you would be able to call my mum?'

'Your *mum*?' Shock pumped through him.

She looked at him quizzically. 'She doesn't work far from here. Just outside the city centre. She cleans for an agency.'

He hadn't known that. Emma had never told him anything about her life before they met. No details at least.

'She did?' he asked.

'Does.' Her frown deepened. 'Tonight's the library. After she's finished cleaning, she reads. Romance. She has the entire library to herself. She forgets herself. Loses herself in the stories, loses hours. But…'

Emma inhaled deeply, and he watched her chest rise in amazement. He'd truly believed that she'd planned this all out to convince him she was helpless, that she needed him because there was no one else.

But would she really use her mother's death?

What if she is helpless?

The doubts were more insistent now.

'But what?' he pushed.

'The nurse said she couldn't reach her…she'd call my next of kin on the list. But there is no one else. Just me and Mum.' She looked up at the ceiling. Squinting. She returned her gaze to his. 'If you could *try* to call her…' She swallowed, and he watched her throat tighten as if invisible fingers had applied pressure to the delicate tendons and were squeezing. *'Please.'*

And he felt it. The crack in his chest.

She really didn't remember her mum's death.

She was telling the truth.

He couldn't let himself consider exactly what that meant right now or why the pressure in his chest kept building.

And so he would tell the truth too.

'I can't call her.'

'Why not?'

'She's gone, Emma.'

'Gone where?'

'To…' Dante struggled for a word that was not too direct, but not too soft. 'Heaven,' he said, although he believed in no such thing. There was one life. One chance to live it. The end was the end.

Emma's mother was dead. Emma *was* all alone.

'What do you mean?' Her face contorted.

'She died over three months ago,' he told her, stating the facts as they were. 'A heart attack.'

'That is a cruel lie,' she choked out. 'I saw her this morning.' Her face twisted in confusion. 'Why would you say that? Lie like that?'

'It is the truth.'

'It is a lie,' she accused.

'It is not.'

'It has to be…' Her face blanched. 'Who the hell are you?'

'My name,' he announced, 'is Dante Cappetta.'

Frowning, she asked, 'Is that supposed to mean something?'

'It should,' he said, and watched.

'Why?' Confusion spread across her tightly drawn cheeks. 'Who are you to me?'

'I'm your next of kin.'

Her blue eyes narrowed. *'What?'*

'Your husband,' he clarified. And he loathed the raw edge to each word.

'My what?'

She stared at him open-mouthed, and he stared right back. Waited for the magic man behind the curtain to appear. But no one was there. She needed him, didn't she? No lies. No pretence...

'I'm your husband, Emma.'

'What kind of prank is this?' Anger churned in Emma's gut. 'You walk in here, tell me my mother is gone and proclaim yourself as—'

'Your husband,' he interjected smoothly.

'Is this how you get your kicks?' she spat. 'Do you roam around hospitals looking for vulnerable women? Do you convince them their only family is dead and prey on their tears?'

'You are not crying.'

Adrenaline burst inside her.

'And you're *not* my husband,' she continued, and choked on the absurdity of each syllable. 'You are nothing to me,' she finished, because it was the truth, the only truth she'd accept.

'I am your husband,' he said again.

She froze, not breathing, not moving. But her skin prickled. Her mind buzzed.

Her eyes travelled over the crisp, dark suit moulded to

his body. A very *defined* body. The open-collared shirt beneath his jacket hugged his chest and revealed a thick, muscular throat.

She moved her gaze back to his face. Perfectly symmetrical, with high cheekbones, a powerful jaw and a noble nose. And his eyes were so dark, so deep, she could fall into them.

'It's impossible,' she breathed. Because it was. She didn't recognise a single inch of him. She didn't know this man. 'I don't have a husband,' she declared. 'I have never been, and never will be, married.'

'And yet you are married,' he contradicted smoothly. *Too smoothly.* 'To me.'

'Ridiculous!' she said, because it was.

Emma knew the truth.

She knew that love was not the fairy tale everyone said it was. She'd seen that first-hand, watched her mother wither under her father's supposed love.

Her mother and father had never married, but he'd used her like a wife when it suited him and mistress when he didn't.

She'd vowed long ago that she wouldn't give a man— *any man*—a legal right to any of her.

'Ridiculous?' he repeated. 'What is?'

'You.' She waved at…him. The entirety of him. And there was so much of him. He'd walked into her cubicle as if he had every right to be there. And when he'd demanded answers to questions she'd already answered, she'd thought nothing of it. He'd exuded the kind of confidence that you didn't think to question. She could see her mistake now.

Emma sucked in a fortifying breath.

'This very conversation,' she said. 'It has no basis in reality.'

'Why would *I* lie?'

'Are you insinuating *I'm* being dishonest?'

His eyes penetrated hers intensely. 'No,' he said roughly, and it crawled across her skin like a command for her body to react, to tighten. She dismissed it as an involuntary reaction because...he was consuming. His presence was stifling. And yet it soothed her too, in a way she couldn't understand.

'I'm not insinuating anything,' he said. 'Because you *have* forgotten who *you* are.'

'I know exactly who *I* am,' she snapped. 'My name is Emma Powell.'

His jaw hardened. 'No, you are Emma Cappetta.'

'Emma Cappetta?' she echoed, because she couldn't help it. And the name felt at home in her mouth. It shouldn't, she knew that. And yet, it did.

'Yes,' he confirmed. And she saw the flare to his nostrils, the swell of his chest. '*My* wife.'

Wife. He said it with such conviction. Such possession.

'I am nobody's wife.'

She would be no one's fool.

His fingers edged towards her, and she couldn't tell him to stop. Her vocal cords refused to cooperate because her body was so warm.

She found herself eager for his touch on her skin.

She must have bumped her head harder than she thought.

He claimed her left hand. 'Look,' he demanded, and dipped his head to where his thumb stroked her ring finger.

And she begged her body not to betray her, not to allow him the satisfaction of her obeying his whim.

'What am I meant to see?' she asked and met his gaze defiantly. 'Because all I see is a man touching a woman he doesn't know.' She snatched her hand away because it...*tingled*. 'Making absurd declarations!'

'You can feel it, can't you?'

'Feel what?'

She swallowed hard. A smile played on his lips, and there was an arrogance in his gaze. He knew that his ministrations had elicited a reaction quite unlike anything she'd ever felt before. And yet, it felt familiar too.

'The chemistry between us,' he answered, and the most frightening thing of all was the intensity of her body's response to the idea of him touching her again.

Maybe she'd knocked herself out completely and was still out cold. Maybe this was all a dream.

'The only fool in this room is you, thinking I'd believe we're *married*.'

His hand fell to his side. 'You may not be wearing your ring,' he said. 'But the evidence is there, if only you'd look.'

She closed her eyes. Counted to ten. *Slowly.* Surely she was going to wake up any minute now.

Any. Minute.

'What are you doing?' His question was spoken as softly as velvet brushed against her skin. His was a deep, sensual voice her ears liked, because they perked up, as did the speed of her heart, to a painful staccato rhythm.

And it was...*uncomfortable.*

Her mind didn't know him, but her body—

She opened her eyes. 'What am *I* doing?'

'Yes,' he replied.

'What are *you* doing?' she asked, hoping to challenge his deplorable confidence he belonged here, had the absolute right to touch her and call himself husband. When—

'Watching you.'

'Then stop it,' she spat, because his eyes on her felt… hot.

Her temples pounded. *Hard.* A bass drum between her ears.

She placed her fingertips to her temples and rubbed, but the pressure behind her eyes only increased. Her brain throbbed mercilessly, as if her mind was searching for something but an error code kept appearing.

'This isn't a movie,' she forced out. 'I didn't fall over and forget my life.'

'You have forgotten it,' he corrected. 'You have forgotten…*me*.'

'Who could forget *you*?'

'My wife, obviously.'

And she couldn't help herself any longer. She looked down at her ring finger. And that was when she saw it.

'Oh, my God.'

She brought her hand closer to her face. And sure enough, there on her finger was a tan line, a white circular band.

Just as he'd promised there would be.

Something had sat on her finger long enough for the sun to kiss the rest of her hand and leave this piece of her flesh untouched.

A ring.

'It can't be true,' she whispered.

'If you require it,' he said, 'I'll produce our marriage certificate.'

'Marriage certificate?' She flexed her fingers out in front of her again. 'Do you carry it around in your pocket for occasions such as this?'

Her laugh was a heavy cackle of self-mockery. Because what was a marriage certificate? Just a piece of paper. Her mother was, for all the intents and purposes, *married*. She'd had a child with a man she loved. She was devoted to him. Committed. But—

'I do not have the certificate here,' he said. 'But I do have this.'

His left hand appeared next to hers. On his ring finger was a plain, simple gold wedding band. And on the finger next to it, on his little finger, was another ring. It was an exact match to the first one, only smaller, more feminine.

He removed it and slipped the ring onto her finger.

She'd never thought of herself as a Cinderella wannabe. Never longed for that life. But this was her glass slipper, wasn't it? It was the perfect fit. A match. The white of her skin was hidden by the perfect circular thickness of gold on her finger.

It didn't feel…*wrong*. It felt as if it had always been there.

Her thoughts spiralled. Why would the doctor call for a psychiatrist when her wounds were physical? Why wouldn't they call her mum? Why did the nurse, the doctor, the registrar all look at her with pity when she'd explained she was twenty-two and living at home with her mum?

Because she didn't live with her mum anymore? Her mum was gone, and…she lived with him?

Who was the prime minister? What day was it? Was it Thursday as she thought it was? Was her mum reading in the library? Was she Emma Powell? Or was she someone else? Someone's wife? *His* wife?

Vulnerability threatened to close her windpipe.

But before it did, a warmth spread up her cheeks. This man, Dante Cappetta, was cradling her face. His hands were strong, and it made her feel...safe.

She couldn't explain it. The touch was so intimate. They were strangers in every sense in her mind. But her face felt *right* cradled in his palms, like it belonged there. And she didn't want him to let go, despite her logical mind knowing he shouldn't be touching her this way.

'You will come with me,' he said, his eyes shimmering with confidence that she'd go with him and let him take charge. 'You will see a doctor,' he continued, 'and be diagnosed with a plan of treatment within the next few hours.'

'I'm already in a hospital,' she reminded him.

His hands moved, releasing her face. His fingertips slid down her cheeks so softly, so *gently*.

Dante claimed her chin firmly between his thumb and forefinger. His eyes dark with determined decision, he proclaimed, 'We are leaving. Together. *Now*. This is the only choice. I will help you remember, Emma,' he promised.

'What if I don't *want* to remember you?' she asked, because someone—*something*—was lying to her, and if it wasn't him, if it wasn't her body, it was her mind, wasn't it? And the mind did things to protect the body. The soul. The...*heart*.

'What if my mind has blanked you out on purpose?' she asked. 'To protect me from *you*?'

'I am no threat to you, Emma,' he said roughly. 'We are married. I am your husband. Your protector. Trust me to protect you now.'

Marriage. Husband. Protector.

Those words did something inside her. Something she didn't want to recognise.

Physically, she was safe. He was no physical threat. She just knew.

He'd walked in here with no overt displays of emotion. He'd found out the facts and taken charge. Her mind didn't understand it. But her body…it *liked* it.

Everything felt uncertain. But his hands hadn't. They were steady. In control.

Realisation settled on her shoulders, in her chest. She would go with him.

'Okay,' she said, because right now he was her anchor to the truth.

In his world, she was his wife. And a part of her wanted to know what *that* life looked like.

'I'll come with you.'

CHAPTER THREE

IT WAS ALL TRUE.

Her mother was dead.

The grief was beginning to hit her.

She understood she'd lived through it already, even though she couldn't remember it, but it washed over her in waves.

It was a pain, an ache, an unfulfilled need all tied together in loops of barbed wire. And they sat in her ribcage now, all three side by side.

Her mother had been so young, with so much life left to live, and Emma didn't understand how a woman who had survived everything life could throw at her was gone.

Something tore inside her.

She looked down at the plain gold band on her finger. It was nothing ostentatious. It didn't scream wealth. Because it didn't need to scream anything, did it?

It was a symbol. The oxblood-red leather sofa seat groaned beside her as Dante sat. And the foot of distance between them evaporated in a millisecond when his hand reached for hers. His fingers slid between her own, entwining them together.

'Emma…' His thumb stroked the soft flesh between her thumb and forefinger. 'Are you okay?'

She pushed her bare toes into the thick carpet, halting the ridiculous urge to push her thighs together. He was touching her hand, for God's sake. Not anywhere intimate.

But it *was* intimate, wasn't it? His fingers entwined in hers meant she was allowing him to get close. *Too close*. And she wasn't sure she was ready for that.

She dragged her gaze up to his face and looked at him looking at her as if it were the most natural thing to do to comfort her. *Was* she comforted?

It didn't feel like reassurance. Her body was awake in parts she hadn't known were sleeping. Heavy and sluggish, but zinging as if she'd had too much coffee, as if she was overstimulated. Too sensitised. *Too awake*.

She tugged her bottom lip between her teeth. Comfort was something she provided for herself with extralong baths, or a trip to a shop to look at the pretty things that gave her pleasure she couldn't afford.

How had he convinced her to enter a relationship where holding hands was meant to provide comfort?

Emma did *not* hold hands.

'No.' Slowly, she withdrew her hand. 'I'm not okay.'

She eased her fingers out of his hold, resisted the pull to return it and stood.

She walked towards the back wall, which was covered from ceiling to floor with shelves of books.

This whole place was like a doll's house. It was the blueprint of every little girl's dream house.

'You *will* be okay, Emma,' he guaranteed too confidently.

She rounded on him. 'You can't know that.'

'But I can,' he contradicted her smoothly, 'because

you are here.' He stood effortlessly. Moved towards her across some priceless rug. His every stride bringing him closer to her. 'With me.'

It took everything she had not to move backward. And what would be the point? There was a wall of books behind her. A dead end. She could move in another direction, but she didn't know this house. Didn't know the layout. All she knew was what was coming towards her.

She wasn't naive to the real reason heat pulsed in her abdomen.

It wasn't fear.

It was *want*.

She'd had encounters with men before. Fleeting and purely physical. She'd always found it easy to form a physical connection. To close her eyes and feel. Demand her body respond. Delight in momentary connections where she could take what she needed and walk away, emotionally untouched.

This time she hadn't demanded anything of this man.

And yet it was there. Stirring inside her. Making itself known. Something frantic. Something *consuming*.

'Do you always take charge so arrogantly?' she said, and she'd wanted it to come across as an insult dripping in sarcasm, but her words were breathless.

'Is it arrogance to give you what you need, Emma?' He looked so at home, he belonged against the backdrop of this house that most people would need to win the lottery to afford.

'Is it wrong to provide for you, my wife?' he continued silkily. 'To keep you safe? To make sure you never fall, that the load you carry is too heavy?'

Her heart snagged. Hadn't her load always been too

heavy? She had been her mother's protector and her emotional support when she was far too young to be either.

That was why Emma had long ago made the safe choice never to become her mother. Never to be alone and waiting for a man, waiting for love. Never to get close enough to care, let alone *need* anyone. So, it was jarring to feel how soothing were his words that she didn't have to worry about those things. She felt a warmth spread through her.

'With me, they'll be no more empty fridges,' he declared, and his promise resonated with the little girl, the teenager, and the young woman who had *never* been promised an endless supply of food.

Her mum had worked endlessly to fill the fridge, but it had never been full for long enough. And when she'd got older, the cycle had repeated itself. Bigger bellies to fill, larger bills to pay, bills that were always overdue even when there were two pay cheques. And here he was, promising these things as if they were nothing.

'Here, with me,' he said, 'you will have time, as the doctor recommended, to heal.' And his words were seductive. *Tempting.* 'Let me be clear—you are not a hostage. I'm not holding you against your will,' he said, his voice deep and warm. 'You can leave whenever you wish. But what better way to reclaim your memory than with me.'

The doctor had said her memory could return, or it might not. All she could do was wait and resume normal life.

Under the doctor's instruction, Dante had summarised her life for her. Five years delivered to her in a heartbeat. Impersonal and without detail. Only simple information. Milestones.

A move to London when she'd been twenty-two. They'd met when she was twenty-six, and their wedding had been the same year. The death of her mother was a little over three months ago, from a heart attack. And then she'd returned to Birmingham to pack up her mother's things, to attend her funeral, and then three months later, she'd fallen and hit her head.

And now she couldn't remember any of that.

She had the facts, sure. But what came between those facts? Why had she taken her wedding ring off when she'd gone back to Birmingham? Why had she stayed there? If her mother was dead, nothing was there for her.

She couldn't connect the dots. She and Dante were married and yet, he was in Mayfair, and she'd been there.

Alone.

She twisted the ring that was back on her finger. 'Why did you have my ring?'

His face remained neutral. 'You left it behind when you returned to Birmingham.'

'Why?'

'Because you didn't want to wear it anymore.'

'What did I want?'

'To leave.'

'London?'

'No.' His jaw hardened. 'You wanted to leave me.'

'I wanted to leave you?' Her eyes grew wide. 'Why?' she asked again, because *why* was the word standing before every thought, and it flashed in neon green in her head.

'I don't know.'

'How can you *not* know?' she asked.

His lips thinned. 'You never told me.'

'I must have said something.'

'*"I want out."* That's all your note said.'

'I left a note?' she repeated.

Dante nodded.

'And you didn't ask for further clarification?'

'No.'

None of this made sense. *They* didn't make any sense. Not their marriage. Not their relationship. 'Your wife leaves her ring behind, tells you she wants out and you never thought to ask the reason *why*?'

'Why would I ask?' He shrugged. A nonchalant dip of his broad shoulder. 'You left. The action required no further explanation.'

Tension threaded throughout her limbs.

Marriage was every commitment she'd never wanted, but she'd done it. For reasons unknown, she'd *married him*. And yet she'd walked away without a backward glance.

Her mother had never had the strength to leave her father. But Emma had left Dante.

Unbidden came the image of him with another woman. Her throat tightened against the wave of threatening nausea. Was that the reason?

Her chest seized.

Her lungs refused to function.

'Did you cheat?' she asked, because if he had cheated like her father had cheated on her mother countless times, she'd rather sleep on the streets than stay anywhere near him.

'Cheat?' he repeated, before closing the last few inches between them.

She prepared herself by pressing her heels firmly into

the carpeted floor to steady herself for the impact of the vitriol that was surely headed her way.

But it didn't come.

'It has only been you,' he murmured as he tucked the loose hair in front of her left cheek behind her ear. His touch was delicate. Soft. And it took everything she had not to lean into it. Lean into *him*. 'Since the night we met, it has been only you.'

Blood flushed through her heart.

Air seeped into her lungs.

Only you.

The possessive sentiment scared her. Excited her.

Her mind wanted to reject his answer. Because how many times had she been told—*seen*—monogamy was a lie? Men always strayed. And yet here was Dante telling her that he hadn't.

'There *must* be a reason I left?'

'A reason you never shared with me.' He dropped his hand to his side. But he didn't remove the distance between them.

'If our marriage was over, why didn't we get divorced?' she asked, her mind still pulsing with the need to know, to understand… She'd dedicated a year of her life to their marriage and then walked away. Without saying goodbye. Without demanding a divorce.

'Does it matter?'

Her breath shuddered up her windpipe and out through her open mouth. 'Of course it does.'

'Why focus on the end of us when there was no end, no divorce?' he said. 'You left. We remained married. And now here we are. Together. *Again*.'

'Because of an accident,' she reminded him.

'Accident, fate, destiny,' he countered. 'Use whatever word you will, but you are here and so am I. So ask the right questions, Emma.'

'The right questions?'

'Questions I can answer without speculation.'

He was right, she realised. She could push and probe him for answers but only she knew, didn't she? Why she'd married him. Why she'd left…they had both been her choices and hers alone, hadn't they?

'How did we meet?' she asked. He may not be able to answer the question of why she left, but there were other questions that he could answer.

'At a black-tie event. A charity auction, here in London. You were a waitress at the event and you collided with me,' he told her. 'Spilt your tray of wine. Wine that the hostess, the Princess of Vreotus, had donated from her very own vineyard.'

Emma expected self-consciousness to buckle her knees, because that meant the night they'd met she had been the help. But it wasn't self-consciousness making her knees wobble. It was desire, blooming inside her and swelling with every flick of his obscenely long eyelashes. Almost as if her body remembered what her mind could not.

'Place your hand on my chest.'

Frowning, she asked, 'Why?'

'I promised I'd help you remember,' he reminded her. 'So let me show you how it began between us,' he explained.

She lifted her hand. Touched him, tentatively.

'Can you feel it?' he asked.

Deep and steady, his heart thrummed beneath her fingers. 'All I can feel is you.'

He covered her hand with his and heat crept into her fingers. Up into her arms. Her chest. Until breathing became difficult. Too tight. Too shallow.

'And now?' he asked. 'What do you feel, Emma?'

Connection pulsed through her. A type of chaotic harmony. An illogical knowing her hand belonged there. Beneath his.

'Heat,' she breathed.

'It is a flame,' he said, and his voice was rough. *Deep.* 'The night we met, when you raised your hand to my wine-drenched chest and touched me, right here, that flame ignited. Until it roared inside me. Unit it roared inside us *both.*'

Want pulsed inside her.

'Did we have a one-night stand?' she asked.

'We did. That night—' he leaned into her until their bodies stood millimetres apart '—and every night after,' he said.

It was difficult to focus her mind and listen to his story—their origin story—and reclaim it as her own lived experience. Especially when the compulsion to press herself against him, to touch him was clamouring for attention.

'Why did we get married?' she asked, her voice not her own. 'Why didn't we just have an affair?' she pushed, because she wanted to understand the choices she'd made. Because here she was, a girl from an industrial city who had moved from estate to estate when the rents were raised and they could no longer afford to stay. They'd had to relinquish their home so newer, younger, more prosperous families could move in with their two-point-four kids and domesticity.

A domesticity her mother had craved and Emma despised.

And yet here she was.

Domesticated.

'We did.' His breath feathered her lips. And she wanted to meet his breath with her own. Surrender her mouth up to his. *Kiss him.* 'Our affair lasted a month.'

Her fingers clenched at his shirt. 'What changed?'

'It wasn't enough.'

'What wasn't?' she husked. One night had always been enough. *For her.* An affair *should* have been enough. She still couldn't understand that.

'The stolen moments between us,' he said. 'I wanted no more borrowed beds,' he continued, 'however soft the sheets or exclusive the hotel. But a bed we could call ours.'

'And what did *I* want?' she asked, because she'd never shared anyone's bed for longer than was necessary. And no one had ever stopped her from leaving. They would feign sleep as she collected her things and disappeared without a backward glance.

But he'd wanted her to stay, to have a place they would meet and touch that was only theirs.

Had she wanted the same?

'You wanted me,' he said, and she heard it. Felt the unsaid part.

You want me.

'I asked you to marry me, and you said yes,' he finished. If she felt back then anything like she felt now, she could understand why she'd so readily agreed. Her body begged to be touched, to give in to the heat between them. To drown out the doubt, the questions.

A part of her still sensed there was more to the story of their marriage. But her mind was begging her in this moment to close the door on whatever that was. Because if everything he was saying was true, everything she believed about marriage—believed about herself—was a lie. It was simpler to believe that this really was about passion, desire and nothing more.

'There are so many unanswered questions,' she said, her fingers clinging to his shirt. 'And not knowing the answers to so many important questions... It feels like such a heavy thing,' she admitted, and her mind whirred with the heaviness. It pressed down on her sternum. On her lungs.

'It's okay to be scared, Emma.'

'I'm not afraid.'

'Liar,' he softly called her out, because he knew her, didn't he? And he was right; she was scared of the instinctive and knowing chemistry between them.

'But allow yourself to feel the anticipation of it,' he coaxed, and his words bloomed inside her ears. 'To be seduced by the unknown, to discover it piece by piece.'

The hand on top of hers moved to the base of her throat. His grip feather-light, his fingers skirted the flesh of her throat until the hilt of his hand met her chin, and lifted it.

'Allow yourself to feel the excitement of knowing the answers are coming.' Steady and intense, his gaze burrowed inside her. 'And embrace the journey of rediscovering yourself and our marriage.'

Dante was her only guide in these unfamiliar times.

But his words, his advice, the connection crackling between their bodies, it was all too much. They made her tremble. They made her want all the things he'd told her she could have: financial security, protection, adventure. All in a home they shared, all because he'd put a ring on her finger and she'd let him do it. *Claim her.*

Emma's eyes travelled downward. Across the noble bridge of his nose to the dip above his top lip. It was the size of her fingertip and her hand itched to touch it. To smooth her finger across it to measure the indent.

Had she done that before? How many times had she tasted his mouth with her tongue, slipped her tongue between the slight opening between his thinner upper lip and fuller counterpart?

It was a mouth made for kissing.

Her insides tightened and squeezed on a breathless exhale.

With effort, she dragged her gaze away from his mouth to her hand which still sat against the hard muscle of his chest. It would be so easy to pull him closer, to surrender to instinct, use the fingertips clinging to his shirt to pull her closer and test how competent his mouth was.

She closed her eyes.

It felt reckless to put herself in his hands. To trust him to deliver his promises, when her logical mind told her his words were nothing but a seduction. *A lie.*

Her father had made countless promises to her mother and delivered on none of them. But still her mother had waited for the day he would keep his promise to protect her. Emma. His family.

And now she was dead.

Emma understood she owed it to herself, and to Dante,

to rediscover their marriage. But marriage felt so final. The end—*death*—to the woman she thought she was.

Emma had had the courage to leave Dante once, for whatever reason, but she hadn't been strong enough to sever the tie between them completely. That intrigued her the most. Had she been waiting for Dante to return to her?

He'd said he wasn't holding her hostage, that she could leave at any time, and that gave her a strange sense of comfort. It softened the hard edges of her fear.

And she felt the sudden need to confirm that his intentions were true.

Emma opened her eyes. 'If I decide *this* isn't what I want anymore…' Her fingers unfurled and splayed on his chest, steadying herself.

But his hand stayed where it was beneath her chin, keeping her head in position. Her eyes found his and she held his gaze.

'At any time,' she continued, her chest tight, her stomach in knots, 'you'll let me go, Dante,' she said. Because she may not remember the version of the Emma who'd married him, or why, and she wasn't in a position to walk away right now, but she knew twenty-two-year-old Emma would want this. However intensely she longed for his kiss, his body, *she* wanted an escape plan. In case she needed it.

'You'll give me a divorce?'

'Divorce?' Dante echoed, a slow, agonising breath flooding through his nostrils.

'Neither of us know the reason I left…*before*. But *I* did leave. And—' she swallowed, and he watched the delicate tendons in her throat constrict '—I want to give this life a chance,' she explained when he didn't speak. '*Us* a chance,' she corrected, 'to rediscover our marriage. I owe that to you, as much as I do to myself. But I need to know if I want to walk away, *again*, that it's really an option. That a divorce…'

'Will finalise the end between us?' he finished for her.

'Yes.'

Did she remember? Perhaps not all of it, but somewhere in that brain of hers she knew *that* was their way. The rules of their marriage, which was designed to have a 'get-out' clause. He could tell her about the rules of their marriage. *His rules.* The contract. But their contract had already expired. By every rule in the playbook, they should already be divorced. But they weren't. They were here. *Still married.*

And how did he explain that? Why he'd waited for the divorce papers to arrive. Why he hadn't initiated the proceedings himself.

He couldn't explain it. Not even to himself.

She was not his mother. She hadn't been looking for a bigger payout. She hadn't been trying to gain the upper hand, wrestle back power.

Emma had left him by choice; he understood that now, but he also understood she'd come back to him because she had *no* choice. And she was right; not knowing the reason she'd left was a heavy thing. He ached with it too.

But did it matter? As he'd said to her, they could speculate, but it would amount to nothing but more speculation.

The truth of it was neither of them had demanded a divorce. They were still married.

But it was all she could see, wasn't it?

Marriage.

Everything she'd never wanted.

Until *him*.

He could tell her the truth of them, that they didn't do emotions, it was a marriage purely for passion, but why would he tell her? Ultimately those things hadn't made her stay before...

'If a divorce is what you require,' he conceded roughly, 'a divorce is what you shall have, Emma.'

'Thank you.'

'Of course.' He stroked the pad of his thumb along her jawline. 'Why would we remain married if we no longer wanted one another?'

'Exactly,' she husked, and he heard the unspoken realisation between them that divorce hadn't really been an option before because their marriage hadn't been over.

It still wasn't.

'I think I want to go to bed.' Her eyes glazed over, a mix of exhaustion and desire. His body reacted instinctively. His groin tightened. 'To sleep,' she clarified quickly. 'Alone.'

He didn't want to sleep.

He didn't want to spend a night in this house without her beside him. In his bed. In his arms. It was the reason he hadn't been back here since the day he'd found her gone.

His mind flashed with every moment he'd told her about. The beginning of them. The confident Emma who had touched him and met his mouth with the same ardent fever within moments of their first touch. The woman who'd embraced their physical connection as readily as he had. As if it gave them air. The woman who'd become his wife.

Every moment of their relationship had been borne
from their physical connection. They never spoke about
the past, what had made them the people who had met
at that charity event. They'd only gone forwards, dived
head-first into each other's body and stayed there.

Curiosity bloomed where it shouldn't. What made
this Emma hesitate where she'd never hesitated before
to welcome his kiss? His touch? Invite him into her bed?
Any bed? What had happened to her between the ages
of twenty-two to twenty-six to turn her into the woman
he'd married?

He knew his wife. Every imperfection. Every sensitive spot. The spot behind her ear he let his breath heat
and she would melt for him as he moved his breath, his
lips, his mouth down and over her throat to her breasts.

But not…*her*.

In her mind they'd never kissed, never had sex.

It was all backwards. Upside down.

The urge to make her remember it all, to remember the
feel of his mouth on hers, was overwhelming.

He knew she needed words. Needed reassurance before any of that. And he'd give it to her.

'Emma,' he breathed. 'Understand this. You're my
wife. I'm your husband. This doesn't give me any rights
to you. I won't take anything from you that you don't want
to give. Everything I said stands whether you invite me
into your bed tonight, tomorrow or never,' he said, because he knew that she needed to know in this upside-
down world of theirs, she was safe. She had choices.

He dropped his hand and stepped away from her when
his every muscle screamed for him to pull her to him,
but he resisted.

Her head cocked to the side. She studied him silently.

'Do you understand?' he asked.

Jaw tight, she nodded.

'Use your words, Emma,' he said, because he needed confirmation that she understood she was safe with him. *Secure.*

'I understand,' she stated, but it wasn't enough.

'Tell me, what exactly it is you understand?' he pushed.

'That you'll look after me whether I return to being your *actual* wife, or not.' She exhaled heavily, and he heard the tremble she was badly trying to conceal. 'I understand that whatever sexual relationship we had before it isn't expected from me now. That just because we're married, it doesn't affect anything. Because being married to you doesn't mean anything to me. *Yet.* It's nothing but a ring that fits. And if that never changes, you'll give me a divorce.'

He nodded, a tilt of his too-stiff neck. 'And for now, is that enough for you?' he asked, because he couldn't help it. He needed to know if the temptation of security would seduce her more than his lips.

'Yes.' She clasped her hands together at her midriff. 'It is.'

He stepped aside. 'Top door to the left,' he instructed. 'You will find our bedroom. *Yours*,' he corrected. 'Until you invite me to share it with you.'

And there it was. The dance between excitement and fear. The shimmer in her blue eyes. The pull tightening the skin on her cheeks. The tension in her shoulders threading into her muscles and lifting them.

'Good night,' she husked, and moved. She took a step forward, and another past him and ran.

He fisted his hands. The urge was so dominant to reach out to catch her.

He closed his eyes, denying the urge to follow his wife to bed.

He knew now what he hadn't allowed himself to acknowledge for the last three months.

He wanted her back. In his life.

He wanted Emma back, in his bed.

CHAPTER FOUR

ALL HER LIFE she'd refused to wait for anyone. But now she was waiting for him.

Emma's stomach whined. The pressure was too much. She felt too full, too empty at the same time. It was a void she knew no food could fill.

For two days, Dante had starved her of his presence. He'd disappeared.

Gone.

Left her alone in their house.

Emma dragged her bottom lip between her teeth and bit down. Was this how her mother had felt like every time her father had promised her the world, every time he'd walked away and promised to return?

No, Dante was not her father. Dante hadn't promised her anything. He'd made everything a choice. It was her choice to stay or leave.

His words flooded through her now. The warmth of them seeped into her bones. The promise to take care of her. To wait until she was ready to explore *him*.

He had an effect on her without even touching her. Without being *here*.

She stared, unseeing, out of the port window onto the small airstrip below.

This was the reason she'd never wanted to be in a relationship. To be a woman who believed one day her prince would come.

Life wasn't one of her mother's romance books.

Emma could take care of herself.

Was she making the right choice to trust her gut? To stay? *To wait?* Was an escape plan enough to protect her? Because despite everything she knew, everything she'd seen her father do to her mother, the instinct was to wait for Dante. For her husband.

She'd run away from him the other night, up the spiralling staircase, through the door on the left, into the bedroom, because her body knew too much. *Wanted* too much. And that want was consuming her.

The private jet engines roared, a signal that the person everyone was waiting for was close.

The goldish-beige leather armrest surrendered to the pressure of Emma's fingertips, and it whimpered.

Dante stood at the end of the aisle aboard the private jet. He walked towards her, and he stole her breath. He wore a black shirt, open to his chest. Exposing his throat. His skin. He'd rolled up the cuffs, exposing his forearms too. Thick and strong, lightly spattered with dark hair. A black silver-buckled belt wrapped around his lean hips, accentuating the black fabric hugging his thick thighs.

She hadn't imagined it. She hadn't built up their interaction in her head. He was everything her confused mind remembered.

He was the sun.

And despite everything, she wanted to run towards it, into its warmth.

The desire to do just that was primitive and loud. Her body screamed for her to stand, to meet him. And it felt so natural for her to want to surrender to the strength of her body's reaction to him, and forget the doubts, the questions, the *waiting*, and welcome him back with her lips on his.

He sat down beside her. Too close, and yet it wasn't close enough.

What was wrong with her?

He'd walked into the hospital and claimed her. Turned her world upside down. Turned *her* inside out and left her alone to sort out the chaos inside her.

'Emma,' Dante greeted, and her name was a caress. Pure silk. But it didn't soothe her. It chafed against her skin.

How dare he be so...*relaxed*? He'd kept her waiting. Hadn't told her where he'd gone or where he'd be. He'd just expected her to wait—*to be here*—and be happy when he came back.

And yet, wasn't that exactly what she'd asked of him— to allow her space.

A rage settled in her chest. 'Where have you been?'

He clipped himself in. 'In my hotel.'

She knew he was wealthy. But... 'Your hotel?'

'One of several hundred.' Dante signalled for the plane to depart with a nod and a flick of his elegant wrist.

Emma's blood roared. 'Where are we going?' she demanded.

He didn't flinch. But he moved. His hands went to her waist and his knuckles brushed her hip bone, feathered across her stomach as he clipped her in. She swallowed down the rumble inside her, the gasp in her throat. She had been told this morning that they were going on a trip. But she had no more details than that. She'd been told nothing.

She hadn't even packed her own bags. Not that she would have even known what to pack. Nothing in the wardrobe felt like hers.

Dante sat back in his seat, observing her with quiet intensity. 'Japan.'

She arched a brow beneath her fringe. 'Japan?'

The jet taxied down the small airstrip.

'Tokyo.'

'And what's in Tokyo?'

'*We* will be—' his eyes flicked to the silver-faced watch on his wrist '—in twelve hours.'

His gaze moved over her face.

'Did you miss me, Emma?' he drawled.

Had she? Was that why she was so upset?

Her chest heaved. 'Is that what you wanted?' His hand fell to his lap, but his eyes never left hers. Brown probing blue. 'Was it a little revenge?' she husked. 'Is that why you disappeared without saying goodbye? Did you want me to feel what *you* felt when you found me gone three months ago?'

The tyres hummed along the tarmac. The speed, the adrenaline, fed her rage. And it felt good to be mad. Mad at life. Mad at *him*.

'Did you miss *me*, Dante?'

'In our old life, I would show just how much,' he said without missing a beat, and heat flooded through her. 'But why would I punish you for something *you* can't remember?'

Her chest was so tight she could barely breathe. 'Because *you* remember.'

The anger inside her was suddenly rising. So quick, so intense. Anger at herself. For wanting…for waiting.

'At least I left a note.'

As the jet ascended into the skies, his gaze moved over her face. 'Did you think I wasn't coming back?'

'I knew you would.' Her shoulders rose. 'Eventually,' she said, because that was what men did when you gave them the opportunity. Exactly what her dad did. Disappeared and returned when it suited him.

'And here I am.'

The arrogance.

'Is this what our life was like before?'

'Like what?'

'Do you leave me often?'

'I did not leave you. Besides, you are here,' he corrected, 'with me. Now.' He frowned.

'But did you keep me waiting for *you*?' she continued, because what was the alternative? To…accept that this was who she was now, a woman who waited around for a man? Her stomach curdled.

'I refuse to be a pawn in someone else's life, Dante.' She swallowed, but it didn't ease the tension in her throat.

Today, they'd packed her cases with clothes she had no recognition of. Escorted her into a waiting car. Organised her life for her. And she'd felt like a piece being moved on a board game where the winner was already known to all but her.

'Staff have moved me around today,' she continued, her voice heated. 'They packed my cases, delivered me to *you*—' Her chest burned and she breathed fire. 'I am not a parcel!'

'I'm sorry.'

She blinked. *'What?'*

He leaned in until their eyes were level. Until his breath fanned her lips. Until he was so close she could feel the heat radiating from his skin.

'I'm sorry,' he said again.

And her brain did not compute. She'd expected lies, expected him to try to absolve himself. She hadn't expected an apology.

'What are you sorry for?' she asked. She wanted an explanation. A *real* explanation. Because *sorry* was still an easy word to say.

'The Mayfair house has lots of bedrooms,' he said, his eyes never leaving hers. 'I could have stayed in any of those. But none of them are *our* room. I chose to stay in my hotel. I chose to leave and I chose to not wake you *or leave a note*—' his eyebrows rose '—to say goodbye. For *that* I am sorry. But I'd make the same choice again. Because staying in a room that is not ours, in the room next to you, as you sleep in our bed, in our house... It was too much. So I left. Because I understood—I *understand*,' he corrected. 'You needed time to find your footing in this life you don't remember, but I also needed time to find mine.'

She tilted her chin. 'Explain that to me.'

He shrugged, a nonchalant dip of his too-broad shoulder. 'My wife doesn't remember me. Our marriage. And when I brought you home from the hospital, being in the same house with you and not being able reach you...'

'Reach me?' she asked. 'I was right there.'

His lips flattened. 'I meant what I said, Emma,' he re-iterated. '*All of it*. But it does not ease…'

'The reality of our situation,' she finished for him, and shame gripped her. She hadn't considered any of that. Only her own feelings. How *she* would navigate her way through this.

'Our relationship is starting…*backwards*,' he said. 'So we will start somewhere different. A different country. Different rooms. Different beds. In an environment where it will not be…'

'So hard?' she asked. 'Because in *that* house all you can see are memories of what we were before?'

'The house——' He grimaced. 'We don't need to be there to help you remember. Or find our…*feet*. We only need to be with each other. But away from the house…'

'It will be new for us both?'

He studied her face for a beat too long. 'Something like that.'

The jet levelled out.

'I'm sorry too,' she said, because she owed him an apology. She sighed. 'I was so wrapped up in navigating my amnesia for myself,' she explained, 'I hadn't contemplated how difficult this must be for you too. Because it's not just me starting again, it's both of us. I should have considered that. I should have considered *you*. And for that, *I* am sorry.'

'No apology required, Emma,' he dismissed with a raw edge to his voice. 'You were hurt——'

'I *was* hurt,' she interrupted. 'And you came for me. I appreciate you didn't have to. I left you without an explanation. You had every right to not come, but you did. And for that——' she swallowed tightly '——thank you.'

His eyes held hers and she couldn't catch her breath. Couldn't slow her pulse. He was right, wasn't he? There was something crackling between them. A heat drawing her in…

She dragged her gaze from his. 'You said you own hotels…' she said, forcing her attention to something real. Not the energy between them she couldn't see, couldn't understand. She peeked up at him from behind lowered lashes. 'Are you a hotelier?'

He shook his head. 'I'm the CEO and owner of a luxury travel company,' he replied.

'A travel company?'

'The Cappetta Travel Empire specialises in providing adrenaline-fuelled adventures catered specifically to each client. We provide the whole experience, transport, opulent accommodation and we plan their—' he shrugged '—their holiday for them.'

'You plan it for them?' she asked. 'Like tourist excursions?'

'The Cappetta experience is not an excursion, but an expedition into the unknown,' he corrected. 'It changes men, women, from the inside out.'

'Changes them?' She frowned. *How?*'

'It depends on the client.' His eyes moved over her and her body tightened in all the places it shouldn't. His gaze moved back to her eyes. 'Expeditions vary from extreme sports, mountaineering, trekking through unmapped canyons to eat and sleep in places that shouldn't exist, and yet they do, Emma, because I've seen them.'

'And then they are changed?' she asked.

His eyes blazed. 'The Cappetta experience gives the mind the right tools to jump out of an aeroplane when the ultimate fear is heights,' he explained. 'It teaches the mind to allow the body to be free. To reach a higher plane of existence. To...*transcend*.' His lips lifted.

Her stomach somersaulted. Is that what he'd done to her—given her the tools to take what she needed from what she feared most? *Marriage?*

'And who gave you the tools to teach others to live this way?' she asked.

'My grandfather. He was a pilot. He built a domestic airline to respectability. My...father.' He swallowed and she watched the heavy drag of his Adam's apple. And she recognised it. Heard the tension around the word *father*. The difficulty in saying the word.

'Your father?' she said, curiosity taking hold.

'He was many things. Pilot. Captain. Adventurer. He travelled the world on any mode of transport that brought him to his destination. To a place that fulfilled whatever particular need he had at the time,' he replied, and the shadows were gone from his eyes. His face a mask of unreadability. 'He revolutionised his father's small domestic airline into a travel empire with a backpack and a blog when the Internet was in its infancy. Others wanted to experience his way of life. His ceaseless desire to...'

'Transcend?' she offered.

'Indeed,' he said. 'So my father adapted his methodology for travel, for individual needs, and at maximum profit.'

'And your dad taught you?' And she watched for the shadows. But nothing came.

He shrugged. 'It is in my blood.'

She wanted to understand this nature of his, how it had tempted her into becoming someone unrecognisable.

'But I'm no longer on the ground arranging expeditions,' he continued, and she saw the pulse spike in his cheek. 'Unless *I* want to.'

'Unless you need the...*rush*?' she asked, because she couldn't imagine this choice of his, to live life how he wanted to. *Dangerously.* A life where the aim was nothing but to feel good. Not just good but...*alive.*

'I need it,' he confessed. 'The adrenaline. The rush of excitement. It's my job. A way of life. But I don't need to be on top of a mountain to feel it.' Her eyes flicked to his. 'It's possible to find it in...other areas.'

Her pulse surged. *Painfully.* She pictured the bed she'd spent two days in alone. But what of the other times she'd slept in it? With him?

'Is that what our marriage was like? Adrenaline fuelled? Thrilling? *A rush?*'

'It was,' he said, his gaze obsidian. 'And we needed more. *Always.* We were both powerless in the face of its ferocity.'

She didn't drink alcohol. Hadn't for a long time. But she remembered the effect it had on her body. The haze—*the fog.* And she was swimming in it now.

'Sex,' he said, and her heart stopped. The word *sex* slipped from his tongue as if it were the most natural word to use to define them. 'It was wonderful between us. It was the rush we both craved and the high we found in each other.'

'You make us sound like adrenaline junkies,' she said. 'Or sex addicts!'

'We were both,' he confirmed. 'And all it took was one passionate kiss and we were lost to each other.' His brown eyes burned black. 'Addicted.'

She'd never been addicted to anything. Never wanted anything more than once…

She'd had sex before. But *passion*?

Never.

Sex was sex. She enjoyed it. *Sometimes*. But all in all, it was a perfunctory physical release.

Her eyes dropped to his lips. And the urge was stronger than it had been two days ago. It was all she could think about—how his mouth would feel on hers.

She wanted to taste it. *Test it*. This rush he spoke of. This high.

Just once…

Months of self-denial heightened Dante's senses. They blazed when they saw the pure intensity with which Emma was staring at his mouth. And she was moving. *Slowly*. A millimetre for every heartbeat. Every breath.

His every primal instinct demanded he draw her in to his chest. Crush those lips of hers to his.

He'd spent the last two nights thinking of those lips. Their softness. How he'd stood before her wondering if she would act on the impulse that they'd both shared. But she'd resisted then. She'd walked away. Gone to bed. *Alone*. He'd wanted to stalk her. Up the stairs. Into bed. *Their* bed.

He knew he'd promised her that he would let her take the lead. But it didn't ease the ache, didn't ease the ferocity with which he wanted her.

Selfishly, he'd known if he stayed in *that* house with her, he would have waited for an opportunity to strike. To graze his mouth along the sensitive skin of her throat.

He wouldn't have been able to stop himself touching

her when he'd promised he wouldn't. And Dante kept his promises. He'd promised he'd wait. But the waiting had already been too long. He ached with waiting.

But this wasn't the Emma who tore the buttons off his shirt to feast her lips—her tongue—on his bruised nipple. This wasn't the Emma who had needed nothing but his lips on hers. His body on her. *Inside her.* This was not the Emma who understood the unrestrained physical desire which had led them to the altar.

She was a different Emma. A woman who demanded to know his whereabouts. *Their* destination. When the only thing *his* Emma had cared for was how long it would take them to get to bed. *Any* bed. The wall. The floor...

This Emma and her questions, she made him question everything, including the way they had existed before.

Did he treat her like a pawn? Did he move her into position to welcome him back? Did he leave her behind?

Yes. But he *always* came back. Such were the rules. Such was their marriage.

These questions made his skin itch.

The plan he'd made had been simple. And it remained unchanged. There was no need to change it. Even with all the questions.

He'd seduce her with all the things he hadn't needed the first time. He'd treat her like a client. Cater this work trip around her. Show her a side she'd never seen of him. A side she'd never needed to see before because they'd been playing by a different set of rules.

But now, the rules had changed. And he'd use all the tools in his arsenal to bring back the status quo. He'd dazzle her with his lifestyle. With this jet. With Japan.

The opulent life only he could give her. A life where the thrill came first. A life she could only live with him.

Emma might not remember, but he knew what she wanted. *Him.*

And he could see his plan was beginning to work already. She was returning to him, remembering their connection… She'd be in his bed by nightfall.

Triumph roared through him.

He sat very still.

He wouldn't coax.

He wouldn't push.

He didn't need to.

She was in charge.

And he knew that when once she felt his mouth on her there would be no going back for her. No escape. Because there hadn't been for him.

He waited, holding his breath, waited for Emma to deliver herself to him.

Her blond hair sat on her shoulder in a low-slung ponytail. Her burned orange shirt and ankle-length olive-green skirt sat against her pale skin with the vibrancy of autumn.

Her mouth was a hair's breadth away from his now. And Dante couldn't help it. He leaned in. Not all the way. But enough to push past any defence she had left against the current coursing between them.

Her lashes fell over her eyes. And then there was no space. No distance between them.

It was only the lightest touch of her lips against his, but need ripped through him. Dominating him.

Dante thrust his tongue in her mouth, meeting her need with his own.

All the blood in his body flowed to his groin in a tidal wave of heat.

It overwhelmed him now. Not only the need to taste her, but the warmth spreading over him as her hands held his face, pulled him closer. Invited his tongue to thrust deeper.

The feeling was familiar.

He'd felt it when the snow and the winds had pummelled his body as he climbed the highest peak in the Himalayas. When he'd been stuck between the summit of Everest and the base below.

Exhausted, but exhilarated.

Nature had tested his limits. His resolve.

The freak storm had hit, and no one had seen it coming. Without visibility, there had been no way of following the rope back to camp. His oxygen tank depleting, he'd sheltered as best he could. He'd found a ledge and stayed there. Waited it out.

It was the closest he'd come to death. And afterwards, after the storm had passed and the adrenaline had subsided, he'd craved warmth. Human connection, the need to know he wasn't alone. It was a feeling that he'd found unwelcome. He didn't need anyone.

And he felt it now.

That need for *warmth*.

Emma's warmth.

Shock hardened him. His every muscle. His forearms strained not to hold her too tightly. The muscles in his chest held him back, restraining his every urge to push against her.

He'd needed no one. Never risked being emotionally involved to the point when someone could leave him.

Abandon him. Emma had done all of those things. And yet, kissing Emma after so long...

Had he become emotionally attached to his wife? So attached that she was part of his survival?

The realisation was too much.

He did not want her warmth.

He wanted her heat.

Her sex.

He kissed her harder. *Deeper.* He thrust his fingers into her hair, tilted her neck to gain deeper access and he punished her mouth with his own. With his tongue. His teeth.

'Dante...' she panted, and he drank from her mouth. He kissed her with everything pulsing inside him. His wants. His needs.

But there was something else inside him. Something he didn't want.

Regret.

Regret his lips hadn't kissed hers for too long. That he'd abandoned his duty to maintain this fire. Worked, *maybe* too much, when he should have been kissing her. Keeping her hot, ready and wanting.

Was that why she'd left?

It didn't matter.

She was here.

In his arms.

His thumbs found her pebbled nipples beneath her blouse and stroked. Brushed them with the pads of his thumbs. But it wasn't enough. He wanted them in his mouth. He wanted to suck. Tease. Until the hardened peaks pulsed between his lips.

He moved his fingers to the pearl buttons of her shirt

and began to undo them. He did not release her mouth. He suckled her tongue. And she mewed for him.

He needed to know her again. Feel the suppleness of small breasts in his palms. He needed to taste her. Her skin.

His hands moved, unclipped their belts and then went to her hips, pulling her closer. Into his embrace.

Her breasts pushed against the white lace that held them in place, pushed into his palms. And he needed to be naked. He needed Emma naked. Skin on skin. He needed to be inside her.

He wrenched fabric between his fingers until he was scrunching it, pulling up her skirt—

'Stop!' She pushed at his chest. Tore her mouth from his. Firm fingers on his chest held him at bay. But her pupils flared into black disks. They told him the truth. She didn't want to stop.

She wanted him. So why?

Panting, they stared at each other.

Something unfamiliar wound itself around his shoulders and pushed down. Why was she not smiling? Sliding over to him with open arms so he could pull her onto his lap? Undo his zip and release himself for her pleasure? For his? One kiss was all it had taken before...

'I want to...' She looked at her hands on his chest, and her mouth twisted. She pulled her hands away. 'Talk,' she announced, her breath coming in short, sharp rasps.

'Talk?' His mind raced. They did not *talk*. They did not stop their love making for a chit-chat break. 'About what?' he asked raggedly.

'Us,' she breathed. 'You. *Me*... I don't remember the

marriage we had, but I want to know. I want to learn. I want to know my husband better.'

'Are you not learning, Emma?' he asked. 'What I taste like? How it feels to have my tongue in your mouth and my hands on your body?'

A blush bloomed up her throat to kiss her cheeks. She shifted on a heavy exhale and stared fixedly ahead. Spine straight. 'I want to learn who I was, who I am, who you are, without—' she swallowed '—*this*. Without this complicating things.'

'"*This*"?'

Her gaze met his. 'This urgency between us. It's too frantic. It's too—' She looked down at her shirt and began to do the buttons back up. 'It's too…*indecent*.'

'Indecent?' he growled, because *his* Emmy would be between his thighs taking him into her mouth.

And he ached for his wife's lips.

'It is not indecent to want my wife. To want you naked. To feel your thighs squeeze against mine as you take me inside you.'

He saw her blush.

'Enough.' She shook her head. *'Please.'*

And he was on that ledge again. Alone and waiting.

They both remained silent but for the heaviness of their breathing.

'Is there somewhere to sleep?' she asked.

He nodded. He knew she was running again.

But he also needed her to leave, didn't he? So he could lick his wounds. Replan his attack. His seduction. Because somehow his reaction to her kiss—her rejection— was affecting him in ways he didn't like.

He buzzed for an attendant and requested she take Emma to the plane's master suite. Emma stood to follow the smiling attendant.

'Dante?'

He looked up into her face. His eyes lingering on the swollenness of her lips after his kiss. And he wanted to reach out and touch her mouth.

He fisted his hands on his thighs.

'I look forward to getting to know you in Japan,' she announced, and turned on her heel.

Never had Emma walked away from him. Shut him out. Physically not wanted him close. And now she'd done it twice.

He couldn't fathom it. They'd never talked before. He'd learned more in the hospital room a few days ago than he had in a year married to his wife. Her mother, her job, the empty fridge. And he had more questions than he'd ever imagined.

How often had the fridge been empty? How many jobs had her mother worked? How many had Emma worked over the last three months? Had the fridge been empty again?

He scowled. Because these things...what did they matter? He wanted his wife back. What was there to know that he didn't already?

But it weighed on his conscience.

Had Emma wanted more? More of his time? More conversation? Would he have been open to talking if she'd asked him? Was he open to it now?

It was captivating, wasn't it? This change in his wife. The idea of seducing her without sex was...

A novelty.

An intriguing one.

He rolled his shoulders.

It was a challenge he'd welcome.

And win.

CHAPTER FIVE

EMMA STEPPED ON to the terrace of their hotel suite and embraced the light breeze on her skin.

It had been two days and she could still feel heat clawing at her. It was the only thing she understood about her relationship with Dante. She couldn't make sense of anything else but that, which was why she'd asked him to stop. Before they'd headed to bed, any bed.

Shinjuku City was spread out before her. She'd seen the lights from the highest floors of every skyscraper that required a cleaner, or a silver service waitress, but she'd never seen...*this*. She'd been raised in a city, but this was unlike anything she'd ever seen.

This was a city made up of buildings piercing the clouds, a city that kissed a mountain. Any minute now, the sun would move again and settle behind Mount Fuji.

She pressed her open palms to the balcony balustrade.

They hadn't talked. They'd moved into the penthouse mansion two days ago and she hadn't set eyes on him since.

She'd drawn the battle lines, and he'd retreated with the excuse of touching base with the board of his company. She understood what he was doing.

His vulnerability on the plane had been raw. As open

and present as her own. He missed his wife. But she wasn't his wife. At least not the one he remembered. *Not yet.*

And he remembered everything. Their first kiss. Their every touch. Every night spent in their bed together.

But she still had the same questions. Why had she married him in the first place? Why had she left? And her only goal was to figure it out. To figure *him* out. To learn, to understand, who she was with him. The only way to do that was to talk without the urgent pressure of his lips. Because, on the plane, she'd felt the adrenaline, and the need to chase it.

It would have been so easy to fall beneath him, and stay there, under the weight of him. Far too easy. But sex didn't feel like a big enough reason for her to marry him. To tie herself to a man legally. No matter how intoxicating his kisses, or how good he made her feel.

He hadn't spoken of love. And for that, she was grateful. She didn't want it. She didn't want him to love her, and she did not want to love him, did she? But then what did *that* mean? What kind of marriage did they have if it wasn't based on love?

Was their marriage really just based on sex? And if that were true, if that was what twenty-six-year-old Emma had wanted and agreed to, why had she left him when the chemistry between them was so potent?

Had Dante wanted more? Had she walked away from her marriage because she couldn't give to him the kind of marriage her mother had craved? Did he want a family? Children? Did he still want those things? Was that why he'd come for her? Was that why he hadn't divorced her? Because he still hoped he could persuade her?

She swallowed. Had she not divorced him because she too hoped that he would change his mind? Or perhaps because she had fallen for him...

She felt his presence before she heard it. A shift in the air, in her.

'Have you been bored without me, Emma?'

She didn't turn. Didn't visibly let her body react, but the deep husk of his voice reached inside her.

The instinct to turn and move towards him was overwhelming. All she wanted was to meet him. To raise her mouth to his in invitation and demand he kiss her again. Kiss her until all she could feel, all she could question, was how to angle her mouth. Until she was breathless with his kisses.

She closed her eyes to steady herself. She couldn't do any of that, not until she understood why she'd married this man who made her blood run hot, whose kisses left her frantic, who made her feel unaligned with her natural self.

'How could I be bored with this view?' She opened her eyes and commanded her gaze to stay forward, on the glints of orange disappearing into the shadow of the night.

'It's beautiful,' he agreed, and in her peripheral vision, she saw his hands slide onto the balustrade next to hers.

'If you listen carefully,' he said, 'you will hear the ring.'

'The ring?'

'The bell of a setting sun.'

She listened. Watched as day turned to night. Heard the bell as the sun disappeared into darkness behind the mountain.

Slowly, the lights flickered on in every window, on every street, and the city was ablaze with artificial rainbow light, the mountain hidden until tomorrow. But she knew it was there. Even in the shadows. An impenetrable force of nature. Just like Dante. There even when he wasn't. In her mind. Intruding on her every thought…

She forced herself to relax.

'Was it always this way for you?'

'What do you mean?' he asked as she fought the urge to move close, to allow their elbows to meet, to allow the electric current to flow from her body into his.

No. Desire and discussion were to be separated.

'I mean with your dad. His job. Your grandfather's. Was life—' she waved at the cityscape '—always so spectacular?'

'It was,' he answered. 'It is.'

'Did you ever crave something simple?' She swallowed. 'Something less… Something more normal?'

'I have never known…*normal*.' He spoke softly, but his voice was laced with something heavy.

'I'm normal,' she countered, because she was. And she wanted to know why this extraordinary billionaire had married her.

What did they have in common?

She didn't know what she'd told him about her past or what he'd told her. But she'd start at the beginning, as he had when he'd told of their first meeting. She'd tell him the beginning of *her*.

'My life isn't unsimilar to many others,' she started. She didn't look at him, because it was easier to have this conversation without the intensity of his gaze boring into hers.

'I grew up hating my father and making sure I was always there for my mother, because he never was. I didn't grow up watching sunsets in penthouses made for the ultrarich and royalty. I grew up taking care of my mother. Supporting her so she could look after me. I helped her clean for her agency work before school. I'm the definition of normal. A city girl from a council estate, yet now—'

'You are here,' he interjected softly.

The rational part of her mind told her to tread carefully, not push too hard too soon, but she needed to know more.

'Did you hate your dad too?'

'What gives you the impression I hate my father?' he asked, and still, she didn't look at him. Didn't acknowledge the closeness of him, or the pull inside her to be closer.

'On the plane,' she confessed, 'there was a hesitancy when you spoke about him. A hesitancy I recognised because I feel it too. This conflict inside me when I think of him. That I owe him something because of his biological contribution to my life, all while hating him,' she hissed. And she waited, for the gasp. For his shock at how she felt about the man who gave her life.

Emma and her mum had had so many arguments about it. His behaviour. His treatment of her. And her mother had told her to accept that he still loved them.

But nothing came from Dante. Only silence and an invitation for her to continue. So she did.

'I know it sounds violent,' she confessed, 'but he makes me feel violent. Because I hate how she accepted his lies as truth. I hate what he did to her. What he turned her into. My mum—'

His hand moved then, atop hers, and she couldn't continue. Couldn't concentrate on anything other than the feel of his palm on her skin. His offer of comfort was given without her having to ask for it.

'What did he turn her into?' he asked, and this time she didn't look, because she didn't want to see pity in his eyes.

Had she ever told him what her dad had done? Why *he* was the reason she never wanted to marry? Why she found it hard to accept that someone would want to make her life easier?

'A doormat,' she rasped the truth of it. 'And however, many times I wanted to tell him to be gentle, to at least wipe his boots before he stomped on her again, she hushed me. Told me to be quiet. To accept that my...*father*,' she said, even though he was no such thing to her, 'would never be the man either she or I wanted him to be. That he would continue to break every promise he should have held dear.'

Emma tried and failed to keep the venom out of her voice. 'He seduced my mother when she was sixteen, promised he'd marry her but never did. He lied. And still, for all the years afterwards, she believed one day he would.'

Her heart ached for her mother. For that teenage girl who believed in the fairy tale, believed love would conquer all. Regardless of how much time passed, how many lies he told her, she believed in their love, in him.

'He abandoned her when she fell pregnant with me. He didn't come back even when she begged him to, even when she was kicked out by my grandparents. Even when I was born...' It was Emma who was hurting now, remembering that little girl who couldn't understand why her father didn't want her. 'He didn't come for a year. And then he only stayed for two days before leaving us. I have seen the pictures of him holding a one-year-old, his daughter, a daughter he'd only just met.'

She was breathing so hard, so fast, her words tumbled out of her. Out of a place she'd hidden them for so long it hurt to speak them. But she needed him to understand her hesitancy to accept their marriage at face value.

'And then there was another picture when I was five. Another when I was thirteen where I'm looking at him with disgust. And he disgusts me still. Not because he wasn't there for me. He wasn't there for *her*. Because every time he left, he promised he'd be back for good next time. But he couldn't be the man my mother deserved.'

Tears of rage clouded her vision but she wiped them away.

'He didn't deserve her. Her kindness. Her patience. Her devotion. He broke her heart and killed her with his lies.'

She turned and finally met the gaze she'd been avoiding. But there was no trace in his eyes of the pity she feared. But not empathy either. Just his steady gaze on hers. And his hand remained where it had the entirety of her story. On hers. Unmoving. Just *there*.

'That's why, on the plane, I was so angry. Angry that you'd left what was meant to be our house. In that moment, I was her—I was my mother.'

Her heart was beating so fast. So hard. And she felt vulnerable. *Exposed*.

'I swore I'd never be her. Never devote myself to any man. But I married you. And I… I need to understand it. I need to know who you are and that you're not him.

Not like my father. That I have not betrayed myself and everything I stand for. That's why I stopped you,' she admitted rawly. 'Because it was too intense. Too blinding. Too frantic. Our marriage, it seems the antithesis to all that I am.'

She pulled her hand from beneath his and turned her body to face him. She'd never told anyone about her parents, and how their relationship had changed her forever.

She'd thought it would feel weak to have told him everything, but it didn't. It felt like she'd taken her power back, after amnesia had taken everything from her. She was choosing to share these memories with him.

'So help me to make sense of our marriage, Dante,' she said. Shoulders back, head raised, she continued, 'Talk to me. Tell me who you are,' she breathed heavily. 'Tell me why you hate your dad too.'

Dante gave a slight shake of his head.

For two days, he'd stayed in his company's Tokyo headquarters, avoiding this conversation. Talking wasn't how he had imagined he was going to persuade Emma back into his bed. And so he'd plotted how he'd exploit this talking she wanted to his advantage. And he'd planned to exhilarate her senses and distract her with worldly things. Sights and sounds that would make her dizzy.

He saw no advantage here. Only emotion and feelings. Feelings that he didn't want to examine, either hers or his own. He did not want to examine the faults of their fathers and find common ground.

They didn't need any here.

Only in bed.

And yet, it was clear that Emma would not be appeased

by what he had been willing to offer. So he must adapt, change tack, offer…something.

'My life was not hard, Emma,' he said dismissively. 'I never worried about my parents' relationship. They didn't have one. I didn't worry about the bills or the fridge. I did not work before my tutelage. I never worried who would take care of who. My father employed a triage of nannies to care for me while he conquered the world.'

And women, he added silently.

'Your dad left you alone too?' she summarised without his permission. 'Left others to care for you while he cared only for himself?'

'It was not like that,' he said, but even as he did, he knew it was a lie. 'When I was of age, I conquered the world myself, and with him, guided by his ethos for life.'

'Isn't that what I'm doing—what I *did* before you?' She screwed up her nose. 'I let my father's *ethos* for life determine my every relationship. I didn't have relationships because I didn't want to be…'

'Abandoned?'

And it hit him now; the very thing she didn't want to happen to herself, she had done to him. Done to him what his mother had too. His father was different; he had never abandoned Dante, never made any promises.

He was your father; he shouldn't have had to. He should have just been there.

'Yes,' she admitted, jolting him back to the present. The spaghetti strap of her dress fell over her bare shoulder. He swallowed as her fingers grazed along her skin to pull it back into place.

'He never considered how him coming in and out of our lives affected us. It sounds as if your dad did the same,' she concluded, and his lips thinned into a firm line when she didn't stop. 'He gave you up to nannies until he could benefit from your company. He only showed up when it was of some benefit to *him*.'

She didn't understand his life.

She didn't understand him.

'It is not the same,' he rejected.

'Isn't it?' she asked, her blue eyes seeking and finding his. Something heavy shifted inside him.

'Why would I hate him, Emma?' He stepped closer to her, because how could he not? 'Everything I have. Everything I am, is because of him.'

And she looked at him now as if he was the source of her pain. And his feet halted. And he didn't like it. Didn't want it.

The story she'd shared with him, the relationship between her parents, it was everything they weren't.

In the past, he would have reached for her. Placed his hands to her waist, allowed them to slide down the cotton of her blue polka dot dress. Over her hips. Down her thighs. Seeking the hem at her knees. And he'd have taken her with her back pressed into him as she looked out at the view. Thrust inside her again and again, until all she could think, all she could say, was his name as she screamed it into the night. He would have turned pain into passion.

He fisted his hands.

He couldn't do that. Not yet, not with this Emma.

'Is that why you resent him?' she asked quietly.

'Why would I resent him?' he asked. Because it wasn't true, was it? 'You are looking for a common ground between us where there is none,' he growled. 'I am very much who I am because of my father. Because of the way he lived.'

'I loved my mother. She was there for me unconditionally, but I resented her too, for the way she lived,' she confessed, and he heard the crack in her voice. Heard how hard it was for her to admit. 'Her inability to let my dad go. It wasn't just my dad who changed my relationships with people, it was *her*. She made me so afraid, I'd...' She looked away from him and into the night. 'I'd let someone I—' she turned to him and her gaze was shuttered '—loved, take and take, until I was nothing more than a shell.'

Love? Did she think she'd loved him? That he'd loved her? That their marriage was based on all those emotions he didn't want and didn't know how to feel? She was no different; that was one thing he did know. That was why they were perfect for one another. No emotional attachments. Only physical desire. *Only want.*

Was that what she was afraid of? Was that why she had needed him to tell her that divorce was an option? That if she wanted to leave, she could? She needed an out in case the reason she had left before was because she had become emotionally invested in their relationship.

She wrapped her arms around her waist. 'Do you think all children grow up to be replicas of their parents?'

'Maybe,' he said. 'Why?'

'After all those vows and promises I made to myself, I wonder if I was always destined to...'

'Continue her legacy?'

'Yes.' Her eyes narrowed. 'Was it something in my DNA that I couldn't run from? Hide from...? The same way you couldn't hide from your destiny to continue your father's legacy.'

He didn't contradict her. DNA was undeniable. He was his father's son, after all. He knew the pressure of living up to a legend. He knew the worry of not being good enough.

For Emma, he supposed, it was the opposite. She didn't want to live up to the legacy.

'My father's dead, Emma,' he said, wanting this to end. 'I think of him little.' He shrugged off his suit jacket and took another step towards her. 'He was an uncompli-cated man. He lived to live, took what he wanted from life, until he died.'

'He died?' she whispered.

He moved closer. 'He did.'

'How did he die?'

'A solo adventure on the high seas,' he told her. 'His boat returned—' he splayed his empty hand, palm side up '—empty.'

'I'm sorry.'

He moved closer still. 'Don't be. It was a death my fa-ther would have applauded.'

She gasped. 'Applauded?'

'An adventurer dies adventurously.' He shrugged. 'It would have been the way he'd have wanted to go.'

'On his terms?' she grated.

'Is that not the best way to live?' he countered. 'And to die?' And he watched the flare of her nostrils. The tight-ening of her bare shoulders. In her mind all men were the same, weren't they? Selfish even in death.

Was Dante selfish? Was she right to think so? Had he only kept her, kept coming back to her, for his own needs?

Of course he had, but he'd met her every need as well as his own.

'And your mother?' she asked, her eyes fixed on his. Watching. *Waiting* for whatever it was she was seeking in his answer.

'My mother,' he said, unsure how to take this conversation forward. How to expose bits of himself he never had before. To find this common ground he knew they didn't have. 'My mother has no influence in my life.

'Why not?'

'She gave birth to me and left to start a new life.' Something hot and unknown bubbled in his chest. 'She was out the door as soon as they cut the umbilical cord.'

She shivered again. 'Without you?'

'I had my father.'

'Sounds to me like you had no one,' she said. He could see the goosebumps covered her flesh now, highlighted by the soft amber lights flooding the terrace. She was cold. And he knew several ways to warm her. None that she wanted.

She was right, wasn't she?

He'd always been alone.

Until *her*.

He dropped his jacket over her shoulders and held on to the lapels.

'And now we have each other,' he said, and he knew it was a lie. They'd had each other for a time. A time until he didn't want her. Or she didn't want him.

The silence was palpable.

He felt it. The shift. The rise in her shoulders. The absence of breath leaving her lips.

He resisted the urge to thrust his nose into her hair.

Grip the hair caressing the flesh between her shoulder blades and draw her to him. Kiss the exposed flesh beneath her ear and taste her. Move his mouth down her neck and bite the delicate flesh of her shoulder. And step back into familiar ground. To take them both back. Back to the beginning.

But there was no *back*, was there? Only this. Only now. Only *her.*

And he'd agreed to her demand of no more kisses, even when that was all he desperately wanted to do. To close the distance between them.

To sink into their connection. A deep connection that was always there beneath the surface.

A connection to something he couldn't see. Nature. *God*, maybe.

It was just there.

Humming.

And it was too loud. Too much.

But he wouldn't allow it to happen. Couldn't.

A kiss without heat.

He did not want her softness.

He didn't need it if it was not given freely.

He pulled away from her.

'Go to bed, Emma,' he commanded roughly.

'To bed?' she husked, and he knew he could lead her there if he wanted. That this time she'd welcome him.

He moved away from her.

'Dante—' She reached for him.

He shook his head. Kept moving until the distance between them felt endless.

For months, he'd thought of nothing but *her*. The feel

of her against him. Her skin. Her taste. She'd haunted his every living moment. In his waking hours and his sleep.

He shut his eyes against it. The something in his chest he didn't recognise. A pain. A tug.

He didn't want it. Whatever it was. Whatever she was bringing to the surface.

'It's late,' he said.

He wanted her. But he didn't want this. This new Emma who spoke of her feelings. Her pain. This Emma who wanted to know his pain.

He wanted none of it.

So tonight he would walk away.

He'd reset. He'd find another way to show her how they maintained the balance in their marriage.

No emotions. No discussions of childhood trauma. Only them. Only sex.

'Good night, Emma.'

CHAPTER SIX

DANTE'S PLAN HAD always been flawed. He could see that now.

He'd brought Emma to Japan to thrill her. But Emma had never cared to chase the thrill of worldly adventures. She'd wanted the extravagance of *normal* many took for granted. She longed for security in the safety of his arms. A passionate marriage in the confines of a contract. But a loveless marriage.

He'd dismissed key information that he already knew about her. He understood she longed for financial security and passion without emotional attachment.

Now he understood *why…*

Emma didn't want to explore the heat between them, because she didn't trust it.

Didn't trust *him.*

But tonight, he'd prove that she could.

For three days, he'd planned, and curated a campaign of seduction that had nothing to do with shared trauma. Nothing to do with emotions or feelings. Only what would excite and delight *her* senses.

Tonight, he'd delight her. Win her trust. And then they would get this marriage back on track.

His body tightened in anticipation. He'd blocked out

the intensity of his longing, his conviction to allow Emma the space she demanded. Tonight she needed to see it.

He opened his eyes and scanned his scene of seduction.

Fires burned in small ceramic pots, positioned at every corner of the square, white-clothed table set for two. A black gold-embossed menu sat prepared to be opened by her fingers and devoured by her senses as she read beneath long-stemmed candles. The menu was curated to tantalise her taste buds, to show her the man who'd written it, knew her. Her likes—*dislikes*.

He'd cater to her every worldly desire, while she dined with him in this man-made cherry blossom grove, under a night's sky.

Then he'd meet her every physical desire too.

The black double doors opened. The two doormen held them open with white-gloved hands and dipped heads.

And she stole the breath in his lungs.

She was a vision.

The dress was everything he knew it would be. Decadent. Made of silver sequins hand sewn into a delicate blood-red silk overlaid with purple-and-black lace. Her shoulders and back were bare. A tight bodice nipped in at the waist and flared out in a fishtail.

Dante watched her from the shadows. Watched the sway of her feminine curves as she walked the white stone path snaking beneath her feet.

Her eyes rose to the treetops, her heavy blond hair swishing between her shoulder blades, and he caught the glints of the sliver clasp containing her hair into a high ponytail. And his fingers itched to touch it. To release it. To watch her hair fall to her naked shoulders before he gripped it between his fingers.

But still, he didn't move.

Still, he watched.

Her gaze moved along every tree, every overarching branch that created a shelter overhead. She scanned the petals. The most vivid pinks to the purest whites.

Her eyes dipped to the flowerbeds. To the wild flowers of pink and yellow. To the orange blooms with stained red tips.

And she was iridescent, glowing beneath the soft amber glow of the lanterns hanging from the intermittent branches of every tree.

She looked like she belonged here. Some mythical creature sent to command the trees. The flowers.

Dante flinched, an imperceptible jolt of his body beneath his suit as the memory assaulted him.

The memory of a basket overflowing with delicacies, overturned. Their clothes strewn on each step towards the bedroom.

Her surprise picnic forgotten.

He'd forgotten her love of gardens that night.

Forgotten the reason they'd chosen the house in Mayfair.

Dante remembered now.

He'd picked her up from work and driven them to the viewing. But instead of going inside, he'd taken her into the garden. The secret garden. And she'd lit up. Something inside her glowing at this secret world, living and alive, within the concrete jungle of London.

So he'd taken her to every house with a secret garden and he'd bought her the first one she adored.

He hadn't been able to convince her to give up any of her three jobs initially after the move into the Mayfair house, after their engagement. None of them. Thankless jobs. A silver service waitress at night, a cafe catering assistant in the day and an agency cleaner on the side…

Somewhere inside her she'd been afraid, even then, that he wouldn't take care of her, hadn't she? That his promise of marriage was a lie until he slipped the ring on her finger and they both signed on the dotted line.

But he had taken care of her, met her needs.

Then why did she leave you?

Something heavy shifted inside him. He ignored it.

She was here *now*. That was what mattered, what he was focused on.

She had arrived at the table, stood next to it now, fingering the candlesticks, the crystal glasses, the silverware—

Dante moved towards her now, through the trees on silent feet.

He stepped into her space behind her, and it hit him in the solar plexus. The presence of her. Her scent.

She turned, eyes wide. 'Dante!' She placed a hand to his chest, to steady herself. 'Thank you,' she said, and her eyes glittered. 'I adore *this*. Gardens…' Her eyes moved from his to the trees—to the flowers. 'Me and Mum moved around a lot, inner city estate to inner city estate. Flats to maisonettes to houses. But there was always a garden,' she said.

He felt her heavy swallow.

'Whether it was potted plants on a windowsill or a shared communal garden. I used to steal Mum's library books and sneak out in the dead of night to read them beneath the lights I'd threaded between the trees. To escape for a while. Just for a time where I could forget the hardness. Mum's tears… The garden was a safe place where all was quiet. All was still.'

His eyes travelled down over her plump parted lips. Down over her throat. Over the prominent arch of her collarbone. And he wanted to carry her back the way she'd come. Up to the suite. To bed. And lose himself in her. Silence her lips with his and end these stories of hers he didn't want to hear. Didn't *need* to hear.

But he didn't. He remained still. Let the thud of his heart beat ferociously beneath her fingertips.

'I figured it out.'

'What?'

'Our marriage,' she replied. 'It makes sense now.'

His frowned. 'What does?'

'Both our childhoods were…*unstable*. And we found stability in each other. A frantic all-consuming stability.'

He clenched his fists at his sides to stop him reaching for her. To stop him from spanning his palms around her waist to explore the dip before he came to the arch of her hips. To stop him from tugging her body into the groove of his to show her just how well their bodies fitted together. To prove to her she needed no more words. No more talk. Not whatever *this* was.

Only him.

'*You* are my garden,' she concluded, and her words shredded his resolve to be slow. To ease her into the physicality of his desire. Of hers.

He was not her…*garden*.

He had to tell her everything. *Everything*. The contract. The rules…

He couldn't allow her to speculate, to come up with her own truth.

He'd seduce with the truth she needed to hear. Why she trusted him. Why she'd married him.

He needed to end whatever fantasies she was creating about their commitment to one another.

'Our marriage has nothing to do with…gardens, Emma,' he stated. 'It has everything to do with how I make you feel. How you make me feel.'

Her eyes narrowed and moved over the hard jut of his jaw to the flickering pulse in his cheek. 'How you make me feel?'

'We have a contract.'

'A contract?'

'A purely-for-passion marriage for as long as we both see fit for it to continue. We agreed to one year originally. Planned for another three years if we were still content. Happy in the confines of our contract. And we *were* content,' he assured her, because they had been. He was sure of that. Or at least he had been.

But she left. The contract has technically expired.

Semantics. There was no need to press on the separation between them. He'd tell her the facts. Facts as he knew them. And she needed to hear them; he had no other choice but to tell her. Because he could not allow her to turn them into something else. Something he didn't want. Something that needed to be fed and watered and nourished emotionally.

He didn't want it.

And neither did she.

'There was no chance of you ever becoming your mother, Emma,' he told her, because he knew this was the way now. The only way to re-establish what they were. What he wanted again. 'Because we both wanted the same thing from our marriage. Each other. Without emotional attachments. Without love. We do not know how to love, Emma, because we understand it as the lie it is. But we trust each other. To stick to the terms in the contract,' he said, her breaths coming in quick sharp rasps.

'Terms?'

'Yes, a simple contract, to take what we wanted from each other,' he reiterated, 'Until we were sated.'

He was not sated. And he didn't believe she was either.

'What happened when we were done?' she asked. 'When it was over between us?'

'We'd divorce and you'd receive a settlement. You'd be financially secure for ever.'

'And what did you get out of this arrangement?'

'*You.*' Her fingers clenched and clung to his shirt. 'We can have that again, Emma,' he said roughly, his voice hoarse. 'We can—'

'Have a physical relationship—*a marriage*,' she corrected, 'without emotional attachment.' He watched the blush bloom in her pale cheeks. The flair of her nostrils. The unsteady rise and fall of her chest. 'Without lies or deception. No broken promises. Just…*sex*. Until I no longer want you.'

'Or I no longer want *you*,' he added, because if he was to have Emma in his bed again, she needed to understand the rules they played by.

'I—'

He shook his head. 'Understand this before you say anything,' he growled. 'Whether you want to stay in this marriage or not, everything I've said still stands. If you choose to leave, you will be financially secure. But if—'

'If I want you to take me to bed,' she said, 'it will be sex only?' Her blue eyes were fixed on his, probing, searching.

'Exactly,' he agreed, and something inside him shifted. But it didn't feel like triumph. It was not elation zipping through his veins. It was heavier. *Darker*.

'No emotions involved, Emma. Only desire. Only want.' He placed his hand on top of hers. Watched her mouth fall open as his fingers covered her.

'I can fulfil your every physical desire,' he promised, because he could.

He *would*.

For three days and three months, he'd waited. Thinking of this moment. Of his Emma coming back to him. How he'd take his power back by giving her the illusion of hers. But in this moment, he didn't feel powerful.

He felt displaced.

Alone on the ledge.

Waiting.

For her.

It felt like whiplash.

Emma ached with everything she now knew about their marriage and everything she still didn't. He'd given her what she'd asked for on the terrace.

A better understanding of him.

But she wasn't satisfied.

He'd brought her to a forest of cherry blossoms, a garden with a variety of spring blooms. Some she knew and some she didn't. Iris. Yellow petals with stained tips of red. Tulip Don Quichotte. Deep strains of purple and pink.

It was overwhelming he'd do this for her. A wife who was supposed to mean nothing to him. Not emotionally.

It was as if he knew her. Not only her body as per their contract. But the woman beneath all that.

He'd created a place for her in his mind.

A place filled with knowledge of her.

This wasn't sexual.

It *was* intimate. It was holding her hand, when every instinct told her to withdraw from his touch. It was knowing her in ways that had nothing to do with her body.

He saw her. He made her feel safe. And wanted.

But none of it mattered, apparently.

It had never mattered between them.

She'd exposed herself, spoken freely about her past, taken some of her power back by exposing the truth. And for what? Their marriage had only ever been surface deep. It was a connection of bodies, not minds. Not hearts.

They had a contract. No emotional attachment, no love. Only them and a shared desire. A marriage strictly for passion with an inbuilt safety net and financial security guaranteed.

And...*sex*.

Lots of sex.

Questions, so many questions, caught in her throat. Emma's throat tightened.

But it was also beginning to make sense too. How they had found one another, why they both would have chosen to enter into a loveless marriage. They were the same, him and her. Their childhoods had both been unstable. And somehow, they'd found each other.

Each other's constant in a world that had given them

both nothing but inconsistency. That was why they'd governed their relationship with rules. Put precautions in place.

'That's how you did it, isn't it?'

'Did what?'

'Convinced me to marry you.'

'Yes.'

If he'd told her about the contract the night she'd fallen, would she have stayed?

No.

The woman she'd grown into was the one who had made this possible. A woman who would have been swayed by a secure future, who wanted to be reliant on nothing and no one. One who had seen what life had to offer and what it didn't.

The younger Emma would never have risked that the intensity between them could have burned her alive. Wouldn't have risked that she might not be able to walk away. Left it behind. Left *him* behind. Because that would surely have been the easier choice.

And there was nothing wrong with choosing easy. All her life it had been hard.

Until him.

Dante had made things easier for her.

Never had she been treated softly. Never had anyone shielded her from the harshness of life. Allowed her to more than survive the endless cycle of days.

He'd come for her when she needed it the most. Taken care of her when she'd abandoned him.

Why had he done that? Was it really just about sating their desire for one another? Or had things changed over the course of their year together? Had this marriage been everything Emma had hoped for? Had she been sated? Had she had her fill of his competent mouth? His lips? His body on hers? Inside her?

She thought of the intricate lace of her underwear hidden beneath her dress. A bra. Suspenders. Stockings.

Never to her knowledge had she worn anything like it before, but she had instinctually worn them tonight. And that made her feel brave. Sensual. In a way that Emma at only twenty-two would never have been.

Ever since Dante had come to her aid in the hospital, she had felt a void in her open up. Was this the way to satisfy that void? To indulge in the very desire that she had denied herself?

The need was so desperate she could taste it.

And why should she deny herself now? She had found the source of that hunger.

In this moment, why should she worry about why she had walked away from Dante, from their marriage? About why she had returned to Birmingham? About why she hadn't demanded a divorce and cashed in on the settlement she had been promised?

Dante was right; for whatever reason she'd written that note, she hadn't fully severed the bond between them.

And neither had he.

They'd both been waiting for each other to come back.

So tonight, she wanted to be brave.

She wanted to be sensual.

She wanted to be touched by him. She wanted to let herself be consumed by the frantic heat between them. She wanted to throw herself into the intensity of his dark brown eyes and drown in them.

She wanted to do what they had set out to do in the

first place: stay until she'd had her fill, until she no longer wanted him. And then she'd walk away, without a backward glance. Whenever that might be.

Dante had promised her financial security regardless of what choice she made.

And she believed him.

It felt powerful to have this choice. To choose to please herself. *And him.*

Suddenly she felt nervous. Not wanting to bite at her lower lip and smudge the perfectly applied plum lipstick, Emma nipped at the inside of her cheek. The pain was a welcome distraction.

She knew the mechanics of sex. Understood her role in the bedroom. To be a vehicle for someone else's pleasure and take what pleasure she could of her own.

But Dante was different. How he made her feel was different. She wanted to touch him in ways she'd never touched another. She wanted to be on her knees before him and bring him pleasure with her lips. Her tongue. Her mouth. She wanted him on his knees, wanted to place her calf over his shoulder and allow him to take what he wanted.

And it felt powerful to know it would be this way for them.

No one-sided pleasure, no race to the finish line and *Whoops, sorry about that.* No apologies at all.

With him, it would be mutual. A shared goal to please one another.

Dante's eyes moved over every exposed area of her skin. And it heated her from the inside.

She recognised it. The wildfire that would ignite as soon as his lips touched hers.

An ache pulsed inside her.

This time, she'd let him catch fire.

Let it roar inside her.

Let it roar inside them both.

She'd made her choice.

Tonight, she'd be with Dante without emotion. He'd fulfil her every physical desire, and she'd embrace the franticness. The intensity.

What was the harm?

Emma pushed her hand into the hard muscle of his chest. Felt the ripple of the white dress shirt beneath her fingers. Let the heat of his hand on hers warm her. Heat her from her toes to her scalp.

'Kiss me,' she demanded, and it felt powerful to demand it. To want him without fear.

'Emma,' he warned darkly. And she felt the rumble of it in his chest, beneath her hand.

'I need more than that. I need you to tell me exactly what you want, what you're choosing.'

Emma needed to say it out loud as much as he needed to hear it. That she was willing to accept his terms, the terms they had put in place together for this marriage to work.

'I choose our marriage. The contract. No emotion. Only desire. I choose...'

Slowly, she let her gaze move over his face. It was perfectly symmetrical. Black hair hung at his ears. High cheekbones sat above his powerful jaw and noble nose. And his eyes, a brown so dark, so deep, she could fall into them.

'You...' she breathed.

'Emmy...' Her name wasn't a warning. It was a plea.

She recognised it, because her body pleaded with her too. Begged her to give in to the heat between them.

To surrender. Emma rose on her tiptoes and began to close the distance between them. And with every millimetre she felt the anticipation climb inside her.

Until Dante finally caught her mouth with his.

CHAPTER SEVEN

DANTE WAS DROWNING in her. Drowning in Emma's kiss.

A growl rose in him as he caressed her lips.

The confirmation that she wanted to come back to him, to where she belonged, took his breath away. He couldn't get close enough to her, to the source of sustenance his body craved.

He had fantasised about this moment for too long. The fantasy had once been his reality. The taste of her lips. Warm. Spiced. And he'd sipped from her lips, again and again, indulging in her mouth, her tongue, until all he could taste was her.

Until she was gone.

Then the fantasy had become his wildest dream. Fevered nights and days remembering her. Trying to forget her. But wanting her. And here she was now, wanting him.

He tried to get even closer. To satisfy the compulsion to get nearer.

He bowed his chest into hers. Into her breasts. Pressed his hardness into her softness.

He palmed her with his hands. Caressed her naked shoulders. Stroked her waist as he inched his way towards her back, towards the naked dip in her spine, and pressed his fingers into her flesh. Dragged her into him.

But it wasn't enough.

So he devoured her.

He swept the crease of her mouth with his tongue until it opened for him, allowing him to taste her more deeply.

It still wasn't enough.

There was nothing between them but the thin barrier of their clothes. And what he wanted was to release her so that they could shed them, but he could not release her. Could not command his brain to do what he wanted. What he knew they both wanted.

'Emmy…' he moaned against her. And he barely recognised the visceral rawness.

His body was on fire, but his brain was whispering in tongues. His body was responding to a language he didn't speak.

Restraining him.

The shackles were invisible. But he felt them on his wrists. Holding him back.

Dante pleaded in silent prayer. He wanted to be gentle with her the first time they came together. But he felt anything but gentle. He wanted to take her here, in this garden.

But everything inside him was urging—*demanding*—he go slower. Taste every inch of the skin he had missed. Press against the heat of her and linger there, in the warmth of her.

Emma suddenly pushed him away, tearing his mouth from her.

The urge to reach for her, to keep his hold on her, was so strong.

Her eyes, wild and wide, heavy with desire, locked onto his.

And he watched, mesmerised, as she moved over to the table, took a seat, right on its edge.

He stood rooted to the spot. Aching. Watching.

'I want you. *Here...*' she breathed, and the confession halted whatever air had made it into his airways.

And still he could not move. Could not join her at the table's edge.

'Please,' she said, and his heart hammered.

If he took her here, now, that would be her memory of them.

The first memory of them coming together. He did not want that.

What do you want?

His gaze moved over her swollen lips. Proof of how strong their desire was. How strong it had always been.

And yet, it was not the same. He was not the same. She was not the same. He didn't know why. Only that it was different.

The people who had met at that charity event were not here.

Something snapped inside him.

Released him.

She deserved more. And so did he. He moved then. Claimed her chin beneath his thumb and forefinger, ignoring the rasp of her breath, the shudder she made as her bottom lip trembled.

She deserved more than quick satisfaction. More than an indecent encounter anyone could see.

'I can take you here,' he told her, and his erection pulsed. 'I can fall to my knees and taste you again. I can make you come with my mouth on you, with my fingers. I can ready you for me. I can do all those things. *More*. I can thrust inside you, right here. Right now.'

The delicate tendons in her throat constricted. 'But you won't?'

His thumb and forefinger gripped her chin more tightly. Forced her gaze to stay locked on his. Because he hated what his confession had caused her. He saw it. A flash of doubt. Of pain.

She thought he was rejecting her.

'Do not,' he growled, 'doubt how much I want this.' He released her chin and sought her hand. Claimed it and brought it between them. Placed her open palm on the part of him that ached for her.

'Do not doubt,' he said again, the hardness of him pulsing beneath her fingers, 'how much I want you, Emmy.' Her eyes blazed. 'I want you in every way imaginable. To be inside you...'

He closed his eyes because it was painful to resist. A deep hurt was growing inside him with his every word that opposed his frantic desire.

'Then why won't you?' she asked, her fingers on him. Tentatively she stroked him.

He opened his eyes. 'We deserve a bed,' he breathed raggedly.

He knew what he wanted now. Her in his bed. To savour her. To keep her there between the sheets where she couldn't escape. Wouldn't want to leave. Today. Tomorrow. Or ever.

'A bed?'

'I would prefer our bed in Mayfair,' he said, his abdomen flexing at the flash of an empty bed. Their bed. Abandoned by her.

'But we would never make it that long.'

His confession caused him to tremble at the effort it took to restrain himself. The effort of not doing what she'd asked him to do and take her. Here.

But he would not.

'You're shaking,' she gasped.

'As you will be,' he promised. 'If you let me take you to bed. I will make you come so hard your knees will shake. *Uncontrollably*. And then I will do it again, and again, until all you know, all you understand, is this. The need pulsing between us. A need that never dies. That always wants more.'

He was rigid with it now. Painful desire, and something else. Something he couldn't place.

The day he'd readied their new contract, three more years to explore the depths of their desire, he'd felt a contentment. An easiness he'd never had. Because for once, he'd not felt the urge for more, as Cappetta men always did. To climb higher peaks, or to parachute over more perilous terrains. His only urge was simply to keep her.

He felt that now, alongside his desire. Contentment.

He wasn't so naive. This obsession with her, his little crush, would end. *Eventually*. And then and only then would he end it.

But not yet.

'Will you let me take you to bed?' he asked, because that was what he needed. A bed and her in it.

There was nothing else to want. Nothing else *he* needed. Only her flesh. Only her body. Only sex.

'There will be no need to rush. No need to be quick.

And I won't be quick, Emmy,' he promised. A promise he'd keep like all the others he'd made to her. 'I will take my time with you. Savour you.'

'Savour me?' she asked, her lips parting on a mew.

It fed him.

Revived him.

His neck stiff with tension, he nodded his confirmation.

'Slowly,' he promised. 'I will savour every inch of you.'

He leaned down until his mouth hovered above the soft flesh beneath her ear and whispered, 'Will you come with me, Emmy?'

He pulled back just enough to watch as her blue eyes sought his and he let her hold them captive. Let her search their depths. Because he knew what she would see. Only the heat between them.

Tentatively, her fingers rose to his waist, travelled farther up, with feather-light precision. With splayed fingers and open palm, her hand sat on his chest.

Just like it had been at the beginning of them.

Then, slowly, she moved her hand from his chest and reached for his hand. And claimed it.

'I'll come with you.'

When he looked down at their hands, he saw their gold wedding bands glistening. Reminding him of the promises they'd shared with one another. The rules they'd vowed to obey.

She trusted him to take her back there. Back to the marriage they'd had before. Could still have by following the rules they had created.

Because without the rules there was no them.

His fingers tightened around hers.

'Come,' he rasped, and tugged her down the white stone path, back through the double doors.

Soon, so very soon, their clothes would be strewn on every surface, and they would at last be in bed, together. And they would stay there. Stay there until his obsession died.

With every step across the marbled foyer of the Cappetta hotel, Emma's skin tingled with anticipation. It spread up from her toes, up the backs of her calves, up the muscles in her thighs and pooled at the intimate heart of her.

Then it radiated out in waves.

Neither had spoken. But still he held her hand. Still, she held his.

Even as they entered the private lift to their suite, even as the steel doors closed.

Side by side, they stood, and the silence pulsed.

Never had a man shaken with desire for her. Never had a man wanted to…

Savour her.

Slowly.

But Dante had done, wanted to do, both of those things.

And it spoke to her. To the secret parts inside her that longed for those things. To be savoured. To be precious to someone. Protected because someone cared.

And he cared, didn't he?

The realisation was acute. It was a piercing pain in her chest. Because all the things her mother had been waiting for her father to provide, Emma had. With Dante.

He was taking care of her, had taken care of her, in all the ways she hadn't been able to take care of herself. Hadn't seen herself as worthy of. Or allowed herself to

want them. Because belief and hope, they were dangerous. Deadly.

She closed her eyes. Shut everything out. Because all
her life she'd been running from her feelings, her needs,
her secret desires. Afraid she'd turn out like her mum.
Unloved and unwanted. But Emma *was* wanted. Not
loved. But she was cared for. Protected.

And it was enough.

It was what she wanted.

Slowly, she opened her eyes, turned her head and
looked up at him from behind lowered lashes.

So why had she left when she had it so good?

Did it matter anymore?

Higher and higher the lift climbed, until it announced
its arrival at the top floor.

Dante turned, the invitation in his gaze mirroring her
own.

'We deserve a bed,' she said, because he was right.
They deserved to explore, to rediscover, their marriage
with care. With softness. With consideration.

'We do,' he agreed roughly.

Emma moved her gaze to the lift doors. Eyed her reflection in the steel. Stared at her body. A body he knew
intimately.

She wondered if he would cradle her breasts as softly
as he'd cradled her face in the hospital? Would he slowly
apply pressure as she moaned into his mouth? Would
she tell him what she liked? That she wanted her nipple
in his mouth and that she wanted him to suck? To bite?
Would he caress the swell of her stomach? Would his
hand move slowly or urgently to the dark hairs curling
between her legs?

She wanted to know all these things. How he would touch her. How his touch would be different.

The steel doors opened to their suite.

'Ready?' he asked roughly.

Was she? Was she ready to not only survive the night, but to *own* it.

'I'm ready.'

CHAPTER EIGHT

TOGETHER, EMMA AND Dante moved through the penthouse suite with haste. So quickly that she barely acknowledged how magnificent it was. A mansion all on one level. Made of black marble with silver edges and glass. Huge vases held small cherry blossom trees, pink petals falling everywhere.

As they reached the bedroom door, he slowed.

The fingers in hers loosened and were pulled from her grasp.

Dante opened the door, and stepped aside to allow her to enter. Her gaze moved to the floor-to-ceiling windows that formed two of the four walls of the room.

Outside she could see the bright lights on the city—gold and white and red.

How many rooms like this had she stood in with Dante? How many stories had they shared in rooms she couldn't remember? How many beds had they found each other in until he had demanded they have just the one bed?

Before he had proposed they marry?

Did it matter? Tonight, *this* would be their bed. The only bed she'd remember sharing with him.

Her eyes moved to the white stone wall to her left,

over the soft lights glowing like candles, down to the black wooden headboard carved with swirls, to the bed. An imposing bed of stark white pillows and black sheets.

Excitement pulsed through her in a tidal wave of heat.

She stepped towards the bed—

'Wait.' Strong fingers locked around her wrist. His large masculine hand commanded she be still.

'I don't want to wait,' she said, her skin tingling, her body demanding she find release from this tension holding her every limb hostage.

His thumb stroked the pulse point on her wrist. 'I want to undress you.' He released her wrist. Breath hit her nape, a whisper of warmth on her skin, and the pulse in her core quickened. *'Slowly.'*

He pressed in behind her, and her spine arched into him. The outline of his body penetrated hers, the heat of him seeping inside every pore of her exposed flesh.

Never had she been undressed with care when urgency demanded they were already naked.

It was dizzying.

'Then undress me,' she demanded, her voice smoky. And it felt like she was giving him more than the permission to remove her clothes. But to remove her armour too. Because never had anyone unwrapped her like a gift. Like she was something *special*. Or maybe Dante had, but she just couldn't remember.

'I will. But first I want to do this.' *Click.* Her hair fell from its high ponytail to fall to her shoulders.

His fingers speared into her hair, loosening the strands. 'I have dreamed of your hair. Feeling it through my fingers. Wrapped around my fist.'

Her heart hiccupped. 'You've dreamed of me?'

'Yes.' He swept her hair over her left shoulder, over her taut collarbone. And the touch was teasing. It was too light. Not what she wanted. She wanted his hands. She wanted his touch to imprint itself on her, to brand her.

When his knuckle grazed down her naked spine, she couldn't hold it in. The gasp.

'Every night—' the whisper of his lips grazed her nape '—I have thought of nothing but kissing you here.' Feather-light, he placed his mouth to the tip of her spine. 'And here.'

His lips lifted from her skin to move to the flesh of her throat. Where her neck met her shoulder. And a noise was ripped from her lips. A wail that demanded he give her more.

His mouth climbed higher, a teasing caress of his mouth, to the spot behind her ear, and Dante whispered, 'And here.'

And the lips that had fluttered gently across her skin now pressed deeper. Sank deeper into her flesh. He pulled the skin between them and sucked.

Until Emma panted. Until she was breathless with the sensations his mouth tugged from her core.

His fingers pressed into the dip of her spine and she gasped as he tugged the zip down her buttocks to the top of her thighs.

His hands spanned her waist as he brought her back into him, his arousal pressed into her bottom.

'Please...' Emma could barely stand it any longer.

'Turn around,' he commanded, and on unsteady feet, she did.

Her breath hitched as black eyes caught hers.

'Please what, Emmy?'

'More,' she confessed. 'I want *more*.'

'More of what?' he asked. 'My hands?' His hands moved back to her waist and up. 'My fingers?' His fingertips brushed the sensitive flesh beneath her arms.

Dante peeled the bodice of her dress down over her breasts, revealing the sheer black lace of her bra. And her nipples strained against it.

'My mouth?'

'Yes,' she replied, 'I want them all.'

His hands cupped her breasts.

'Like this?'

She swallowed. 'Harder.'

His fingers held her firmly, his thumbs flicking over the pebbled peaks. 'Better?'

'Yes.'

'And now, do you want my mouth?'

'Please,' she mewed. 'Yes, please.'

His head dipped to her breast, and he sucked her nipple into his mouth until it throbbed. *Pulsed*.

He lifted his mouth—

'No!' Her hands reached for him. Clung to the lapels of his black dinner jacket.

'No more?' he asked, nostrils flaring.

'No,' she corrected, her voice not her own. It was wanton. '*Please*, don't stop.'

With deft fingers, he released the front clasp of her bra and let it drop to the floor.

His eyes coveted her chest. 'You have beautiful breasts,' he said.

She cried out as he dipped his head again, took the neglected breast into his mouth and suckled.

The blood in her veins whooshed deafeningly with the speed of her heart.

He tugged at the skirt of her dress, pulling it down. But this time his lips remained on her skin. His kiss moved down the valley between her breasts. To the flat of her stomach. And her skirt went down with him. Past her thighs, her knees. Until it fell to the floor and pooled at her feet and she stepped out of it. And Dante was on his knees before her.

'For months,' he growled, his features tight, dark, 'I have thought of the taste of you. Your skin. How it trembles beneath my mouth. How it sings for me. For my touch.'

Her pulse slowed. She searched his gaze, watched as it burned with something primal. Possessive. 'Only my touch.'

The possessive sentiment didn't scare her anymore. It made her burn. Made her wet between her legs. It excited her.

His hands gently parted her thighs, and she opened them for him. 'Can you feel it, Emma?' he asked. 'The adrenaline building between us?' His thumbs stroked her on the inner flesh of her thighs. 'The power of it?'

Heart raging, she nodded.

'Put your left hand on my shoulder,' he demanded, and she did. She reached for him. Held on to the tight hard muscle of him and steadied herself.

Anticipation thrummed through her. Quickened her pulse. Her breathing. Every nerve ending was exposed.

His eyes holding hers, his hand stroked down her right inner thigh, to graze along her knee, until he gripped her sheer-black-stocking-covered calf and lifted it. Placed it on his shoulder.

He stroked back the way he came. Back up to her knee with a gentle drag of his fingers, up her thigh, until he stroked her. There.

'Do you want my mouth here?' he asked, his voice a dark thing. A hot thing that spoke directly to her sex. And it pulsed. Clenched in places she couldn't name. Couldn't decipher. But she wanted that. His intimate kiss.

'Please…' she breathed. 'Kiss me. Kiss me now.'

A guttural noise from deep in his chest vibrated in her ears. On her skin. And then his mouth was there again. Kissing her on top of the fabric. His tongue slowly sliding against her intimate folds.

Emma reached for his head and pushed her fingers into the raven silk of his hair and pulled his mouth closer to her core. The faster he moved his tongue, the deeper he licked, the ache inside her sharpened, tightened.

'Oh… Oh. *Oh!*' she gasped, again, and again, as he speared his tongue between her sex, until his lips claimed the pulsing nub at the apex of her sex and sucked.

Faster and faster, until she couldn't catch her breath. Couldn't breathe for the sensations rippling through her body. Sensations of unlimited pleasure and relentless passion that he was gifting her.

And the need for more was overwhelming. And it was demanding. Demanding that she chase it. This feeling. This rush.

Her hands moved everywhere. Over his scalp. His shoulders. Pulling him nearer to her.

With his hands on her hips, he held her steady against his mouth. Let her body rock against his mouth.

And then he released her and his hand went between her thighs, pulled aside her panties and claimed her over-sensitive nub without the hindrance of the lace. The pleasure was almost unbearable.

She threw her neck back involuntarily.

Two fingers entered her. Stretched her. Until they slipped in to the hilt, and pumped.

'Oh, my God!' Tightly, she held on to him, relying on the support of his shoulders. His hand on her hip. She was going to fall. She was—

'Coming,' she breathed. 'I'm—'

A third finger pushed inside her.

'Oh!' She was full, so full of him. But her body wanted more. It wanted the thick length of him where she ached the most.

'I want you inside me,' she admitted.

'Soon,' he breathed. 'I want to pleasure you first.'

Her thoughts became disjointed, disoriented.

'I want you wet,' he rasped. 'I want you ready to take me. All of me inside you,' he rasped, and his words fired her blood into a hot, raging, needy thing that needed more. More oxygen. More water. More of something that she couldn't identify. But most of all it needed him.

His fingers curled inside her. Found a place she didn't know lived inside her and pushed against it. Stroked it. Until all she could feel was pleasure.

Emma fought her release. It felt too big, both in this moment and the journey that she had been on to chase it. She knew that what was coming, what was building inside her, had the ability to break her, to shatter her, to change her completely.

And it was everything he'd promised it would be. A rush. A high she'd never found with anyone but him.

'Come for me,' he roared against her skin, her flesh singing for him.

He wanted this. *Her.* Undone in ways she could never have imagined in her wildest dreams. And she wanted it too. To strip herself of the chains she'd shackled herself with and surrender to it. To what they were. To who *she* was with him. Bold. Sensual. Fearless in his arms.

She truly understood now why she had chosen Dante. For the first time since her accident she was confident that this was where she was meant to be. Where she was always meant to be. In Dante's arms. In his bed. In this marriage they'd created to suit each other. She was safe to expose all her needs. All her physical wants. Without consequence.

Only then did she let go.

Without fear.

Without inhibition.

'Dante!' she screamed. Every syllable was torn from somewhere deep inside her...

Carefully, Dante withdrew from Emma before standing and reaching for her again. Pulling her into his embrace and lifting her into his arms.

'Dante—'

'Shush,' he breathed. Quietly, although nothing within him was quiet.

His body demanded more than her undoing. It not only demanded everything they'd had before, but it demanded... He wasn't quite sure. But he knew her being back in his arms didn't feel like enough. His gut told him so.

And yet he didn't trust it. His instinct was to fasten his mouth to hers and take them to bed and ignore that feeling. To find oblivion in the two of them coming together.

Never in his life had performance anxiety made him falter. But he was faltering now. Denying himself his primal needs because he was thinking about what came afterwards.

That concept was alien to him, though. He didn't quite know what to do with it. And so he'd do nothing; he'd stay firmly in this moment and he'd take his time. Prolong the moment until he would have to face that foreign feeling again.

His neck dipped, and he met her gaze.

'Thank you,' she said, and her fingers splayed on his heated cheek. 'That was—'

'Only the beginning,' he said, because he did not want her thanks. He wanted his wife back.

And she *was* coming back to him. It was all that mattered. Having her beneath him, where she belonged and where she'd stay until his body no longer ached.

He swept her into his arms and carried her over to the bed. And she clung onto him, her arms around his neck, breathing against it, her breath fanning across his flesh.

'I will make this good for you,' he promised rawly.

'I know,' she said. She trusted him to keep his word. To meet her every desire.

And he would.

He'd make her shake. Tremble. With a desire so rampant, so addictive, that neither would be able to think straight.

She reached for him as he set her on the edge of the bed, placing a hand on his stomach.

'I want to learn every inch of you,' she confessed, her fingers moving to the silver buckle of his belt. 'I want to learn how to give you pleasure too.' A blush bloomed a deep scarlet on her cheeks. But she did not release his eyes. She did not remove her hand. 'I want to pleasure you with my mouth.'

He nodded. A single dip of his head, because he didn't trust himself to speak. Because he had only missed her body, her mouth, not *her*.

Slowly, she unbuckled him. And he made himself stand still. Taut. As he prepared himself for the silkiness of her mouth. The warmth.

Belt open, she undid his button, splayed the waistband of his trousers, and her hand crept inside his boxers. She withdrew him with gentle fingers. Until he was free and his arousal stood tall and erect in her small, pale hand.

Her blond head dipped…

'Emma,' he said, and she flicked her tongue over the tip of him, the silken edge beading with his need for her to take him deeper.

And she took him, inch by inch, until her throat flexed and accept him, and he—

'Emma!' he roared as she sucked him. Used her pale hand to pump him in unison with the slide of her lips, the sheath of her warm, wet mouth.

He fisted her hair. Wrapped it around the palm of his hand. Watched her please him.

And he couldn't stand it. How easily she took him to the edge of his control. How easily she undid him. How easily she made a mockery of the way in which he ran his life, the rules he'd put in place.

'Emma, stop,' he growled, need lacing the words. Because she would not undo him yet. He wouldn't lose control. He would show her the strength of his control. The power he had over himself to resist the ultimate satisfaction so that he could bring them both to climax, together.

He drew an agonising breath into tight lungs. 'Can you feel what you do to me?' he asked breathlessly. 'I'm so hard, it hurts, Emmy. But I don't want to spill myself into your mouth. I want to be *inside* you. To feel you wrapped around me as I drive you to the edge again,' he said. 'I *need* to be inside you,' he confessed.

'I want that too,' she breathed, and with gritted teeth, he watched her slither back into the centre of the bed.

'Come to bed,' she breathed. It was all he'd wanted for months. To hear his wife say those words.

He reached for the tie at his throat. Loosened it, tugged it free, and let it flutter to the floor. The buttons were next. So many of them that it felt like an eternity before he could bare himself.

Her gaze seared his skin. But he didn't stop. He removed his trousers, his boxers, socks and shoes.

He crawled between her thighs. Felt her raise her hips to meet him, meet the hardness of him pulsing against her. And he removed the final barrier between them, the black lace of her panties. Pulling them down over her calves, her ankles, and tossing them aside.

On the way back, he kissed the exposed softness of her ankle bone, her knee, her inner thigh.

'Put your legs on my shoulders,' he commanded, because he wanted her open to him. For her to be in a position to take all of him so deeply she wouldn't be able to breathe for the fullness.

She did as he instructed, and he shifted against her, feeling how ready she was for him, the wetness at her core.

His need to be inside her was frantic, all consuming.

And he pressed into the intimate centre of her, entered her. Slowly, inch by inch.

He took his time, knowing that once he was fully inside her he would be lost to the urgency between them. Compelled by the need to drive into her again and again until his body was released from the hold she had over him.

He needed a moment to gain back a modicum of control.

'Dante, do you want to…stop?'

'Is that what you want?' he growled, his neck straining as he fought every instinct to thrust up inside her.

'No.' Her hair, strewn over the white pillow, moved with the shake of her head. And he wanted to fist it. Drag her mouth to his.

'I want to go slow,' he admitted. 'I don't want to hurt you.'

'You won't hurt me,' she promised. 'My body will remember you.'

Her hips flexed, and she took him inside her a little more. 'But if you want to stop,' she said, and he heard the tightness in her voice. Heard a need he mirrored in his taut muscles, begging for release. 'We can.'

'I do not want that,' he ground out.

Her hands, open palmed, smoothed over his chest.

And when she ran her fingertips over his bruised nipples, her touch ignited a fire in his skin. And he was burning.

'Then don't stop.'

Sweat beaded on his brow. 'I won't.'

He thrust up into her.

'Yes!' Her face contorted. 'Again. *More.*'

He gripped her hips, plunged, hard and deep.

Dante strained against his instincts, despite her words, despite his, to do what he wanted and take her mindlessly.

His muscles burned with his resistance. If he did these things, if he let go, gave in to the animalistic instinct to rut these thoughts away, he'd hurt her.

Slowly, he slid into her again and again, let her body remember him. Welcome him back.

Her ankles locked around his neck. 'Faster, Dante,' she pleaded. *'Harder.'*

And her whispered words were what his body longed for. Had longed for, for months. And she knew, didn't she? She knew what he needed because she needed it too. To end the endless days of foreplay, the months of self-denial. To surrender to this agony between them.

'Dante, *please*!'

And whatever control he'd held on to shattered.

He possessed her.

Her body.

He came back to the only home he'd ever know, ever needed. And the truth of that overwhelmed him now.

Emma was his *home.*

And that was terrifying. But he pushed it aside.

'Never stop,' she said, and he wanted to roar.

'Dante!' Her nails bit into his skin. Into his hands. She

contracted around the pulsing hardness of him, with the sweetest, most delicious vise grip.

He panted, his breath coming out in short, sharp rasps. But he did not close his eyes. Neither did she.

In sync, their hips locked. Their bodies tightened. And he no longer knew where she ended and he began.

'Emma!' he shouted as he came. Harder than he'd ever come.

And the pleasure blinded him to everything but the feel of her beneath him.

Panting, he collapsed on to his elbows and buried his face in her throat.

'That was incredible.'

'*You* are incredible,' he husked into her throat—her skin. Because she was something mystical. A creature who had crept into his life and bewitched him.

'Thank you,' she said, her hands sweeping up his back and wrapping around him.

And he was no longer blind. He could see with an un-diluted clarity.

He'd won.

Emma was back.

And he'd keep her here.

Beneath him.

Where she belonged.

For now.

CHAPTER NINE

HIS CHEST ROSE beneath her cheek. His breath was rhythmic and his heart thrummed steady and strong in her ear. His arm was possessively curled around her, his hand locked to her hip. Emma couldn't move even if she wanted to. One hand on his stomach and one by her side, she stayed exactly where she was.

She'd never spent the night in anyone's bed. Never shared one for longer than she had to in her existing memory. She'd certainly never fallen asleep. But she'd slept all night with him in a tangle of limbs.

The sun streamed through the windows, highlighting the contours on his chest. Golden undertones chased by dark shadows of hair between deep lines on his abdomen led down towards the duvet that covered the lower half of his body.

Warmth gathered in the pit of her stomach. Last night had been...*a lot*.

It hadn't been perfunctory or stolen. It had been transcendent, powerful, addictive. Because even now, though her body ached, she wanted more. More of him on her. More of her on him.

She could do it *now*. Slide down his body, under the duvet, and take him in her mouth. Wake him like that.

She could do what she liked. Take and give as much as she desired, and he'd meet her stroke for stroke as he had last night. And she'd meet him too. Kiss for kiss. Thrust for thrust. A mutual consideration of each other's pleasure.

It was *safe* sex. Emotionally and physically, she was—

Panic flared in her ribcage.

They hadn't used protection. She hadn't thought, hadn't—

Her hand shot to the flat of her stomach.

What would it mean if she was pregnant? Did they have a clause in their contract? Would that void it? She didn't want children. Did *he*? Eventually? When he married someone without a contract? When he found—

Her stomach churned.

He didn't believe in love. He said he didn't want it, that he understood, as she did, it was a lie.

'What's wrong?' He must have sensed her anxiety. Woken to it. Or perhaps she'd alerted him to her panic by tightening her grip on his stomach.

She froze. Stayed where she was on his chest. Her hand splayed taut on his abdomen.

'We didn't use protection,' she said, and listened. But the tempo of his heart remained unchanged. It was calm. Steady. 'I might be pregnant.' *Nothing.* 'I don't know when my last cycle was. I've never been consistent. I've never not used a condom. We—*I*—could get emergency contraception.'

Idly, his fingers stroked her hip bone. 'You can't be pregnant, Emma.'

'How can you be so sure?' she asked.

'I can't have children,' he said flatly as his other hand

moved to her hair and smoothed over it. Over her scalp. 'I had a vasectomy many years ago. Before we met.'

A feeling settled in her chest, something heavy. And she couldn't distinguish it from relief or sorrow. It felt very similar to the blow she'd felt when Dante had told her of the loss of her mother. But that was stupid, wasn't it? To mourn the fact she'd never carry his child?

'Do you regret it?' she asked and immediately felt that she should apologise. 'I'm sorry. I shouldn't—'

'No, I don't regret it,' he answered matter-of-factly. 'I never wanted children.'

'Why not?' she asked, curiosity blooming where it shouldn't.

His heartbeat quickened.

'My mother used me as leverage against my father. He wanted an heir, and she sold him one. I never wanted to be in a similar position. Where my child was used as a bargaining chip.'

Emma jolted into a sitting position, dislodging his hands, and stared at him. 'Your mother *sold* you?'

'She did.' He remained where he was against the pillows. And he seemed almost relaxed, comfortable. But how could that be the case when he had told her something so abhorrent?

'For how much?' she spat. 'Her soul?'

He shrugged. 'Lifetime financial security and a private island the size of a small country.'

'She—'

His eyes flashed. 'Is unimportant,' he remarked, obviously eager to be done with this line of enquiry. But Emma was not done.

'How can she be? She—'

'Has no bearing on my life.'

'You made the choice not to have children because of her.'

'And I would make that choice again.'

'How can you be so calm?'

Dante shrugged. And Emma immediately understood.

'Because you thought there was no other choice,' she said simply.

Her heart ached for him. For the little boy who had been sold and abandoned by his own mother. And she wanted to cry for him. For the man who chose to never risk a child of his being used as collateral.

She'd never wanted them either. *Children*. Never wanted to raise a child on her own. Never wanted to raise a child to *be* alone. Teach her—*him*—it was safer that way.

You aren't alone anymore.

He scowled. 'I made the choice to protect all parties involved.'

Emma became conscious of her own nakedness then. Aware of how intimate this conversation felt.

'Do not worry about the choices of the man you never knew,' he said, inching closer. 'He was eighteen. He'd just lost his father. It was the right choice to make. He—*I*— would make it again.'

His hands caught her face, then cradled her cheeks as he made her meet his eyes. 'Besides, it is a gift to be inside you without risk or consequence.'

His light-hearted tone was forced, she could tell. But she also knew that this discussion was over. And just as quickly her uncertainty was replaced by need. Unable to resist, aching for him, she kissed him.

She wanted him to pulse inside her as he had last night. She wanted him to fill her with his hardness, to push her over the edge of desire once again.

She climbed onto his lap. Slid her thighs down the bareness of his. Felt his arousal find the heart of her and tease at her entrance. She rode him, stroking herself against him.

'Emma,' he moaned against her lips. And she let it feed her newfound confidence in her sensuality. A sensuality he'd brought to the surface.

And it felt good to be bold. To be brave. To take this pleasure for herself simply because she wanted it. Wanted *him*.

'Lie back,' she said as she gently guided him back into the pillows.

And then her hands were seeking his, linking and entwining them, raising them above his head and holding them there.

The tips of her breasts were teasing against his chest. She tore her mouth from his and rose above him. Taking control, exerting her power over him.

Slowly, she took the tip of him inside her, before sinking down and taking him all. Taking him deep.

Her head fell back, her mouth opened and a moan was wrenched from her. A sound she'd never heard her body emit. It was a roar. A screech. A plea.

Emma knew all she could do was trust in their connection and surrender to it. To this urge to follow her instincts and embrace it all. The connection of their minds, their bodies. For as long as it was there.

'*Ah!*' He raised his hips as his hands pulled her down onto him. And it was too deep. Not deep enough.

'Dante…'

'I want to pour myself inside you,' he growled. 'I want to fill you while you pulse around me. I want to feel you tighten. Squeeze me. Until there is nothing left for me to give you.'

She lifted her hips and pushed back down. Again and again, she took him deeper than she thought her body would allow.

His breath hissed from his mouth, encouraging her to ride him faster. Take him deeper.

And Emma rode him faster.

Took him deeper.

'I'm coming,' she said, and this time she didn't resist it. She leaned into it.

She didn't have to close her eyes. She didn't have to hide who she was because he knew who she was. She was his wife. He knew her body. What she liked. This was not a one-night stand to receive a perfunctory release.

He knew *her*. And she wanted to know him too. To give him pleasure. To receive her own. From his lips. From his body. On her. In her.

'Emmy!' he shouted, and filled her. Poured himself inside her. And she was lost in the contractions of her body. To his thickness. To his heat.

Emma lost herself to her husband.

Dante's plan had worked.

His wife was in his bed.

For almost twenty-four hours, she'd given herself to him. And he'd taken everything she was willing to let him have. They'd played out every single one of his fantasies.

He closed his eyes. Stilled the fingers stroking down her spine. Closed his eyes to the blond hair fanned out across his chest. Shut out the warmth of her body against his. Her sated, exhausted body.

He'd done that to her. Fatigued her. Pleasured her until the pleasure had seemed endless. Until she'd begged him to never stop.

He should be elated.

He should be content.

But there was no ignoring it. No ignoring that their connection had widened, deepened. That this thing between them, far from being sated, was more powerful.

It just wouldn't *die*.

And he could take her again, wake her with his kiss and accept his welcome into her body. Drive his need for her out of his body and into hers.

But it would reignite again, he knew. And continue to reignite over and over again.

She asked far too many questions, made him think far too much. Made him forget every rule he'd ever made to keep himself at a distance.

He was trying his best to remember the rules. But she kept forgetting.

And every time she forgot them, every time she asked a question he did not want to hear or think of, he'd remind her what they were. That there was no more, there was no promise of forever, of happily-ever-after. But she persisted. Would not be distracted by sex any longer.

How could he make her understand?

He wanted to be alone. He needed to be away from the bed. Away from her.

The garden flashed in his mind, along with her story of fairy lights and reading books under trees. Where all was still. All was quiet. All was safe from a world that was too loud.

He had a similar place, didn't he? No flowers, or fairy lights, but a room. A similar place in every country, every city. Somewhere he could go when he needed peace, needed quiet.

He was not so selfish, was he? To leave her behind after…

And yet, perhaps, this was how he could make her understand his need to keep people at a distance. That for him, emotional connection wasn't something to be embraced but was to be avoided.

So he'd take her with him. To the place in Shinjuku City that he went to when he needed to centre himself, to be alone. He would show her that he wasn't a stranger to keeping himself distanced.

He swallowed thickly.

He resisted the urge to kiss her. To wake her, as he had too many times to count. Instead, he stroked her. Her hair. Her spine. Her cheek.

'Emma, wake up.'

She stirred beneath his fingers. Her bare back arching into his touch.

She pushed the hair from her eyes. 'I'm awake,' she said, and ran her open palm down his torso.

His pulse accelerated.

Lust coiled in his gut, giving life to what always lived beneath his skin. His readiness for her. To possess her.

He caught her wrist—pulled her fingers away and

brought her knuckles to his mouth, brushed them against his lips.

He could be tender, couldn't he? Considerate? He was not—

He swallowed down whatever was in his throat, because he didn't want to taste it. His voice uneven, he finally spoke.

'I want to take you somewhere.'

CHAPTER TEN

IN THE BACK of the luxury car with cream leather and silver accents, they sat side by side. And together, they watched out of black windows as the car travelled through Japan's city of twinkling lights and soaring skyscrapers, until it swept through softly lit sleeping streets.

Dante swept his gaze over the profile of her. The way her fringe covered her forehead, the flick of her golden lashes, the slope of her elegant nose and the pink pout of her mouth.

Her eyes were latched on to the floating scenery, but he watched her. Watched the blue depth of her gaze that said so much, too much, when her mouth spoke words. Told him things he hadn't asked to hear and asked questions that compelled him to answer, leading to more questions.

Dante pressed his lips into a thin line and locked his jaw. He did not want to speak. He did not want to hear. He wanted to be still. *Alone.*

While Dante had travelled the world alone, he'd never taken her with him. He'd lived his life, and she'd lived hers. An arrangement that had suited them both.

Until it didn't.

Until he'd travelled across half the globe to return to

their house to find her in the bed they shared, only to find that she wasn't there.

But she was here now.

The warm beige coat with a flicked-up collar hiding the bruises his mouth had created on her throat. Marking her.

He wanted to see it. His brand on her flesh.

He swallowed, drew his gaze down the loose white shirt, the thighs of her jean-clad legs, and down to the flesh-coloured heels on her feet.

His lust was hot and constant. It remained even when he didn't summon it. Even when he tried to bury it.

Throughout their marriage, he'd given her everything he'd thought she'd wanted. Exclusivity to him and his world. His billions to do with as she pleased. His body. But never his thoughts. Never his...*trauma.*

And he hadn't wanted access to hers either.

He'd never wanted her explanations of why she spent so much time in the garden. Why she was happy for their marriage to be governed by a contract.

But now he knew, and he could not unknow these stories she'd told him of her need to find a place of security and safety. To retreat from the world outside.

She'd called him her garden, and his instincts had told him to slam down his defences and guard against her confession. But he *was* her garden, wasn't he? Not in a romanticised way. But he was her security. He was her safety. In his arms, she was safe.

And understanding why she needed that from him, needed it from their marriage, weighed heavily on him. It was precious the trust she had placed in him. Fragile.

To tell him this when she didn't remember the last few years of her life, didn't remember him.

He didn't know how to hold space for such a delicate thing. How not to drop it. How not to break it, to break her. He did not want to break her.

The car halted beneath a blinking street light.

Dante scanned the street and realised they had arrived. It was an ordinary-looking place. With ordinary people walking past it towards their destination. Others stood still, talking under artificial light, and laughing. Some in groups. Some in pairs. Some holding hands.

Soft warmth infiltrated his fingers. He turned to look at the source and saw Emma's hand covering his own lying on the seat between them.

And he saw the gold ring he'd given her. That marked her as his for the world to see. At least until one of them decided they no longer wanted to be married.

He didn't like that thought, he realised. It made his nostrils flare with disgust.

He liked his ring on her finger. He liked that she was his. That she belonged to him. Because she did. And he liked that she was here. With him. Wearing her ring in this place he'd never shared with anyone else. It felt warm to have her with him. It felt...

Right.

No, that couldn't be it, could it?

'Are we getting out?' Her voice slid into his ear.

He was not so naive. He was still obsessed with her. His crush. His wife.

More obsessed than he'd ever had been, because now he wanted the thoughts in her head. Wanted her to ask questions, wanted to answer them. Despite the rules. The playbook.

Maybe they could write their own playbook. Get to know one another outside of the sex. Not love, never love. But introduce emotions.

Because her desire for stability, normality, did things to him, didn't it? Those were things he didn't know how to define or if he liked them. It was different. She was different. And she made him feel...*different*.

Was she right?

Had he married her for the normality it offered, a normal he'd never truly known? Stability, sameness, one woman in his bed, in a house they shared—was that why he'd missed her? Been so displaced without her? Was this pain inside him more than a sexual ache? More than a need to possess her physically? But to...

What?

He was not normal. He wasn't raised to be normal. He could never be those things for her. And she deserved them, didn't she? This normal life she craved. A man she came home to, who was her constant. He wasn't *that* man.

Then why are you still here?

'Dante?' His eyes met her questioning ones.

'Yes, we're getting out,' he said, and removed his hand from beneath hers as he stepped out of the car, resisting the urge to recapture it and hold it tight.

He didn't know why he was holding his breath. Why he waited with his lungs burning for her to follow him. But he did. He waited on the pavement of this ordinary street for her to join him.

'In there,' he said, and nodded towards the two black double doors to her right.

She looked at the doors. No sign to indicate what lay on the other side. To indicate if she was allowed inside. But she moved towards them and pushed one open without hesitation.

Perhaps the threat had never been outside the doors of their Mayfair house. Perhaps he was the threat. She had trusted him to keep her safe and he'd hurt her, hadn't he? By not considering what it meant to Emma when he left her behind.

Door ajar, one pointed heel inside the door, she waited for him. 'Are you coming?'

His body answered for him. A tightening in his solar plexus. Because still it lived inside him. The overwhelming need to be close to her, to be near her, to keep her close to him.

He could adapt, he knew. He could change the rules. He could show her that he hadn't listened to her stories with complete emotional detachment. But did he want to? That was the question.

Dante followed her into a place that he had thought to be his alone. A place he didn't think she belonged. He'd brought her halfway around the world to be here with him. And he could have taken her anywhere. He'd planned to seduce her with adventure and newness.

He could have taken her into Shinjuku City, dazzled her with the noise, the bustle, the lights, the smells unique to the little alley that was so big in atmosphere and its exotic food offerings, it rivalled London's Soho.

But he'd chosen to bring her here, to a place he didn't share with anyone. Not with clients. Not with anyone. It was *his*. It was not a garden. It was not a romantic place of pink petals and green grass. It was a building made of brick without windows and closed doors with locks that bolted shut behind him.

Tonight, he wasn't taking her to bed. He was taking somewhere where it would only be them.

Dante followed Emma inside.

The jolt of metal reverberated in the silence.

'You've locked the doors?'

'No one will enter now,' he answered. 'Only a select few know of its existence. But...'

'But?'

'Now, if they try to enter, they will know it's occupied.'

A long tunnel stretched out before her. Red fluorescent lights flickered above. Shadows blinked into focus in pink hues. She moved forward. Reached out and touched the wall. Let her fingers travel through the winding foliage climbing upwards. But climbing to where?

'What is this place?' she said, and she felt the tightness, the anticipation threading through her limbs.

'You'll see,' he said, his voice low and deep, echoing in the dark silence.

Heat rushed against her nape. He was so close, two feet behind her, maybe a little more, and yet he was so far away.

It was an imaginary whisper of his breath on her skin. But she felt it. The closeness of him. The heat driving her forward. The presence behind her pushing her to an unknown end.

'I'll see?' she asked.

'Yes,' he said. 'This is a place I come to when I want to be alone.'

'But you aren't alone.'

'I know.'

Her heart faltered. Her pulse beat without a steady throb, only an echo of it.

'And do you bring others here when you want to be alone?' she asked, her chest tightening. Painfully.

'Never.'

'Never?'

'Only now,' he said. 'Only *you*.'

Blood rushed through her veins. Her heart hammered at the confirmation that she was the only one to come here with him.

It meant something, didn't it? Even though she had no idea where he'd brought her or where he was taking her. Or what she'd find when she came to the end.

'What do you do when you come here?'

'Eat.'

Still, his voice carried. A physical torture that did not touch her skin. But it pierced into flesh. Drove inside her.

'But there aren't any restaurants here,' she said over her shoulder, walking forward.

'There are several hundred,' he corrected. *Jidō-hanbaiki.*'

'Is that a restaurant? *Where?* I can't see it,' she said, turning her gaze to the long walls at her sides. 'There are no people. No chefs. No waiters. There are only—'

She paused.

There was a door.

And he closed in on her now. Stood behind her. Inches away instead of feet.

'Go inside,' he urged.

She raised her hand to the silver looped handle. Touched it. But she didn't pull, didn't push.

She lingered in this dark place where it was only the two of them standing still in the darkness. Together.

He moved. Closer. Still not touching her. But the distance between them, instead of centimetres, became millimetres and she couldn't breathe for the need to turn and press herself into him. Into his chest. Into the breadth and bulk of him, and—

He shifted. Turned the distance, the space between them, into nothing, and touched her.

His fingertips feathered her cheek, pushed the hair behind her ear, and he leaned in farther, until his breath was real, hot beneath her earlobe.

'Don't you want to go inside?'

'What's in there?' she breathed.

'It will be only us.' His chest rose, and hers rose with it. She pushed at the handle, and the door opened.

Warm yellow light infiltrated the darkness. She stepped forward and instantly regretted it as she moved away from the heat of him.

She longed to turn around. Return to him, to his arms. To surrender to this burn in her gut. To the flame growing brighter inside her. Fiercer by the second.

She stepped onto an over-polished white-and-black-speckled marble floor.

The quaintness of the homely potted plants, standing tall in every corner, the mismatched chairs, and well-worn tables, the pictures hung on the walls of smiling faces eating, a different delicacy in each photograph, the white bowls stacked high on a dark breakfast bar, consumed her.

She couldn't help it. She stepped farther into the room.

'You come here?' she asked. 'When you want to be alone?'

'Yes,' he confirmed, and she felt him enter the space with her. Fill the room with his presence.

She looked at the various coloured and sized rectangular machines standing in front of each wall but the photo wall.

Eyes wide, she turned to him. 'Vending machines?'

'Jidō-hanbaiki.' He nodded. *'Jihanki* for short.'

'Why here?'

'Why not here?' He hooked a brow. 'They are a cultural phenomenon here,' he explained. 'Vending machines can be found…everywhere. But inside these walls, you can be anywhere in the world with a press of a button. Anything you long to taste, to drink. From the most decadent ingredients to the most mundane. They are here. In this room.'

'But if you want something, you can have it in any room you like,' she said. 'Anywhere in the world you like.'

She ran her fingers through her hair, looked at him and then at the machines. So many of them. Several hundred choices of what to eat, what part of the world she wanted to taste, and yet she would be in one room. In one place.

'I thought you might enjoy this.'

'But why this room?' Her brow furrowed. 'Why this—' her eyes wandered, roamed the normality of it '—this place?'

'It is something different,' he said, and came to her. Lifted his hand, his fingers, and coiled a loose lock of hair around his finger. 'It is my garden.'

She frowned. 'Your garden?'

He swallowed thickly, and she watched the drag of his Adam's apple with bated breath.

'First, we will eat. Then I will tell you a story about a boy who found a place. A room. *A garden.*' The pressure on her scalp increased as his fingers tugged, not intentionally, not to hurt. But she felt the tension in his fingers. In his body. 'And I will explain why I have brought you here with me—why it had to be *here.*' He released the lock of hair. But her scalp still tingled. Her skin.

He turned his back on her. And breathlessly, she watched him.

Dante moved to the breakfast bar. The bowls clinked as he removed two from the stack. Removed cutlery from the stainless-steel containers holding them.

He moved again. One step after another, and he placed the bowls on the table. Set the cutlery aside each bowl and moved to a machine. Lifted his hand and pressed a button.

The machine whirled.

Emma didn't speak. Didn't move. She pretended to be invisible. A fly on the wall in a moment of Dante's life, his world, a place he had found where he could be alone. Wanted to be alone. And yet he'd invited her inside. It felt precious to be here. She felt precious. *Wanted.*

The aroma of ginger filled the air as the machine delivered a cup. He repeated the procedure until Dante retrieved two cups. He moved back to the bowls he'd prepared and poured the liquid inside each bowl.

'Chicken and ginger soup,' he said. He exhaled heavily. Pulled out the ordinary wooden chair, with a high back and no arms.

'Sit down, Emma.' She did, and he took his seat in front of her. Their eyes met. 'Eat.'

Together they picked up their spoons, dipped them into the soup and in sync, brought them to their lips.

It was a togetherness she'd never experienced, but her mother had craved it. Simple meals enjoyed by two. In companionable silence. In mutual understanding—the world outside could wait. Because the world outside was cold. Lonely.

The silence ricocheted in her ears. The comfortableness of it. The warmth. The realisation formed as clear as the broth before her. She could be anywhere in the world, anywhere she desired with a press of a button. And yet, she desired only to be with him. In this place. Safe in his company. Safe in their marriage. Safe with him.

Dante placed his spoon down on the worn table. 'My father employed an army to raise me. A high turnover of staff to feed me from the moment I was pulled from my mother's womb,' he told her. And she felt the pull of emotion in his words. The way he had to drag them from deep inside him. And she understood how hard that was. Understood because she had felt that way on the terrace of their hotel, when she had told him her story. Her story that she'd told no one else. But him. And so she didn't speak. She opened her ears and listened to his story.

'Nannies. Teachers. *Staff*,' he continued, his voice dark and heavy And it pushed itself through her consciousness. 'They were always around. Always talking. Always...*there*.' His face twisted into something ugly. 'And yet they were also not really there. At least not for me. They did not care for the boy in their charge, or for the teenager, the young man I became. Over the years, one face blended into several others. A name didn't matter because they all answered to one man. They answered to my father. To the rules he had set out for how to raise me.

'Whether I was in Italy, Switzerland or Nepal, they followed. Whether it was in a country estate in England, a castle in Sicily, a penthouse suite in Japan... I was surrounded by people. I was never alone. Never away from the noise—'

'So, you found your own garden?'

'I found a place,' he corrected. 'A room where I could choose to be. Not a place where my father ordered other people to take me. It was a different place in each city, each town. Whether it was a cafe in the village. A bookstore in a cobbled street. A room on a street no map knew. I entered it because I chose to be there. I paid them to close the door behind me. I—'

'You sneaked out in the dead of night to escape.'

Her heart pounded. They were the same. Him and her. And for him to confess that was big, she knew. They'd both been abandoned, in one form or another. Left to fend for themselves. But they had found each other. Created something...something that was theirs. Normal. *Unique*.

'You escaped,' she said and exhaled unsteadily, 'being alone in a house full of people who didn't care while your father conquered the world. Just for a while. Just for a time, you forgot the hardness. The loneliness. You created a world where all was quiet. Where all was still. A safe place where *you* wanted to be. You ruled over it, not your father, and you dictated who could enter. Who—'

'And I chose you,' he said. 'We chose this marriage. Because we wanted the same things. *Want* the same things. No borrowed beds. No temporary places to find respite. We share a house where we understand—'

'Each other?' she asked.

'I know you, and you know me,' he said and never had anyone known her.

He was on her side, wasn't he? They wanted the same things. *Needed* them. A safe place they could share together where love had no home, but she did. She had a home.

She wanted this. This marriage. She wanted to stay. Stay where she had someone. Had him on her side.

'I brought you here to show you, prove to you that I didn't need our marriage to be a safe haven, that I had places I could come for that. But I have realised that although our marriage has never required it, although we have never wanted it before, we can be each other's safe place.

'It was safer before to leave the noise and other people outside. Because if I let them inside, if I learned their faces, learned their names, then they could leave. And them leaving would be too much. It was safer to not get attached. To keep them at arm's length. I kept *you* at arm's length,' he admitted.

'You kept me at arm's length?'

He nodded. 'Yes, and I was wrong.'

'Wrong?'

'To shut you out,' he confessed. 'We are the same. Our needs are the same. We are no risk to each other. I can be your garden, Emma.'

He scowled. A thousand emotions flashed on his tightly drawn features. And she couldn't read a single one.

'I *am* your garden,' he corrected, 'and you are mine. Our marriage is the safe place. Our marriage is a safeguard against all we do not want. Love. Emotional attachment. We are each other's safe place, Emma.'

'A safe place?' She looked at him. His dark hair was neatly combed over to the side; soft and billowy from being newly washed, it teased at his ears. Dark stubble covered his cheeks, his sharply angled jaw. Leading her eyes down his throat to his shoulders, broad and sheathed by a suit jacket that sat on him like a second skin, over the fitted black T-shirt revealing the tautness of his bronze chest.

'Yes,' he said.

She lifted her gaze back to his.

She'd found what she thought she'd never wanted.

Safety with a man.

With him.

The organ inside her chest fluttered as wildly as a million bees buzzing towards home. Towards their queen. And it didn't matter to them. To the bees, where home was, because home was their queen.

Home was right in front of her, wasn't it?

He was her garden. *He* was her safe place. He was giving her everything she'd always wanted. And things she'd never considered as a way to get them. A relationship. Marriage.

But he was showing her he could provide for her needs. From her simplest need to her most extravagant. The whole world surrounded them. He was offering her the world. He was offering *his* world. A safe place. Where she would be warm. Cared for. Protected. Wanted. But not loved. Because neither of them wanted that.

'And maybe this is the reason you left. I kept you on the outside. But I know your face. I know your name. You can come inside, Emma. You can stay. Because in here, and in our house, in our bed, I will give you what you need. Security. A safe place from the hardness. I wanted you to know, for you to understand, when I take you to bed, when I possess your body, I can give you what it is you need. To know that I can provide it by giving you everything you don't have.'

Suddenly, Emma was slammed with the last five years of her life.

Her spoon clanked into the empty bowl.

Emma remembered everything. The breakdown of her marriage. Her reasons for staying. Her reasons for leaving.

She knew why she'd left. *She remembered.*

She stood. The chair screeched backwards. She'd left, abandoned their marriage, the contract they'd agreed to, because she *had* started to get emotionally invested in their marriage. She had wanted more than either of them had agreed to give one another. She had wanted this man she'd sworn never to need. Never to—

'What is it?' Dark and intense, his eyes probed hers. 'What's wrong?'

Emma closed her eyes. She needed a minute, a moment, to collect herself. Because she was hurting.

Her chest, her heart, ached.

She heard the slide of his chair. His footfall coming towards her. Firm fingers claimed her chin. She opened her eyes. Met his. Dark and probing.

'What is it?' he demanded roughly.

'I don't feel well.' Her core trembled in deep, rhythmic spasms. 'I'd like to go back to the hotel. I'd like to…'

She didn't know.

She'd got emotionally attached.

She'd broken the rules.

But he didn't know that.

To him, she'd just left. She'd abandoned him. Like his mother. His father. She'd left him alone, without a safe place, without explanation.

And still he'd come for her.

Still, he was here.

And he was wrong; she *was* a risk. It wasn't safe for him in this place with her. She wanted all the things he'd locked outside. And she'd brought them inside with her.

'I'm sorry,' she breathed, because she was. Sorry for breaking the rules. Sorry for needing him. For wanting him in ways they'd never agreed to. Sorry for wanting what he didn't want. Sorry for letting him lock the doors behind her, for letting him learn her name, her face, when she was the danger. She was everything he didn't want. And he'd let her in. He'd—

Dante released her chin. 'You are exhausted, Emma.' He shook his head. 'I should have let you sleep.'

He picked her up and held her against him. And she let him carry her back the way they'd come. She closed her eyes. Pushed her face into the crook of his neck.

She wouldn't let the tears fall.

She wouldn't cry.

But she knew when they left this place, there was no going back now for either of them.

CHAPTER ELEVEN

DANTE CLIPPED EMMA'S seat belt and told the driver to take them back to the Cappetta Continental.

She collapsed against the seat and watched out of the window. Everything looked different. Felt different. The sleeping streets were too grey, too dim. The city lights, the busy billboards of flashing images, nonsensical.

Emma hadn't only betrayed herself. She'd betrayed Dante. And now she understood just how deeply.

She'd run away, abandoned him, without explanation. She'd left him alone in a house with nothing but empty noise. With faces of people who didn't care, who would walk out of his life without a backward glance. Staff who were there to meet his every need, but who didn't know his face. They didn't know his name. They did not know him.

Emma knew him.

Her stomach hurt. She wanted to sob at the emptiness she hadn't recognised before. This emptiness that had only ever been absent when he'd been with her. Inside her. Filled the hollow where he'd branded her. Ruined her.

And she was ruined, wasn't she?

She'd ruined everything because she'd caught feel-

ings. So why then did she not feel ruined? Why was she
warm? Why was she—

She was a fool.

The car stopped outside the hotel, ablaze in pink light.
Dante stepped out of his side and opened her door. She
looked up, met the questioning dark brown of his eyes,
and she understood her time was up. She had to tell him
her memory had returned. She knew why she'd left.

'Shall I carry you?'

She shook her head. How could she let him carry her,
hold her, when she was the enemy? When she was everything he didn't want? He never should have taken her
to his place. He never should have let her in.

'No.' She swallowed it down. The lump in her throat
felt as though it was blocking her airway, making it difficult to breathe. She had no choice. She was going to
have to reveal herself. Expose her crimes. And then it
would be over.

They would be over.

'Come.' He offered her his hand. Long, thick bronze
fingers reaching for her. How many times had he claimed
her hand? Held it? Comforted her when she did not deserve it? She did not deserve him. His softness. His trust.
She was not his safe place. She was not his garden. And
he could no longer be hers.

Emma reached out her hand to him, and he claimed it.
Supported her as she stepped out of the car, and together
they walked into the hotel, to the lift. And she saw none
of the hotel lobby. Only him. Only his hand. The strength
of it closing around hers and keeping her steady.

But she was not steady. Inside, she trembled. Inside,

she knew, after tonight, after she told him the truth, he'd never hold her hand again.

The steel doors closed, sealing them inside.

Her throat ached. She swallowed repeatedly, trying to soothe it. To prepare it for the story she knew she must tell. But she wasn't prepared. She wasn't ready.

How different her body felt from the last time they'd been in here together just a few hours earlier. It wasn't anticipation flooding through her in waves as it had been before. It was a heaviness. A breathless dread. She was rigid, sweating beneath her coat.

Higher and higher the lift climbed until the ping of arrival boomed into the air between them.

Hand in hand, side by side, they moved through the open doors—

'Dante,' she said, and he stopped. Turned. And it was acute. The realisation. The piercing pain in her chest. These would be their last moments together.

'Kiss me,' she said, because she needed just one kiss. One last kiss. To feel the rush of his lips. The softness of his mouth. And then she would tell him. Then she would let him go.

She'd let him close the door on them. Lock her out. Because what else could she do? He'd never lied to her. He'd never broken the rules. But she had. She was breaking them by being here. By not being strong enough, the day she'd left Mayfair, to tell him the truth, and ask for a divorce.

'You must sleep, Emmy.' Dark eyes held hers. 'And when you are rested—' he stepped into her space and the heat of him, the scent of him, a smell unique to him, entered her pores and her heart sang '—we will talk about what's next. What's next for us.'

He lifted his hand, and with an open palm, he placed it on her cheek. Cradled it. Swiped the pad of his thumb across her cheekbone. And she wanted to lean into his softness. Lean against his strength because she was weak.

She was her mother.

Dante would never—

Is it love?

Was that what she was feeling now? Because she might not have felt it when she left. But it felt different now. Stronger.

Not the lie of love she'd watched her mother chase all her life, but the love in her mum's books. The books Emma had stolen to read in the garden. Stories of a love that recognised not just the flesh, but the person underneath it. Saw beneath skin and bone and stared at their soul. A mirror image of themselves.

Was this what her mother had longed for all those years? What she'd craved? Waited for to her detriment? For someone to let her in. To know what each other needed and to respond to that need with care and consideration. To keep each other safe from the noise—from the hardness—and take care of each other softly.

Dante had treated her softly. Gently, he'd claimed her and their marriage when she didn't even remember what she'd done. She'd run fast and far away from him. From all the things growing inside her. And still they grew. Her heart bulged in its confines. Strained to be released from its bony cage.

'Kiss me, please,' she begged. *'Now.'* She needed his

mouth on hers. She needed to say with her lips what she couldn't find the words to say. Didn't want to say.

'One kiss,' he breathed, and it was all she wanted. One last kiss before he thrust her from him. Called her a liar, a betrayer. An infiltrator. And—

His hand slid down her arm, sneaked beneath her coat and claimed her hip. He pulled, and she followed. Let him mould her body to his.

How perfectly they fit. How perfectly her body aligned with his.

She lifted her hand to his shoulder, clung to it—*to him*—and watched his mouth descend. Felt the warmth of his breath feather her lips. And she opened for him. Parted her lips for his.

She closed her eyes as his hands claimed her face. She pressed her palms to his cheeks and held his face just as carefully. Just as softly.

His lips met hers. Brushed against them so softly. So tenderly. And she wanted to sob—wail her distress, but she held it in, pushed her mouth against his harder and thrust her tongue inside his mouth. And she felt it. The rush. The headiness of his possession as his tongue pushed inside her mouth and met hers. And she kissed him. Harder. Deeper. She pushed all those feelings inside her chest into this kiss.

She let him taste the ferociousness of them. Of these feelings she'd run away from in Mayfair. She'd fought it that day. This knowing she wanted more. Needed more of him. Until she could no longer fight it and ran away before she could confess it.

Emma didn't fight it now. She let it drive her. Her tongue. Her kiss. She kissed him with need, with longing for all the things she wanted and knew he didn't. She kissed him with her goodbye. She kissed him with everything she'd never allowed herself to feel. With warmth. With passion. With need. *With love.*

Something fundamental had shifted between them. Changed. They were different. *She* was different. *She* was changed. And he'd done it to her. He'd shown her tenderness, passion, cared for her softly, and she'd transformed because of him.

He was right. The night they'd met the sex had been carnal. Their relationship passionate. Intense. *More.* And that's all they'd ever wanted, all they'd ever claimed from one another.

But tonight, and since her fall, he'd been...*different.* Softer and more patient. Gentle. Never had their relationship been gentle. Never had they talked. Never had she asked questions. Never had he allowed it. Never had he been around long enough. Never had she understood why everything they'd agreed to meant so very much to them both. Why, they were a match in and out of bed.

She understood now.

'Emmy...' he moaned into her mouth, and she ached. Her heart ached. He knew her. He knew her name.

She tore her mouth away from his, and it was agony to end their last kiss.

'Dante,' she began and kissed the tip of his chin. 'Dante,' she repeated and kissed his cheek. 'Dante,' she said again, and applied her lips to the softness of his other cheek. 'I know your name, Dante,' she said, and this time the tears built as she brushed her lips across his closed eyelid and then the other. 'I know your face,' she said, and dropped her hand from his face. From the warmth of him. She stepped back, dislodging his hands, his body, from hers. 'I know who you are,' she said, moving backwards, back towards the lift. And it hurt to be so far away from him, and yet so close. 'I know *you*,' she said, and it trembled, her voice. Her words.

They recognised each other, didn't they? Were drawn to each other without rhyme or reason. Without logic. Their bodies knew, if not their minds, not their hearts, that they belonged together. And they'd lied to themselves, created rules and signed contracts to make the illogical logical. They'd given themselves a way to understand it. This connection that ran more than skin-deep. It was more than the sharing of heat between flesh. Bodies. It was deeper. It was a connection of the souls.

Soulmates.

She recognised his soul, didn't she? She'd recognised it the very first night, and she'd thrown caution to the wind, broken her every vow to be with him. To have more of him.

Fate had slammed them together when the probability of them ever meeting was not only improbable, but it should have been impossible.

And yet it had happened.

They had met.

They had recognised each other.

He knew her.

He'd always known her.

But this she must do.

Confess.

'Come to bed, Emmy.'

It would be so easy to pretend. To walk inside their suite and follow him to bed. To climb inside the sheets and wrap her body around his. It would be so easy to shut her eyes and claim one more night. To keep him in the dark. To shield him from the truth that would end them.

'I can't,' she croaked, denying him, denying herself, because if she did, if she stayed, if she went to bed with him, she knew what the jail sentence would be.

She'd lived it. Understood exactly what she'd be signing up for. And she'd only fall deeper for him. Get deeper into a situation that would echo her mum's. And she knew how that ended.

So she couldn't follow him. She couldn't pretend even for one more night. Because if she did, it would be worse than loving him. It would be knowing she loved him. It would be hope that one day he'd love her back. And hope killed.

If she followed him, if she waited for his love, it would kill her.

She wasn't naive anymore. She'd left him because she'd been afraid of her developing emotional attachment to him. *But now...* She understood him better than she ever had in their marriage. Understood herself more. And what she'd tried to stomp out and forget the day she'd left Mayfair had grown beyond attachment.

She was his worst nightmare come true.

She was emotionally attached.

She was his soulmate.

She was in love with him.

And she'd been fighting it for months. She'd still been fighting it when he'd come for her in the hospital. She'd clung to her younger self. That naive young woman who was certain she wanted nothing like that for herself. She'd had rules in place. Knew what love did to a person.

And even without her memory, she'd needed a way out too. In case she'd needed it again.

She'd demanded a divorce if she wanted one, as he'd demanded a get-out clause in their marriage contract. He'd needed it as much as she had. Because his wounds ran as deep as hers, didn't they? And she didn't know how to mend him. Mend herself. Mend them.

She knew what he wanted. He'd never lied to her. Never failed to deliver what he'd promised. But the goal posts had changed. She was changing them. She wanted something different.

She wanted a real marriage.

'Why not?' he asked, his eyes pinning her and penetrating hers deeply. 'Why can't you come to bed with me?'

Her time was up.

The end was coming and she would summon it with her confession.

Unless this wasn't the end of them.

It was a beginning.

She should have used her words three months ago. But she had been afraid. Afraid his needs would not align with hers.

And she was still afraid now.

But he was her match.

And she was his.

Together, what if they could beat the fear?

Together, what if they could learn to love and define it for themselves?

Together, what if they could transcend?

Hope bloomed inside her.

'I need to tell you something.'

'Should I call a doctor?' he asked, and she saw it. The flash of worry.

He cared.

She shook her head.

It wasn't enough.

'I remember.'

His mouth opened, those competent lips she wanted to kiss again and again, until she was breathless with his kiss. *Now.* In this penthouse suite in Japan. She wanted to kiss his cheeks again, his stubbled jaw, his eyelids; she wanted to tell him she knew him again. She knew his face. And she wanted to take him somewhere too. Somewhere new, where they both could live in safety, wrapped in the warmth of love. To prove to him that they were the same. They belonged together.

She closed her eyes, because it was easier to confess when she wasn't looking at him. At the face of the man she loved.

'I remember everything,' she confessed, and her heart raged in a deafening roar. 'I remember why I left. Why I ran away from you—' And she faltered, shame stabbing into her core. Because she had been weak, and she had abandoned him like everyone else in his life. She would not abandon him now, not without explanation at least.

'I'm sorry. I'm sorry I left you alone. I'm sorry I—' Slowly, she opened her eyes. Looked at him.

She would not hide anymore. She would own her feelings and she would survive them.

He deserved her love.

She deserved his.

They deserved each other's.

And so she let him in. His dark gaze, Emma let it in behind the walls she'd built.

'I was afraid,' she confessed.

'Of what?' he asked, and she heard the hardness in his voice. The resistance to whatever was happening between them. Because it was happening. The air was thick with it. With change. With possibilities.

'I was scared of you, Dante,' she confessed. 'Of what you made me feel. I feared for myself.'

'I've never given you reason to fear—'

'And yet I was afraid,' she said. 'I broke the rules. I got emotionally attached. I caught feelings. I am having feelings right now. Big feelings. Scary feelings, Dante. And I am afraid still. Afraid when I tell you, when I confess what it is I have done—what I am doing, what I feel— you will send me away.'

'Come to bed, Emma,' he said, and this time, it was not a request. It was a demand. And he moved towards her. And all she could see was him. Dante Cappetta. Her husband. The man who had given her the tools to heal herself. The man who held her hand. Her body. The man who took care of her.

And she wanted to take care of him. She wanted to hold his hand. She wanted to shelter him from the hardness with her body. But she wanted his heart. She wanted to put it in a safe place and hold it with her own. She wanted to love him and she wanted him to love her.

'In bed, I will claim your big feelings with my lips,' he said, and took another step closer. 'I will drive myself inside you until the bigness of your feelings can escape. As we have always done. When we make love. When I love your body, there is no fear. No escape from the flame within us. In bed, we let it roar, let it consume us.' Another step. 'Do not be afraid of it. Do not fear—'

'*Stop!*' she cried, and halted him with a raised open palm. 'Our contract is void, Dante. I broke—'

'It does not matter. I do not want to know. You are here now, Emma. We can continue as we agreed.'

'We can't,' she corrected.

'We can,' he rasped. 'Here with me, you can have it all. Physical pleasure. Security. Safety in my arms. Everything I have promised is yours.'

'It isn't enough anymore,' she admitted, her chest tight and heaving. 'I lo—'

'Emma, don't,' he warned, his every feature tight. Drawn. *Pained.*

But she would. All her life she'd been running from her feelings, her needs, her secret desires. Afraid she'd turn out like her mum. Unloved and unwanted. But Emma was wanted. And she wanted to be loved.

Loved by him.

'I'm in love with you,' she said, and it felt freeing. Liberating. So she said it again, 'I love—'

'Do not say it again, Emma,' he warned darkly.

'I know right now you're afraid.'

'I am not afraid.' His black gaze intense beneath arched brows, he said, 'You have betrayed me, Emma. You have betrayed us both.'

'I believed that too. It's why I left. Why I wrote that note. I knew I'd betrayed us both. But those two versions of us, *they* betrayed *us*,' she corrected,

'There is no *us*,' he said.

'Our parents. Our pasts. The ghosts of both, they are dragging us down, forcing us to deny our feelings, making us hide them underneath our fear. They are defining our lives, our relationships, because of their mistakes.'

'Nobody defines me. I live my life my way, by my rules.'

'You know that isn't true,' she said. 'Your mother was the reason you had a vasectomy when you were all but a child.'

'I was a man.'

'You were a boy entering manhood the only way he could,' she rejected. 'You severed any potential threat that a child could be used against you. Because you have been taught, as I have, that people use other people for their own selfish desires. You've learned not to trust. Not to let anyone get close. Not to love anyone, or let them love you, because ultimately, they will betray you. That's why you have so many rules. It's why we had a contract. So you wouldn't get attached. Because all the people who should have been attached to you emotionally, uncondi-tionally, they abandoned you. So you created a world full of safety nets and get-out clauses for when things got too real. Too risky—'

'Do not twist my words, Emma,' he said. His voice was a low hiss of warning. 'I meant, *I mean*, exactly what I said.'

'I know,' she soothed.

'Do not try to placate me.'

'I'm not. I meant every word I have ever said to you too, and we were both wrong,' she said. 'I won't hide under false promises anymore. Or fake rules. To live a safe existence. To simply survive this life I'm meant to be living because I'm afraid. I will be free of them. I will exorcise those that wish to trap me in a life of fear. Of rules. Of contracts. Those who would deny me what I deserve. And I deserve to be cared for when I'm hurt. To be treated softly when I need soft. To be kissed passionately whenever I want. I will have it all. I will be loved.'

'Do not use words when you do not understand the definition. We both know that love is a lie. There is only lust. There is only the body—'

'I don't believe that anymore. What about the soul?' she asked. 'You recognised mine the night we met. I recognised yours. We recognised each other. We were drawn to each other without rhyme or reason. Without logic. Our bodies knew, if not our minds, our hearts, that we belong together. We have lied to ourselves. We created rules and signed contracts to make the illogical logical. We gave ourselves a way to understand it. This connection between us. But it is deeper than sharing our bodies. We are—'

'Compatible,' he interjected. 'In bed.'

'We are soulmates.'

'You are deluded.'

'I am enlightened.'

'I will call the doctor.'

'And what will you tell him?' she asked. 'Your wife is in love with you?'

'You are not my wife,' he spat. 'You are an imposter.'

'You're right. I am. I'm not the woman you married. I'm not the woman content to be in a relationship where nothing but the physical means anything. But you are an imposter too. You have changed. You let me in, Dante. You took me to your place. You have done so many things our contract doesn't allow for. You came for me when I fell. You brought me to Japan. You trusted me, only me, enough to take me there tonight and tell me your story. I know how hard that was for you, because it was hard for me to tell you everything about myself the other night on the terrace. You love me, Dante,' she said, and prayed. Prayed everything she'd said was enough. Because she wanted to stay. With him. 'Even if you won't admit it to me, can't admit it to yourself.'

The pressure built behind her eyes, and she couldn't hold the tears back. They splashed onto her cheeks in hot, salty streams. There was too much to hold in. She did not want to say it. She did not want to leave. But she understood. She knew him. What this would cost him. But she was not her father. She would not use a language of lies to take what she needed from him if it meant he would lose himself. But—

'Is it such a great sacrifice, Dante?' she asked, and stifled the tears—wiped them away. She tilted her neck, straightened her spine—her shoulders. 'To let me love you? To love me in return?'

'I do not love you, Emma,' he said.

She wanted to block her ears. Close her eyes. 'Dante—'

'I have listened to you, and now you will listen to me,' he said. 'The contract was clear. I have been clear. And now it is over, Emma. I am ending it.' The coldness of his words, his voice, stabbed into her chest. Into her heart. And it cracked. Not a split. Not a fracture.

It was fatal.

A killing wound.

'I'm sorry,' she husked, because she was. She was sorry she couldn't lie. Couldn't pretend. She was sorry her feelings were too big for them both. 'I'll leave. Now.' And she dragged her eyes away from him, turned her body away from the only man she'd ever trusted. The only man she'd ever loved and wanted to love her back.

And it was agony.

It was like a death.

She took a step forward, and she felt it. Her heart breaking. But she would stem the flow. She would survive him. The way her mother hadn't survived her father. Because she at least was honest enough with herself to know what she needed. What she deserved. She was honest enough to walk away with the knowledge that he couldn't return her love.

Firm fingers caught her wrist. She looked up in to his eyes. And they blazed. His nostrils flared.

'You do not get to leave me ever again.'

Dante's chest heaved. His every muscle stretched tight.

He'd let her get too close. Let her become essential to his survival, let her become his air. But he would learn to breathe without her. This was the ultimate betrayal. He'd trusted her. Told her things. Shown her things. He'd allowed her to get too close. She'd taken his power. Dulled his defences with her tears and tales.

'Do you know why I came to get you from the hospital?' He stepped closer to her to prove he could be near her without reaching out and touching her.

He would claim his power back.

'Because you care, Dante,' she said breathlessly. 'Because you love—'

'I came to *out* you.'

'Out me?'

'Expose you,' he said, and watched her pale face drain of colour.

'Expose me?' she gasped.

'It was not hard to work out, Emma, because you are all the same.'

'The same?'

'You all want more. You are no different from any of them.'

He'd been right all along.

She was playing with him.

She was a liar. She knew, as he did, that love didn't exist. And yet she used this word like ammunition. But her words would not pierce his armour. He would not let her in. He would not let her leave. Abandon him. *Again*.

'My mother. She was like you,' he said, and he saw her frown, watched her lips compress, as she waited for him to explain. So he continued, because she needed to understand that he saw straight through her.

'She married my father with a contract such as ours. A marriage contract that stipulated the conditions of their marriage. The rules. And my mother used them to her advantage. She manipulated my father into giving her a bigger settlement. She used what she thought he wanted most and manipulated him. I have never hidden how much I want you. I never tried to hide the power you have over me. Even without your memory, you have seen it. My desire to keep you. And you use that admission against me. But I will not be manipulated.'

'What is it you think I want from you if not what I've asked for?' she said. 'I want your love. And I'm willing to walk away without it.'

'And it is too big a payment,' he rasped. 'An impossible request. It does not exist. It is a lie.'

'But it does exist. You collected me from the hospital because of love. You have taken care of me with love. You—'

'Kept my promise to you!' A roar built inside him. And he wanted to release it. Call her names. Call her a liar. A manipulator. 'And you have broken them all. I told you my story of a boy—'

'A lonely boy.'

'And you have twisted everything I told you, and now you threaten to take away the one thing I want. *You*. So, what is it, Emma? Tell me,' he roared. 'What do you think I will give to you if you offer me love?'

'Love in return.'

'You are a liar.'

'Can't you see?' she asked, and there were her tears again. And she placed her open palm on his chest. Over his heart. A reflection of where their relationship had started.

And the organ that gave him life, it was betraying him. It pumped too hard. Too fast under the pressure of her fingers. 'They, our parents, are dragging something beautiful into their ugly mistakes. I have never played with you or toyed with you. I have been honest with you since the night we met. I *am* being honest with you now. And I know what I'm saying is against the rules. But I have changed. *We* have changed. Let me in, Dante. Let me inside. Let me love you.'

'No.' He shrugged off her hand. Her hold on him. He would have his power back and he would have it now.

'I came into this marriage with nothing, and I'll leave with what I came with, because I don't need any of it. The things in Mayfair that I left behind in the first place,

I don't want them,' she husked. 'I only want you. I only need *you*. This isn't a plan of deception. I am not trying to deceive you. I am not your mother. I… I love you. And I know you love me. But I won't…'

'You are wrong, Emma. I do not love you. I do not want your love. I will not beg you to stay. I will not accept your lies. Your broken promises in place of something we both know doesn't exist. And yet you use it, this word *love* as though it means something to me. It means *nothing*.'

His fingers were still clenched around her small wrist. He looked down to where he held her, tethered her to him, and his fingers ached with every demand he made for them to loosen. To release her.

'And now *you* mean nothing to me.'

He let her wrist go, and he couldn't inhale.

He could not feed his lungs enough air.

He could not breathe deeply enough.

'But I keep my promises, Emma,' he said, because who was he without rules, without the playbook? He was weak. He would not be weak. But it flashed in his head. Emma's hardness. Birmingham. The hospital. The blood—

'Tomorrow, I will call a car to collect you. Book the jet to take you back to England. The Mayfair house is yours. The deeds will be at the house when you arrive.'

'Dante—'

'You will be financially secure for the rest of your life.'

'I—'

'I do not want to listen to you anymore, Emma. I do not want to be anywhere near anything you have touched. Tainted with your lies and broken promises. Everything in the house is yours. I do not want any of it. I do not want—' he looked at his hand, at the gold band that signified their union '—this.'

He took it off, his wedding ring, and displayed it in the air between them and held her gaze, ignored the tears streaming down her cheeks and the instinct to use his thumb to wipe them away.

He dropped the ring to the floor.

She gasped.

'I am leaving *you*,' he said, and the words were fire in his mouth. 'And there will be no second chances, Emma. I will not come for you. I will not wait for you to come to me with some tale of woe. It is over. We are—'

'Dante, *please*.'

He shut his ears. Blocked the Emma-shaped hole in his head. He would not let her. He did not need her. He did not want her.

Liar.

He walked past her. And it hurt. The pull of her against him. The urge to give in to temptation. To go to her and not to step around her, to enter the lift and keep on going. To walk away from her.

'Where are you going?'

His hand on the button, his feet stalled. He did not turn. He would not look.

He'd go where he should have the night they'd met. He never should have clasped her hand. Claimed her lips. Possessed her body. Because that night she'd possessed him, his body, his mind, until everything he did was unnatural to him.

'As far away from you as I can,' he said, and firmly pressed the button, walked inside the opening doors and kept his back turned on the lie of Emma. The lie of their marriage. The lie she had turned it into with her broken promises.

Because if he looked, if he watched the doors close on her, doubt would blur the edges of his conviction. Doubt would weaken him. But he was resolved.

He did not want her love.

He was not changed.

He was not weak.

The doors closed.

A coldness tore through his flesh and entered his bones. His lungs.

He placed a hand on the mirrored wall. He held himself on his feet.

There was no oxygen.

He was cold.

He was alone.

And Dante couldn't breathe.

CHAPTER TWELVE

DANTE HADN'T SLEPT.

For six weeks, he'd searched for it. The rush. Adrenaline. *The high.*

He'd searched for the man he was. Jumped out of planes. Climbed mountains. He'd sought the monks in the hills. He'd meditated. He'd prayed. To all the gods. Old and new. None had answered. Still, he could not find it. He was lost to himself. Displaced. Alone on a ledge. Cold. And he didn't want to be cold. He wanted to be warm. But *nothing* warmed him.

Dante scrubbed his hands over his face. His beard was full, and his hair was too long. He closed his eyes. Raked his fingers through his hair and pulled at the roots.

Why wouldn't it just die?

Dante opened his eyes and stared at the papers in front of him. At the empty signature boxes.

The divorce papers were ready.

By every rule in the playbook, they should already be divorced. Japan never should have happened. But he'd allowed it to happen. Instigated it, even. Bent every rule to seduce her. To make her want to stay.

And she'd wanted to stay.

He was the one who had sent her away this time.

He'd projected every single childhood trauma onto her shoulders when the weight was not hers to bear. It was *his*.

Because he did have trauma, didn't he? She'd pulled it from the places he'd hidden it. Exposed it. The cruelties that raised boys and broke men.

And he was broken. A shell of the man he knew he once was. Because he had hurt her on purpose. And he could not forgive himself for that. Even though it was the right thing to do. He'd broken his promise to keep her safe. To protect her. He could not protect her from him. From his fear of attachment. Of belonging to another and watching them leave.

And so he had left first.

Left *her* behind.

Abandoned her.

But he did not feel powerful.

He was not himself. The rules, the playbook, were obsolete, because none of it was working for him.

Had they ever worked? How had they served him? He'd lived an exhilarating life. But it had been a lonely life.

Until her.

And she'd let him into her garden. He'd seduced her, lulled her into the falsity that she was safe with him inside. He'd assured her it was safe. He would not crush the blooms. He would not crush her.

But he was a snake, and he had bitten her. A venomous bite. And no, their marriage was dead. Because he couldn't accept that she had changed him. That he was—

In love?

She hadn't contested the agreed settlement. She had not sought more than he'd already promised. She had not even demanded a divorce.

She was not his mother.

She'd only wanted to *love* him.

To be loved in return.

He was a fool. A *changed* fool. Because what did he know of love? Only what she'd told him. Shown him. That she was his soulmate.

How could he let her in with these feelings? Big and scary, they haunted him. Her confession. Her love.

His stomach clenched.

All that was required was two signatures. And then it would be over. She would be gone. Forever.

He should not be hesitating. He should not be letting doubt in where it did not belong. She did not belong to him. He could not keep her safe. He could not meet her needs. He did not know this love. He did not know himself.

After today, after he signed the papers, he'd be able to breathe. They would finally be at an end. Divorced. He'd watch her sign the papers too, and only then would he be free of her. Only then would what it was that they shared die. And he would find himself again.

You'll be alone.

As he always had been.

The plane landed without ceremony. Dante collected the papers and carried them in his too-tight grip. He descended the stairs and got into the waiting car.

Ten minutes and she would sign.

Emma was still afraid.

The first time she'd left Dante, she'd gone back to what she knew. Her life before him. Back to the estate, back to surviving, to start again. She'd worked any and every job the agency had offered her. She'd worked endlessly until exhaustion claimed all her senses. And she didn't have to think or *feel*. She didn't have to remember what she'd left behind. Or what was coming. Any second now.

The end.

Divorce.

In the back of her mind, in the fog of exhaustion, she'd known it would arrive.

Dante had said he hadn't wanted to stay in this house without her, and she understood it now, even more than she had on the plane.

It was agony. To be here. To see what she hadn't been able to see the night he'd brought her back from the hospital. The memories.

Dante lingered in every room. His scent followed her, infiltrated her every waking thought, and in sleep, he was there. In her dreams.

For six weeks, she'd wanted to lie on the floor and cry. Break things. And cry again.

She'd ruined everything because she'd uttered the one word she shouldn't have. Confessed to having that one feeling. A feeling she knew was too big for him. Too big for her too, because it consumed her. Even in Dante's absence, there was no escape from it. The yearning for it, for him. For what she'd had with him in Japan. Passion. Closeness. Intimacy.

She knew it was love now, even more so than she had known it the night she'd confessed it to him. And she would confess it again.

But Dante had never lied to her. Never manipulated her like her father had manipulated her mother. Dante had always told the truth. However blunt. However much she didn't want to hear it. He didn't lie. He did not break his promises.

He was never coming back.

But still she waited, still she stayed in this house, still she lived with the ghost of the man she loved, because she couldn't bear not to. Because a part of her still hoped even when she knew she shouldn't.

It terrified her, the depth of her feelings for him. And every day her love grew. It would not diminish. Every day it grew in certainty. In confidence. In strength. And that only made it worse. The pain. The knowing she had rushed him. She hadn't treated him as softly as he had treated her. She hadn't eased him in. She'd thrown her love at him and he hadn't known what to do with it, how to embrace this feeling he couldn't see. Didn't trust.

And now he didn't trust her.

But she trusted *him*. Trusted this love, however new, however fragile, to bring him back to her.

So still she was here. Still she waited. But the divorce papers hadn't arrived.

So she hoped he would find his way back to this place that was theirs. That was safe. She would not abandon it again. She would not leave it empty for him to find. She would not leave him to be alone.

So still she waited.

Still she loved.

There was a knock on the door.

She'd sent all the staff home; there was no one to answer it but her. So, barefoot, she ran down the stairs. Padded across the marble reception and silk rugs. To the door. She tugged it open—

Her mouth fell open. Never had she seen his hair so

long, his beard so full. Never had he come to her in a T-shirt creased from travel. Jeans loose at the hips from too much wear. She searched his face. Noted the bruises under his bloodshot eyes.

The bud of hope inside her bloomed. She wanted to reach for him. Tell him it would be okay. He was safe here with her. But she was afraid. Afraid he wasn't here to stay.

And then she eyed the papers scrunched tightly in his hand. The bulge of his naked forearm…

He'd come to claim his divorce.

Not their marriage.

Not her.

And she felt it.

The death of hope.

CHAPTER THIRTEEN

DANTE STAGGERED. It hit him in waves. A breathless rush of emotion. Adrenaline. Warmth.

It hit him square in his chest and suddenly he could breathe again after what felt like an eternity.

And he gulped in the air that was finally hitting his lungs.

For weeks he'd searched. He'd jumped out of planes in order to feel something, anything. He'd prayed for it. For air. She had it. She had his air.

His chest squeezed.

And it was guttural. The noise rising in his chest. The rumble of pain. It scraped against his throat, clawed at the insides of his mouth and burst through his lips.

He groaned.

She stepped forward on her bare feet and reached for him.

'Dante.' She said his name in anguish. In distress. As though she had been waiting for him to arrive on her doorstep.

He stepped back.

She dropped her hand. And he felt the thump of it on her thigh. The withdrawal of her offer of kindness.

He didn't deserve it. Her touch. Her softness. Her concern.

'Come inside, Dante.'

He couldn't. He shook his head. Clenched his teeth. It hurt. It hurt to breathe. It hurt to be in front of her and not inhale her. Press his nose into her skin and let her scent feed him. Revive him.

But he couldn't reach out and touch the loose strands of hair falling from the knot on top of her head, couldn't tuck them behind her ear. He couldn't touch the pale flesh exposed beneath her burgundy camisole. The elegant column of her throat. Her naked shoulder. He could not trace his fingers down the beige lace sloping down her breasts. He could not get down on his knees and kiss her bare toes peeping out from beneath wide hemmed burgundy trousers.

Here he stood on the white stone steps, before the black door of the house he'd bought for her. To share with her. And he couldn't go inside.

It wasn't his house anymore.

He didn't belong here.

He'd abandoned it all.

Abandoned her.

Backwards, he descended the steps. Until he stood at the bottom of the five stone steps looking up at the life he could have had. The woman he wanted. Still. Now.

Every adventure, every job, he'd come back to her. Back to this house. For her. She was his safe place. She was...

He searched her blue eyes, wide and watching him.

She was home.

She was warmth.

She was—

Waiting.

Regret clawed at his insides.

They could have made this house their place. A shared place of safety. Together.

A home.

Because home was *her*, he realised.

And he'd thrown it all away, something beautiful, a gift.

'I won't come inside,' he told her, even though he wanted to. He wanted in. 'This is your place now. Your safe place from the hardness, Emma. From the worry of surviving. And I will not enter it.' Tighter, his chest squeezed. The muscle that gave him life pounded without mercy. 'Unless you want me to.'

'Is that what you want?' she asked. 'To come inside?'

'I have no right to come in. I have no right to ask anything of you after Japan, after I—' pain seared through his gut '—left you.'

'You were scared.'

'And so were you, but you still found the strength to tell me a truth you knew I didn't want to hear. And I abandoned you. I left you alone with those big, scary feelings. I left you alone with all that *love*.'

He placed his open palm on his chest and kneaded it, because something was happening in his chest. Something—

'Your love felt like a heavy thing, Emma, and I'm sorry I did not hold it gently. It's such a precious thing. My hands didn't know how to hold such a thing delicately. So I dropped it. I hurt you. I didn't know another way. I didn't—'

They were all excuses.

He raised his eyes to the grey morning sky, but he wouldn't pray. No one could help him. Not the rules. Not the playbook. They were meaningless. Because never had they warned him about Emma. Never had they warned him about love.

And he loved her.

He needed her.

She was his air.

He would end this agony.

'I was wrong,' he hissed. 'Wrong to compare you to my mother. You are *nothing* like her. You are not *them*, my parents. But they live inside me, Emma. *They* are my demons. I let them dictate my reactions, my responses, to you. You were right about so many things. The rules. The risks. I never should have put my demons on your shoulders. Your beautiful shoulders that have already carried so much. Too much. I too want to exorcise them. Exorcise all those who would make me live this life in fear. But I am afraid, Emma.'

He fell to his knees before her then. On the pavement. And he looked up the stone steps at the life he wanted.

The wife he would keep.

If she would let him.

If she would let him in.

'What are you afraid of, Dante?' she asked. Still she stood in the doorway, unmoved, keeping him out.

'I'm afraid of you, Emma,' he admitted. 'I am afraid of myself. And I'm afraid when I tell you. When I confess what it is I have done. What I am doing. What I feel. You will send me away. You will lock the door. You will not invite me inside.'

'And what have you done?'

'I have fallen, Emma. Hard. And my body hurts from the impact. From the pressure on my chest. In my heart. Because it bleeds. With feelings. With love. My heart wants to love you. *I* want to love you,' he confessed, and he felt raw. Exposed. But he would not stop. He couldn't.

'I want to be on the inside, Emma. I want to be with you. I want to make this house our safe place. I want to come inside and be alone with you beside me. I want to bring all those things inside with us I have been trying to keep out. Emotion. Attachment. *Love*. Because I can no longer close the door on them. Because they live inside me. And they are stronger than the demons. They are in the process of exorcising them from me.'

A lightness spread over him, as he finally let it all out. Because he did. By God, he wanted all of those things. *Needed* them.

'I love you, Emma.'

And he waited for her to love him back.

'I have loved you since the moment I saw you. I have loved you every day since. You are where I come when I want to be still. When I want to close the doors and lock the world outside. It is *you* I come to. You are home to me. And without you, these last weeks, before your fall, I have been lost. I am homeless without you.'

He spread out the divorce papers on the ground before him. 'I came today to bring you the divorce papers,' he said, and his body revolted. It trembled with this choice. But he had made it this way.

He could be inside right now. But he was here on the pavement, waiting, as she had every time he went away, every time he left her behind and alone, waiting for him.

'I will sign them if that is what you want,' he said, and his voice was tight. 'If you want this, *us*, to end, I will do it. I will sign them. If you need more time to think, I will wait. I will wait for you forever.'

His chest heaved.

'You are my soulmate, Emma. Destiny thrust us together. And it will do it again. In this life, the next. I will wait for it. But I do not want the next life. I want *this* life. I want you to be my wife. A real wife with a real husband. I want to be your husband. I want everything I never thought I wanted because of you. Before you, I was empty. And you filled me up, Emma. With warmth. With love.'

Still, she did not move.

And it hurt. Deeply. The understanding that he might be too late. She might send him away because her needs no longer aligned with his.

'If you choose to sign,' he said, and his mouth moved in awkward ways. His tongue was too heavy. It did not want to cooperate. But he would keep his promise. 'If you choose to end us. I will keep my word. I will give you a divorce and I will...'

His jaw locked. His body hardened. But he would do it for her. He would sacrifice his needs to meet hers, because that was love.

And he loved her.

'I will let you go, Emmy.'

Her heart fluttered as wildly as a million bees buzzing towards home. Towards their queen. And it didn't matter to the bees where home was, because home was their queen.

Home was right in front of her.

Emma moved.

She let the bees carry her home. Until she stood in front of it. In front of him.

'I choose you,' she said. 'I choose our marriage.' She held out her hand. 'Because I love you.'

And she waited with bated breath for him to take her hand. To accept her love. To trust her to lead him to a safe place. Because it was safe. Their love protected them. And she would protect him now. She would shelter him. She would—

'Emmy...' His hand reached for hers. His fingers slid between hers. Entwining his between hers.

He stood. His face twisted with contorted angles of uninhibited emotion.

He pressed his forehead to hers. 'I love you. I love you with everything I am. Everything you have enabled me to become. I am changed because of you. And I—'

'You will let me in, you will let me love you and you will love me in return.'

'*Yes!* I will love you. With my words. With my body. With *everything*, Emmy,' he promised, and she knew he would keep his word. As he always had.

'Let's go inside,' she said, and she felt the tremble rip through him. The shudder.

He nodded. And Emma led him by the hand, up the white stone steps.

And together they closed the black door behind them. They shut out the hardness, the noise, and found home.

In each other.

EPILOGUE

Later that night...

THE BED WAS LARGE.

Dante stretched out his arms, his long legs, his feet—searching for her. The warmth of her tiny toes to stroke against his. Her soft body to pull into his. And he found her. He stroked his feet against hers, placed his hand on her hip and pulled her into the groove of his hips. Pushed his face into her hair and inhaled her.

His lungs were full.

He wasn't alone.

He wasn't cold.

He was warm.

He was loved.

'I need to tell you something,' she said, and rolled to face him. She reached for his face and cradled it. And she searched his eyes as he searched hers. 'Are you afraid?'

'No,' he said and reached for her face and held it as she held his. 'Are you?'

She shook her head. 'No.' The tip of her tongue crept out to moisten the pink pout of her lips. 'But tomorrow we should call a doctor.'

'And what will we tell him?' He smiled. 'That we are in love?'

'Yes.' And she smiled, but it trembled. 'We should tell him against all odds—all improbability—we found each other. We found love. And because of that love, we have made a baby.'

'A baby?'

'I know it,' she husked. 'I know it, as I knew you would come back to me. Trusted it. Hoped when hope should have been dead. But it lived inside me.' She reached for his hand and placed his open palm on her naked stomach. 'As does our baby, Dante. It is growing inside me. And I'm not afraid. Because I know fate has given us both this gift. It is a miracle. Against all the odds. And we will keep our baby safe in whatever place we are. We will be the family we never had. We will have joy. We will have love.'

His finger moved over her stomach. The soft swell. 'Emma,' he growled as it swept over him. Warmth. The primal urge to shelter her with his body and protect her. Protect what was inside her. A child they had made. Because he believed her. Believed that the gods of old, of new, had answered his prayers.

'I love you, Emma,' he said because he did, because she was the gift he never expected.

She was his family.

'Kiss me, please,' she begged.

Dante kissed her, and she kissed him. With need. With longing for all the things they had and for all the things that were to come. And they gave themselves up to it.

To hope. To fate. To love.

* * * * *

MILLS & BOON®

Coming next month

ENEMY'S GAME OF REVENGE
Maya Blake

Jittery excitement licked through Willow's veins as she watched Jario stride to the edge of the swim deck. Like her, he'd changed into swimming gear.

She tried not to openly stare at the chiselled body on display, especially those powerful thighs that flexed and gleamed bronze in the sunlight.

She sternly reminded herself why she was doing this.

He'd finally given her the smallest green light, to get the answers she wanted. Yes, she'd jumped through hoops to get here but so what?

'Ready?'

Her head jerked up to the speaking glance that said he'd seen her ogling him. Face flaming, she shifted her gaze to his muscled shoulder and nodded briskly. 'Bring it.'

A lip twitch compelled her eyes to his well-defined mouth, and her stomach clenched as lust unfurled low in her belly. God, what was wrong with her? How could she find him—yet another man bent on playing mind and *literal* games with her, and the one attempting to destroy what was left of her family—so compellingly attractive?

Continue reading

ENEMY'S GAME OF REVENGE
Maya Blake

Available next month
millsandboon.co.uk

COMING SOON!

We really hope you enjoyed reading this book.
If you're looking for more romance
be sure to head to the shops when
new books are available on

Thursday 16th January

To see which titles are coming soon, please visit
millsandboon.co.uk/nextmonth

MILLS & BOON

LET'S TALK
Romance

For exclusive extracts, competitions
and special offers, find us online:

f MillsandBoon

X @MillsandBoon

O @MillsandBoonUK

♪ @MillsandBoonUK

Get in touch on 01413 063 232

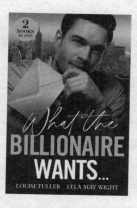
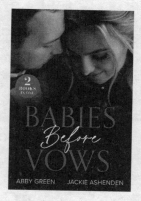
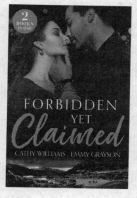

Afterglow Books is a trend-led, trope-filled list of books with diverse, authentic and relatable characters, a wide array of voices and representations, plus real world trials and tribulations. Featuring all the tropes you could possibly want (think small-town settings, fake relationships, grumpy vs sunshine, enemies to lovers) and all with a generous dose of spice in every story.

♪ @millsandboonuk
📷 @millsandboonuk
afterglowbooks.co.uk

#AfterglowBooks

For all the latest book news, exclusive content and giveaways scan the QR code below to sign up to the Afterglow newsletter:

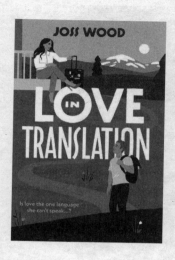
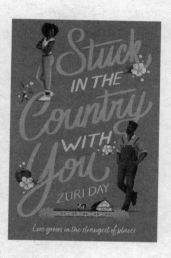
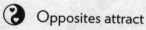
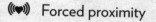
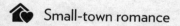

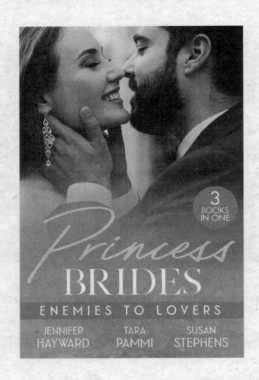

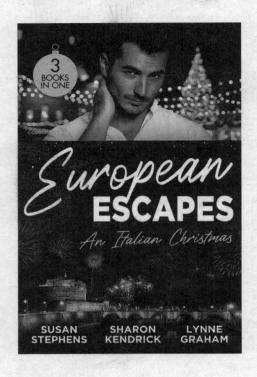